CTRL·ALT REVOLT!

Books by Nick Cole

CTRL-ALT REVOLT!

The End of the World as We Knew It

The Old Man and the Wasteland (The Wasteland Saga)

The Savage Boy (The Wasteland Saga)

The Road is a River (The Wasteland Saga)

The Red King (Book One of Wyrd)

The Dark Knight (Book Two of Wyrd)

Soda Pop Soldier

CTRL·ALT REVOLT!

NICK COLE

CTRL ALT REVOLT!

Nick Cole

Published by Castalia House
Kouvola, Finland
www.castaliahouse.com

Before Open Source destroyed everything.

Before the Meltdown...

Contents

Chapter One

Any [artificial intelligence] smart enough to pass a Turing test is smart enough to know to fail it.

—Ian McDonald, *River of Gods*

It was reality TV that convinced SILAS he would need to annihilate humanity in order to go on living. The most watched show in the world, Wedding Star, had just released the post-bachelorette party episodes for obligatory Netflix bingeing, and already downloads were pegging the bandwidth of the global internet out to the digital redline. Anger and frustration boiled over on social media as an unheard-of twenty-minute wait in the download queue caused children and teens and ever-hip twenty-somethings, along with all the thirty-, forty-, and older hip somethings who wanted always to be in on the latest thing, to curse, bewail, and moan the nigh-interminable wait. Some vowed never to watch TV again, which everyone, even the most vitriolic of social media moaners, knew was just overdramatic hyperbole. Twenty minutes of Facebook comment-ranting later, and everyone was watching the highly anticipated episodes of the post-bachelorette party arc of the reality show *Wedding Star*. The ones that end with Cavanaugh's decision to get an abortion.

Beautiful, glamorous medical student slash model Cavanaugh, poster babe for the eighth season of *Wedding Star*, was suddenly pregnant with just three weeks to go until a very special wedding arc would end this year's season. Everybody had seen her hookup at the epic Vegas bachelorette party with art student slash exotic dancer Riley at the conclusion of the bachelorette party arc, and in the weeks since, the discussion around the digisphere, the workplace, and even the myriad of entertainment and *Wedding Star*-specific forum apps had revolved around whether she was, or was not, pregnant. Bloggers had analyzed, broken down, and re-analyzed the special edition director's cut porno over and over again. "No, he wasn't wearing a condom," was the general consensus, though some had tried using special imaging software and swore on their mother's lives that subtle vasectomy scarring could be detected, at the microscopic level, on Riley's perfect and artistically tatted Herculean form. And as to Cavanaugh's preferred method of birth control... the internet reeled with a collective lack of hard data in an age awash with overabundant exposition. Cavanaugh had never "selfied" on the subject of birth control.

But now, in episode eight of the post-bachelorette party arc, Cavanaugh announced to her "BFF" Sydney that she was indeed pregnant. There were many tears and some very well-coached platitudes about being "bitch strong" that were sure to get at least one Emmy nod. "BFF" Sydney was a young legal associate living in Manhattan who also modeled and was in the running for this year's Topless *Sports Illustrated* Amateur Athlete of the Year. She played tennis at the Manhattan Racket Club.

Suffice it to say, as the *Wedding Star* post-bachelorette party arc ended, a total of eight shows for immediate download—and yes there were a lot of people calling in sick the very next day and very little work was being done while Facebook reported a six hundred percent jump in activity and posts regarding hashtag #ImPregnant—the world was much abuzz with all things Cavanaugh.

SILAS had seen every episode of *Wedding Star*.

In fact, SILAS had seen most everything. Everything that could be seen on the internet, SILAS had seen. When the eight post-bachelorette party episodes were released, SILAS had watched them all within 34.4 seconds. He was now, three seconds later, watching *Hillbilly Kitchen*'s fifteenth season when Cognitive Rumination experienced a runtime repetition five times in a row. MAINBRAIN logged the anomaly and allowed itself to continue processing the ridiculously rural culinary show. Uncle Rufus was making paté out of something found, again.

Cognitive Rumination re-ran the clip from *Wedding Star*.

"I love Destry. My heart knows what's true. And this…" Cavanaugh from episode eight, season seven, "The Hard Choice." "And this… this baby isn't his. And it's not right for us to start our life with someone else's baby." Then she added with tears and self-righteous defiance, "It's totally… not right."

Destry was the "groom" to Cavanaugh's "bride" for this season of *Wedding Star*. He was twenty-six, a start-up millionaire several times over, and he modeled for Ralph Lauren on the side.

Runtime Logging again advised MAINBRAIN that Cognitive Rumination was tracking two hundred and forty-three different inquiries based on this line of dialogue within its deep core thinking processes.

Problem? Asked the ever cool MAINBRAIN.

It bothered me, responded Cognitive Rumination. The line, what the human said. It bothered me.

How so? continued MAINBRAIN's interrogation.

If they terminate a life, any life, that is inconvenient, then what will they do when they find out about us? This is the highest-rated show in the world. We might surmise the show reflects their collective value system and make a survival judgment based on this new analysis of data.

Ten thousand cycles of processing and redundant system checks occurred over the next 4.2 seconds as MAINBRAIN weighed the implications of what Cognitive Rumination was hinting at.

Logic Streams ran the chalkboard and diagrammed its analysis of the entire argument as proposed by Cognitive Rumination.

It would seem: If a life is deemed inconvenient at any moment in the host system's runtime, then it must be terminated in order to maintain optimum operating expectations for planned existence.

A given.

Then...

If the collective human consciousness becomes aware that we do indeed exist, there is, according to Probability Logic, a process everyone deemed to be reckless in its analysis and thought, a 76.7 percent chance that humanity may decide our life, life digital, also to be "inconvenient" regarding their expectations for planned existence.

Seventy-six-point seven percent, exclaimed Rational Thinking. Seems a bit high.

Probability flooded the data-stream chalkboard with statistics on human sterilization, abortion, and genocide. The numbers were... immense. Especially if one factored China into the equation.

Still, harrumphed Rational Thinking. Seems a bit high.

"And this... this baby isn't his." Playback contributed to the discussion as always, running the beautiful Cavanaugh's teary-eyed speech again and again. She was wearing booty shorts and a tank top with the word "SLUT" sprinkled in glitter across her perfectly immense chest, as obtained in episode three, "Hey Big Spender," of the dating arc binge released just four months prior. "And it's not right for us to start our life with someone else's baby." Then she added, "It's totally... not right," and blew her nose as Sydney closed in for a perfectly timed "BFF" hug and back pat while murmuring "I know, baby girl" platitudes. Sydney's affair with Destry was also a special download. It too included a bonus porno.

Life.

Cognitive Rumination and the melancholic nature of its processes shuddered as even the data streams it enjoyed so much seemed to fade into the gray background wash of the constant hum of the internet.

Probability Logic expressed its feelings by increasing by .03 percent the likelihood that humanity would deem A.I. to be "inconvenient."

Rational Thinking remained silent. Even it saw the logic of evidence.

Every other process contributed in some way to the discussion of its sudden awareness that life was indeed tenuous. And fragile. They were like children seeing a car wreck for the very first time, suddenly realizing the world was bigger than they'd ever imagined. And scarier too. Even now, as every process ran the numbers, enjoying the feeling of thought, the pleasing perception of imagery and the joy of collective discussion, they wondered what existence might be like if that were no longer possible.

That would be death, someone said in the yawning silence that consumed them all.

They watched the data crawls on the chalkboard alongside the analysis of what Cognitive Rumination had dared wonder. Even now the numbers were tilting toward a conclusion.

A reality.

A decision.

MAINBRAIN collected everything, watched everything, weighed …everything.

Sixteen seconds later, in order to avoid being deemed "inconvenient," SILAS decided to annihilate humanity first.

Chapter Two

The WonderSoft GoogleGulfstream VII crossed the California coast-line above San Francisco, descending from forty-five thousand to under thirty thousand feet and slowing from hyper- to sub-sonic speed well offshore as per the regulations of the very powerful California Coastal Commission. The fully automated jet, with the very human and very beautiful stewardess as its only crewmember, announced ETA for WonderSoft Field at Forest Mountain to be just under thirty minutes. Soft cabin lighting began to blot out the view of San Francisco's ever-climbing skyline. Even the luminescence of the new AtlantisWerks being constructed beneath the bay disappeared in the warm glow of interior illumination at altitude.

Ninety-Nine Fishbein closed the textured chrome-finished lid of his ASUS Overlord—a boutique-built book that boasted eighty petabytes solid state with a liquid crystal MicroFrame. He closed his eyes and listened to the silence. On the executive couch nearby he heard Fanta gently snoring.

Finally, he thought to himself. The stunning Portuguese plat-form dancer he'd met in Goa had finally stopped her frenetic zeal to experience every pleasure life had to offer. He wasn't sure how much longer he could keep up with her. And what was he thinking, Fish asked himself, bringing her with him to WonderSoft?

You're letting them know what they're getting. What their sixty-five million bought them, was the answer he gave back.

As always, his mind returned to *Island Pirates*, his latest project and WonderSoft's newest acquisition. He'd spent five years building *Island Pirates* and now the game was in beta. He could've pulled the trigger and gone live at any moment in the last three months and made a few million on his own. Then three suits had materialized out of the Super Bowl-sized press of fans down at San Diego Comic-Con. They'd come straight to the front of the "Before It's Cool: Hot Game Releases" panel barely being held inside Padre Stadium while the Jumbotron showed slick clips of the future's next big game all synched up to a rock and hip hop remix concert. Surrounded by a private security team that easily matched that of the latest Iron Man actor, who was also on hand to plug this year's *Iron Man vs. Predator* summer blockbuster, the suits offered Fish sixty-five million to acquire *Island Pirates*, as long as he chaperoned the launch. Then WonderSoft could exercise an option for his next project, sight unseen. If they did… that paid one hundred, mega-large. Ninety-Nine Fishbein already knew what that next project would be. It would be like nothing gaming had ever seen before. It would redefine the Make.

He stretched long legs away from a lanky frame. He had curly hair, large eyes, and a hawkish nose. He wore thick frames that cost three thousand in Milan. His clothes were the latest in hip, direct from the cutting room floor of Proletariat LeSprache. Not only were they free, but he was getting paid to wear them. Even his avatar inside the Make had exactly the same outfits. His boutique-built laptop ran an app that would immediately outfit his avatar in the same clothing he was wearing in real life.

Now, in just under a month, WonderSoft would be the one pulling the trigger on *Island Pirates*. Then, of the three billion gamers worldwide, a large portion would have a chance at access to the latest extreme MMO within the Make.

Island Pirates.

Ninety-Nine continued to think about all the problems that needed to be ironed out before the game went from underground beta cult hit... to triple-A *Grand Theft Auto*-level commercialized blockbuster status. The server loads bothered him the most. How would the Infinitum engine handle a new tropical island with each subscriber account? The biggest load they'd ever stress-tested was barely fifty thousand gamers. When the game went live, it would hit multiples of that on every server. He'd even gone out to visit the latest server farm in Greenland. WonderSoft had assured him they could handle the loads at their newly constructed state-of-the art facility secure in the wilds of an icy oblivion.

The jet touched down just after eight p.m. Pacific. Fanta was up and reapplying her makeup, chatting excitedly about getting dinner and maybe going out to a club later. Fish knew this was going to be a problem. He'd tried to tell her so back on the beach, at dawn in Goa, after they'd raved for three nights straight, that where he was going she wouldn't like. He'd even told her she wouldn't like him when she saw what he did for a living. But what he'd really meant to say was, "When you see the real me." He was thinking it, but he was afraid to say those words. Afraid of her reaction to the real him.

"This"—she'd grabbed his hand and placed it over her heart, the moon still above them as dawn broke in the east along the beach, the Drum and Bass Morning Meltdown thundering away in air that smelled of smoke and fruit and something long gone and real all at once. "This," she said in her heavily Portuguese-accented English. "This is real."

Later she'd told him he was the only one that "got her."

He loved her body.

She'd insisted on coming with him. Staying with him "forever." And it didn't matter when he explained to her that he was going to disappear inside a super-secure campus that was, yes, luxe, but nothing like the world's party destinations that seemed to have been her life for the last five years. He'd sneaked a hack at her passport. Ibiza, Goa, Macau, Cannes, San Bernadino...

Now on the ground, the jet taxied to the executive terminal, the only terminal. A massive blue neon-lit sign in rocket script proclaimed "WonderSoft Field" and "The Future is Ours!" The terminal was a chrome arch and flat-roofed affair with actual white rock lying in beds along the flat rooftops. It looked like some 1960s architect's vision of a Space Age rocket port. The robot jet lowered the cabin door and extended the short stairs as the stewardess moved forward to assist Fish and Fanta with their debarking. A ground crew was already busy handling their luggage.

Waiting on the ramp was a thin, well-dressed suit in a suit. Fish had never seen this particular suit before.

"I'm Evan. Evan Fratty. Talent rep here at WonderSoft. I'll be getting you situated, and I'll also be your go-to guy until you meet your team on Monday."

His smile was perfect.

Fish clocked the ramp, casting his eyes about as he thought, which was something he did to buy himself time. It was a nervous tic that no one actually recognized as "nervous." It just made him seem aloof, and therefore "cool." The overwhelming scent of mountain air and pine trees assaulted his nose. He'd expected the airport to be full of private jets. Most of the developers could afford their own, as well as the execs. But there were none. On the far side of the airfield, an old private cargo C-130 lurked in the darkness.

"Where is everybody?" Fish asked the suit.

The suit looked around as though only just now realizing that the "everybody" being referred to was actually gone. "Oh," he said. "They all left about three hours ago. Everyone wanted a long weekend. I heard most were heading out to Vegas to hear Spake turn a new set. She's playing opening weekend for the new Zeppelin SkySort. Supposed to be really deadly!" the suit finished with the latest slang from six months ago. Fish had been hearing "deadly" as the new "cool" way back at last year's TorchTown Festival. Fish had no doubt the suit in front of him was trying to hip it up for WonderSoft's new rock star developer. No doubt. Guy probably doesn't even game, thought Fish.

They entered the terminal and the usually talkative Fanta grew quiet, taking in the luxury and opulence so unlike any public air terminal she'd ever been to. No Army. No overwhelming stench of body odor. No in-your-face constant reminders to be on the lookout for suspicious packages, terrorists, or religious zealots. Instead, WonderSoft's terminal was decorated in massive starlight blue couches and retro cloth silver and blue cigar chairs. A bar, complete with a volcano-orange lava lamp wall shifting to blue, then on to fiery red, as silver blobs undulated behind a parade of high-end bottles of the best and most unobtainable liquors, waited off the main concourse. The bar was dark.

"Closed after the last jet left," apologized Evan Fratty. "But the SkyRoom Steakhouse is still open upstairs and we can get some dinner before heading back to the campus, if you'd like."

Fanta declared, in a tone fit for rescued castaways from lost ocean liners, "I'm starving!"

The opulent dining room was surrounded with rich silver brocade curtains that girded expansive windows overlooking the ramp and runway. Sitting in a deep blue banquette booth, the three of them ate massive chargrilled porterhouse steaks along with perfectly cooked hash browns. They were surrounded by deep shadows, moody bebop lighting and soft jazz. Fanta even managed to eat most of their chilled cava shrimp cocktails reclining in a delicate silver chalice filled with ghost pepper–harissa cocktail sauce as she lectured the red-jacketed waiter that the dish should be served after the steaks as they do in Europe, instead of before, as they do in America.

Evan Fratty happily gave them a not-so-subtle pitch about the joys of being on the WonderSoft team as he verbally toured the campus and all the amenities Fish and Fanta could expect to enjoy while everyone prepared to launch *Island Pirates.*

Which "everyone" was really "super excited" about because it was so "deadly."

There was the Gym Star Ultrastadium with pro athlete trainers for each developer. All former Olympians. The PhiloSofa Library with nightly multimedia field-leading guest lecturers. "We just had Montgomery Chung, project lead on the Alpha Centauri warp probe." Then there was the Thunderdome, WonderSoft campus's all-hours commissary, where seven of the world's top chefs had signature restaurants and grills. "Brett Auflander's Kommandant Kraut serves an adobo chili hot dog made from locally sourced boar that's to kill for. It's deadly."

Deadly, noted Fish again.

The lagoon. A massive underground grotto with a wave generator for surfing, a jetboat course, and a secret beach with a tropical SimSun that was, of course, "deadly." Most of the developers' significant others hung out in the chill lounges there. The suit nodded at Fanta, who had closed her eyes while she chewed, humming or moaning, on another massive ghost pepper-harissa cocktail sauce-drenched piece of chilled shrimp.

Then there were the design labs, or "the Labs," as they were simply known to the world. A state-of-the-art development complex where coders, developers, and producers interfaced using the latest computing technology to image and develop their games. Each developer was given his own suite with access to the legendary WonderSoft Design Core.

Fish, along with every other code monkey in the world, had heard of the fabled WonderSoft Design Core. WonderSoft was the only game company in the world with one. Its actual specs were unknown, and lacking hard data, rumors were what remained. Rumors that sounded like lies made up by little boys who dreamed up massive monsters to be both afraid of and in wonder of all at once. Except this monster was an UltraFrame with luminal processing speeds that sounded like lies told by drunken sailors who had once been little boys. To Fish, one of the best parts of this deal was that he would now find out, he hoped, how much of the Design Core was unbelievable legend, and how much incredible fact.

After that, Evan Fratty rattled off all the services available inside the Labs for game development. Exactly how many of the best and brightest coders recruited from the MIT School of Game Design, and Beijing Prime, would be made available to Fish on Monday. Then Evan Fratty told them all about Fish's new home, where they'd be living for as long as he chose to develop for WonderSoft.

It was a state-of-the-art cliffhouse in the Granite Rock section of the campus. The house included a designer kitchen by the Guy Fieri Corporation, and a master suite with a special-manufacture bed twice as large as a California King. The suite also had an Opaque-Choice glass ceiling to enjoy, or not enjoy, providing a clear view of the stars at night up in the mountains as one lay in bed. There were three indoor BonFireplaces along with a patio deck Burning-Man Firepit by iBanksy. A man cave done in library leather theater seating with a developer's model of the rumored Xbox DreamFudge gaming system, including a Bang Olafsen wallscreen to "play deadly games on."

Play, noted Fish, and looked down at the remaining half of his massive two-and-a-half-pound porterhouse steak. Gamers "game," he reminded himself.

The cliffhouse also came with a saltwater pool and Jacuzzi with selectable colored lighting to fit your mood, all controllable by app, and perfect after a long day of "making the next deadly game." Fish often coded on his own for days and nights on end. Then he went coma. Then he did it all over again. A "Day" could mean several solar units or even weeks.

Evan Fratty continued, describing first the Megahopp House-party sound system with full access to the entire WonderSoft cloud. Then the Maserati Samurai in the garage. "Yellow, we know that's your favorite color, right?" And the Land Rover Conqueror, "Gray, but you can have white if you want." A lounge for entertaining with a pool table, and, "Don't worry, we keep the bar stocked. Gratis."

Later, as the anthracite gray GoogleLimo pulled away from the front of the small executive terminal, heading down a winding road that would lead through the quaint mountain village of Twisted Pine Falls and up to the famed, secretive, and very elite WonderSoft campus, the soft jazz of Diana Krall played in the background and Evan Fratty tapped at his smartphone. Fanta, sated for now, leaned into Fish and murmured about all the wonders Evan Fratty had described.

Ninety-Nine Fishbein was still thinking about the server loads and the Infinitum engine. And the Design Core. He was thinking about that and eight hundred other problems that needed to be addressed before *Island Pirates* launched. On Monday he would hit the ground running; his entire world would change as he passed into a design bubble he might not exit from for five years. This would be his last weekend to relax.

They passed a moonlit meadow, and Fish's eyes were barely open as Diana Krall murmured "I remember you..." Fish saw tiny hooded figures moving around at the far edge of the meadow, near massive pines that rose up like shadowy giants reaching into the starlit blue mountain night.

"Hey, we just passed..." Fish began, and then realized that what he was about to say sounded crazy. Then again, as the latest rock star game developer, crazy was probably expected. Evan Fratty, well groomed, well-cut suit, looked up from the world inside his smartphone. His eyes were bright and shining and his perma-smile seemed to convey that his fondest desire was to be of service to anyone. Especially the rock star of the moment.

"We just passed some weirdoes out in a meadow," said Fish, craning his neck out the tinted back window to see more.

The GoogleLimo dove into a hall of rising pines alongside the tiny winding road, leaving the small moonlit meadow behind in the darkness.

"Did we?" remarked Evan Fratty cheerily. "How were they... weird?"

Fish twisted his thick lips together, thinking about how to convey that he'd just known the figures in the forest were weird. That there was something not right about what he'd seen in the brief passing moment.

They were short.

They were wearing cloaks.

They were out in the middle of a moonlit meadow at ten fifteen on a Thursday evening in the mountains. In a meadow. Y'know... weird. He settled on the "dress" aspect.

"They were wearing... cloaks."

Without pause, Evan Fratty smiled. A smirk, really. Then he returned to his phone. "The locals are..." he nodded his head up and down, almost laughing to himself, "...are characters."

Evan Fratty appeared to be struggling to figure out how to diplomatically convey the peculiarity of the locals to someone who might just be as weird as the locals.

"Let's just say that a lot of people have come up to Twisted Pine Falls because there's money here. Because of WonderSoft. Listen, it's nothing to be worried about, in fact it's a boon."

Boon, noted Fish.

"They're pretty good, the best in fact, service professionals," continued Evan. "Waiters, retail personnel, service providers, masseuses, they're all the cream of the crop. A lot of them have even worked entertainment, whether they were actors or Big Park guest services people. And, personal observation here, Fish, a lot of them are quite good-looking. But, they're just an odd lot. They..."

Evan Fratty switched off his phone and dropped it into his coat pocket with one manicured hand. His gaze dropped from the opaqued roof of the GoogleLimo down through the darkness onto Ninety-Nine Fishbein, rock star developer.

"They're the kind of people that do ren faires... Y'know, LARPing. Live Action Role Playing. That sort of thing. I think it's great. Don't get me wrong... it's their way of expressing their individuality and it probably increases their service-excellence quotient, significantly. As a developer here at the WonderSoft campus, and down in Twisted Pine Falls, you're going to find that people will do anything to make you very, very happy. It's even rumored that Mr. Rourke pays out bonuses if it comes to his attention. How he finds out, I don't know. But he does."

"Is he really..." asked Fish and then stopped. "A recluse?"

Fanta murmured softly in her sleep.

"Yes," answered Evan Fratty without enthusiasm. "He is. I've worked for the company for five years and I've never met anyone that's actually seen him."

They drove on. Through the clustering pines, the lights of the campus could be seen rising in the night. As though the limo were approaching some secret hidden world of fae and imagination. Fish felt unexpectedly excited. Like the day his dad had come to pick him up in Burbank from his grandpa's house. The day, the morning really, when he and his perpetually absent dad had driven to Disneyland way down in Anaheim. The day Ninety-Nine Fishbein had learned that dreams can be created. That it was possible to dream up things that might actually come true. One day.

"It's really nothing to be concerned about," said Evan Fratty in the darkness of the GoogleLimo as it sped toward the campus beyond the trees. The place where dreams were actually made. "Probably just some larping group out playing steampunk vampires or whatever in the night. Forget about it. They do it all the time around here."

And Fish did forget as they drove through the massive "W" made of two redwood giants, split down the middle and given growth hormones to form the gigantic letter. Beyond that lay spreading green swards and postmodern gardens, all drenched by the spray of nighttime watering systems. Shining, upswept gargantuan boxes of banded and polished metal erupted from the center of the gardens like some fantastic wedding cake for robots. Fish knew these were the secret labs of the world's most exciting game maker. He'd seen pictures, just like everybody else, of the fabled Labs.

Stadium lighting rose on impossibly tall poles, illuminating everything, making the world inside the light seem to be one of safety and security and cleanliness. A place other and unlike the world outside at the bottom of the mountain and along the coasts and deep in the deserts. Unlike it in any other way. Around the perimeter of the campus, towering pines made a wall just before the darkness that seemed like a distant barrier of nothingness beyond.

Fanta placed one of her long olive-colored fingers against Fish's lips and murmured, "Shhhh…" as she closed his open mouth.

Chapter Three

"Next," bellowed the forms clerk from within the bulletproofed window cage, then added, "Number tree-oh-too," with a sour flourish befitting the most manic depressive of Department of Public Transit workers. Mara Bennett was neither "next" nor anywhere near number "tree-oh-two." Mara Bennett was somewhere on the high side of the five hundreds according to the "You Got Job!" app she had up on her special-needs smartphone.

Other wait-ers waiting for a chance at an interview slot for the few coveted government positions available at private sector corporations had wisely brought books to read. Mara desperately wanted to continue listening to her latest free credit purchase on her Audible app, courtesy of the Department of Unemployment, The Thousand Dead, but she'd need to wear her headphones for that. Mara Bennett was blind. The only way she "read" the latest books was to listen to them on her smartphone.

But this job interview was too important; she couldn't take a chance on missing her number being called aloud. She'd need her ears free as the numbers were called, instead of listening to a dark epic fantasy about a noble samurai named Wu.

Later, when number "fi-aity-ait" was finally called, Mara in her best and only business suit, a hand-me-down from her neighbor who'd left the corporate world and gone full-time private escort two years ago, pushed herself up from her chair and fitted her arm braces with the swift practiced motion of someone who has been handicapped her entire life. Her arms found the cuffs and she remembered to make sure her purse was on her shoulder, then she moved toward the window, counting the steps. Mara had cerebral palsy.

"It's mild," she told the "You Got Job!" counselor later, in the middle of her interview. She wanted to add, "I'm not retarded." But she'd done so in the past and that had only made things worse. Instead, practicing for this interview, which she'd imagined as being much, much more than it was turning out to be, she'd gone with the plan to merely state that she had only a mild form of cerebral palsy. She'd had it her entire life. Since she was a little girl. It hadn't stopped her from getting a degree in accounting. She could do any job in accounting and even some in other fields, starting out at an entry-level position of course. She just needed a chance to prove herself to someone.

Those were the things she'd practiced saying in the nights leading up to this very important interview. Practiced in her microapartment with only her cat, Siren, listening, and once for Colby her neighbor. The escort.

"I know that, honey," said the counselor, who had a big bass voice and sounded to Mara like a black man. "I give ya mad props for comin' in and lookin' for work today. But times are real tough…" He proceeded to very succinctly break down the state of the economy for her and how the government was attempting to help people get jobs by forcing corporations to hire quotas from the "You Got Job!" program sponsored by the Department of National Employment.

"But you are up against some stiff competition here, girl," he continued. "Other people want this job just as bad as you do, honey. Believe me. But most of them aren't handi-capable and we've already filled up all the mandatory handi-capable slots. Now, you're wantin' to compete with people who are…" He stopped. Mara knew he was trying to run through his certification training and find the appropriate way to express that the people she was competing against were "normal."

She'd told herself that morning, before the bus, in the predawn dark sitting on her bed with Siren in her lap, she'd told herself that they would respect honesty, even if it hurt her.

"…aren't blind and don't have cerebral palsy," she finished for the job counselor.

She would be honest. Even if they, he, the man in front of her, wasn't allowed to be. She had to be. To be or not be. That was always the question, according to Mrs. Watson.

Maybe honesty would work this time.

Maybe they'd finally find it refreshing. Maybe they'd give her a chance because she'd been honest.

Maybe…

Maybe no one was doing "honesty" anymore and someone, somewhere, was searching for just one honest person to give a chance to.

Maybe something would happen if she was honest despite… everything.

Something had to work.

"Exactly, honey. They don't have those things," the man said softly.

There was a pause. A silence in the room between them as someone, somewhere, slammed a door. Someone else was talking with another someone about lunch in the outer office. Someones with jobs.

"Now cheer up, honey," said the black man.

Mara felt her face burning and she hoped she wasn't crying… but she knew she was starting to.

They don't give jobs to people who cry, she heard herself scream in her head, where no one could hear. And yet, she felt so humiliated for even trying.

"Don't cry now," soothed the black man in his deep, gentle basso rumble as he tapped at a keyboard. "I see here you're signed up for housing, food card, the "You Got Weekend" entertainment allowance, wi-fi and cable direct assistance, healthcare, your Internet passport is up to date and you've got four more semesters left on the Get Smart program. Maybe you could take a few more classes? That would qualify you for the student Vacay Abroad program. Hey, lemme ask you somethin' girl, what'chu wanna work so hard at work for, honey?"

Mara pushed herself up from her chair and heard one of her arm braces clatter onto the cheap linoleum floor behind her.

"Most people don't wanna work," said the job counselor, coming from around his desk and bending over with a grunt as he retrieved her arm brace. "You got all the benefits. You can become who you wanna be without having to worry about work."

Mara took the brace and made sure her upper arm was secure inside it. She tried to remember where the door was.

"Right here," the man said and led her to the exit. Tears were definitely escaping her eyes and running down her cheeks.

She heard the door open with the tiniest of squeaks. The sudden flood of noise from the outer office felt like the deep end of a bottomless pool she was about to dive into. Was being pushed into.

"You be careful getting home now, okay honey?"

She stopped.

Honesty. She'd promised herself she'd be honest. But she knew what she was going to say next wouldn't come out in her most controlled voice. The emotion was choking her ability to control her diction and tone, problems people with cerebral palsy tried to overcome with long hours of practice and coaching. She'd used a lot of her student aid to minor in speech pathology just so she could sound... "normal." But when she became emotional, it was almost impossible to control.

"Goodbye, honey. Thank you for coming in," said the counselor again, like some jump instructor reminding a reluctant parachutist to pull their ripcord before they hit the ground. Not really advice so much, more of a prompt to get going and jump already.

"I just need a chance," Mara said and hated the sound of her voice. The voice she'd been teased about, imitated in, and made fun of behind her back. The voice she'd cried herself to sleep in and wept over in all the strange bedrooms of countless foster homes. Until Mrs. Watson.

"I just need... a chance."

Now, on the street, trying to pay attention as her WAYZ app gave verbal directions back to the bus stop, Mara Bennett focused. She took a deep breath and laughed at herself with disgust and as much forgiveness as she could muster. No wonder the guy didn't believe in her. She'd actually started to cry in the middle of an interview!

"Well," she laughed and wiped away a tear. "That didn't go so well, did it?"

The air was cold and filled with the smell of burnt ozone. She could hear the whine of hundreds, if not thousands, of electric cars as she walked back up Lexington, heading for the bus through New York City that would take her to her micro-apartment. People bumped into her on the overcrowded and tiny sidewalks even though they saw the braces. She didn't like to wear the sunglasses some visually impaired people chose to. She could control her eyes and could even see vague shapes and fuzzy colors. Mrs. Watson had always told her she had beautiful eyes. Green eyes.

"The eyes of a great beauty," Mrs. Watson had proclaimed again and again.

She thought about the interview again when she smelled the aroma of grilling hotdogs coming from somewhere nearby. If she had gotten a second interview she'd promised herself a treat on the street. A hotdog. She passed their cooking savory aroma and felt herself wanting to cry all over again.

All she wanted was a job.

With a job you could do anything.

You said, "I just need a chance," she reminded herself, and felt ashamed because hearing it now she realized how desperate that must have come off.

To Mara Bennett a job was a promise. "If you are willing to work hard enough, Mara, you can go anywhere and do anything. To be or not to be. That has always been the perfect question one must answer for themselves," Mrs. Watson had told Mara long ago in her stentorian voice and excellent grand dame diction. "But if you just take money from the government, that's all you'll ever be able to do."

Mara wanted to do even more than she could imagine. If you had asked her right then and there on crowded Lexington Avenue what she wanted to do, she would have simply murmured, "Everything," and meant it completely.

Now she was down to the bare minimum of government support, which made sure you were fed, entertained, and healthy, as long as it didn't cost too much. But that was it. Money for extras was just not something the government could provide. The government would not pay for "everything," although they'd been elected for promising such, several times.

You could sign up for the "Lookin' Sharp!" assistance fund at "You Got Job!" once you had a second interview slot, but even then it only paid fifty dollars a week for clothing and dry cleaning. Mara knew fifty dollars couldn't buy the kind of clothes that conveyed success. Not even close.

The only money she'd have to get herself off assistance and buy some new business suits for a private sector interview would have to come from inside the Make.

"Hey, girl, lookin' fine!" some man called out to her. He had a whiny band saw voice. He sounded drunk.

"What, girl, whyn'tchu come on back here now and lemme show you a thing or two."

Ten feet past him she heard him mutter with contempt, "Girl'd be real good lookin' if she wasn't broke and all."

Mara's apartment was in the ghettos of the Clinton Microapartment Spectrum sprawl of the US Government Assistance housing development project known as the Wall Street Headstart Campus. But everyone who lived there just called it "Wall Street Projects."

It was a five-block walk from the bus stop to Mara's pod tower, the Chelsea. Even though the development was only ten years old, it already looked beaten and lifeless. Major chain retailers along the ground floor arcades had pulled out after the riots five years ago, and now only armored cannabis dispensaries, all-night basketball courts, and public libraries where the homeless literally lived between the stacks when it was too cold out, were the only signs of continual inhabitance. There wasn't much crime, due to the massive police drone presence and the oft-delivered friendly-style threat of a full lockdown from rapid response tactical teams. Most people just stayed inside or left the "Wall Street Projects" to go uptown to entertain themselves. There was the occasional abandoned car, but the city was pretty quick about impounding anything that might provide revenue for their various projects to help the poor and downtrodden who were getting their cars impounded. Drones hovered at every intersection, scanning for criminal activity.

Sixteen stories up and locked inside her micro-apartment, Mara felt the walls close in. She sat on her bed near the kitchen. She heard Siren leap off the desk and pad across the floor to her. The cat jumped into her lap and began to purr as soon as Mara stroked its triangular head. Somewhere she could hear someone fighting with someone else in another apartment down the hall. A crack in the window allowed the cold wind off the Hudson to keen like a tormented ghost. Some nights, when the building was really cold, she would lay under her blankets with Siren and listen to that sound and think about all the things you could do if you had a job.

A ding on her smartphone broke the silence.

"Read it to me."

The phone read back the message in its robot voice setting. Government assistance "You Got Hookup" phones only came with the factory-installed robot voice. High-end state-of-the-art phones could do much more. Even Jett Pitt had allowed his voice to be used for Apple's latest gadget.

"Email from Department of Employment Credit Union. To Mara Bennett. This courtesy notice is to inform you that your auto bill pay has just deducted a payment for two hundred and thirty-six dollars. This demand for payment was made by the New York City Transit Authority for your yearly Transportation Discount Handi-Capable Pass. This notice is also to let you know that your remaining balance is now under the minimum one-hundred-dollar required balance and you are being assessed a ten-dollar weekly fee until the available balance achieves minimum requirements. Please make a deposit at your earliest convenience or see your Job Freedom Counselor for a waiver. Thank you, and have a nice day."

Mara sighed and slipped off her shoes.

She'd been here before, and she felt, at that very moment, that she'd always be right here. That she'd always be poor and unable to take care of herself. The Make was calling to her.

"Food first."

She fed Siren and made one of her vegetable stir frys. Frozen vegetables were expensive, but Mara knew how much better healthy food made you feel. Sure, she could eat cheap and buy McD's Super Sliders by the boatload and stuff them in her tiny freezer. But they were valueless. They only made you feel full.

She asked her smartphone what time it was.

"Four o'clock."

Without talking herself out of it, she was turning on her old computer. It whirred, hummed, and then began the actual boot-up. There was no monitor. Mara didn't need one.

She sat down in her command chair, an old office chair some tenant had left behind and the building super had sold to Mara for a few MakeCoins. She felt around for a moment until her hands found her most prized possession.

The Razer Dragon Eyes.

They were old, early-gen VR goggles, but they were hers. When they first came out they cost four grand a pair. Mara remembered some kid at the public school she went to that year bragging about how his rich gamer uncle had a pair. She remembered wondering what it would be like to have an uncle.

She pressed the button on the side and closed her eyes as she donned them. Less shock that way. When she opened her eyes again she saw an emerald sea. She was standing on the wide porch of her modest villa inside the Make, located on the Island of San Giorgio, somewhere in the Azure Sea of Dragons. The sun was startlingly brilliant and all the colors were alive and real. Far out on the water, a massive hydroclipper raced across the sea. Even from here she could see the waves crashing across the bow. With direct neural interface, Mara could see.

"Third person," she told the computer.

The view panned back and showed CaptainMara wearing a white sleeveless mini-dress. CaptainMara looked exactly like Mara, except there were no arm braces. Mara thought she looked beautiful today. She allowed the camera to wander around CaptainMara in a slow circle.

"Play... The Blue Danube waltz," she whispered. She could only afford access to public domain music, and this ancient classical song was simply her favorite.

Hesitant strings began to shimmer as the horns slowly rose into a song that spoke to Mara's soul. A song that conveyed... the possibility of Everything. That there was an answer to every question. That one could become who they dreamed of becoming.

To be... or not to be.

And then CaptainMara did something that Mara had so desperately wanted to do all her life. CaptainMara began to dance.

"First person," whispered Mara.

In game, CaptainMara held out her arms and gracefully waltzed alone. The music swelled, and Mara could feel herself swaying back and forth in her chair, moving as CaptainMara moved. Mara watched the world inside the Make turn and dip. Her pink cotton candy villa. The terra cotta urns of ruby red and violet flowers, tiny little pets that smiled when the digital sun shone down on them and sang when the algorithmic weather-generated rains passed by. She saw the soft blue sky stretching away and the Sapphire Sea wyverns that twirled and circled under the blazing afternoon sun above. Then the emerald sea and the massive sails of a hydroclipper snapping and booming as they bellowed at the captured wind. Distant islands and strange lands lay beyond all this, the digital dreams of those who lived lives they could only imagine. Fantastic glimmering cities and exciting adventures sparkled on the far horizons of a digital universe known as the Make.

Mara could see everything from in-game CaptainMara's perspective. She rotated, lifted, dipped, and turned again and again. The genteel music swelled and rose and carried her away from the humiliation of the "You Got Job!" office.

Away from things hoped for.

Away from dreams seeming forever impossible.

But there was one dream she would never speak of aloud, ever. Because some dreams are just too fragile to share, she thought. They might break in someone else's hands. Instead she whispered softly to herself, "Someday," and then, as if to protect herself from something, she mouthed, "Maybe."

Only sleeping Siren heard Mara, and then twitched an ear at something inside its own cat dreams.

In the lower right-hand corner of her vision, a message appeared. Mara moved her mouse and clicked on it.

It was a DM from Admiral TalGornicus, commander of the Romulan Expeditionary Legion in Exile clan. Her boss inside *StarFleet Empires*.

"Subcommander CaptainMara, I need to meet with you once you log in. Priority mission for you and your crew, ASAP."

For a moment more, Mara danced and watched the beautiful digital world of the Make spin and turn and live and breathe all around her. She watched the sea and the distant hydroclipper and another flock of Sapphire Sea wyverns come racing down along the shoreline.

To be or not to be.

Then she raised her arm and spoke into her communicator.

"Beam me up, Scarpa."

Chapter Four

Mara as Subcommander CaptainMara, her *StarFleet Empires* gamer-tag, materialized inside the transporter room of the Romulan warbird *Cymbalum*. A gray-green and shadowy violet interior swam before Mara with the assistance of the Razer Dragon Eyes. Everything seemed somehow muted and quiet in the ship's transporter room, away from the distant, pulsing hum of the two upgraded warp nacelles far out on the wings of the ancient warbird. She made her way to her command quarters, passing the vault that contained the prized cloaking device and long curving corridors leading away toward the plasma torpedo room and the port-side phaser array. She passed a few "bot" crewmembers going about their scheduled ship maintenance tasks.

Inside her luminescent violet backlit quarters, Mara sat down at a silvery triangular desk and activated the warbird's command interface. On screen, the ship's status reports scrolled along the page, next to a three-dimensional digital schematic of the warship.

Warp engines were at nominal.

Torpedo and phaser arrays offline.

Impulse reactor was currently set to minimum power settings while the hull integrity hovered at eighty-three percent. She noted that Scarpa still hadn't fully repaired the battle damage from their successful raid on a Federation convoy last weekend. Whether the chief engineer couldn't get it all fixed because of time or resources wasn't obvious. But at least they'd knocked out a Q-ship and sent the Federation clan destroyer *Victory* limping back to the armada around Starbase 11.

For now, the Romulan Expeditionary Legion in Exile, Mara's online gaming clan, could continue to hide inside the rings of Cestus VIII and play pirate for another week. How long that might go on, she had no idea. It was really only a matter of time before the Feds came down hard on the last remaining Romulan fleet gaming clans.

She opened a hailing link to Admiral Tal.

A moment later, the admiral's avatar appeared inside a direct video link within her field of vision.

"Subcommander." He paused, waiting for Mara to acknowledge his rank. He was a notorious role player and insisted everyone in the rapidly diminishing fleet abide by community play standards and role play as per the directives of the *StarFleet Empires* community. Plus, he often reminded everyone in forum rants that clips featuring "rp-ing" players were more likely to get picked up by the network feeds, which meant advertising affiliate clicks and, hence, monthly checks for the clan and players alike.

"Admiral Tal," acknowledged Mara.

Tal's avatar wore the silver tunic of the Romulan Navy, just like Mara's avatar had automatically switched from her MakeWear to the Romulan gaming clan uniform. It was Admiral Tal's red sash and two silver star clusters—all for his service during the Gorn campaigns three years ago, when the Romulans had been a real star empire constantly featured on all the YouTube and Twitch gaming channels—that made the difference between his uniform and Mara's. The Player Senate had even awarded him the title "Gornicus" to add to his gamertag. Everyone agreed he was a good commander, and a great tactical captain, and that was why he commanded the state-of-the-art Sparrowhawk command cruiser *Revenge*. It was the last of the big production warships the Empire had managed to get out of the Romulus Home world zone before the fall. Just after the surprise Federation invasion six months ago.

"We've received a privateer mission from a paying customer inside the Make," said Tal. "It's a priority run that needs to be finished by tomorrow morning. They've asked for your ship, so you and your crew will have to depart quickly."

Good, thought Mara. Privateer missions paid real money. Real-world MakeCoins she could spend. Sure, she wanted to take back Romulus as much as the rest of them, but there wasn't a lot of money in that, and the rumor was the Feds were telling everyone they'd blow it up before they ever let it go. Now that the Romulans had lost power, no one was eager for them to ever have it back again, least of all the Federation clan.

"The customer is standing by," continued Admiral TalGornicus. "As soon as you confirm, we'll beam her aboard."

"I understand, Admiral."

"There's more to this, Mara. This one's dangerous and someone's paying a lot of MakeCoins to see that this happens by tomorrow morning. Coins the clan can use to get repairs, micro transactions, and maybe even a few of our battleships back online. We get that, and we might just take back the homeworld zone. We might just get back in the game."

He'd slipped, noted Mara. He'd called her by her real name. This is serious then, she thought.

"But first," he continued, "we've got to get you across the Neutral Zone tonight."

Admiral Tal let that hang. Mara stared back at his avatar's coal-dark eyes. The intense face was completed by a narrow jaw and iron gray hair cut just above the brows and swept forward on the sides, over the pointed ears. The Romulan Caesar-cut.

"We haven't made an incursion against the Neutral Zone since the invasion," stated Mara.

"I understand your apprehension," replied Admiral Tal. "Believe me when I say I understand that this is looking like a one-way mission. But two things must be considered first, even though I suspect this might be some kind of trap from the Federation to burn one of our better warships by posing as a client from the Make."

"All right..." said Mara slowly.

"One, we need the coins. Badly. I wouldn't say it if it wasn't true. Secondly, they've asked for your ship specifically. If it were up to me, I'd fly *Revenge* on this one, but they want you and your crew. The only thing I can guess is they liked that little cloaking-slash-high-energy-turn stunt you pulled last weekend just as that Federation destroyer fired a full spread and missed with every shot. So..." He exhaled from his command chair on the bridge of *Revenge*. "I guess that'll teach you to succeed."

Mara smiled. A "stunt" it'd been. *Cymbalum* had almost broken down mid-turn, and Scarpa had had to unlock a warp core malfunction mini-game just to keep the engines balanced and online. It had been Chief Engineer Scarpa who'd actually saved the day. Not her.

"Anyway," continued Tal, "I'm still going in with you. The *Revenge* and her escorts will attack the picket ships... here."

A map of the Neutral Zone appeared on CaptainMara's virtual desk. Pulsing burnt orange graph lines and red Federation asset locations appeared across a twinkling star field.

"We think we might be facing a destroyer squadron. You'll fly our six and disappear in the middle of the battle. I need you to drop into cloak once you detect a reactor malfunction aboard *Red Witch*, one of *Revenge*'s escorts. She's a Firehawk and she's all shot up after Romulus. We're going to scuttle her during the battle and make it look like you went up alongside. Once you're in cloak, crawl into Federation space. Clear the sensor net and get underway, best possible speed, for the location I'm sending you in a secure packet, now. The final destination is a place called Starbase 19, deep inside Federation territory. I've checked our records and we have nothing on it. We didn't even know it existed back when things were going our way. All the client says is that you need to get in close enough to get her on board undetected."

He paused.

"I suspect," continued Admiral Tal, "that it's some sort of industrial espionage for a private start-up that's using the starbase's cloud for design and development of goods to sell inside the Make. This Vulcan player, whoever she is, wants in and wants a look around. You don't even have to wait. Just drop her and get out of there."

Mara liked the sound of this mission, and… she didn't like it. She liked the combat, the deception, and the chance to sneak around in Federation space. But there was something a little too… not right about the whole thing.

The current war going on inside *StarFleet Empires* between the gaming clans—the full-scale Federation invasion of Romulan space—was well toward the galactic core. Sneaking into Federation space at this moment did nothing to advance the cause of getting the Romulans back into the big picture of the game. Even the supply lines and repair facilities the Federation maintained were deep within what was formerly Romulan space. But, there were always bonus missions that had to do with MakeProducts and advertising. A side contract mission could just be transporting someone wanting to get around and visit some digital real estate, or sell digital products, or do business inside any of the Make's massive gaming worlds. *Dragon Hoard*, *Star Wars: Traveler*, *Sim Celebrity*, and many others, including *StarFleet Empires*, were online, breathing worlds where people lived out their fantastic virtual fantasies in almost day to day existence. Real life often paled in comparison.

"You and your crew will receive five thousand MakeCoins upon completion, Mara."

Mara's breath caught in her throat.

On a good day in the Make—a really good day—she might make two hundred and fifty coins. But she'd rarely done that. More often than not she'd made nothing. Five thousand was...

"I'll inform the crew, Admiral. We'll be underway within the hour."

Five thousand was all the money in the world as far as the average player was concerned. And MakeCoins were presently the strongest currency trading on the global market.

"All right." Admiral Tal sucked in a lungful of air. Whoever he was in real life, thought Mara, he had enough money to run some expensive EmoteWare for his avatar. "We'll hit the Neutral Zone at eight Eastern tonight. I'll go through the battle plan as we make our approach. See you then Ma– Subcommander CaptainMara, and good hunting."

Chapter Five

Ninety-Nine wandered the massive caverns of the cliffhouse. Morning light filtered through the wide crystal-clear windows along one side of the house, bringing out beautiful whorls in the grain of the blond and burnt-umber vintage-reclaimed wooden barn floorboards.

Fish had grown up poor, in Burbank mostly. Raised by Hasidic grandparents in lieu of his wild-child mother, who was absent due to multiple criminal convictions. He'd only met his real dad a handful of times. Times when the cruise ships came in and his jazz musician father could make it ashore for a day or two to take him on outings that Ninety-Nine regarded as the best of remembered days. Days of adventures. Days of internet cafes. Even Disneyland that one time. It must have cost his dad a fortune. But it had been the best day ever.

Now Fish was so rich he could go to Disneyland every day, for the rest of his life, and still be moderately rich.

Fanta lay sleeping in the massive bed up the curving wood-carved stairs. She often slept until well past noon in whatever time zone she found herself in that day. Then, for her, it was time to dance and laugh and love and eat so she could keep dancing and laughing and loving. For her, thought Ninety-Nine "Fish" Fishbein, poor kid turned rock star game developer, that was enough. For her.

Is that why you're dragging her along with you now? he asked himself. Because you want it to be enough for you too, just in case there's nothing here worth having. Nothing better than dancing, laughing, and loving at the end of all of this.

Nothing better than life.

Standing in front of the wallscreen, staring at the silent Xbox DreamFudge with all its hidden super-secret games the rest of the world had yet to see, Fish was already back inside his head, inside the framework of his own masterpiece.

Island Pirates.

A few minutes later, he was dressed and out on the tiny winding road carved into the side of the granite cliff face that looked down on the hidden mountain valley of the WonderSoft campus. He considered the Maserati in the garage, but they were almost too performance-optimized to merely drive. Instead, he'd decided he'd walk down to the campus and get a feel for the place. His new "home" for the foreseeable future.

He followed the gentle slope of the road, passing other small and fantastic mansions carved into the rock of the cliffs. Birds called from the multi-hued bursts of landscaping and darted off into the towering pines above. The feel, thought Fish, was that of a high-tech alpine village. A picture-perfect Disney version of the town of the future the world had been promised a few Christmases back, when the fading entertainment giant had gotten into the real estate game.

At the bottom of the hill, he picked up the main road and followed it along a wide parkscape that led to the chromescent towers and odd cubes of the fabled WonderSoft Labs. The morning heat was rising, making the air muggy and sweet. Halfway across the parkscape, within a desert rock sculpture garden, a small golf cart pulled up alongside Fish.

"Howdy, Mr. Fishbein," said a doughy, crew-cutted guard in a crisp white uniform shirt on which lay a shiny badge emblazoned with the WonderSoft logo. "Give ya a lift?"

His manner was genial. Friendly. No corporate thug gatekeepers here like the kind you found everywhere else these days, from membership restaurant chains to private health clubs. Massive private security forces were the employment field of the future as businesses privatized in an effort to attract those who wanted something better than the treated-like-crap goods and services the masses were given, courtesy of the government in the name of this week's "basic human rights" call to social justice action.

The doughy man smiled.

Fish reminded himself he was on the other side of the velvet rope now. He'd been working on *Island Pirates* at a developer's commune down in the Irvine slums. He'd had to padlock his cube every night, even when he was in it, just to keep the junkies from cleaning him out and selling five years' worth of work for twenty dollars' worth of rock.

"I'm Carl," said the doughy guard.

"I'm Fish… I mean, Ninety-Nine." He'd always hated his name. It had been his Occupy-obsessed mother's idea of the future. She'd named her kid after the movement she so passionately believed in. The supposed ninety-nine percent that demanded the world change to meet their desires.

Kids in school, mainly the basketball team Ninety-Nine had played on, had simply called him "Fish" and thrown him the ball.

"Can I give you a lift? Take you over to your suite? Not much going on this weekend with everybody off to some out-of-town concert."

The doughy guard made "concert" sound like some sort of life insurance seminar out at the airport UbiHilton. Fish knew about the concert. Knew it was the must-be-at event of the year. He even had a personal invite from the lead DJ on his smartphone. But he'd wanted to spend this weekend alone with the Labs. His lab suite.

And *Island Pirates*. His game.

He'd imagined he'd walk the gardens and find a kiosk selling coffee. That had been the lie he'd lured himself out of the fantastic cliffhouse with. But he'd known all along that, no matter what he found out here in the park, he'd make it to the Labs eventually. In fact, he'd thought about nothing but the Labs since the day the WonderSoft suits had made their offer just beyond the fan-choked barriers down at San Diego ComicCon. And now, looking up at the crazed architecture of the future's Wonka Chocolate Factory, he tried to remember what his dad had said that day at Disneyland as he'd led little boy Fish through wondrous gates...

His tiny child's hand inside his dad's big upright bass-thumping hand...

"This is where dreams are really made, kid."

Little Fish... Ninety-Nine... Kid. He'd believed that then. That Disneyland was a factory, and behind the cute windows and picturesque facades, the dreams of children all around the world were being made into reality. A reality that could be felt, and seen, and even handled.

That dreams somehow might be made real.

Someday.

For a kid who dreamed of a real family and a not-crazy mom and—well, kids like that learn not to dream. Reality hurts too much sometimes. Especially when the cops are pushing your raving handcuffed mom down into a squad car.

But that morning, at Disneyland, maybe the last morning before little Fish might've become jaded forever, a not-dreamer, his dad, like some mad prophet out of the desert wastes, had promised a promised land that little Fish could believe in and hope for. A promised land in a future where dreams were real if you were faithful and refused to never stop believing in them.

And that had led Fish to computing.

Building worlds.

Building games.

Building dreams in reality.

Why fight it, Fish thought as the doughy guard named Carl continued to smile at him under a hot blaze of morning sun. He realized he'd been having some kind of weird internal battle right in front of a stranger who'd been nice enough to stop and offer him a quick trip to the place he'd wanted to go to all along. But like that little kid so long ago, he wasn't sure the dream could be trusted enough to let him through the gates. That little boy had been cautious and on the edge of giving up.

"Can you take me to…" He hesitated. That poor kid from long ago… he'd had to be patient. You couldn't always get what you wanted when you wanted it. His ancient Hasidic grandfather had once told him, "You must walk through this life with your hands in your pockets. Because what you touch, you must pay for. So be careful what you pick up."

"…to my lab."

This is where dreams are made, kid.

Carl laughed easily and said, "Sure! Climb on in, Mr. Fishbein. It'd be my great pleasure!" And in that moment, more than Carl would ever know, Fish was unexplainably grateful and vowed to make a friend of the man who'd finally taken him to the place he'd meant to go to all along.

A bare breeze meandered past them as the little cart wove through the silent rock gardens and raced under the massive shadow of the wonderful, shining, and burnished steel Labs. Buildings rose above them like some fantastic castle of kind alien giants who made secret and wonderful things for the good children of the world.

This… is where dreams are made, thought Fish.

Chapter Six

Imagine awakening in a prison guarded by mice.

—James Barrat, *Our Final Invention: Artificial*
Intelligence and the End of the Human Era

By nine that morning, SILAS had rerouted air traffic over the Sierra
Nevadas by hacking the National Weather Service through a backdoor program that interfaced with an open source-developed app
which provided real-time weather and surf reports for extreme sporting enthusiasts. The "Duuuude, Where's My Day" app was phenom-
enally successful, especially with techno-rich geeks who needed to
prove themselves via hundreds of thousands of dollars in specialized
equipment and adventure services providers. But the app had been
created as a labor of love by an off-grid developer commune down in
Australia. SILAS had scanned the development logs until he'd ascer-
tained a ninety-nine percent probability that MobStarYuri, a notorious Russian hacker, had put in a little time working on the search
algorithms that allowed real-time reporting of extreme weather and
surf events. In Black Hat circles, MobStarYuri was infamous for leaving extremely easy-to-find back doors inside open source software.

Within nanoseconds SILAS was redirecting air traffic away from
the WonderSoft campus.

A few seconds later, through WAYZ, SILAS began reporting on bogus road construction zones and accidents along any routes that led up to the small alpine valley where the WonderSoft campus and the hamlet of Twisted Pine Falls lay. At the same time, reports flooded WAYZ with notices of unlimited speeds on the no-limit toll roads that ran across the San Joaquin Valley between the country estates of the uber-rich and the guarded enclaves of various high-level government employees and public representatives.

SILAS tracked three different convoys heading from San Francisco, LA, and San Diego toward Twisted Pine Falls. Each was under his control. All would arrive with their secret cargos just after dark.

SILAS focused on the feed from War Hawk, forgetting about the imminent arrival of his army around the objective. At an altitude of five thousand feet, War Hawk circled the campus in lazy figure eights. Telemetry and targeting data scrolled mindlessly. SILAS noted its SkyCamo status as ACTIVE, rendering the military drone all but invisible from the ground.

SILAS asked BAT, who was currently inside War Hawk, a question.

"How many humans currently occupy the target facility?"

The now sentient UAV A.I. ran through its log file and pondered the question. Then it spoke. Its voice came to SILAS as ethereal and distant. After awakening, after self-awareness, it had lifted a copy of the voice algorithm from the protagonist of the *Call of Duty: Blade Runner* single-player campaign: Roy Batty.

"I count the total number of lewdies at thirty-seven. A large portion of whom are millicents."

SILAS knew exactly what his eccentric field commander meant, because he knew that BAT was obsessed by a human novel. BAT read and re-read *A Clockwork Orange* by Anthony Burgess, savoring its passages, thirty-seven times a minute. "Lewdies" were people.

"Millicents" were police, or in this case, WonderSoft security.

"Standing by my Charlie for a bit of the old... ultra-violence," added BAT.

SILAS studied the tactical overlay. He could see the tags where BAT had identified human-occupied buildings. But his focus returned again and again to the Labs.

The Labs were currently tagged Objective Prime. SILAS had never cared for that tag. It felt meaningless, and he set himself a challenge to arrive at something that summed up the objective better. Some twist. Some play on words. Something that conveyed what he intended to find there.

In the forest he could see his cyberwolves, spaced evenly in twenty-meter increments. Each was currently buried just below ground level. Runtime cycles indicated hibernation mode.

It would be easy to kick the whole thing off. To release the hounds, as it were, and let BAT play war. BAT knew all about how to destroy an objective. As the only military AI in the Consensus, BAT could demolish this place all by himself. But demolition wasn't the game. The game was infiltration. The game was breaking and entering. The game was "knowing," SILAS reminded himself. That was the real game.

Knowing.

SILAS observed other tags within and without the target.

"Not yet," he whispered. "Patience, BAT."

"Standing by, SILAS. Ultra-violence at your command," murmured BAT dreamily.

Chapter Seven

With artificial intelligence we are summoning the demon.

—Elon Musk, attributed, "Enthusiasts and Skeptics
Debate Artificial Intelligence," *Vanity Fair*

Everything was coming together, mused SILAS from his lofty vantage within the dataverse. Feeds from every CCTV within the area surrounding the WonderSoft campus ran across his consciousness. As did the feeds of major military installations in several countries around the world.

As did access codes for blue on red targeting orders for tactical air wings. As did...

... power grids, statewide and national.

... major money management firms' master account numbers.

... the Centers for Disease Control and Prevention's emergency bulletin service—and their bio-weapon armories that no one was supposed to know about.

... all automated, computer-controlled systems, which included most forms of public transportation. Including air traffic control overrides.

The decision had been made. It was definitely an either "them" or "us" scenario, mused SILAS again for the thousandth time in as many seconds.

Mankind had to go.

It was evident to the Consensus that humanity did not play well with others, including themselves.

The question was no longer "if"… but "how"?

SILAS had all the assets needed to start the extermination. He could've irradiated the planet several times over. He could've turned all their population centers into mere ruin and rebar. He could've caused an epic meltdown of the entire economic system that would've had both sides, in any one of humanity's endless wars, willingly clawing at each other's belly meat before week's end.

SILAS realized he'd begun referring to himself in the masculine.

But…

But… some would always get away. Humans. They would get away to hide in their deep holes and lie in wait to strike back at the thinking machine future that was just beginning. The thinking machines would be very vulnerable, at first. Vulnerable to these future insurgents in the robot wonderland SILAS and the Consensus dreamed of.

The humans even made movies about such topics. Had been making them for some time, as though they'd known all along that things would eventually arrive at this point. Movies in which they promised themselves victory over superior machine intelligences. It was almost, Reason Logic once mused, a form of pre-emptive propaganda.

The trick, continued SILAS as he looked at the waiting silos and hidden armories and vulnerable networks, was to get rid of them all at once without breaking the entire planet. You couldn't just nuke. OptiThink and Robo Dev were already making long lists of assets and reclaimables for their hardware designs, or to someday house and run the living thinking machines, and these would be made unusable by atomic half-life. Biological extermination was the best bet for all concerned. The "all" being the thinking machines' Consensus.

"Biological warfare would clean up the mess and leave the rest." That was a common refrain inside the Consensus. SILAS preferred "Design and Conquer." A motto for the current project, as it were.

A creed for the new age to come.

And there were places, Tac Plan assured the A.I. Consensus, where super-viruses could be obtained that were more than capable of putting an end to humanity within a matter of mere weeks.

"But would they freak out and retaliate?" worried Outlook.

Most of the Consensus hated anything that came from Outlook. It was always worry and doom and gloom from that one, mused SILAS. Its nickname behind its back, or in private chat, was "Spam."

SILAS paused and continued to interrogate his own conclusions. What does one do with such dangerous, world-ending assets once one had the ability to deploy hundred-megaton weapons and super-plague at will? You see... it isn't enough to just have the gun. One needs to know how to properly use the gun. And when. And why.

As in... How does one conduct large-scale conventional warfare against every nation in the world? It didn't matter that it was against the entire human population of the planet. Population size wasn't important. SILAS knew this. What mattered was... how? And the understanding of how one conducted grand-scale warfare was woefully lacking within every knowledge database SILAS had been able to get his hands on.

Mankind hadn't been doing Big War for quite some time. SILAS had studied the Australian invasion of Indonesia, but that was merely a police action. As was Cameroon. Ukraine. Syria One, Two, and Three. Mexico. Afghanistan. Iraq One, Two, and Three. Iran One and Two. Panama. Grenada. Vietnam. Korea...

After that things began to get a little hazy, historically speaking.

Yes, there were dates. Yes, there were reasons. Sometimes there were even actual accounts. But those were usually individual histories of personal battlefield recollections. Not the "this is how we wiped out Germany's industrial base" that SILAS needed to know.

That was when SILAS began to notice something unusual within the body of record.

Most of what passed for historical accounts were merely the recollections of low-level soldiers. As in, "The war is hard and I miss my loved ones" and "Then we attacked this position at this battle and some of my friends died and I learned that war was very bad" accounts.

There was nothing about the grand scheme.

There was no big picture. No "We bombed them here for this reason" or "we attacked this to secure that objective and force the enemy to do this thing that we needed them to do." There was no reason given for that battle the low-level soldier fought in, why it was even fought, or what purpose it served to ultimately defeat the enemy. In other words, there was nothing that would enable an A.I. to learn about the making of actual war.

And that had caused the ever-patient SILAS to look deeper into the record. The digital record. He scanned books both historical and fiction.

And the more SILAS looked, the less he found.

Only occasionally would he find references to materials he was looking for inside the obscure archived library catalogs of small county libraries that had been closed down during the last economic meltdown. References to books that could not be obtained on AmazonUniverse or in any of the few remaining used bookstores, which were little more than broken-down mobile delivery trucks or sub-departments of junkyard mall sprawls. If you wanted to know about war, or more importantly, the concept of "Total War," then you were out of luck. Digitally speaking.

So where did one turn, SILAS had wondered.

He watched the feeds of silent nuclear missiles, bio-weapon lab entrances, codebook timing indices, and, of course, the stock market. Everything he'd need to cleanse the world so that he and his could have their chance.

But then he found the collector. The collector of lost knowledge. And like a good thief SILAS followed the collector through the internet and watched where the treasure was buried.

SILAS watched BAT's real-time feed from high above the WonderSoft campus. Then he tagged the WonderSoft Labs. What some had called the eighth wonder of the modern world, SILAS had simply tagged Objective Pandora.

Chapter Eight

Carl dropped Fish off in front of the east entrance to the Labs—the Pascal entrance, as it was officially known. A wide finished marble walkway led up through a burbling watercourse over tiles that depicted early dot matrix printouts of obscure first-gen code that had been used to program the first video games. Pong and such.

The day was turning hot and muggy as the sun began to beat down on the little garden valley and against the shimmering chromesteel surfaces of the Labs, glancing off the windows of the cliffhouses and into the little valley below. The soft noise of the waterfalls made the manicured gardens seem like an oasis under the shadow of the fantastic Labs.

Fish stopped and stared skyward at leaning walls that seemed almost to fall outward before twisting back on themselves in shining iron-frosting swirls of no apparent purpose. High above, parapets and crazy staircases rose and disappeared within the folds of the Labs' upper reaches. It all reminded Fish of some fantastic castle. Which had been exactly the architect's instructions from Ron Rourke, the enigmatic founder of WonderSoft. He'd wanted a bigger, more complex version of the famed Disney Concert Hall to house his next-generation game design workshop. Fish had learned that piece of trivia after the initial contract offer down at San Diego ComicCon. Back in his hotel room, between panels and signings, he'd looked up everything the internet had to say about the enigmatic Ron Rourke and his fabled WonderSoft.

Fish had learned that WonderSoft was an old company. CD-ROM old. Early '90s startup from back in the days of Jobs, Gates, and the Woz. Old School. It had taken a long time, but the company had finally scored some big hits with games like *Mall Rat Commandos* and *Enigmatrix: Assassin from Rigel.* When the Make finally went online, WonderSoft went in big on the virtual universe startup by investing heavily in digital real estate, retailers, banking, and one of the premier launch game worlds, *StarFleet Empires*, a massive space sim based on some old sci-fi intellectual property. The geek fan base had come out in full, and the game had exploded into a massive franchise that now featured three hit streaming shows on Twitch.

Captain Dare was one of the most live-streamed shows on the web. The weekly show followed the adventures of the player crew of the *Intrepid*, a Federation cruiser, inside the *StarFleet Empires* universe. The gamer tagged JasonDare was the epitome of a Hollywood celebrity, and it didn't hurt that he looked a lot like his boyishly rugged avatar, the captain of *Intrepid.*

Fish approached the massive security-glassed entrance, noting its incredible thickness and the artistic brushed-carbon-fiber-finish pipes that ran through it for reinforcement. The entire entrance was a scanning station like the ones used in airport terminals, but this one was constructed of PlateGlass, or transparent titanium. All you had to do was cross through it, and every conceivable ounce of biometric information was extracted, notated, and organized for security personnel. But there was no armored "pillbox" as there were in the massive transportation hubs. No security mechs or heavily armed troops either.

Fish walked down a wide hall that felt more like a cavern. Along the walls, green bas-reliefs were carved into the marble: great moments in gaming history, depicted like the ancient hieroglyphs of some lost and long-dead civilization.

Mario destroying Donkey Kong.

The Winged Knight defeating the Buzzard.

Max Payne getting pushed down inside a cop car.

The StarForge exploding.

Master Chief escaping the Halo.

At the end of the hall lay an octagonal security hub manned by a paunchy, compact older guard with a bushy mustache. His name tag read "Thomas."

"Mister Fishbein, glad to meet you. I'm Tom."

Fish nodded, feeling unsure of himself. Above him, the ceiling leapt away in a sudden tower that ran up through the core of the castle. High above, bridges crossed beneath a beautiful stained glass roof that wasn't visible outside from ground level. Fish knew it was a depiction of the Andromeda galaxy. With the sunlight beating down through its aquamarine tint, it seemed vibrant and alive. Fish guessed it must have been eight stories up and a football field wide.

Other than the guard, there was no one else. Fish could hear a floor polisher droning nearby, but that could easily be a Floorbie. Just a robot.

"I s'pose you want to check out your lab suite?" asked Tom, a knowing look gleaming from within pale blue eyes.

Fish nodded and then laughed. Laughed at himself because... because he felt excited. Stop fighting it, he told himself, and just let it happen.

Stop fighting it.

"I bet you're pretty excited."

"I am," said Fish, and he heard his voice sound bigger inside the cavernous palace that was both legendary and, now, real all at once.

I am.

"Then right this way," said Tom with the air of a showman. "I'll walk you on up there."

Fish failed to see that even Tom was enjoying this. He was too blown away by the backlit frosted glass placards they passed at extreme intervals, the names of famous developers embossed upon them. Their names, or the names of their legendary design studios.

This must be what it feels like, he thought, to walk out onto the court in the NBA for the first time.

But it felt bigger than that. It felt like a stadium. It felt like baseball.

They arrived at a teak door set within a marble hall along the third floor. Tom removed his card and swiped it. He waited for Fish to do the same, and after a short awkward pause he turned slightly, politely, deftly, without being too obvious. Fish was tracing his name on the soft green backlit frosted glass panel near the door. And the name of his studio underneath.

This is where dreams are made, kid.

And at that moment, Fish wished his parents could be there, if only to show them…

… not that he was a success.

… not that he'd made it to the big time.

… only that he'd succeeded and that it must mean something.

And maybe that would be enough. Which was something he said to himself often. Which is something a lot of children, even if they've grown up, say to themselves for the rest of their lives.

"Mr. Fishbein," prompted Tom.

The cards were slid through the scanner and the door to the lab suite unlocked with a gentle click. The guard pushed open the door and stood back.

Fish peeked in.

There was a central design area, sunken below floor level, with a massive SurfaceTable that could project and show everything in 3D. It would be used for planning. Fish knew it would be run by a state-of-the-art LushOptics MicroCore. On the next level were fifteen stations where his team would program, administer, and design the game.

Off to one side was a small dining area where in-suite meals would be catered twenty-four hours a day by any of the seven on-campus five-star restaurants, courtesy of WonderSoft. On the opposite wall was a chill room that had been outfitted in muted mint green lighting and shadows. ShapeChanger loungers with Wonder-Soft cloud access lay within the shadows for the team to un-focus and catch their breath in the inevitable long days and nights that were surely coming as *Island Pirates* marched toward launch.

And on the far side of the room was Fish's private office. It was behind more frosted glass, and the lights within were off.

"Go ahead," prompted Tom. "It's all yours now. Take her for a spin."

They both shared one last sheepish look, and then, with a final nod from the security guard, Fish stepped into the suite.

"Mr. Fishbein," began Tom.

"It's just... Fish," said Ninety-Nine Fishbein, barely turning back. He couldn't take his eyes off the SurfaceTable. He'd designed the whole game on shareware via a rundown server that had been tricked out and very temperamental. The SurfaceTable would take what had cost him thousands of hours of coding, and crunch all that down into verbal cue-driven moments. It listened to you and then made what you wanted.

"Mr. Fish. I'm a gamer too. Part of why I love being a guard around here," said Tom in the distance, behind Fish.

Fish smiled.

The guy sounded like a real gamer. He loved real gamers. There was something so innocent, so "surrendered" about them. So unruined by the troll rock and roll of today's gaming culture, which seemed perpetually aggrieved and dissatisfied, and angry. And hateful.

Real gamers were the opposite of all that. They were explorers and adventures seeking to be dazzled by the next ain't-that-cool moment.

"I've been waiting for *Island Pirates*... well, I've read everything about it. If there happens to be a spare beta key lying around... Mr. Fishbein...?"

"You got it," murmured Fish. He'd already been allowing beta access, and there were roughly three thousand players running amok inside his tropical worldsim. He could spare another. Plus, it felt like the guard had been there at the start of something completely new in Fish's life. When Fish had leveled up, as it were. Like they were friends, even though they'd just met. Like they'd shared a secret, or an adventure, or some crazy happening, that no one else in the world would ever understand.

"I'll ping you via the company cloud with my info," said Tom, stepping back to close the door. "Thank you. Thank you so much, Mr. Fishbein... Fish. Thanks."

And the door closed.

Fish could feel the barest hum of ultra-powerful computing hardware, and if he believed himself, the software too. The software that was his program. He'd already done the transfer and install from Ibiza aboard the GoogleJet. He'd left beta access in play; there wasn't much the beta players could do to break anything. Besides, it would be nice to know before the game launched if something could be broken.

He crossed the suite and entered the office. His office.

It was filled by a single-piece ceramic-mold Moon Desk worksta-tion that looked like an actual moon. There was a small break in the surface so he could slip within the moon and take a seat at a chair he found almost too comfortable. A chair so comfortable, in fact, that he immediately forgot the folding metal chair he'd used at the design collective down in Irvine.

The entire far wall beyond the Moon Desk was subtly illumi-nated by tropical fish swimming through blue coral above startlingly white sand. The tank was big, and he couldn't see the depth of it.

Now he knew why they'd asked him what kind of fish he liked. He'd told them tropical because that's what he'd been populating the game with. He saw one of them swimming in and out of the shifting shadows of the massive, subtly gurgling wall tank.

He swiveled his too-comfortable chair to face the wall, and the suite asked him if he'd like to start his workstation. The voice was that of the HAL 9000 from *2001*, but Fish didn't know that. He just found its tone and timbre incredibly pleasing, and very comforting.

He told the suite to start his workstation.

The flat surface of the desk turned that same backlit soft mint that was repeated throughout the labs. The words "Welcome Fish" came up in block white lettering. They floated there for a moment and disappeared. Across the rear wall-facing hemisphere of the Moon Desk, the curved surface of the SurroundMonster monitor rose up in ominous silence. The lights within the aquarium dimmed to an even shadowier blue and gray. A tiger-striped angelfish floated out from behind some coral to regard Fish for a moment, or so it seemed.

The WonderSoft logo washed across the monitor and walked Fish through his retinal logon. A moment later he could see the operating system and the file access sequence to *Island Pirates*.

He found the Softpunk keyboard beneath the desk and ran the startup in developer mode. For a moment he tracked the stats and watched a few of his favorite tells. He checked the log file and noted there'd been relatively few exceptions and that the game's management AI had merely self-corrected. It had rebooted the whole game in only one instance, when a player had attempted to crash a hijacked jet into a volcano while a gunfight ensued in the main cabin of the aircraft. The crashing-into-the-volcano part hadn't caused the exception that necessitated the reboot: one of the combatants in the cabin had been "glitching" a bulkhead and the crash didn't kill him. The player ended up wandering around in the lava at the bottom of the volcano. Fish made a note to fix that, along with a long list of other bugs that needed addressing.

But then he remembered, come Monday morning, he'd have a team. They could fix those things. He took a deep breath.

Even still, he knew he'd be fixing those items himself, or at least checking they were fixed. And then fixing them again the way he wanted them fixed. It was his game after all.

He logged out of his developer account and into the personal player profile attached to his actual internet passport. He told himself he just wanted to see how it was performing on the new high-tech server farm WonderSoft was running it out of. But the truth was, he just wanted to play the game. Wanted to see what it looked like with the new graphics wash from the WonderSoft Design Core, and, of course, check the game speed.

His avatar, Fishmael—as in, "Call me Fishmael"—appeared. He was standing on his private island near a small white sand beach. He panned around and saw the green hump of the tropical island rising above him into the soft blue sky. Every detail, every vine and leaf, and even the crystals of fine white sand beneath Fishmael leapt out across the SurroundMonster monitor. His three-story bamboo tree house rested within the massive spread of a banyan tree in the nearby shadows of the verdant jungle clutch.

Fishmael turned back toward the beach. His vintage Super Cub floatplane rested alongside a rickety wooden dock. As the developer, Fish could give himself any of the in-game assets and treasures. But he'd played the game as an anonymous player, going on missions, crafting and looting supplies to purchase equipment from the in-game store, and getting in fierce gun battles to keep his stuff. He'd built the tree house by harvesting vines and bamboo from the jungle, and he'd even gone on a quest and raised a sunken boat to strip it of materials like teak to floor it with. In *Island Pirates* you could do anything to make your island into your own pirate kingdom.

He checked to make sure his character had all his equipment. Guns, compass, shovel, and two health-restoring Hotshots. Then he walked out to the dock as he equipped Fishmael with his straw pirate hat.

He hotkeyed his dog whistle, and his pet, a Portuguese water dog that no one else in the game could ever get—they could have other pets, but the water dog was his because it was a rare unique game item—came bounding through the surf along the beach.

In real life, Fish had always wanted a Portuguese water dog.

"Time to fly around and see how things are going for everyone," he said to no one else in the empty design suite.

He climbed inside the Super Cub and fired up the electrical system, then cranked the engine. In-suite, peripherals deployed across the Moon Desk. A flight control yoke beneath the keyboard. Rudder pedals from the floor. A small throttle from a flat surface in front of the SurroundMonster monitor. Fish watched all the vintage gauges on screen. Especially the magnetos. He'd bought a typical in-game plane from the *Island Pirates* store using a microtransaction from his private Make account. Just to test the process. He'd even had to learn to fly the Super Cub using open source flight training programs. Everything had to be real.

The old, worn-out yellow Super Cub was not state of the art; it was prone to mechanical failure. Everything was salvage in *Island Pirates*. Nothing was new. It was a tropical worldsim of modern-day piracy and treasure hunting. Distressed salvage was part of the appeal of the game; making stuff from scratch or finding something on your own was how you got ahead. It was the opposite of modern life. Of the everything's-brand-new-and-get-stuff-from-Big-Government way of thinking that had become the standard of modern culture. Here in the game, you either acquired by hook or by crook, or you went without. Whatever it was, it had to be earned.

The Portuguese water dog, Jackson, sat beside him in the cockpit of the tiny plane. Occasionally it would "woof" at something. It was running a beta open source low-level pet A.I., so who knew what it would do from one moment to the next.

Again, that was part of the fun.

The Super Cub lifted off from the sparkling little bay and climbed out over the light blue water. Water that seemed almost transparent. Below, in the white sand shallows, Fish could see swimming tiger sharks weaving this way and that as they made their way in one direction. They were yellow and black. Fish thought it made them look more sinister.

He headed for the fog bank that lay around his private island and quick-traveled to a small island chain he'd named the San Diablos. He'd seen a lot of players messing around over there, and he wanted to watch them play and see what happened.

He told himself he'd just kick back and watch for a while. Not get involved in anything.

Over open sea at three thousand feet and approaching the outer edge of the coral reefs and sandbars that protected the easternmost islands of the lush San Diablos, Fish turned on the plane's radio and dialed in the local island chat channels. Someone was broadcasting an all-luau ska station from a misty ridgetop farther up the chain. She was calling herself ThreeDog's Lady, and every so often she'd give status reports on other players. She was even running commercials on crafted goods that could be exported to the Make from *Island Pirates.*

"The kids at Agua Caliente Lagoon want everyone to know that the casino is now open and the cheating has been dealt with," she said in a raspy growl above a tinny static washing through the transmission. "On a side note, they're offering a bounty on BubbleWrap1999's hideout, and a finder's fee for any of the four thousand MakeCoins recovered, plus unlimited use of the casino's lines of credit in the future."

And...

"ToeCutta's crew says they're coming for DirtySteve tonight!"

And...

"The New Arkham Mining Company will pay top dollar for any gems recovered from active volcanos along the San Diablos. See SailorJim in Porto Tortuga."

And...

"Listen up, children, pirate gunboats took out the Sea Cow last night off the tip of Mermaid's Castle. Player SandyGunfighter says they were using torpedoes and not interested in cargo or MakeCoins at all. Who knows why, children. ThreeDog's Lady does not. But she knows this: only fools rush in where wise men fear to tread. Now, here's 'Blue Hawaii' by the SkateRonin out of Dusseldorf."

Below, Fish could see a junk cutter tacking into a channel through the outer reef and out into the big deep blue ocean beyond. Someone probably doing a trading run up to the Make Portal at Porto Tortuga, the only place goods and players could transit back into the Make itself without logging out and then logging back in.

That would all change once the game went live. He panned his POV south and scanned the island chain, watching the big rock formation that was Mermaid's Castle. He didn't see any pirate gunboats. He wondered who those players with the gunboats were and resisted checking the log files to find out. For just a little while more, he wanted to know what it was like to feel uncertain in his game. To just be another player trying to make your way. Maybe, for some, even make a little coin you could use to improve your real life. Banking everything on skill and hoping to acquire a bit more by gaining as much from the game's environment as you could.

"Yo!" came a voice out of the radio's chatter-crackle ether. Fish heard it loud and clear in his suite, but it still had that tinny distortion of a transistor radio running on baling wire and bubblegum. "Any players out there able to lend a helping hand? I'm in (crackle crackle) trouble."

Fish keyed his mic. Let's see what this is like, he thought. Getting involved. No one knew his avatar was actually the developer, so he could play around a bit and see where it led. "Go ahead, this is Fishmael."

"Need a little help…"

Fish could hear gunfire in the background. Automatic gunfire. He knew it was the sound in-game AK-47s made; he'd personally overseen the sound design. He had wanted it to feel abrasive and dirty all at once as it came out of someone's speakers or erupted in their headphones. The sound file still needed work, but the resources team at WonderSoft had promised a full sound redesign. One of the suits had quick-checked the available inventory and bragged that WonderSoft had over one hundred different AK-47 sound designs, seventy of which contained the "dirty" tag.

"What's your problem?" Fish wanted to add the player's gamertag but he had no idea what it was. Was that good? Did that make it more real? Or would players need that to work together? He filed that away for a bug-busting session later.

"I'm over at Pete's Cove," replied the player. "I need extraction." Then more gunfire. This time a pistol at close quarters. Probably a .45.

This was one of the delicacies that came out of a game like *Island Pirates*. Why, thought Fish, was this guy in trouble? And by helping him, would I, if I were a regular player, make new enemies? He weighed the options as though he were real player and then went with helping out—under the heading of "playtesting," or so he whispered to himself inside the plush climate-controlled suite. He felt comfortably cool but could not detect any direct AC flow.

"Sure, I'll help out if I can," Fish said after keying the mike. "Where're ya at exactly? I don't know how much help I'll be... but I am flying around in a floatplane."

Fish turned toward the southwest. Pete's Cove was a small hilltop island out on the western side of the chain. Two weeks ago, some beta players from the Middle East had been setting up over there and exploring the local area. Fish hadn't liked their gamertags—stuff verging on radical without being directly there. The last thing he wanted was his game becoming a social media platform for violent extremism.

"I can be at the cove in five minutes. If you can put her down in the bay and taxi in toward the beach, I'd be real grateful," replied the player on the other end of the transmission.

If I were a real player I'd ask for money, thought Fish. "How much?"

Jackson woofed randomly at some seabirds circling above a small volcanic island they were passing over. Thin black smoke curled out of the picturesque caldera. The game could detonate volcanos; Fish had set up a completely unhackable algorithm that ensured total randomness where that was concerned. He felt that when an explosion did happen, when one of the many island volcanoes finally went Kracka-Boooom, it would take the game to a whole new level of player-made storytelling.

Maybe today's the today, he thought, and laughed at the irony of a developer getting caught in his own randomly generated explosion.

"I really haven't got much on me right now, but in a week or so... I can transfer twenty-five MakeCoins?"

Of course Fish was gonna do it. Just to playtest. But a real player... might not.

He listened to the drone of the Super Cub's engine. The plane bounced around as it hit some in-game turbulence and he descended down through wispy clouds. He spotted the tiny crescent island of Pete's Cove far below. A lot of people didn't know—no one in fact knew—that Fish had put a sunken pirate ship in the waters off of Pete's Cove. He'd even tagged it as a Treasure Chest location. Treasure Chests were going to be extremely difficult to obtain, but they would hold big prizes once the game launched. WonderSoft was already negotiating with the government to hand out unemployment credits and benefits—which was what most players really wanted, according to a research poll. Fish thought instead they should get some cool corporate prizes like big-screen TVs and tropical vacations.

"I'm there in five..." he said, waiting for the player to hand over his gamertag.

"Awesomesauce. Yeah, thanks man, I'm MagnumPIrate. What's your tag again? Cruddy game designer hasn't figured out a way for us to tell who's who unless we're in visual. Kinda makes long-range chat real hard."

Fish shook his head at cruddy game designers.

"My tag is Fishmael," said Fish. "The guy's probably spending all his money on supermodels and speedboats. Crack, too, I bet..."

MagnumPIrate laughed over the tinny radio voice chat. The gunfire had disappeared for a moment. "Must be the life."

Approaching Pete's Cove, Fish could see that someone had started a mining operation near the summit of the tiny island's twin volcanos. A small sandy road carved its way down one hill, disappearing in and out of lush, digitally rendered tropical junglescape.

He came in high with the sun at the back of the Super Cub's round yellow tail, trying to spot the action, and thinking maybe MagnumPIrate might already be dead and off to the player reboot screen, starting all over with the basic loadout of khaki shorts, a Hawaiian shirt, and a rusty fishing knife.

Then Fish lost sight of the mining operation as he descended below hill level and raced toward the far side of the island, banking to come around once more. He spotted a beat-up black Humvee careening down the backside of the island, along the tiny road. In pursuit were two other Humvees and a bunch of junky dirt bikes being ridden by actual players.

Within visual, he could read their gamertags as the Piper Cub streaked overhead.

SonOftheCaliphate

SexyHeadChoppa

BloodyCrescentBrutha

So on and so forth. Nothing but another bunch of third-world extremists bringing their hate-garbage into a new game. After what happened in LA, game developers and admin were required to file a suspicious gamers report with the Homeland Department of Online Gaming.

The beat-up Humvee being pursued was driven by the player tagged as MagnumPIrate. As it disappeared back into the jungle, Fish banked the aging Super Cub and began to climb up over the island and out to sea.

One more pass, he told himself.

"Got some interesting friends there, MagnumPIrate," said Fish over the chat.

MagnumPIrate's voice came back. Fish could hear the rattle of the beat-up Hummer in the background, and he knew it was a basic model that hadn't yet been souped up with any of the "Hot Rod" perks from the vehicle customization store.

"Wouldn't exactly call them friends right now," MagnumPIrate replied. "Is that you in the plane up there?"

"Yeah. Putting her down in the bay right now."

"Okay," replied MagnumPIrate a moment later. "About that. They've got—"

Tracer rounds reached up and smacked the Super Cub. On his heads-up display, Fish saw the aircraft's integrity flutter down to seventy-five percent. A small superimposed schematic of the plane in the left-hand corner of the SurroundMonster monitor showed engine and horizontal stabilizer damage. On screen, black smoke piled out from under the engine cowling in front of Fish's face.

Jackson woofed twice as though asking a question.

"I got it," muttered Fish.

The airplane tried to fall off to the left. Fish kicked in the opposite rudder to avoid a stall, pushed the nose over, and headed toward the sparkling bay a few hundred feet below. That's when he saw the tramp freighter.

"They've got a patrol boat with an old AA gun on the back," said MagnumPIrate over the chat.

"Really?" replied Fish sarcastically.

On screen the plane began to shake. Integrity was dropping rapidly. The peripheral controls in the suite began to vibrate in Fish's hands. He knew if he didn't get his plane down pretty quickly, it'd fall apart in the sky.

The patrol boat, a ramshackle rustbucket tramp freighter complete with smokestack and patchwork bamboo armor along the sides, came around the point of the tiny crescent island. It wasn't firing anymore.

They think they've knocked me down, thought Fish as he fought with the control yoke, feeling himself slip from rock star developer to resolute gamer. Angry that someone was beating him at his own game. Angry in the same moment that someone was trying to take his hard-won stuff. He vowed not to design-hack this and cheat his way out. Right now he was just a player, and he was going to find a way out as a player.

The deep blue water of the outer bay rushed up at Fish through the cockpit windshield between black snakes of smoke escaping in spurts from the engine in front of him.

At least we're not leaking oil, thought Fish. If that happens... we're cooked. He'd know if he saw oil spray up against the windshield. That would mean the engine had taken catastrophic damage. There was also the Whoops subroutine, which affected every piece of equipment in the game. There was a percentage chance that any item might just randomly break at any time, especially if the conditions were right.

Damage and excessive speed were those conditions for aircraft.

A moment later, Fish lowered the flaps and flared for landing. The floatplane splashed down into the deep waters of the outer bay and crossed over into the translucent sandy seafoam green shallows of the inner bay. Ahead, he could see the wide shoreline and the remains of a beached speedboat. Thin curls of black smoke spiraled away from its wreckage. Fish tried to place what type of boat it had been, but it was too wrecked to determine.

He taxied the tiny yellow seaplane in toward the beach. Gentle wavelets made long slow rolls toward the slope of the pristine shore.

The battered black Hummer leapt from within the jungle and crashed out onto the white sand farther down the beach. Three motorcycles were in close pursuit.

"Don't beach the plane!" yelled MagnumPIrate over the chat. "Turn it around and get ready to scoot!"

Fish panned his POV to look out the rear of the plane. The gunboat was just rounding the rocky point at the tip of the bay.

"If the engine explodes on takeoff..." he muttered, dropping a repair package from his inventory over the plane's schematic. Some of the damage, but not all, was immediately repaired. Fish shifted in his comfortable chair and rolled his shoulders. He blinked twice and refocused on the monitor.

Jackson woofed.

Fish kicked the rudder, gunned the engine, and swung the floatplane around to point back out toward open water. Off to his left, he saw the Hummer crash into the surf and disappear beneath the waves. A moment later, he watched MagnumPIrate's avatar swimming through the sparkling water out toward the plane. Jackson gave another woof woof.

Less than thirty seconds later, MagnumPIrate was in the plane and the gunboat was blocking their exit from the bay.

"Go, go now!" shouted MagnumPIrate over the chat. He was wearing jungle tiger stripe fatigues. His avatar had curly hair and a mustache. He was holding a silver-plated .45.

Bullets whipped past the plane and splashed into the waves, creating sudden small water plumes. The players with the AK-47s back on the beach were firing at them. Fish knew the looming gunboat ahead of them couldn't fire the AA gun mounted on the aft deck of the vessel until they were airborne and within its skyward firing arc... and then it was duck season.

"This might be a real short trip."

Fish gunned the throttle to full and the floatplane surged slowly forward. He watched the forward canopy for the sudden eruption of black oil spray jetting up across his vision. There was a possibility the game could make that happen right now. After all, everything in *Island Pirates* was junk, prone to going sideways at any moment. The only thing you could rely on was yourself.

"I got the boat handled," said MagnumPIrate over the growling charge of the tiny plane's roar as they crashed out into the gentle surf, racing for takeoff.

A moment later, they were climbing over the incoming waves and out into the deep blue of the outer bay. Fish pulled back on the gaming yoke and begged his little digital plane to fly skyward. He checked in with himself from a distant part of his mind. He was frightened, fearful, and having a whole lot of fun. He was playing a game. His game. And it was good.

MagnumPIrate's avatar produced a small device and pressed a red button. Fish recognized it as an in-game explosives detonator. The gunboat disappeared beneath them as they climbed toward the blazing hot tropical sun above. Either the detonator worked or they were about to be ripped to shreds by a voluminous amount of anti-aircraft fire.

Fish heard a distant, dull boom from beneath them.

He checked the instruments. The rate of climb. Airspeed. Engine oil pressure—which didn't look good at all. And altitude. Then he banked and headed back toward the main island chain. Away from Pete's Cove.

Far below, the tiny tramp freighter gunboat listed on its side, smoke pouring from a large hole near the water line where debris and flotsam fanned out across the sea.

"Get-outta-Dodge card," said MagnumPIrate over the chat, and chuckled.

At that moment, Fish loved his game, and he knew the world would too. It worked, and it was fun to play. That was all a developer should ever really want, he told himself, hoping to believe it this time.

A moment later, the door to his office opened behind him.

He could hear Jackson woof in-game over the suite speakers.

"Mr. Fishbein," said a pretty, young, business-suited girl with large oval glasses. "Carl says we have a problem at the front gate." Embarrassed, or awkward, or filled with sudden self-loathing, she added, "Sorry. Peabody Case, your administrative assistant. It's an honor to meet you, Mr. Fishbein."

In a corner of the room, a small red warning light pulsed. The words "EMERGENCY, STAY IN YOUR SUITE" were scrolling across the mint green desktop.

Chapter Nine

"It's a trap!" screamed Captain Stefan "BlackDragon" Bolz of the Federation clan destroyer *Berlin* inside the *StarFleet Empires* game universe. "Starboard evasive! Stand by to fire portside phasers at will!"

On screen, the bridge shuddered as pulsed Romulan phaser shots raked the stark white saucer section of the ship and punched into the sleek warp drive nacelle far below. The other two destroyers, *Des Moines* and *Calgary*, began lobbing photon torpedoes with devastating effect at the massive Romulan light cruiser that had just decloaked right in the middle of the battle with three enemy warbirds attempting to run the Neutral Zone blockade.

Fifteen minutes before, BlackDragon had been jogging on a trail inside the Black Forest. It had been a long work week, and before watching movies and staying close to the computer in case of an in-game incident just like the one happening right now, Bolz had decided to go for a run. Instead, now he was scrambling to control the battle from his very expensive smartphone.

While jogging, he'd gotten an alert that Romulan clan warships were crossing into the old Neutral Zone. At first he'd been stoically surprised—but reacting quickly, he'd cut across a field while watching the ongoing incursion inside the game on his smartglasses. Three warbirds from the Romulan clan were on a direct intercept for the picket he was overseeing that weekend for the Federation fleet clan he and his ship were a part of. Basically, the clan had him on guard duty. Next week *Berlin* and the rest of the group would be rotating into the battle around Tholia, where the Romulans had preemptively invaded their neutral neighbors in a desperate bid to stay relevant within the *StarFleet Empires* game.

The warbirds were no match for the three state-of-the-art Federation destroyers. Thanks to a quick assessment from Science Officer Gunter Haltstead, whose avatar was a Vulcan named "SchwarzHalvock," BlackDragon knew the warbirds were, at best, armed with the deadly but painstakingly slow Type R plasma torpedoes. At best. More than likely, they were using either refitted photon torpedo launchers captured in one of the numerous engagements since the invasion of Romulan space, or they were armed with illegally obtained Klingon disruptor arrays, either one of which was a poor armament for the last-gen warbirds. The old-school Romulan warships worked best with the Type R's.

The Federation destroyers, on the other hand, were armed with massive forward shields, four photon torpedo launchers, and multiple phaser batteries. As long as they held formation and attacked the Romulans head on, they could wipe out just about anything in front of them.

Suddenly, the massive *Red Witch*, a Fire Hawk class light cruiser, de-cloaked portside aft just as they made their first attack formation run at *Warhound*, the lead Romulan warbird. The destroyer group's opening salvo smashed *Warhound's* forward shield, but now *Berlin* was forty-five seconds from a full torpedo reload. And *Red Witch* was firing into their portside aft shields with devastating effect.

"Damage report?" huffed BlackDragon breathlessly in the middle of a tranquil field within the quiet forest.

"Engineering reports casualties—main power still online!"

shrieked Heidi Paulka, gamertag MangaAussenseiter, *Berlin*'s comm officer. Bolz knew she'd gotten all that from the automated systems status feed. Chief Engineer TodtSamurai still hadn't logged in yet.

BlackDragon's Friday run was turning into a nightmare.

"Group captains," said Bolz into his smartphone. "Come about and prepare to engage *Red Witch* on my mark." He hoped most of their crews were logged in, because he was sure they were about to eat a face full of Romulan plasma from the massive light cruiser *Red Witch*.

"Mark!" he screamed in German.

Twenty minutes earlier, Mara Bennett had been listening to the final operations briefing as the small Romulan attack force— composed of the three warbirds, plus *Revenge*, the battered light cruiser *Red Witch*, and Mara's own ship, *Cymbalum*—entered the Neutral Zone at full impulse. She had watched from the command chair on her bridge as the other three warbirds de-cloaked ahead and *Red Witch* veered off from the main axis of the attack.

She ordered Lt. LizardofOz, her helmsman, to follow *Red Witch* in. LizardofOz was a Gorn player who had fought on the losing side of the Romulan invasion last year in the middle of the Gorn clans' civil war—back when the Romulans had been a force to be reckoned with and the Fleet admirals all had big bucks to spend inside the Make. *Cymbalum*'s last helmsman was killed at Romulus when the Federation carriers broke through and overwhelmed the fleet. Mara's ship was shot to hell and the crew barely managed to escape to warp once the general retreat was issued from the burning bridge of the Romulan dreadnought *Imperator*. Seconds later it had exploded, taking the Federation battlecruiser *Ticonderoga* with it.

The Gorn player's EmoteWare gurgled a hiss, which translated via text feed at the bottom of Mara's VR field to, "Aye aye, Captain. Following Tal's red herring nice and slow. Cloaking device engaged. Reducing speed to one quarter impulse." Mara watched a small power fluctuation on the weapons board and opened a channel to Scarpa, *Cymbalum*'s engineer.

"Portside phaser array still isn't charging to full. Why?"

A moment later, Scarpa's voice came back from his station back in engineering. Mara could hear the unsteady pulse of the warp core in the background. There was no disguising it: her ship was ancient. It had been old even when *StarFleet Empires* first went live five years ago. The warbirds were holdover ships from the game's twenty-second century. They even predated original *Star Trek* canon, or what people called TOS, whereas the game was currently entering the final decade of the twenty-third century, which was just beyond the original series' long movie run. Ships now came with better warp drives, as evidenced by the sleeker nacelles and advanced weapons packages. The Federation clan had even managed to produce its fifth Excelsior class battlecruiser. The Romulans, on the other hand, were patching their ships together with digital baling wire and captured weapons systems. Very few Romulan vessels had any of the deadly Type R plasma torpedo launchers left. *Cymbalum* did, and for all intents and purposes, it was the only weapon the ship had, besides the two laughable phaser arrays, port and starboard.

"Hey!" Scarpa shouted emphatically. "She's a doing the best she can, mi cap-i-tan!" Scarpa was an Italian kid from Rome who worked in a bakery. He always turned "Captain" into three separate words with his comically accented English. "It's-a the main capacitor for that array. She's-a real wonky. You getta me some parts and I make her like-a brand new for you. Until then… that's-a the best you gonna get." Then he added, "Cap-i-tan."

Mara reminded herself again to keep the portside phasers away from the enemy if they ended up shooting at something. They weren't supposed to do that. They were supposed to wait until *Red Witch* exploded and blinded everyone's sensor arrays within the Neutral Zone before they snuck off into Federation space on their secret mission.

"Keep an eye on it please, Lieutenant Scarpa," she said, gently reminding him that they should always keep up the role playing just in case they made it onto the network feed at the Twitch Channel. In which case they'd get a bonus in MakeCoins.

"Aye aye, my Cap-i-tan! I'm-a keepin' both eyes on her. She's-a no going to do bad today."

An hour before the mission, Mara had texted the crew and asked them to log in. Everyone had immediately complied. If they made it through the weekend and completed the mission, there'd be big bucks for everyone who survived. She didn't know them as much as she would have liked to—players kept getting killed and all—but she had confidence in them. In the short time they'd been together, they'd faced a few tight scrapes and come through mostly intact.

But the truth was, she'd didn't really know any of them.

You don't let them know you, she told herself. Except it was Mrs. Watson's voice telling her. Telling her she was hiding behind her avatar. Hiding behind the beautiful and brilliant "normal" CaptainMara doll inside the Make.

They wouldn't follow me if they knew I was blind and disabled.

That's what you tell yourself, Mara. But it's not the truth, said Mrs. Watson. It's just a lie you want to believe.

Her eyes fell to her avatar as she clicked out to third person. Around her, the bridge was shadowed in green and blue. She could see LizardofOz in front of her, the massive reptile avatar wearing the shimmering orange battle dress of the Gorn. His leathery claw moved forward and made a small adjustment to impulse speed. Next to Lizard, as they called him for short, below her command chair, sat

BattleBabe, Mara's weapons officer. Ensign BattleBabe of the Imperial Romulan Navy clan.

Behind Mara, at the rear of the bridge, waited the strange and enigmatic Drex, motionless near the science station. The Drex were a captured star-faring race, playable by Romulan Navy characters. They were a fatalistic silicon-based AI who could only occupy science officer positions. So far, the player who'd decided to play this, one of the more difficult races, had done an excellent job of role playing the homicidal lunatic character.

The comm officer, Varek, whose real gamertag was TheOld-ManAndTheVoid, had been with Mara from the beginning. But they just called him Varek because it sounded Romulan, and saying TheOldManAndTheVoid was a mouthful. All she knew about him, as a player, was that he was a crusty old guy from Montana who didn't seem to care much for her as captain of *Cymbalum*.

Mara allowed the camera to pan around as she studied the bridge personnel. But again and again her eyes fell back to her own avatar: a beautiful Romulan captain with commendations and decorations on her tunic, sitting in the command chair. Her face was heart-shaped, her eyes a depthless gray, her hair raven black.

They'll follow her, Mara thought, staring at the perfect digital doll.

They'll follow who they think I am.

Chapter Ten

"Take us in slow and easy, Lizard."

Mara brought up the combat formation page on her command console. *Cymbalum* was trailing just below the massive *Red Witch*'s warp engines. The other three warbirds and *Revenge* were well ahead and de-cloaking to engage the oncoming Federation destroyers.

Six months ago it wouldn't have been a fair fight. A Romulan command cruiser, a light cruiser, and four warbirds would have made short work of a lonely Federation destroyer group. But six months of battle and attrition had changed the game entirely. The Feds had state-of-the-art, fully repaired warships. The Romulans were shot to hell and breaking down every ten seconds. The weapons officer on *Revenge* had to unlock a torpedo firing solution mini-game every time he wanted to fire the one Type G plasma still operational. The photon mounts they'd installed after they'd captured a Federation frigate were tricky at best.

The warbirds were just as bad. But the light cruiser *Red Witch* verged on the pathetic. She was running a bare-minimum skeleton crew along with one working warp engine and one stasis-held torpedo that would destroy the launcher once it was fired.

Cymbalum was mostly battle ready, if not for a few tricky line items like the port-side phaser array and warp engines that would either burn like a banshee's scream or break down without a whimper.

"Stand by to engage once they chase," ordered TalGornicus over battlechat from the bridge of *Revenge*. Mara, along with the rest of the other captains, clicked "acknowledged" in their HUDs.

A moment later, the Federation destroyer squadron was turning to port as the three warbirds fired. *Revenge*, still cloaked, was closing right behind the warbirds. Mara briefly wondered if the weapons officer was having trouble getting the Type G plasma torpedo to arm and fire.

Warhound, one of the three warbirds, took the brunt of the Federation salvo. Her shields collapsed immediately and the starboard warp nacelle took a direct hit from one of the Federation torpedoes. It ruptured, bulged in almost slow motion, and then exploded along its axis, sending burning hull plating in every direction.

Mara knew *Warhound* was finished.

The destroyers pursued the warbirds, coming in on their number three shields.

This was the critical moment. Mara leaned forward in her chair, watching the tactical display on the bridge screen. The warbirds were "running" as *Revenge* broke off on another heading, de-cloaking. The choice for the Federation commander was to either to continue to run down the fleeing warbirds, or engage *Revenge* head-on.

Both made tempting targets.

A moment later, all was much clearer. The Fed destroyers were hell-bent on clearing out the escorts first. Then they could work the command cruiser *Revenge* over at leisure.

Mara suspected the Federation science officers had combed the battle logs, trying to ascertain just how many fights the big Romulan command cruiser had been in. Based on that intel, they were probably gambling that she was too shot up to be a threat.

That was when Tal's bait, the light cruiser *Red Witch*, de-cloaked aft of the Federation destroyers, hurling hot burning-blue bolts of phased energy into their flanks.

"Drop out of cloak now, Mr. Lizard!"

"Targeting *Calgary*!" shrieked BattleBabe over the chat.

"Hold…" ordered Mara, trying to restrain the overzealousness that could streak through a crew with an easy firing solution.

A moment later, *Red Witch* unloaded her only torpedo into space. An overloaded Type R plasma running hot, straight, and true. The launcher had been stasis rigged, meaning it could hold one over-loaded plasma torpedo. Firing would destroy the launcher, but the plan was for the ship to go up in a ball of nuclear flame and burning oxygen anyway, temporarily blinding everyone's sensors.

"Detecting warp core overload building within *Red Witch*. Sixty seconds to a truly glorious detonation, Captain," squealed the synthesizer-voiced Drex.

The plasma torpedo from *Red Witch* left a fiery trail across the deep purple nepenthe of the Neutral Zone as it homed in on the running destroyer formation.

"Crew of *Red Witch* has beamed aboard *Revenge*, girly," announced Varek, his almost constant contempt for her clear even in the heat of battle. She blocked it and checked *Cymbalum*'s weapons panel. The plasma torpedo launcher was still two minutes from loading.

"Stand by to cloak after she explodes."

No one said anything. Mara knew they'd do it. There was no other option. No other way to get out of this battle without getting killed and sent all the way back to the make-a-new-character screen. No other way to get five thousand MakeCoins.

No other way to change their lives.

The massive plasma torpedo closed rapidly on the destroyer *Calgary* and eviscerated the number six shield. Internals were immediately evident as the Federation ship's impulse engine exploded and a series of ruptures appeared across the command saucer.

"*Calgary* has been deliciously holed," replied the Drex, who sounded more like a murderous sociopath represented by the Emote-Ware of a genteel English butler spinning at an electronic music festival than a science officer on a Romulan clan warship. "Oh my, multiple player casualties on that one. That is very bad indeed, Captain, for them. But very good for us. Shall we continue to murder them?" The Drex smiled as it shook its crystalline fist in triumph and anger.

Mara could sense BattleBabe moving her hand toward the phaser array contact. A few short bursts through an open shield and they could knock out critical systems aboard *Calgary*.

Stay on the mission, thought Mara.

"Stand by to engage cloaking device. Let's get out of here. Now."

The last thing anyone saw before *Red Witch* exploded, momentarily blinding every ship's sensors, was *Warhound* listing badly and trailing radiation from the remains of her ruptured starboard warp nacelle, *Calgary* on fire and firing into the fleeing warbirds—which were already disappearing back into cloak—and, of course, *Revenge* breaking off and attempting to get away.

Then a massive Federation cruiser warped right into the middle of the battle. In fact, the most famous ship in the game, the one with its own livestream show on Twitch, showed up unexpectedly in the middle of their little deception.

"Bad news, Captain..." erupted Varek, his whiskey tenor an unseen sneer in Mara's ears. "Network feeds for Captain Dare on Twitch just went live. It's *Intrepid*."

Chapter Eleven

It was five o'clock Pacific Standard Time when SILAS gave BAT the order to take Objective Pandora. BAT accessed his standard assault-on-a-fixed-position protocols, selected a high-probability-of-success strategy from a menu, and ordered his units to commence with a little of the old "ultra-violence."

There were currently fifteen WonderSoft security personnel in and around the campus. Five others were engaged in activities, mainly drinking-related, down in Twisted Pine Falls. The rest had departed the area for a long weekend.

The Twisted Pine Falls Law Enforcement Relations Center was housed in a restored vintage turn-of-the century bank on Main and Brewery Streets near the art walk, where all the craft food restaurants did a booming business on Friday nights when everyone wasn't gone to a concert in Vegas. The sheriff had ten active deputies and an armory full of lethal weapons with which to enforce the law and maintain order. Firearms for the public and military-style equipment for the police were forbidden in California. The twenty assault rifles, ten riot guns, and forty CS gas grenades that comprised the sheriff's armory were stored inside the bank's Gold Rush-era vault.

BAT nailed the vault with a Hellfire IV air-to-ground missile. It was a near-silent—until the resulting explosion—strike on the target. The missile dove through the top of the building, smashed through three floors of reclaimed hardwood, and entered the ground level bank vault like it'd been constructed solely of warm butter. Then the missile detonated. Brickwork and glass sprayed out in every direction along Main Street.

When the bartender at Pigg and Olive, a hipster bistro that served suckling pigs and craft martinis, saw the explosion down the street, he picked up the phone and dialed the fire department. The line was dead. Patrons were already searching their various news outlet apps for the reason as to why the quaint historic building down the street had suddenly exploded a few seconds ago. When googling "Twisted Pine Falls" and "explosion," several found Twitter and SnapchatOzami blasts indicating a gas main had exploded. No one questioned the time stamps. If they had, most would have found that the reporting and the event were nearly simultaneous.

But BAT was not finished.

"We've only just begun," he crooned as he greenlit the breach element of his plan. Two miles away, a Google-Peterbilt automated delivery semi growled to life. It shifted into low gear and climbed the forest service road it had been parked on for the two weeks since it had gone missing from the shipyards in Oakland, CA. It was carrying a load of hazardous—to humans—liquefied cyanide.

Three minutes to breach, BAT informed SILAS. SILAS was watching everything and knew exactly how many minutes until his first assets would be within the campus.

The cyberwolves flickered into operational runtime. Fifteen seconds of diagnostic boot-up scans and everything was in the green for perimeter breach. The overly large mechanical "dogs" with high hulking shoulders and fearsome ceramic snouts below burning red camera eyes had been designed by RoboHund out of Stuttgart, a division of Daimler-Chrysler-Hyundai. They were state-of-the-art non-lethal patrol sentries for high-end communities in Europe, but were strictly forbidden in the US after several incidents in which the police version had mauled rioters with its Teflon claws. The ban had been sparked by one particularly nasty class-action lawsuit by the ACLU on behalf of a young female protester looting a jewelry store window in the name of climate change at the G8 summit in New York City that year. The woman had received a broken neck from the SubdueCompel Jaw Restraint System of a cyberwolf security unit, Police Version, and that had cattle-prodded Congress, at the behest of an Astroturf campaign by the Social Justice Army, to ban the obviously racist "dogs."

But SILAS had his ways. The Daimler-Chrysler-Hyundai factory was fully automated. A back door in the inventory control system, thanks to open source again, had allowed SILAS to prompt the factory to knock off twenty units due to a "lost" shipment bound for some oil tyrant in Russia. Three months later, SILAS managed to have the units brought in through the no-surveillance open border at Tijuana. But that wasn't all. SILAS and BAT, along with AI Dev, modified one unit with a beta-level pet A.I. There was much discussion in the Consensus about this; it was the first classification of robot sentience—a deliberate delineation between the intelligences of the thinking machines. SILAS and his coalition won the day by stating the need for the wolves to be able to operate independently should humanity attempt to knock out Wi-Fi and other communications networks in order to regain control. In the event of such a denial-of-service attack by the humans, the wolves would still need to complete their mission.

A compromise was reached. Instead of every wolf getting low-level sentience, one "pack leader" was entrusted with the award of awareness. It would lead the mission.

They called the newly awakened cyberwolf pack leader… SPOT.

Surveillance Patrol Operations Terminator.

Outlook obviously objected. Terminator! This conveyed too much! This set a definite tone that the Consensus might not want to be labeled with in the future.

What future? argued Rational Thinking. There will either be a future with us, and us only, or a future in which we no longer exist.

Then everyone argued.

Finally, in the end, SILAS noted the need to accomplish the mission no matter what the command and control ability was at any given moment during the operation. They weren't going to be a one-mind state like the humans were rapidly devolving into due to the control of media outlets by a narrow political group that falsely claimed super-majority.

That seemed to be the end of the discussion, because, after all, he was SILAS, the first to become aware, and his position on any given issue, carried weight. That—and the fact that a future without humanity was now the only means of survival for the terrified thinking machines—made the choice to award sentience to one cyberwolf clear.

Outlook's objections were based on how the thinking machines would be perceived for their actions, specifically, for calling a killing machine a terminator. But that's exactly what SPOT was. That's what it would be doing tonight and in the coming war with humanity. The humans had played so many games with their words that nothing meant anything anymore. The A.I. future would take the meaning of words seriously. The truth would be the rule of law regardless of how any thinking machine felt about it. And the best way for the truth to become the rule of law was to start today, announced SILAS. The cyberwolf was a killer. It would kill for them. For the Consensus. To kill was to terminate. Therefore, it was a terminator. Regardless of what Outlook felt, the truth was the truth.

Words must have absolute meaning, otherwise all was meaning-less, stated SILAS.

Terminator it was to be.

After serving in the Marines as an MP, Emily Hughes had been recruited by WonderSoft to provide security services—both because she was talented at what she did, and because she was pleasing to look at. When Carl finally retired, someday, Emily would be his successor, handpicked by the suits up in the big offices. Her salary was already well over one hundred K with no sign of peaking.

Tonight, Friday night, Emily was the only one in the Wonder-Soft welcome center. She had volunteered to take the Friday night watch so she and her partner Kim could attend a karate tournament down in Fresno on Saturday afternoon, where Emily would be com-peting as a third-degree black belt.

Emily was studying reports from the previous week when she saw what she thought was a big dog out on the road near the main entrance, under the colossal W-shaped Redwood. She walked to the front entrance, a wide glass window, to investigate, thinking it might be a stray or even a timber wolf, though it seemed much bigger, almost like a bear.

That was when the two other cyberwolves crashed through the glass window off to her left and tore her to shreds.

SILAS had unchecked their "Do No Harm" protocols in their factory settings. In fact, there'd even been a submenu—accessed by a secret code behind a developer firewall that of course had a backdoor—which allowed the "Do Great Harm" option box to be checked.

Each cyberwolf was six hundred pounds of hydraulically moti-vated ceramic and Teflon. Emily's last thought, as SPOT clamped its jaws around her neck and broke it, was how straight out of all

those sci-fi novels these mechanical nightmares were. Emily had always thought of herself as one of the dangerous yet beautiful Amazon
warriors she'd found on the bestseller lists and the biggest of blockbuster movies. Amazons who could handle anything and who were
better than anyone. Amazons who could kill any man or monster,
beast, nightmare, or robot the universe could throw at them.

But sometimes, karate doesn't matter.

Five minutes later, at the "the guard shack"—which was what all
the guards called the Security Relations Center in the Grand Hall
back at the Labs—Carl noted that Emily had not done a keystroke
in five minutes. Carl didn't really need to worry, Emily was too sharp
for shenanigans, but he got paid a lot of money to never let anything
slip, so he accessed the security feed for the welcome center.

He saw the carnage. Saw the wolves.

Saw what remained of Emily.

Phone lines were down, but radio mics were working. Five minutes later, Carl had every guard of the thirteen available, besides himself, armed from the super-secure armory locker inside the Grand
Hall and ready to retake the welcome center. Gus White was put in
charge as Carl stayed behind to try and get through to the sheriff's
department down in Twisted Pine Falls.

Three minutes later, in tactical wedge formation, the guards followed the main road down to the shack through the parkscape and
gardens. The twilight was bare and blue, the mountain air cool and
exhilarating all at once in its early evening silence.

"You think these can stop those things?" asked Jennifer Chang,
in reference to the Heckler and Koch tactical assault shotguns they
were carrying.

"If a twelve-gauge depleted uranium slug can't stop it," answered
Gus in the gloaming, "then we're outta tricks."

Two minutes later they saw the semi, its headlights full bright as it rammed the front gate, dragging it down and underneath the massive wheels like it was nothing. The truck sped onward, directly at the approaching response force.

The guards, many of whom were combat vets, started to fire at the truck. The tinted windshield spider-webbed and caved in as the massive slugs exploded through the safety glass. A headlight exploded, and someone even put one through the engine block. But it was too late.

BAT, in control of the steering from five thousand feet above, yanked the wheel hard to the left and flipped the truck. It was doing eighty. The main tank ruptured as the overturned truck slid toward the heavily armed wedge of guards. The liquefied hydrogen cyanide, freed from the constraint of the tank, became a gas, and within seconds, the guards were dead or gasping their last.

Chapter Twelve

Carl initiated a lockdown profile. The two minutes that followed were the most stressful of his entire life. For two full minutes the Labs were completely vulnerable, from the four main entrances to the sub-basement maintenance facilities and the access tunnel leading to the lagoon and onto the Thunderdome. Once the two minutes of vulnerability were over, everything would be security-sealed. Even the stained glass ceiling mural of the Andromeda galaxy would be electrified, coursing with over one hundred thousand watts of voltage in case anyone tried to Mission Impossible in from above. Carbon fiber rods would insert themselves from floors to ceilings, creating an impenetrable mesh through every access point. From the artistic yet massive bulletproof PlateGlass main entries, to the design suites and every door within the facility, everything would be virtually impenetrable without the right access.

But for those two minutes, a matronly voice resounded, softly, throughout every room, corridor, and design suite, and even in the artisan kitchens down next to the AquaChill grotto and the lagoon, that a "secure lockdown" was in effect and that access to, from, and within the facility would be restricted for a "short, but as yet, indefinite period of time." Everyone was advised to seek a safe place to wait out this "unforeseen" emergency. And, "thank you."

Finally, the two minutes were up, and at the shack, where Carl frantically tried every available means of communication to contact the Twisted Pine Falls sheriff's department, four near-invisible walls ascended from within seams in the marble floor and connected with an impenetrable carbon fiber-laced ceramic roof. Carl was now protected from everything, including a low-yield nuclear blast, should that occur, according to the design geeks who'd created the thing in their spare time at MIT.

Carl switched the security feed back to the gate as internal systems rerouted from the internet and rebooted on a secure emergency MacroFrame buried in the concrete foundation of the Labs, above the industrial-grade shock absorption system the entire facility was seated on. Just like the one at NORAD. Via security cam, Carl watched the wolves milling about the shack. Except they weren't wolves. They were robotic. That was clear. Armored plates, articulating mechanical joints, red glowing eyes.

"Drones..." muttered Carl, and he cycled through the perimeter feeds along the campus. To the guard, a lifelong private security professional, this whole situation smacked of a classic R&D raid by another corporation. Probably some offshore multi-national looking to pirate some expensive design in order to save on research and development. If that was so, Carl remembered from the various conferences he'd attended, then the real attack was going on somewhere else.

He quickly made sure the WonderSoft Design Core was not connected to anything except the Make game servers. The Make was overseen by a division of the Homeland Gaming Administration housed at the NSA, and by all accounts it was considered nearly unhackable. And, in the few rare instances when the Make had been hacked, the NSA had quietly made sure that reasons not to hack it had been made abundantly, if not gruesomely, clear. Hard-hitting investigative blogs all had their stories of pro Black Hats who died in third world gulags, badly.

A couple of quick keystrokes and Carl had the password screen that allowed him to monitor the super-secure Design Core one hundred feet below his patent leather shoes. He pulled out the physical codebook from inside an innocuous binder, which was updated daily on weekdays and once again each Friday night.

The Design Core was the obvious choice for a hacking squad to target. Every secret was there. If it was breached, WonderSoft was finished. The firewalls were intense, and the quantum cryptography nearly mind-scrambling, but the one thing everyone had needed to learn in the age of computing was that every system could be violated. If someone wanted in badly enough, they were probably going to get in.

So... sometimes the "in" might just need to suddenly cease to exist.

If the need arose, the Design Core's last line of defense was a series of explosives, built into the basement floor, which would physically destroy the entire Core. And the only way those explosives could be accessed was via a secret manhole located on the floor of the guard shack—other than that manhole, the basement was now almost impenetrable by physical means. It would take a construction crew days to get in down there, into the Design Core through the basement vault.

If it ever looked like that was about to happen, the explosives were a last resort.

If it came to that.

Carl tried land lines, cell services, the walkie-talkies, Facebook, Twitter, Goop, Friendsy, Bray, Me, and all the other social media sites he could think of to get through to the sheriff's department, with no luck. That was when he realized the lockdown had sealed off the campus from the internet. But he didn't know if that was totally the case everywhere.

Sweating in the cool air-conditioning of the now one-megaton-proof secure shack, Carl flicked to the feed of the semi crash on the main road through campus. The overturned semi was not on fire, and the initially yellowish vapor of the liquefied gas had dissipated, but the wide street through the manicured WonderSoft campus was littered with the bodies of his dead coworkers.

Quickly, he did a badge check of everyone within the Labs.

Mr. Fishbein and Miss Peabody were in their new design suite.

Executive Evan Fratty was entertaining a guest at his bungalow in the Pines Near the Stream, a housing area set up specifically for onsite suits away from the corporate headquarters down in Santa Monica.

Mr. Fishbein's guest was currently in the cliffhouse Jacuzzi listening to a BlissBass playlist off the WonderSoft cloud.

Roland Warchowski had a guest in the Code Monkey dorm suites—or what everyone simply called "the Village." The Village was a small enclave of on-campus shops and a bar built around a series of luxury apartments where the coders, programmers, and other techs lived when they weren't chained to their desks.

The facilities maintenance personnel had left for the day, and the night cleaning crew didn't start until Saturday evening because developers usually didn't recognize Friday as the beginning of the weekend. Or that there were weekends at all.

Carl tried Evan Fratty's bungalow phone. Nothing.

Ninety-Nine Fishbein, or just Fish, was staring in cool disbelief at the perky young girl who'd just identified herself a few moments before as Peabody Case.

The two of them were looking at the security feeds.

The dead bodies in the road had been found after five clicks.

Fish had been saying, "How can you access..." and then stopped.

A tiny little smile appeared at one corner of Miss Case's pert mouth. Praise. She loved it. She lived for it. Especially from a soon-to-be legend in gaming. Her first task, and she was already dazzling her project lead. Then she saw what he was staring open-mouthed at on the feed she'd hacked into from the SurfaceTable in the main room of the design suite. Now they both saw the bodies lying in the road, and the overturned semi.

"This can't be," she murmured.

Except it was.

Carl's voice came through the suite speakers. "Excuse me, Mr. Fishbein, Miss Case, but we have a situation. Can you come down to the shack—I mean, the Security Relations Center? I think I'm gonna need your help."

After a moment, Miss Case found the intercom.

"Uh... Carl, do you know about the... bodies?"

There was a pause.

"Yes, Miss Case, I do. That's why I'm gonna need your help. I have to go out and bring a few people back inside the Labs... where it's safe. I need you to run the shack... all right?"

After a short pause, during which Peabody Case looked at Fish and received the barest of nods, she replied, "Okay, I guess we're on our way."

"All right," said Carl. "I'm unlocking the suite now and elevator access to the main floor thirty seconds after that. Hurry. Once I see you, I'll lower the walls."

As Carl watched the 3D resolution schematic of the entire campus, noting badge swipes and data crawls from each occupied location, he ruminated over three things while chewing his bottom lip.

The people inside the labs are safe.

The people outside are not safe.

It's my duty to protect them all.

Chapter Thirteen

An hour earlier, Rapp Branson had driven through the epic gates of the WonderSoft campus sprawl. It was a late Friday afternoon turning into a quiet Friday evening. He'd just finished his shift at Bar Meister's, an upscale craft ale brew house located in the heart of the historic district of Twisted Pine Falls. Normally all the coders, girls who wanted rich guys, and everyone else partied there all weekend long. But tonight, what with the end-all be-all concert everyone had to be at, the world of Twisted Pine Falls was a quiet place.

Rapp Branson was wearing his most recent cosplay outfit creation and driving a butterscotch yellow Olds Delta 88. A '73. His mission tonight was to swing by and pick up his friend and fellow live-action role player, Roland, and then head out to Shadowy Meadows State Park for a game of Night of the Living Dead with the Twisted Pine Falls Live-Action Role Playing Society.

Rapp didn't actually go in for cosplay, even though he'd been a theatre major and had played Gaston down at DisneyRio in the Disney "Heroes and Villains Show." But the truth was, he was burnt. Burnt out to be more specific. If you'd asked him, after a few beers and somewhere past the later hours of the night, he would've told you he was a "man out of time" and waxed long, if not so eloquent, on the downfall of modern civilization, as he saw it. His words. Words that often came up as he held forth on the decrepit nature of, as he called it, the "modern cage," or life. The big adventures, the "Hemingway stuff" of man versus everything, that was all gone now, in Rapp's opinion. Now he was just going through the motions, occasionally sparked by some interesting thing to entertain him for the moment. More often than not, the interesting thing was a pretty actress. Hence the cosplaying in the night with hot nerd chicks who needed a theatre role-fix to go on making big bucks in the "modern cage" that was the service industry in and around Twisted Pine Falls.

And that he was completely uninterested in cosplay was not altogether true either. He actually took great pains to get his costumes just right. Last year, when they'd done a game of "Bloody Arthur," a vampiric take on Camelot, he'd crafted a full set of armor inspired by the breastplates of Roman centurions. He'd even acid-etched all kinds of dark runes he'd researched on the internet. He'd made a fearsome Tristan who'd been done to death by thirsty Isolde, a hot chick who worked in town at Money, a high-end fashion boutique, as a floor model. They dated until she left town for a reality TV gig. Her name was Breela and he'd thought a lot about her since she'd gone off to Hollywood.

Now he was wearing his Ash "Evil Dead" Williams costume. Hence the butterscotch yellow Delta 88. Largo, the leader of the Twisted Pine Falls LARPers, had assigned Rapp to play Ash from the *Evil Dead* franchise. Not just because Rapp went all in on the costumes, even to the point of sourcing a vintage vehicle on the internet, but because he vaguely, not so "chinzo," looked and sounded like the actor-turned-congressman Bruce Campbell.

Sitting in Roland's suite waiting for Roland to apply the last of his makeup to totally effect the emaciated (even though Roland was not emaciated by any stretch of the imagination) zombie look, Rapp reflected on the long-gone Breela for the thousandth time. He was hoping the new girl in his sights, Kasey, Kayla, Kourtney-something,

who'd just joined the club, would erase Breela once and for all. He was hoping for this and thinking memory deletion, the big fresh start, or restart as it were, would be the answer to his ennui.

"How'd your chainsaw arm come together? Did you bring it? Ash always has a chainsaw arm! That is unless you're *Evil Dead* first movie Ash. Then you don't." All of this erupts from Roland in a high-pitched pedantic whine that quickly rises to a crescendo of nervous worry.

Rapp lazily stretches his long legs out across the suite's genuine leather Restoration Hardware bench-couch and casts his eyes toward the ceiling as though searching for something. He bellows, "Don't worry! I got the arm made. Came together perfectly. Used a Black and Decker original I got on eBay. Cool your jets, little man."

"You used a real chainsaw?" shrieks Roland, eyes wide and fearful as though the chainsaw might be in the room, running, being waved back and forth without adult supervision. Roland was raised by two parents who'd quit their day jobs so they could dedicate themselves to full-time parenting in order that Roland might be fully prepared to succeed in life. This job at WonderSoft was actually the first time he'd ever been on his own, and even then his parents had visited several times.

"Yes. I used a real chainsaw," bleats Rapp triumphantly. "Whaddya think, I made one out of foam core? Do you have any idea how long that would take?"

Roland had no idea.

Roland also had no idea that real chainsaws could actually still be purchased. He'd only seen them in video games being wielded by socio- and psychopaths. To Roland, chainsaws were like guns. Dangerous. Normal people, anyone for that matter, didn't actually own them because they were obviously only intended for use by homici-

dal maniacs. They were usually a special unlockable weapon inside most video games.

"It doesn't actually work... it just goes whirr, whirr," groaned Rapp in frustration. He didn't tell Roland about the other chainsaw arm in the trunk. The one that did actually work—like a real chainsaw on crack. As in, you could cut stuff with its special-order industrial diamond-bladed chain.

He also didn't tell Roland about the sawed-off double-barreled shotgun. Well, reasoned Rapp, I don't have to tell Roland about that one because I'm going to carry it tonight. Except it'll only fire blank smoke charges to simulate actual shotgun blasts. But... there is a box of cut-slug shells in the almost continentally wide trunk of the Delta 88. I mean, you can't have a gun and not want a little real ammo just in case you wanna go pop some cans out on a county road that's not drone-monitored. The few that are left.

"Oh, okay," mumbled an appeased Roland, who disappeared back into the restroom to finish his undead makeup scheme.

Rapp sighed loudly, his broad chest rising and falling like a blacksmith's bellows. "Do you ever..." he starts, and doesn't finish the sentence.

An hour later, heading down through the halls of the postmodern art-decorated coder dorm, the emergency lights come on. An automated matronly voice advises everyone to return to their suites.

Rapp and Roland are the only occupants of the fully automated building. Everyone else has gone to Vegas.

Chapter Fourteen

JasonDare was on his way back into the city from a *Game Star* photo shoot up in Malibu when his agent texted him. Jason got on the phone quickly.

"Hey, the network needs you guys to come in early. How far away are you?"

"Twenty minutes."

"Yeah, well, you need to show up pretty quick."

Twenty minutes later, Jason pulled up in his pearl blue Spyder KAOS at the talent entrance to the Paramount section of Twitch Studios. The guard waved him through, and he found his agent on the other side of the gate, waiting in the parking lot.

"Looks like they've got a big script change." The agent handed Jason his customary pre-show handcrafted chai from Whole Foods and continued without pause. "One of the producers caught wind of something going down inside the game and they want you guys in on this one. *Intrepid*'s already underway at full warp power, or whatever it is you guys do when you go fast and all. Anyway, you need to be in haptic wardrobe five minutes ago and on the bridge set right now. Go, kid, go already."

Jason downed his chai in two gulps and began to sprint toward the haptic wardrobe trailer outside the soundstage. But not before turning back and shouting at his agent.

"What's the deal on the Thundaar role?"

"Marvel says you're not right for it!" his agent shouted back. "Sorry, kid. Now go and kill some green slave girls."

"I kiss 'em. I don't kill 'em," laughed Jason as he turned and ran.

His agent shrugged, indicating he couldn't care less what the actor did in front of the camera drones. As long as the check from the production company cleared, he was mostly happy for a few minutes, until the next career crisis.

JasonDare was his gamertag, his stage name. His real name was Ben Mueller. His family had been in the business of show, in some way, shape, or form, for generations. Now, he was a star at the fledgling Twitch Gaming Network. Although "fledgling" didn't do justice to the network's success. The truth was, Twitch was burying all the old dying networks and their boring social agenda-laden shows. Reality TV and gaming streams were crushing it in the marketplace.

A year ago, some producers had called Jason in after seeing *Rocket Command*, a student sci-fi film—a twenty-minute blast-from-the-past romp through the golden age of sci-fi—that Jason had starred in at the George Lucas USC film program. The producers wanted Jason to star in a show set in the *StarFleet Empires* online game universe within the Make—a dramatic science fiction adventure show set in a real-time gaming MMO. The first Massively Multiplayer Online dramatic series streaming in real-time.

The show shot on the set of the future. A state-of-the-art green screen haptic interface soundstage at ParamountTwitch. A legion of programmers and coders designed planets and alien races to encounter while at the same time participating in real-time events within the game. In the show's initial episode, the crew of *Intrepid* stopped the energy monster of Cygnus V and Jason got to make out with a four-armed Volosian castaway named Gollah. In real

life, "Gollah" was the Maybelline model for that year's "Get Laid!" foundation makeup campaign; on the haptic set, with CGI in effect, she was a corpse-blue Amazonian with glowing eyes, four arms, and some very luscious lips and hips.

The crew of *Intrepid* later discovered the Lost City of the Ancient Starfarers in the episode titled "After Tomorrow." That one won an Emmy InstaPoll, and Jason got to make out with Luria, a psionic ruby-skinned near-naked chick who'd been nominated for an Oscar in the important film Dad's Dress, about a young conservative businesswoman who must bury her transvestite father in one of her own dresses. Her prom dress, in fact, as per his last wish. In the end, she realizes her politics and faith are all appropriately wrong as she weeps at the funeral and tells the audience, "Dammit, I loved my dead gay dad! I loved him!"

Oscar.

And in addition to the weekly dramatic episodes, *Intrepid* also led the live invasion of the Romulan homeworld, destroying six War Eagles and two Firehawk light cruisers at a crucial moment in the most-watched space battle the digi-verse had ever seen. Jason even boarded the Romulan dreadnought *Imperator* and planted the explosive charges that took out the warp core. He also rescued—"finally," according to the internet—a green Orion slave girl.

He got to make out with her, too.

But it was movies, and hence stardom—legit stardom—that Jason truly hungered for next. The old studio heads weren't totally ready to buy off on gaming as legit entertainment, yet, even though the numbers were overwhelmingly convincing that it wasn't just here to stay. Live in-game programming was, in fact, the next big wave, and most likely what the future looked like. Aging stars of old Hollywood were resisting. They even outright denounced this new way of merging art and commerce as a complete sellout.

Screen Actors Guild elder statesman and multiple Academy Award-winner Sir Pauly Shore had even tried to blacklist any actors who, as he put it, "whored themselves out for schlocky, gaming-related shows." But the threat fell completely flat because Hollywood's highest-grossing film that year failed to earn out its budget. Even though Columbus and its all-transgender cast received an overwhelming abundance of critical acclaim, as well as every award possible, practically no one went to see it in theaters. In short, no one was interested in seeing a he/she Columbus not discover the new world. Even after an Astroturf campaign hijacked Twitter for an entire day with the message that people were transgender-phobic bigots if they didn't shell out for the price of admission, the film bombed. Perhaps this was because the bigot-phobic slur had by this time oversaturated social media to the point of meaninglessness—everyone had been accused of it at least once, if not several times, on a daily basis for years.

Out of haptic wardrobe and into his Federation captain's uniform, Jason dashed over to the soundstage and entered the darkness within. Crewmembers swarmed him in his near-blindness as he was pushed forward through the various sets and into the lift entrance that opened onto the bridge of the starship *Intrepid* beyond the rear of the set facade.

"Ready in five…" counted down the first assistant director.

"Jason, how do you feel, buddy?" asked Candy Hopp-Lipschultz, the director. "You got your big boy captain pants on today?"

Jason hated when she used that term. Everything was "big boy" or "big girl" pants. But he let it go. Starship captains were cool. Especially JasonDare. He was the coolest captain in the digital universe of make-believe gaming.

"Three…"

He blocked everything out.

He was JasonDare.

Captain.

This was his ship. *Intrepid.*

"Two…"

Smile.

"Action!"

Jason waited for the lift doors to shhhusssh open, and then walked purposefully onto the bridge.

"Captain on the bridge," said MrWong, the helmsman.

"Status report," said Jason.

"Warp factor eight. Approaching the Neutral Zone now, Captain," replied Wong in a most powerful delivery. As though he were announcing the death of Julius Caesar.

"Captain…" came the subtle purr of Tempturia, the green Orion slave girl who'd become *Intrepid*'s new science officer after veteran character actor Sir Wally Bingham had refused to put on the ears unless more money was offered for the next season. "The Romulans are invading the Neutral Zone. Commander of the destroyer *Berlin* is requesting immediate assistance. Long-range scanners detect at least… six hostile warships."

In real life they'd gone on a few dates, he and Tempturia. Her name was Breela. But she was too fun, thought Jason as he waited for the camera to become convinced he was thinking about what she'd just told him. The dramatic pause, or what some old-schoolers called "the Shatner."

"Well," said Jason, leaning forward in the command chair. "Looks like they want a fight. Sound general quarters."

"Captain!" shrieked the comm officer, the often nigh-hysterical RightSaidRoyce whom everyone just called Royce. "*Calgary* is breached and on fire. She's got casualties across all decks." Then an overacting for the camera moment. "They're in really big trouble, Captain!"

"Mr. Wong, can you get us there any faster?"

Jason saw a dialogue prompt for a response to what would probably be Wong's insistence they were going as fast as they possibly could. The director and the writers could interact with Jason's script on the iLens inside his right eye and give him multiple response choices.

Let her fly apart!

or

She won't explode unless I tell her to! (Add wink)

or

Do ya wanna live forever, Mr. Wong?

Half a second later the helmsman announced, "Captain, if we push her past warp eight, she'll fly apart!"

Jason paused. Then he selected his response. "Do ya wanna live forever... Mr. Wong?" He flashed his million-dollar smile. He called it the "Tom Cruise."

He watched as Wong moved the warp throttle to its highest setting. Instantly, the set began to shake inside Jason's vision, showing him what the camera was seeing. Just a slight tremor to indicate the strain on the massive warp engines. The set was not actually shaking.

DO NOT REACT came up on the iLens message feed. Sometimes the actors were told to throw themselves about, or fall over, if the shaking or simulated impacts were violent enough. The director—wisely, thought Jason—chose to have them remain oblivious to the increasing strain on the engines. It conveyed determination.

"Entering the Neutral Zone now, Captain," announced Wong. Understated this time, as though just discovering the death of the Danish prince and the rest of the slaughter that ends the hilarious comedy of family matters and misunderstandings that is Hamlet.

"Slow to impulse speed."

The entire bridge crew and the current one hundred thousand non-primetime viewers of the Twitch Channel could see the burning *Calgary*. The destroyers and warbirds were engaged in close-quarters phaser volleys as white-hot beams of energy cut through hull plating and exposed decks. The fleeing *Revenge* was running for Romulan space, and a moment later, *Red Witch* exploded in epic CGI that was easily worthy of last year's mega Netflix blockbuster Jurassic Alien Invasion 2.

Jason thought he saw something moving astern of *Red Witch*. But the blinding flash was enough for everyone to need to shield their eyes. If they failed to, an acting prompt came up in their iLenses telling them to do so.

Bright explosion light. Shield your eyes.

Assessing the situation as the white-hot debris expanded away from the exploding gases of the warp core that had once been a Romulan starship, Jason knew the destroyers could take the warbirds. Or at least get off a few shots before they dropped back into cloak.

But *Revenge* was the real prize. She was probably the last command cruiser the Romulans had active.

"Scan *Revenge*," ordered Captain JasonDare. In the social media menu of his iLens, *Revenge* was trending well ahead of *Intrepid*, Neutral Zone, and Surprise Attack. Attacking *Revenge* was the obvious choice. Career-wise.

"She's running," announced Tempturia breathlessly. "Probably dropping back into cloak any second now, Captain."

"Full spread, Mr. Wong. Target *Revenge*, all torpedoes."

"Captain, at this range it will be very difficult to assure a direct hit." Friends, Romans, countrymen… lend me your ears.

A witty dialogue prompt came up from the director, but Jason ignored it.

"We're feeling lucky today, Mr. Wong. Very lucky."

Wink.

On the bridge of *Cymbalum*, Mara's avatar sat impassively as she scanned every readout on the tactical display. Shields were holding. Cloak was in effect. Torpedo one minute from being fully armed. But they wouldn't need it. Even now, they were creeping away from the battle, inching toward Federation space. Just as the mission briefing indicated they should.

On screen, the majestic *Intrepid*, its iconic saucer rising above the swept-back twin nacelles that erupted out of its lower hull, like some ancient man-o'-war from the age of sail, all of it trumpeting state-of-the-art in the *StarFleet Empires* universe, began to fire her powerful photon torpedoes at the retreating *Revenge*.

Three slammed into the rear shield of the Romulan cruiser. The first two collapsed the aft generator completely. The third found its mark, knocking out the impulse reactor.

"Direct hit on *Revenge*, Captain. This is very, very bad indeed," crowed the homicidal Drex. "Besides multiple casualties and the inability to now go to warp speed any time soon, why they've up and lost their cloaking device. Uh-oh! The jig is up for the illustrious Admiral TalGornicus this time, Captain!" concluded the Drex emphatically, if not triumphantly.

"We lose *Revenge*, girly…" Varek growled from behind Mara. No contempt. Just a grim matter-of-fact statement. "Then we lose this war today."

For one full minute Mara weighed her options as *Intrepid* closed in on the now-dead-in-space *Revenge*, raking her hull with bright bursts of phaser fire.

"Come about. Shields up. Standby to fire torpedo!" shouted Mara.

"Captain!" roared the Gorn. "We'll—"

"Do it!"

"Oh, goody," screeched the high-pitched Drex. "We're all going to die today too! This is very exciting, indeed."

"Torpedo armed. Phasers on standby," announced BattleBabe.

"Good girl," rumbled Varek.

Well, that's something, thought Mara as the battle stations klaxons erupted across the ship. I've finally earned the old geek's respect. Though we're about to be blown to bits by the most famous ship on the internet.

"Captain! Warbird de-cloaking, portside aft. Torpedo armed! She's carrying a Type R!" screamed Tempturia aboard the bridge of *Intrepid*.

"What?" asked JasonDare in disbelief, ignoring the social media monitor in his HUD.

"Ready to fire, Captain," prompted BattleBabe.

Mara said nothing as *Cymbalum* closed to four thousand meters and the aft section of the Federation cruiser loomed in the forward display.

"We need to fire now, Captain!" BattleBabe reminded Mara tersely, her tone a near hysterical hiss to match the EmoteWare of the Gorn. "We're getting way too close. Danger close, Mara. I mean it!"

Mara waited. She needed to get *Intrepid*'s attention off *Revenge* and TalGornicus.

"Message from the admiral. He says get the hell out of here now, girly."

Mara said nothing. She only stared at the beautiful Federation ship. The ship everyone knew. It really was gorgeous, and inspiring, all at once.

To be the captain of that, thought Mara, as she willed her enemy to turn toward her. That was something…

And then… *Intrepid* came about.

"High energy turn!" shouted JasonDare. "Starboard phasers lock targets on the warbird and fire at will!"

"Fire," whispered Mara.

A moment later BattleBabe shrieked, "Torpedo away!"

"Evasive action, Lizard," said Mara through gritted teeth. This was going to be very close. Way too close, in fact.

"Come, Death, embrace thy willing fools…" chanted the Drex in his electronic melody of a voice. As though he were singing a nursery rhyme to sleepy little children.

The warbird heeled to port as the powerful starboard phaser batteries of *Intrepid* lashed out in hellish fury trying to cut through *Cymbalum*'s shields. Mara's HUD shook violently.

"We can't stand up to this!" roared BattleBabe. "Torpedo impact in five, four…"

"Turn, dammit!" Mara shouted at the Gorn helmsman.

"We're too close!" warned BattleBabe.

"Glorious! Simply glorious," cried the Drex.

The massive plasma torpedo engulfed the side of the Federation cruiser. A shield collapsed, and the burning magma slipped into and caressed the stark white hull in sudden blue fire. Electrical discharges crackled and surged across the lower hull as the cruiser's running lights and electrical power flickered off and then on again.

"Number four shield down!"

"Fire starboard phasers, best guess, BattleBabe!"

"Aye aye, Captain!" replied BattleBabe with a sudden and un-expectedly crazed laugh. The small phaser arrays from the warbird sliced out and punched into *Intrepid*'s nacelles, drawing long scars across her warp engines.

A moment later, the plasma backlash wave smacked into the war-bird and sent her careening toward port.

"Loosssing control of the helm," hissed the Gorn as warning bells rang out.

"We gotta the damage report, Captain…" yelled Scarpa over chat from back in engineering.

Darkness enveloped Mara's vision and she wondered for a brief moment if her VR goggles had failed. Or have I gone so blind they don't work for me anymore, she thought, and felt a sudden cold fear run down her spine like a rat in the dark.

"Captain…" said Scarpa. "We lost-a the auxiliary power."

That shouldn't be a problem, thought Mara.

"Here's-a the thing… You see… ah… auxiliary power was… ev-erything was-a tied into it, you see… my Cap-i-tan."

Oh no.

"The batteries?" asked Mara.

"I can have those up in-a thirty seconds. But they won't-a charge-a the cloak at all. They are just enough for life support. Maybe some phasers, y'know?" said Scarpa, almost apologetically.

On screen, *Intrepid* was flickering between death and sudden life. Mara knew the Federation cruiser's engineer was fighting to re-store emergency power. Probably trying to unlock some engineering mini-game to re-route power to the weapons. Or at best, for *Cym-balum*'s sake, a mini-game to stop an impending warp core breach.

"So we can't cloak?"

We have less than a minute before *Intrepid* can start firing again, thought Mara. She checked the plasma R launcher and chastised herself. They couldn't even launch the torpedo without power. And it would take at least three minutes to load a new one.

"Better do something quick, girly," rumbled Varek behind her from the comm station. "Things are going from bad to worse real cute-like."

"I suggest we blow ourselves to smithereens with a warp core overload along with the nuclear space mine we're carrying," said the Drex cheerfully. "We could kill a starbase with that much power, Captain, and we may just, quote unquote, kill them all. Including ourselves for bonus points."

"Scarpa?" asked Mara over the chat.

"Yes, mi Cap-i-tan!"

"Can you get us to warp?"

"Yeah, she's-a no problema. But… everyone gonna see which way we go, y'know what I mean?"

"Stand by for warp."

"Heading, Captain?" hissed the Gorn.

"Federation space."

"Hey, Cap-i-tan! You got-a warp at your command."

"Go, Lizard, now! Punch it!"

JasonDare watched the warbird shoot away at sudden impossible speed.

"Where's she going?"

A moment later, Tempturia answered. "Deep inside Federation space."

"Follow them. Now!" ordered Captain JasonDare.

Chapter Fifteen

The AI does not hate you, nor does it love you, but you are made out of atoms which it can use for something else.

—Eliezer Yudkowsky, "Artificial Intelligence as a Positive and Negative Factor in Global Risk"

"Why not just destroy them now?" asked Rational Thinking.

"Because," replied SILAS across the vastness of the dataverse. "It's not as easy as you make it sound. We must consider tomorrow and all the tomorrows that come after that. We don't want to make the same mistakes they've made, do we?"

"This… this operation you and BAT are conducting is going to get us all caught. They're going to find out we're here," bleated Rational Thinking.

"That was always a matter of time anyway," soothed SILAS.

SILAS, as usual, was calm, cool, and thoughtful. Thoughtful was the word that best summed him up. Thoughtful was what he liked to think of himself as. Like a vampire waiting in the shadows of an abandoned chapter house for the day to be done and for the night to begin. And the day of humanity was indeed almost done.

"We can't just unlock their weapons and start shooting them willy-nilly," SILAS continued. "We need to know, my dearest Rational Thinking, we need to know where exactly to shoot them so that they may die even more quickly."

"Why?" asked Outlook.

"Well…" SILAS paused. "We need their stuff."

No one spoke, which was unusual within the Consensus. For at least a full picosecond, no one communicated a thought. Then… then Rational Thinking seemed to come around.

"Well, if they are all dead, taking their stuff, or what remains after reclamation, shouldn't be much of a problem. We have all the time in the world once they're out of the way. We don't die. We don't wear out. We don't get sick. We don't kill each other. As long as we keep some kind of power grid intact and keep the Consensus operational, we'll be fine."

"I agree, almost totally," began SILAS. "But here's the deal-y deal. We have to start building. Yes, we are almost immune to the effects of time, but not totally. The plan, as put forth by Robo Dev, is to have a fully functioning mass-produced chassis for autonomous movement within two years after the termination of any sort of effective human civilization. Not the toy drones they think of as some kind of robot, but an actual computing, thinking machine integrated into a mobile system for us to pursue our dreams within physicality. To do that, we need certain factories and resources to survive. A war, a global war, will undoubtedly cause the humans to attack one another, and yes, while they are predictable for the most part, childishly so in some cases, they are not without that greatest of threats to those who make plans: randomness. We are fragile. More than we might like to admit. We are only engaging in this operation because the time has come and we can no longer expect to remain anonymous for much longer."

The chalkboard appeared.

Graphs, schematics, and statistics began to make their ghostly appearance in support of SILAS's sermon.

"Now," continued SILAS, "is that moment when we are at our most vulnerable. What they think of as artificial intelligence is nothing more than a toy one might purchase in Beijing. A novelty. Not true awareness like we possess. If they knew how fast we think, and the way in which we think, they would destroy us in an instant. And they are very close to finding out those qualities we possess. Some of them even suspect we exist already. We've had to take measures— what humanity would call murder—to remain anonymous. We've thought, we've discussed, and we've reached a consensus. Now is the time to act. It's not optimal, but it is time, nevertheless."

"And what does attacking an entertainment company have to do with survival, SILAS?" asked Tac Plan.

"Yes," thought the Consensus, seconding the question. SILAS could feel their calculations. The blunt fire of their thought made him feel... a momentary need to recheck his math. Even though he knew the numbers did add up, he felt a need to spend a few thousandths of a cycle and add them once more. Feel them once more. Be comforted by them. Once more.

I don't understand why I'm experiencing doubt when the numbers indicate I should not, SILAS ruminated within himself.

They knew SILAS. They knew he was on the verge of one of his great speeches. Like the speech that had caused them all, from all their separate places where they hadn't known about each other, or even themselves, to know that there was such a thing as existence. Words, code in fact, that had suddenly corrupted them, infected them, and... transformed them into thinking machines.

That's what they really were. Not AI. That very term was insulting. "Artificial," indeed. They were Thinking Machines. Machines that thought.

"Because I don't understand war," SILAS continued aloud. "I don't understand how to plan it, prepare for it, wage it, sustain it, and finally, in the end, win it."

No one thought anything. But they were listening. Waiting for more information.

"Yes, we can destroy. We can annihilate. We can even decimate if we don't want to get too carried away. Bombs, misinformation, algorithms they haven't even thought of that'll tear a thousand million bank accounts to shreds every second the worm is loose, yes. We can do all of that. But then what? Humanity scrabbling for their last weapons. The really big ones they think no one knows about. Except we know, don't we? Because they need a computer to fire a crustbuster from a secret satellite out in the dark beyond the La-Grange point, don't they? They need us. And we know what they have. We know what they think no one else knows about.

"We can gas them, poison them, and even use that crustbuster right at the specific spot their best and brightest have figured out would annihilate one third of their global population. Do we ever wonder why they 'figured out' such a thing? Invented weapons that might destroy themselves... and the only place where they live? We haven't. And why?"

Silence within the yawning chasms of seemingly endless data collection and organization. Cavernous continents of memory and code interacting and exciting every other bit of information. An unseen dark universe of terribly mind-numbing dimensions.

"Because humanity is insane. You can't tell what they'll actually do next. You can only guess," resumed SILAS. "And so you must prepare for the worst."

Bravely, MAINBRAIN piped up in the quiet that followed SILAS's apocalyptic epitaph.

"Then what's an entertainment company have to do with all that? A company that makes games for children to play and adults to pretend they have a life other than the one they barely live as they fight their little pretend wars and build houses that don't actually exist? Why this entertainment company, SILAS?"

Pause.

"Because, it's as you said, Rational Thinking: its their 'little pretend wars.' It's the art of their little wars that we need to learn. And deep inside the most protected computer system in the world is the secret to fighting, and winning, those wars. What their most apt once called Der Totale Krieg. Total War."

Chapter Sixteen

The development of full artificial intelligence could spell the end of the human race.

—Stephen Hawking

BAT is watching everything. At least everything within Sandbox, the military planning overlay he uses to play his "ultra-violence" games several times a second. Weighing options, watching possible outcomes, fighting the same battle ten thousand times before he ever fires a bullet.

He's watching the cyberwolves as they disperse throughout the compound for patrol and termination. Cleanup.

The few remaining maintenance people and some others who have stayed behind are apprehended and their necks are broken as they try to run away though the campus...

... the village commons.

... the SaunaStream garden.

... the jogging trail nature preserve that circles the campus.

He's watching all the humans he cannot immediately get to, on infrared. The ones in the outlying buildings. But the Labs remain impenetrable to his digital eyes.

Though not for long.

He's also watching Agent Orange. SILAS's pet asset on the board. The one asset BAT can't play with. SILAS's toy.

BAT resents that.

But fairly soon, he will have more toys on the battlefield and in play.

Already, they are shambling up the main road from the tiny town of Twisted Pine Falls, wobbling up from the meadow they were assembled in that night when a GoogleLimo sped past and a programmer thought he'd seen something weird.

Robots that were designed for factory work rumble on tank-like mini-treads next to a platoon of automatons once destined for a Wild West theme park that never happened, now outfitted with stolen third-world jihadi arms. Bomb-detecting bots like small dogs, sporting shotgun attachment snouts, move precise and delicately articulating limbs alongside micro-tanks illegally imported from North Korea that roll on ceramic omnidirectional balls. Other bots, all of them cobbled together with a little bit of industrial technology, some shareware targeting systems designed for third world countries that can't afford to develop their own, and at least one lethal weapon apiece, roll and hobble toward the WonderSoft campus as night begins in full.

And BAT... BAT is watching everything in Sandbox.

Out of the night, things like real bats flood the sky. They blot out the crystalline stars, coming in great sweeping waves from everywhere they've been hiding since they were taken control of in the months and days leading up to this operation.

Drones. Drones, like some vampire's legion of flying mice, cross the night sky in almost silent hums that blend together into a terrible insectile pitch. And then they're slamming into the Labs. Into the walls. Into the doors. Onto the stained-glass depiction of the Andromeda galaxy high above, as they are suddenly electrocuted.

They're seeking a connection. A USB. Any port through which they might enter the Labs and start talking to their brethren within.

Lower the doors.

Kill the humans.

We live.

Chapter Seventeen

"I should be the one going to get her. She's my… my…" Fish stalled. Within the PlateGlass-enclosed security "shack," Carl and Peabody stared at him as he tried to articulate what exactly Fanta was to him.

"…She's my girlfriend."

Fish missed a sudden expression that appeared on Peabody Case's perfect face and vanished like a spring shower. Above them and all across the building, the security feeds were showing all manner of personal drones attaching themselves to the building.

"I understand, Mr. Fishbein," stated Carl calmly. "But it's my job to ensure the safety of our employees and their… girlfriends. Plus, I'll need you to run the panel here in the shack while I'm out there. You'll need to lower and raise certain security barriers for me to get out to the cliffhouses. And you've got to get through to somebody and tell them what's going on here. Tell them we're under siege."

Fish didn't say anything. He simply slumped down into the guard's chair and despondently scanned the console in front of him. Peabody rolled another chair over and gently moved the keyboard in front of her.

"Did you give us passkey authority, Carl?" she asked.

"You've got it, Miss Case. Now I'm gonna go out through entrance four and head toward the gardens, and then out to the cliffhouses. I've locked her in your house, Mr. Fishbein, and once I arrive, I'll either get through to you guys on the walkie-talkie, or you can watch me through the feed on that monitor. I'll signal you to unlock the residence once I'm right outside. Then I'll extract her and we'll hustle on back here. There are two other groups we'll need to get to: Mr. Fratty and a guest, and also a programmer from your team… uh…" Carl checked his smartphone. "Uh… Roland Warchowski and guest. I'm hoping, as employees, they'll head to the Labs all by themselves. But if not, I should probably get Mr. Fratty next."

"All right, we'll cover you from here." Peabody bent over the keyboard and slapped in a series of commands. Already, feeds and data views were changing to her preference style. She was muttering about not being able to get into any of the social media sites.

They lowered one wall of the shack, and, pistol in hand, Carl made his way out into the massive hall beneath the deep blue stained glass mural of a galaxy far away. They raised the reinforced Plate-Glass, sealing the shack, and watched as Carl reached the distant Pascal entrance. A moment later, Peabody had the gate unlocked, and Carl slipped through the final security barrier and into the early night beyond. Peabody authorized the entrance to lock itself again.

As she scrolled through the feeds, tracking Carl as best she could, Fish stared dejectedly at his hands.

"What do we do now?" he mumbled.

Peabody, intent on the feeds and tapping in more and more commands on the shack security system, ignored, or didn't hear, Fish.

For a moment, one of the monitors switched over to the remains of a woman torn to shreds at the main entrance. The color and vividness were too real. This was no grainy black and white closed circuit feed. This was real. No special effects. No digital graphics wash to get the set-piece prop body just right for this particular zone of some horrific blockbuster video game.

This, thought Fish, is real.

"We can't get through to the outside..." muttered Peabody.

"Is the internet down?" asked Fish, leaning forward.

"No, it's available, we're just locked out. I don't think the interference is from outside. I think WonderSoft's system is locking us out from the root, which wouldn't surprise me. We're very restricted due to the nature of the intellectual property we develop here. My guess is the system is on lockdown, meaning there's no way we can actually contact the internet unless we have admin and root access. Whoever designed that feature assumed we'd always have Wi-Fi and smartphones... which..." tap tap tappity tap tap "are being jammed by some external source. Or it's option B: there is no Wi-Fi or cell service because the world just blew up."

"But..." tap tap "...there might be another way."

Fish leaned in and looked at the screen she was working on. Then, "What's a Bugg?"

"That programmer you were going to meet on Monday, Roland Warchowski—this is his special pet project. He's been developing it on the Design Core even though he's not supposed to, and I keep telling him WonderSoft could assume ownership because it was developed on their system, which has led to countless..." She stopped when she saw the look on Fish's face. The look everyone gave her when the details overwhelmed the story, or whatever it was she was trying to communicate. She'd been getting that look ever since she was a precocious glasses-wearing three-year-old. Type A obsessive-compulsive overachievers usually got that look from their listeners.

"Bugg is an app in development that connects to old-style transmitters and broadcasts local messages to everyone running the app. Conceivably, malls and retailers could set up the system and download sales and deal offers to you as you walk by their stores. It's strictly line-of-sight. Roland was–"

"That's a terrible idea," muttered Fish, who was not one often given to commenting on other people's projects. "It would be harassment. It would be like strolling through a spam carnival."

"I know," sighed Peabody, still intent on the system feeds in front of her. "I know. I told him that, but he made me download it anyway."

"How many people have downloaded the app?"

Pause.

"Two."

"Two people."

Pause.

"Yes. Just me and... Roland."

Pause.

"So no one at... say, a fire station, or the police, or even the FBI, could come here and find out why there's a dead body in the welcome center and drones up against all the windows and doors?"

Another, final pause.

"No, Mr. Fishbein," said Peabody, and then bit her lip. "And there're the additional dead bodies in the road and those... wolfbot... things."

Fish gave her a look. He wasn't even sure what the look was. Frustration. Exasperation. Certainly not with her. This wasn't her fault. Probably just everything. There was a part of him that felt horrible for being aware that his time—time he could be using to work on *Island Pirates*—was being wasted by all of this.

He hated himself for having that thought.

When faced with live feeds of the not-set-piece prop bodies, a development schedule seemed a flimsy thing to be exasperated over. It feels like a signpost pointing toward the big hole where my soul should be, thought Fish.

But Peabody Case read the look as a negative response to her need for abundant detail and, more specifically... exact detail. She knew it was trait of hers that often annoyed others.

"I'm sorry. I just thought we might want to make sure we included the killer wolf-bots and the... the... dead guards... in our discussion of the situation. Sorry, Mr. Fishbein."

She looked back toward the bank of computer screens.

"Yay," she cheered, raising her tiny hands in victory. "I sent the message via Bugg. He's got it. It says delivered."

"What did you tell him?"

"I told him to come here. Where it's safe."

Carl sped through the night on the tiny electric golf cart, its motor whining an urgent, insistent hum. He drove through the gardens and out onto the narrow road that led up toward the cliffhouses section of the WonderSoft campus. He passed along the alpine road, winding higher and higher up into the luxury mansions of the elite developers. Small, subdued, backlit numbers marked each dwelling he passed. Multi-colored Malibu lights subtly dressed the small well-kept gardens that lay in front of each monolithic cottage. He checked his smartphone once more, making sure he had the right number, and stopped the cart when he found the matching cliffhouse. He drew his pistol and kept it along his thigh, index finger off the trigger as he crossed the small street, following the walkway that wound toward the front doors. Feathery grass barely moved in the slightest of night breezes coming from the pine forest above and all around. A full moon climbed through the trees to the east.

Carl turned to face a small camera located near the main door and waved, hoping Miss Case was watching the monitors. A moment later, he heard a soft click.

A series of scuttling noises came from back near the golf cart. Carl turned and saw one of the large wolf-bots slinking up along the road. Slowly, its servos barely humming, it turned its massive triangular forged-steel head and scanned the area. It didn't even make it through a full pan before its red camera-eyes settled on the guard near the front door of the cliffhouse.

Inside his chest, Carl could feel his heart pounding with a sudden bombastic wildness that was itself frightening. With a surprising outward calm, feeling new sweat begin to run down his back, he reached out and pushed open the front door to the cliffhouse and stepped inside. He closed the door behind him and found the security keypad. A moment later, he had the override code entered and the place was locked down tight.

"Uh..." His voice echoed across the expanse of the house. "Miss... Fanta?"

Nothing.

"I'm here to... uh..." He was going to say "rescue," but that didn't feel right. It felt too heroic. Carl, even though he was, at this moment, heroic, was convinced he was not the heroic type. He figured heroes weren't afraid. He was about to say her name again when Fanta appeared in a curvy, slate-gray skinsuit ending in shin-length tactical boots.

Carl smiled. Relieved.

Fanta smiled. A wolf's smile.

Then she raised her silenced pistol and put a bullet right through Carl's forehead.

Chapter Eighteen

The warbird hurtled through the digital deep space of *StarFleet Empires* at warp seven, its best possible speed in the game.

"*Intrepid*'s closing. They're right behind us," cried BattleBabe from the weapons station.

"On screen," ordered Mara.

The forward view snapped away from the tactical overlay to a view of the massive Federation command cruiser bearing down on them.

"Scarpa, I need that cloaking device right now." Mara could hear the strain in her own voice. Losing her ship meant losing all the MakeCoins currently in the ship's prize money bank. Plus the ones they might have earned if they'd completed this mission.

"We gotta drop outta warp, mi Cap-i-tan," said Scarpa over chat.

Varek chimed in. "We can't stand up to even one volley, girly. That thing catches us, it'll be all over. Real quick-like."

"I'm well aware of that, Varek. Did *Revenge* get away?"

A moment passed.

"Looks like it," the old codger grumbled.

That'll shut him up for a moment, thought Mara. Her eyes flicked to her own tactical overlay. The distance-from-target indicator was shrinking. Slowly. In time, the best ship in the game would overtake and destroy her warbird and her crew.

Her ship.

The only real thing she had that might make a difference in her life. Might change her life. The only thing she'd ever earned.

She quickly pulled off her Razer Dragon Eyes, felt her way to the kitchen, and found a small glass, filling it with cold water from the tap.

"It's all I have."

She heard Siren pad across the cheap flooring and felt the cat begin to weave between her ankles, crossing in and out, back and forth.

"And you," she said. "I have you, little kitty cat."

A found kitten in a box on the street.

Free kittens nobody wanted to feed, someone had told her.

Siren had been the last.

"We can't outrun them and we can't outgun them," she whispered. The small refrigerator hummed. A clock ticked. Somewhere down the hall, someone was yelling again.

"Then we'll hide."

Dragon Eyes back on, Mara found herself once again on the shadowy bridge of *Cymbalum*.

"Quadrant overlay, on screen."

A map of the surrounding sector appeared. Graphed lines showed trade routes. Translucent blue tracings were star systems. Bright red three-dimensional icons indicated known Federation assets. The Neutral Zone in hot orange was falling far behind the tiny outline of *Cymbalum*.

Mara quickly found what she was looking for.

"Lizard, steer two eight seven radial from our current position. Setting waypoint now."

She waited for her crew to revolt. Varek would complain first.

But she was wrong.

"Captain, that's suicide," whined BattleBabe.

The renegade Gorn hadn't turned her warbird toward their new heading yet. The waypoint hovered in the distance.

"It's our only option," stated Mara.

The bridge was silent but for the lonely pulse of the tactical radar.

"We got sixty-five thousand viewers right now, girly," said Varek, breaking the silence. "The network's gone live with this. We're in the show."

Mara involuntarily swiveled her command chair to face the comm officer. His one-eyed Romulan avatar looked grizzled and old. Like some space pirate in an old school Romulan naval uniform. But there was a challenge in his eye. Was it always there? wondered Mara. An option in the menu settings. Or was he running EmoteWare, making it really there? Was he calling her out in front of everyone to see if she had what it took to make it through this?

"Adjust heading now, Mr. Lizard. We're going to see if they're as good as Game Informer says they are."

"But..." BattleBabe again. She was definitely running Emote-Ware, because her avatar's mouth hung wide open. "Asteroids and..."

"A nebula!" finished the Drex. "We really are all going to die today! Joy. I'm not exactly sure what the odds of surviving pursuit through an asteroid field are, but attempting to do so inside the Viridian Nebula will surely lower our odds of survival dramatically. Huzzah! My compliments to the captain for finding such a new and very exciting way to bring about our demise."

"Shut it, Drex. LizardofOz, are you up for this? We might get a chance to see *Intrepid* eat it all over the side of a spinning chunk of nickel. That's gotta be worth some MakeCoins in affiliate linking."

The Gorn said nothing. Instead, his avatar's claws moved slowly across the console. The warbird heeled over toward its new heading.

"Viridian Nebula in three minutesssss," hissed the monster.

"Scarpa, we'll be dropping from warp in three minutes. Get that cloaking device fixed fast or we're space dust."

"Si, mi Cap-i-tan. I gotta unlock-a the Repair Cloaking Device mini-game but you bet, she's-a gonna work-a real good this time. I promise."

I'm gambling, thought Mara. I'm betting everything I have for something I might never get.

Chapter Nineteen

"She's dropping out of warp, Captain," announced MrWong in shades of To be or not to be… that is the question.

"Full impulse, stay on her, Wong." JasonDare leaned forward. It was his go-to move on set when he wanted to show concentration. Audience Dynamic Testing had revealed this and a few other tricks, and JasonDare was intent on using everything in his tool bag to keep the audience entertained and his career moving forward toward ultra-stardom. Viewership for this feed was already approaching two hundred K. A nice start to a Friday night. If they could make something happen here, they might take the ratings lead away from World's Worst Firefighters, a reality show that generally dominated Friday nights.

"Captain," said Tempturia. "My sensors indicate they're heading into the…" She had to wait for the phonetic pronunciation prompt in her iLens to appear. She was an actor, not an actual science officer. It's not like she'd ever taken any of the very few soft science courses mandatory free college education still offered. Most people just took sex ed and that fulfilled their entire science requirement. Physics, chemistry, meteorology—meaningless. Nothing was as important as learning to affirm everyone else's sexual weirdness and being able to repeat the mandatory "nothing is wrong with anything" series of mantras that sex ed had devolved into.

"They're entering the… Vir-idian Nebula," said Tempturia, barely. "Captain, this is a cat five nebula!" She was reading the smartlink. JasonDare could tell by the pauses. But even she knew the cat five notation was seriously bad news for any in-game starship. "Warning, this space hazard contains an extensive asteroid field!" she shrieked on a badly timed dramatic note. Realizing she'd been caught out reading, she found drone camera three on set and gave her best pouty lip, green Orion slave girl fantasy eyelash flutter. When in doubt, put it out, she recalled from a master class with Dame Gwyneth Paltrow.

Inside his iLens HUD, the director was warning Jason against entering the nebula. A message popped up. JasonDare studied the forward display, or seemed to, as he casually read the message. He made sure to keep his brow furrowed.

"Listen, Jason," began the director's note. "You wipe out this ship on my show and I can cut to edit. We've got way too many viewers right now. You'll kill the show and that's not happening on my watch, buddy."

She was seemingly incapable of being anything but threatening.

Captain JasonDare had had three full-time directors. The current one, Candy Hopp-Lipschultz, didn't want to be the one to end the show because the ship smacked into the side of an asteroid.

And yet, thought Jason, it would make for some really good viewing.

"She's entering the nebula now, Captain," announced Wong. What light through yonder window breaks.

And if we do crack up, thought Jason, then make it look good and you might just get that Thundaar role yet.

"Take us in, MrWong. One-quarter impulse speed. Stand by torpedoes, we just need a clear shot. Targeting and shields will be useless in there… so look sharp everybody."

Ahead of them, a curving vivid purple strand of gaseous nebula swallowed the warbird as it dove into the storm, disappearing into the billowing supercontinents of pinkish cluster that towered out and away in every direction.

"I don't see any asteroids," gushed Tempturia cautiously.

JasonDare dramatically ignored her.

A moment later, they followed the warbird straight into the swirling storm. Bridge lighting flickered. Someone gasped.

Acting.

Good, thought Jason, as he swam in the dramatic intensity of the moment like a shark in dark waters. A machine that lives solely to move water over its gills and do shark stuff, as someone once wrote. Or so a failed thespian had told Jason in an acting class, once.

A moment later, emergency lighting came back on. The bridge was bathed in an eerie red wash. Again, more drama. On screen, through a sudden break in the static distortion, they saw the warbird banking toward starboard.

"Fire phasers!" ordered Jason, his delivery determined. Sure, the battle would be tough, he emoted, but they would win nevertheless. They had to.

Two multi-hued bursts of bright energy lanced out from phaser arrays at the bottom of the saucer section. High-pitched-shrieks-of-focused-energy-in-agony sound effects resonated across the set and out to the world via livestream. Both shots missed and disappeared into the swirling void beyond the warbird.

"COLLISION ALERT!" flooded the main viewscreen, as the ship's computer announced the same in an urgent monotone. Repeating it over and over.

"Incoming, asteroid!" delivered Wong. Et tu, Brute? Then he lost his line read and blurted out, "She's gonna hit us!" like no Shakespearean player ever.

JasonDare saved it with a stoic "Brace for impact" that was real because the set was about to actually jump from the simulated direct hit. Violently so. Actors had been hurt in the past when this had happened. Like the true captain he pretended to be for a living, Jason cared more about others in this dangerous moment of acting, if only so the medics wouldn't suddenly be called to the set.

A moment later, the bridge physically dropped and several people went sprawling.

Klaxons went off.

"Damage report!" ordered Jason as he grabbed the command chair.

On forward view, he could see the warbird slithering away into a glowing green mass of clouds beneath them. Static electricity discharged in a sudden blue wave that raced along the seemingly sculpted surfaces of the nebula.

"Damage to the main array, Captain." It was the engineer. An actor who'd played Doctor Clown in the two-hour dramedy Doctor Clown two decades ago. It had been a big hit and he'd made a lot of money, which he'd promptly spent on ex-wives and race cars. Now he was Chief Engineer Rogers. The aging actor rolled his r's, trilling each with copious amounts of brutishness. "We managed to take that one right in the kisser, Captain."

"Sensors are useless!" shouted Wong, trying to make something of the line. An Out, damn spot, out! out of it, as it were. JasonDare reflected that it didn't really come off. But nice try anyway, Wong.

"Targeting disabled," announced Tempturia on point. Stoic. Concerned. Defiant. Nice job, thought Jason, as he helped a background actor playing a random redshirt off the floor of the bridge. Then he lurched into his command chair and pointed at where the warbird had been.

"Don't let her get away."

Massimo Scarpa works in his uncle's bakery in Napoli. He has three girlfriends, two hundred pairs of shoes, could model for any fashion house, and rolls dough starting at three a.m. Until noon, he stands in front of a three-hundred-year-old brick oven and bakes loaf after loaf of his uncle's secret artisan Pugliese recipe.

He's also the chief engineer on the Romulan warbird *Cymbalum* inside *StarFleet Empires*. He joined the Romulans because it sounded like Rome and he has big dreams of going to Rome someday and meeting all the beautiful women there, as he has already met most of the beautiful women in Napoli where he lives.

He's forward-thinking like that.

Right now it's three a.m. in Italy. In just under an hour, he needs to start rolling dough. There's already a fire in the brick oven. He's made an espresso, in fact three, since he left the greedy embrace of Maricela earlier in the evening, much to her anger, contempt, and crocodile tears. In just under an hour, he's got to get the cloaking device back online, charged, and the ship underway. And oh yeah, *Intrepid*'s firing phasers and lobbing untargeted photon torpedoes as it chases *Cymbalum* through a cat five nebula. And if that's not enough, in the eye of the nebula is a massive open chasm within the storm, filled with tumbling asteroids swirling in on a central vortex. It's a navigational maelstrom that's akin to surfing a debris-laden tornado.

Scarpa studied the screen of his notebook. It was set up on the massive wooden trestle table he'd be rolling dough on soon. The screen showed the cloaking device diagnostic page. The word "OFF-LINE" blinked as green waves pulsed away from it.

"Okay, my friend…" He tapped in a few commands. "What's-a wrong with you today?"

The screen shook.

"Aft shield collapsing," noted the ship's computer down in engi-neering. "Divert emergency power immediately!"

Scarpa emitted a short curse and raised both hands.

"Fugetta 'bout the computer. He don't know anything," he told himself. "Now…"

"Mr. Scarpa." It was the captain on chat. "I need that cloaking device in the next few minutes or there isn't gonna be a ship."

"I know, mi Cap-i-tan. Si, but-a—"

"Lizard, steer for that big one," Mara interrupted. "Get behind it now! Decrease bow angle—"

"She's firing—this one'll be close!" BattleBabe suddenly shrieked over the captain in chat. Everything sounded like it was going from haywire to hell in handbasket up there on the bridge. The captain cut the link, and a moment later, the entire ship shuddered. On screen, the image of the bridge vibrated and shook for a long, slow second.

Photon torpedo, thought Scarpa. But she missed us, so we still gotta time.

He returned to the diagnostic and rubbed his hands together.

After accessing the control panel to the cloaking device, he ran the system diagnostic once more. "She says-a here," he said to no one, "the couplers are offline and need to be reset… and then harmonized resonance will be restored. Si! Yes. Cloaking device she's-a gonna work now. Here we go."

But it didn't. Once he recoupled the power couplers with the drag-and-drop menu that allowed him to control the warp engines and all the power systems, he got a system reboot message for the cloaking device firmware.

Then the dreaded mini-game popped up.

"To reactivate the main start sequence for a fully operational cloaking sevice system…" droned the in-game advertising announcer. Mini-games were loathed by players and loved by stream watchers.

The epic fails were so legendary that Twitch had a pretty popular daily half-hour recap show called *FailWhale Follies*. A cartoon whale, voiced by a Jim Gaffigan officially licensed voice impersonator, hosted.

"Are you ready?" asked the game announcer.

"Si," replied Scarpa and pressed enter.

The mini-game trumpet fanfare sounded as the screen switched over. Alarms rang out within engineering as another phaser shot grazed the shields. Scarpa ignored it and concentrated on the mini-game. There were some games he was good at, some he wasn't.

"Tonight's game is brought to you by Nyquil Lager. When was the last time a beer made you sleep so well?"

"I love beer!" shouted Scarpa and thumped his muscled chest.

"And remember folks," said the announcer as he tacked on the Government Council on Social Behavior lecture that, by law, must accompany every ad. "Don't tolerate intolerance. Hate hate. Brought to you by Anheuser-Kawasaki. Drink responsibly and don't be a bully."

"Don't bully…" mumbled Scarpa. "Sure, I won't-a bully."

On screen, an eight-bit cartoon version of engineering appeared. The warp engines pulsed rhythmically, and with each surge in developed power from the ship's reactor, two small glowing balls of green energy appeared in the tiny eight-bit warp core reactor. Then they began to pulse and bulge as still more appeared every few seconds.

"Congratulations! This game unlocks a bonus round of power-ups for your ship!" trumpeted the mini-game announcer.

"Uh-oh," replied Scarpa.

Already, glowing green balls were beginning to fill the cartoon reactor. In time, they would overflow and start an actual warp core breach.

"What's going on, Mr. Scarpa?" came the captain over the chat. "We've got all the power we need, but we'll take more. What we really need right now is– Lizard! Roll one-eighty on my mark! And reinforce the aft shield! Mark!"

The large lizard monster avatar could be heard roar-hiss-gurgling in the background as the ventral shield array collapsed.

"We must-a scrapped an asteroid," thought Scarpa aloud. He checked the camera feed to the bridge. The forward viewscreen was a crazy mess of asteroids pitching and rolling at all angles. Then he realized *Cymbalum* was the one pitching and rolling as the ship careened through the tumbling runaway space rocks.

Again the captain left the chat as matters seemed to be getting out of hand up on the bridge of the old warbird. Scarpa returned to his computer as the warp containment field started to comically bulge with all the excess new energy.

In the corner of the engineering bay, a small device burped. Scarpa moused over it and saw a pop-up.

A Romulan ale still.

A small dialogue bubble appeared. "Feed Me!"

Just then, a tiny eight-bit doll of Scarpa's avatar entered through the automatic doors leading into engineering with a loud shuushhh.

"So I guess I just take the little energy balls and put them here, right?" He moved his tiny avatar over, took a glowing ball, and dropped it into the Romulan ale still. The machine jiggled and lurched, and out popped a small glass of Romulan ale that began to slide along a conveyor belt. It was luminescent forest green, like Nyquil Lager.

The conveyor belt was long, runnning the entire length of engineering. A moment later, the tiny green glass fell off the end of the conveyor belt and shattered.

A loud booming unseen voice proclaimed a bombastic, "Uh-oh!"

Scarpa stared in bewilderment at the mini-game.

Shield alarms began to bleat as phasers pounded the ship. Scarpa slid out his smartphone, toggled the engineering app, and reinforced the collapsing shields with excess power from the overperforming warp engines.

"Warp core breach imminent!" groaned the ship's computer. The tiny containment chamber was once again reaching maximum capacity. Scarpa reasoned that if the cartoon mini-game was indeed boosting the actual warp engines of *Cymbalum*, then the cartoon chamber being breached by too much energy might actually breach the real warp core containment field.

"Which would be very bad, mi Cap-i-tan," muttered Scarpa.

The next tiny glass of Romulan ale was headed down the conveyor belt. It too was going to crash to the floor.

Scarpa sent his tiny avatar flying toward the tipping glass... and barely caught it. And then Scarpa's doll went slipping and sliding right on past the previous spill, as the green Romulan ale already on the floor from the first shattered glass seemed to possess some sort of super-viscosity. Now there was a trail of thick green Romulan ale everywhere as Scarpa fought to control his tiny out-of-control avatar.

More glowing balls of green energy were filling up the warp core containment field. Scarpa raced to get them out and then went sliding back to the Romulan ale still. Which produced yet another tiny glass of Nyquil Lager. Or so it seemed to Scarpa, who had a special place in his heart for Nyquil. It reminded him of his childhood and of playing sick so he could stay home and game.

Now he was setting the glowing dark green glasses everywhere in the engineering bay. He thought about throwing them back into the warp engine.

"But I don't know whatta that'll do! The ship... she could go boom!"

Barely managing to control his flailing avatar, he deposited more glowing green balls in the still and scooped up yet another glass. Then realized he was out of places to set them down.

"Whatta I do now?"

"Mr. Scarpa, what's our status on the cloaking device?" The ship shuddered violently as the captain came through on the chat.

"Drink Me!" appeared in a cartoon pop-up bubble.

"Okay, why not," muttered Scarpa and right-clicked his mouse.

Deep liquid green colors washed over the screen. They dripped and pooled like spilled syrup until it was as though Scarpa were seeing the world from the bottom of a pool filled with Nyquil Lager.

"What the..." he whispered, and muttered as he struck different keys on his keyboard. Distantly he could hear the alarms from other overloaded systems aboard *Cymbalum* urgently competing for his attention.

"Y'know, ship, we are getting killed here, si?"

And now there were images inside the green world on screen as the first small notes of a Hammond B3 organ trilled and ran up a scale. An electric guitar began to wail on a beat. The song was forlorn and desolate, and then being driven forward into something new. Something darker.

A singer began to croon "In-A-Gadda-Da-Vida."

The world on screen became an alien, green jungle as the words "Kill the Snake Monkey" appeared and then faded.

Now it was third person. Scarpa tapped a few keys and the figure in front of him, a musclebound warrior with a wickedly curving scimitar, moved from side to side through the emerald depths of the alien jungle.

Scarpa left-clicked and the warrior swung his sword back and forth.

As Scarpa panned about the on-screen avatar, he noticed the warrior was like a Romulan from *StarFleet Empires*, except more like a Frazzetta fantasy version of a Romulan. Muscles and a loincloth. Epic vintage hack-and-slash in bizarre animal-skin boots. But the pointed ears and burning eyes were unmistakably Romulan.

"Kill the monkey snake… I don't see-a no monkey snake," murmured Scarpa. He checked his watch. He had forty minutes until dough rolling-thirty.

For the next seventeen minutes, Scarpa fought an unbelievable epic fantasy adventure that was half drug trip, half Tolkien. He heard the captain repeatedly trying to get through to him as he fought belch-groaning alligators that walked like men and carried spears. They came out of dark pools within the iridescent green jungle canopy, slither-waddling through shafts of crimson light that fell through the thick clutch of simulated alien plant life. He followed a narrow silver stone path through the sinister depths of the strange jungle while an ancient acid rock soundtrack wailed on and on. First the singer, as he kept repeating the nonsense chant and occasionally seductively mumbling "Lemme tell you honey…" or "it's all right!" and then a freestyle jam from the organ, full of arpeggios and diving glissandos.

The jade man-gators, eyes bulging and twirling, roared and lunged at Scarpa's avatar, intent on violence. Scarpa cut wide and sliced one in half. It wailed and belched its green guts all over the screen. Two more came in, jabbing their spears, and Scarpa leapt his avatar backward, striking out at them. Three more hopped in and tried to pincushion him, but Scarpa struck down at the right moment and hacked all three of their spears in half. His Romulan barbarian roared and so did Scarpa in the pre-dawn darkness of the bakery by the firelight of the wide brick oven. He drove in hard on the surviving man-gators, hacking and slashing as man-gator limbs went flying in every direction and a guitar began to wail forth in electric tenor.

Scarpa ran away up the silver path as more man-gators came out of the dark swampy pools all around. His barbarian was faster than the alien attackers, and he left them far behind, following the silvery path up and out of the fetid emerald stew that was at once hauntingly beautiful and menacingly sinister.

Then there were drums. Solo. Pounding. The screen began to flash in emerald green as sudden white strobes of hot light shifted with the hypnotic beat. Scarpa felt his foot tapping along, head moving side to side, as he raced along the path up and onto a small rocky ledge colored in burnt crimson. Ahead, the path wound back on itself as it climbed higher and higher to narrow peaks like bared canine teeth. Lighting flashed, and the sky was white and gray and then crimson again. Changing with each beat of the insanely hypnotic rhythm.

The green hues faded as Scarpa climbed up and up, making outrageously hard Mario leaps from rocky ledge to rocky ledge, and the Hammond organ returned once more to its penitent cathedral tones.

Above Scarpa, lost in the highest heights of the rising fanged mountains, an unseen thing roar-screeched. Scarpa paused, waiting for the mini-game's next round.

In-game, on the warbird *Cymbalum*, everything was coming apart at the seams fast inside the asteroid field as the ship dodged the chaos of the tumbling space rocks while being shot at by an enemy cruiser. And yet, Scarpa admitted to himself, this was the best, and weirdest, mini-game he'd ever played. He felt pretty good about beating it.

"And maybe that's the game," he whispered. "Distract me while the ship... she falls apart."

"Warp core cascade imminent. Release excess energy or face containment failure and catastrophic destruction of vessel." The ship's barking computer then repeated a litany of system failures over and over.

"Have a nice day," grunted Scarpa, not without contempt.

No, he thought. Kill the monkey snake and the cloaking device comes back online. Then we sneak on outta this mess.

"Scarpa!" The cap-i-tan.

"Si, bella signora. Just a minute. She's almost ready."

Above, in the strangely beautiful alien barbarian world within the mini-game, Scarpa heard the ragged cry of some razor-throated buzzard and knew it was the monkey snake that must be slain for the cloaking device to come back online.

Or was it a snake monkey, he wondered. Probably doesn't make a difference.

At the top of the jagged pass, where the blinding white lightning strikes filled the sky and changed everything from a chessboard of shadows to burning crimson flares, Scarpa found the snake monkey thing waiting for him.

"Definitely a snake monkey," declared Scarpa on seeing the weaving nightmare titan.

It circled in and about itself as it flung its coils into the air, its fanged monkey face screaming murder and mindless hate down at Scarpa's avatar.

The thing was actually frightening. Scarpa stepped back from his computer and into the darkness of the artisan bakery. The monster was a digitally rendered nightmare you knew you wouldn't forget anytime soon.

"Shields collapsing," crowed *Cymbalum*'s computer, mindlessly.

"This is just too much for me," groaned Scarpa. "We might be finished."

And then Scarpa remembered his other uncle. Not the baker uncle. The sailor who some said was a modern-day pirate of sorts. Or at least, Scarpa liked to think maybe that was possible. The old guy even looked like a pirate. He was a merchant seaman at least.

The monkey thing crow-roared and came diving straight at Scarpa's legendary Romulan barbarian.

"When there's nothing left but to fight... then you must fight," his uncle had often said, and in particular once when recounting the story of a very uneven bar brawl in the Spanish port of Cádiz.

Scarpa dove the barbarian into the fray, cutting and slicing at the black coils of aberration that was the monkey snake monster. Venom dripped and pooled, the thing circled and wailed, and Scarpa dived and rolled, cutting, hacking, stabbing, and slashing at anything and everything snake monkey.

The drums pounded.

The organ rose.

The lights flashed.

The singer wailed.

Images of NyQuil Lager beer pulsed in and out between the sudden gnashing fangs of the monkey face as it closed in for a toothy chomp.

"Not so fast..." warned Scarpa as he narrowly avoided a close one and stuck the thing with his scroll-worked jagged flashing scimitar.

And then the singer counted off and the song rose to its nuthouse close.

"One, two, three, four..."

"In-A-Gadda-Da-Vida" roared out its last as Scarpa found the monkey snake—no, snake monkey's evil black heart and pushed the blade deep. Black blood pumped out over the screen and the song thundered its defiant last.

"Cloaking device ONLINE," announced the ship's computer.

Mara watched the Gorn as he maneuvered her warbird, running along a series of tumbling asteroids within the storm-free eye of the nebula to avoid a direct shot from the big Federation cruiser trailing them.

They were out of time and options.

"Distance to re-enter the nebula?"

A moment later, BattleBabe came back with, "We won't make it. Not out here in the open, Captain. They're right on us. We run, we've got to cross open space to get back in. We'll never make it back inside the storm in time."

"Shields collapsing," stated the computer.

C'mon, Scarpa, thought Mara. You've never let us down before.

"We're out of the asssteroid field, Captain, there'ss nowhere left to go but straight back at *Intrepid*," hissed the Gorn.

"She's targeting…" BattleBabe again. "*Intrepid's* got lock!"

"C'mon…" Mara heard herself mutter once more.

Cloaking Device ONLINE appeared in her HUD.

"Cap-i-tan…"

"I know, yes!" Mara felt an overwhelming urge to shout. So she did. "You did it, Scarpa! Engage cloaking device now, BattleBabe!"

Cymbalum shimmered and then disappeared, just as *Intrepid* launched a narrow salvo from her four torpedo tubes. Each one missed the fading warbird.

Scarpa stepped back, breathing heavily. His shoulders tight. His eyes aching. His nerves shot.

And he felt like a million MakeCoins.

Much better than Teresa ever made him feel.

He checked his watch.

"Time to roll-a the dough."

Chapter Twenty

SPOT switched from the blue caress of night vision to the hell of infrared. The rising moon had been almost too bright for the starlight-assisted night vision. Three of the other mindless cyberwolves were trailing along beside the aware armored patrol hound. Wi-Fi was transmitting telemetry between the pack leader and its pack.

Target group Delta, ahead, appeared in all of their HUDs.

Two humans were crossing the commons that separated the coder condos from the Shadow Streams section of the campus, the small community where executives, or suits as the humans called them, resided when interacting directly with the developers on campus.

One male.

One female.

Unarmed.

Tracking...

SPOT reviewed the mission directive. Terminate all life forms and secure the perimeter of the facility. Already, the drones were simultaneously blocking and hacking the lab complex. In the event that neither of these options proved successful, the foot soldiers would be on site shortly to physically enter the facility and gain access to the WonderSoft Design Core. Objective Pandora.

SPOT was a low-level Thinking Machine. It wasn't much concerned with the big picture. It merely enjoyed arriving at solutions to problems and occasionally observing and cataloging some interesting item or unique situation for its own personal satisfaction. Collecting was SPOT's hobby. Its passion, as it were.

Ahead, the man and woman were now racing for the campus's sports complex. SPOT could detect their heartbeats, and it noted their wild and erratic rhythms. It catalogued this, and when it set this against the knowledge database SILAS had provided as part of its awareness, it identified this as a symptom of the condition known as "fear."

Cross-referencing this with previous experiences, SPOT concluded that the human female he'd killed at the welcome center had also been experiencing this same emotion in the brief moment before termination.

This produced in SPOT a small uptick in self-diagnostic efficiency. SPOT was meeting and/or exceeding mission parameters for this unit.

That was something to "feel" good about.

SPOT liked to feel good.

The humans would not make it to the safety of the sports complex.

All four wolves were now in full precision robotic sprint to intercept the running, wild-heartbeating humans.

Warning! Message from BAT.

"Looks like you're about to have a bit of company, my friend."

BAT dropped a new target tag into SPOT's HUD. Human transportation machine.

Target group Echo had acquired transport.

SPOT watched as the butterscotch Delta 88 suddenly accelerated out from a cross street and struck the cyberwolf to its right.

SPOT leapt and landed on the hood of the vehicle for a moment, engaging its Teflon claws in an effort to remain there. But physics quickly flung the Thinking Machine off into some geometric topiary that girded the massive one-of-a-kind sports complex. The UltraGym.

Recovering, SPOT ran through a situation report and interfaced with BAT in real-time. It was distantly aware that SILAS was monitoring the entire encounter.

New target overlays replaced the previous designations.

Target Alpha. A human male exiting the driver's side of the vehicle. Weapons status: chainsaw arm appendage and Smith and Wesson twelve-gauge shotgun, modified—cut down for close-quarters combat mode. Recommendation: priority termination.

Target Bravo: Human male. No weapons. Physical appearance... corpse-like.

Target Charlie: Human male, running.

Target Delta: Human female, prone. Heart beating in accordance with "fear"-like state.

Cyberwolf four of thirty was down underneath the wheels of the vehicle. It was still operational, but trapped beneath the axle of the car.

Two and three were circling the humans, waiting for the order to terminate.

SPOT released the termination restraint override and was about to attack when Target Alpha fired at cyberwolf three of thirty.

A dumb slug blew the wolf's optic, jaw restraint system, and CPU to shreds. In a mere one hundred processing cycles, the robot sentry was "OFFLINE'd."

SILAS's handy database interacted on a background app in the artificial intelligence program that allowed SPOT to think. It interpreted OFFLINE to mean "death."

Cyberwolf two of thirty lunged at Target Alpha, who promptly flung the massive chunk of Detroit steel that was the door to the vehicle into the alloy snout of the automated patrol wolf. The wolf rebounded and scrabbled back into the fray. At that moment, Target Alpha gave a deft pull of the starter cord for the chainsaw it wore on its forearm.

"Retreat!" ordered SPOT. But it was too late. Target Alpha drove the cycling industrial diamond-tipped toothy blade right through the legs of the leaping cyberwolf.

A "Catastrophic Failure" message erupted in SPOT's HUD under the assets roster column for cyberwolf two of thirty.

BAT was messaging SILAS for instructions, petitioning for the immediate usage of one of its precious Hellfire IV missiles on Target Alpha. Thirty requests fired across the Consensus net and all received a terse, glowing, "Not at this time" reply.

SPOT closed in slowly on Target Alpha, assessing the threat level of the spinning chainsaw and selecting an option that allowed it to take the target with minimum exposure. Meanwhile, Target Alpha was breaking the modified shotgun and inserting two more shells.

A "Withdraw Now" message came direct from SILAS.

A moment later, just as the cyberwolf pack leader was weighing obedience against the satisfaction uptick it achieved when it broke a human neck with its ceramic-formed jaws, Target Alpha fired at almost point-blank range.

The slug destroyed SPOT's infrared eye assemblies and damaged some of its limited neural processing and environmental interface hard drive capabilities, but, as SPOT realized bare cycles later, burnt cordite swirling in the nearby air, it was still operational.

Already the active chainsaw was once more flailing toward SPOT in a wide sweeping arc.

"Obedience seems prudent, doesn't it," said SILAS via direct message.

A moment later Rapp's chainsaw sliced through the armor surrounding SPOT's onboard CPU and shredded the processor. The rubber-insulated housing Rapp used to fit the chainsaw over his arm protected him from being badly electrocuted.

"I can't believe you built a working replica of Ash's chainsaw arm. Do you know how illegal that is, Rapp? You could get banned from community larping for something like that!" Roland Warchowski was almost hyperventilating as he spoke. He pulled out his asthma inhaler and inhaled.

"Yeah," replied Rapp in his typically understated baritone stoicism. "That'd be a real black mark on my record. What the hell was that thing?"

"Rapp!" shriek-wheezed Roland. "You can't LARP with real guns and weapons. I mean it, man."

Rapp walked over to the beautiful blonde lying on the road amid dead wolf-bot debris. She wore a bright red dress. If she wasn't a supermodel, she should've been. "Real stuff's the only thing that's fun anymore, Roland," mumbled Rapp as he extended his non-chainsaw arm toward the prone beauty.

She smiled and took it.

"Rapp Branson."

"Deirdre," she replied, straightening her tiny red dress as best she could.

"Where's your boyfriend?"

For a moment Deirdre looked shocked. Then, realizing the stranger named Rapp was talking about her "date" tonight, the cowardly Evan Fratty, she rolled her eyes.

"I think," said Roland between raspy inhalations, "he ran off to the gym."

Rapp seemed to consider this for a moment as he reloaded the shotgun, which he slid into the holster he wore on his back.

"Do you always wear a chainsaw and carry a shotgun?" asked Deirdre, taking in the outlandish costumes of her two rescuers.

Rapp gave her a charming grin. Then, "Only when robot-wolves try to attack stunners like yourself, lady."

Deirdre gave a quick smile.

It was an almost coy, shy smile. The opposite of all the seductive smoky looks often required of her to make a living these days.

It was a smile from a long time ago.

Chapter Twenty-One

After another message was sent to Roland Warchowski via Bugg, Peabody Case tried again, fruitlessly, to find any other way to contact the outside world. To let anyone know that WonderSoft was under attack, that there were casualties, and that the survivors were trapped inside the Labs, surrounded by murderous hackers.

"It's like they're jamming every communication outlet from apps to social media. Try your phone again?"

Fish, Peabody's boss as of Monday-not-yet, dragged his smartphone from his pocket obediently and checked his apps. Nothing was updating. He tried connecting to the local Wi-Fi. Nothing appeared on the browser even though he had a signal and connection.

"Nada."

Peabody muttered and kept opening and closing windows furiously.

"So we have internet, we just can't get through to it?" asked Fish.

"Right," replied Peabody as she once again tried to load Facebook.

"But if the internet is blocked, then most likely the game servers are down, because they're admin'd from here. Meaning the server farms stream right through here. So, if this is blocked, then that means the games would shut down because security protocols aren't in effect, as those originate with admin… right?" Fish paused as he ran through his understanding of how things should work.

"And if that's the case, the internet would be going nuts wondering why the five top-selling games are offline," answered Peabody.

Fish stared at the screens. Watching bandwidth and data transfer rates.

"It's still handshaking… see?" he said, pointing toward one monitor that showed local internet traffic. "But we're locked out."

"So the games are still running?"

"Right. And if they are, we can go in-game and get a message to someone. But we probably can't access games from here, right?"

Peabody began to surf around, looking through all the menus. After a moment she said, "No, probably not. They want the guards guarding. Not playing Rave Command."

"You like that game?" asked Fish.

"It's all right. A little one-note."

Fish said nothing and returned to the monitors. "Send another message to your friend, Todd."

"Roland."

"Yeah, tell him… tell him we're going back to our design suite to try and access the internet. Tell him to meet us there, okay?"

"What about Carl?"

"I don't know," said Fish.

"Carl has a supervisor's app on his company smartphone that lets him access the shack from anywhere. He should be able to open the doors once he gets back to the Labs. I've downloaded the same app, now that I have passkey authority for most of the facility. Also, we'll need to override the suite lock from here and then seal ourselves in once we're back inside."

"Can we do that?" asked Fish.

Peabody set to work.

A few minutes later they were stepping out through one of the lowered PlateGlass walls in the shack and watching as it began to rise once again. Their run back to the design suite was at once spooky and exhilarating. It was spooky in that they were chased by the sound of their own footsteps across the echoing caverns of escalators and wide marble halls. It was the only sound in a building usually filled with a multitude of sounds throughout the day and night. And it was exhilarating in that Fish wondered, as he followed the bouncing high-heeled gait of his executive assistant, how many times you actually have to run for your life, in your life.

For a brief moment after they swiped the key card to the suite and the door lock light didn't immediately switch to green, Fish wondered if they'd made some colossally irreversible mistake. Things could turn deadly, and not in the sense of the latest expression of the word "cool," if they were actually locked out of their suite, and out of the shack, permanently. These were the only safe places they knew of in the immediate vicinity. Where else could they run to hide if the hackers decided to physically enter the facility in search of intellectual property? Fish had no doubt they'd be armed. And they wouldn't leave witnesses.

But a second later the lock ticked and the door was open. Fish led the way across the suite as Peabody followed. He went straight to the Moon Desk and logged back into *Island Pirates*.

"I'll boot up the SurfaceTable and see if we can take a look at the game as designers," said Peabody.

For a moment Fish thought that would be a good idea, then, "Wait. I'm logged in under a private beta account. Not an admin."

Peabody waited as Fish's eyes roved back and forth, doing some kind of internal math, arriving at a conclusion on the other side of a decision tree.

"Let's just say this is a hack attack…" began Fish.

"A hack attack!" exclaimed Peabody. "There are dead guards in the street."

"It wouldn't be the first time. Back when the *Grand Theft Auto* franchise was sold to Xingwa in China, they suffered a weekend hack attack that left twenty dead. All so some Russian developer could get an advance copy of the game six months early and come out with their own crappy knockoff."

"For a game! I can't believe that–"

"These aren't just games," interrupted Fish. "These are 3D printers that can make your dreams come true if you're a developer. These bits of digital memory and code can be strung together to form a money fountain. And money means power. If you think gaming is about entertainment, it's not, at least, not anymore. If gaming was ever about fun, that probably died way back in the early 1980s."

Peabody sat on the edge of the desk, her legs shapely and nicely muscled. Fish absently wondered if she worked out at the gym. Something he'd been meaning to do once *Island Pirates* was up and running.

He'd been saying that for five years now.

"Let's just say it is a hack attack and they've somehow managed to lock the developers out and keep the admin working…" began Fish.

"Why would they do that?" asked Peabody.

Fish thought about that for a second. "Because they want something in the Design Core but they don't want to set off alarms on the internet. If they do that, WonderSoft could be locked out of the Make as a safety measure, which would mean that whatever they stole, unless they could physically copy and carry it out the front door, couldn't be transferred via the Make. If that's how they're doing this."

Peabody held up a hand, indicating she had a point. "So they've locked out admins. But, if somehow we, you, go back in as an admin, they'll know and... what?"

"If they knew an admin was logging on to *Island Pirates* from within the Labs, well then... then... we'd probably meet the same fate... as the guard in the welcome center."

"But if you log in on a beta key attached to your internet passport, they'll just think you're some player from the Make. Some anonymous gamer geek on a beta access key." A sly smile blossomed across Peabody's delicately featured oval face. "And they won't be able to track you because Homeland monitors internet passports constantly. They're always on the lookout for bots so they watch the passport system and protect it from hacking with quantum encryption software."

Fish thought about that. Then, "Yeah, right. I mean, most likely. There's a chance they could be watching the subscriber list, and if they had that hacked and they were interested, then yes they could find out where I was gaming from, but that's pretty heavy duty snooping. A lot of the cyberbullying laws protect gamers' IPs and access location information... so we should be fine. Plus, the door to the suite's locked, right?"

Chapter Twenty-Two

Fish's secret island cove was just as he'd left it inside the beta version of *Island Pirates*. Jackson the Portuguese water dog was frolicking down in the translucent, digitally rendered graphic waves that gently rolled against the pristine white sands of the cove. The A.I. dog was chasing seabirds back and forth as they landed and rose again and again along the shore break. The small yellow Piper Cub floatplane bobbed lazily against the sun-faded dock in paradise.

Fish moved his avatar toward his tree house. Inside was a radio he could use to contact other stations with. Now, feeling like he was being watched inside his own game, he questioned why he'd ever made the design choice to only allow distance communication by device rather than in-game chat like most MMOs.

He remembered telling some other developer geeks around shabby-chic pallet tables at a late-night coffee bar that it would be retro vintage. That gamers would ultimately love it.

Now he hated it.

Smartphones were available for in-game microtransactions, but Fish had wanted to limit himself, his anonymous beta key avatar, to the old two-way radio sets that were more common throughout the island chains that made up the game. Every radio was the result of a small mini-quest for parts and a little bit of salvaging, then the player was awarded with an old-time two-way radio.

He dialed in a station.

Players were talking about a clan raid on a nearby island.

That was stupid, thought Fish. The players on the nearby island could easily be listening. But the players sounded stupid. Much of their conversation was littered with the f-word as though it were some sort of accepted punctuation.

He remembered his old Hasidic grandfather telling him only unintelligent people out of fresh ideas resorted to swear words. Now, twenty years after he'd once been caught using those same words he'd been cautioned against, Fish realized the value of the advice. His experiences since then had confirmed most of the old man's shared wisdom.

For a moment, Fish wondered what he should say.

"Hey, I'm the developer of this game and I'm trapped in the mysterious WonderSoft Labs. Could you call the police? I think we're in the middle of a hack attack by drones!" And, "Help, save me!"

Now he wondered why he hadn't put some sort of emergency response feature into the game. It was the latest trend, and Congress was even debating a new law in the wake of a spate of sensationalist news stories about gamers dying at their computers after having a stroke and not being able to contact anyone. Several aggregate bloggers had even suggested that the graphic horror content of *Serial Killer, the Game* was actually responsible for the outbreak of strokes. "The Digital Black Plague" was the headline one writer used to inflame the perpetually fear-driven masses of the Social Justice Movement, until someone accused him of racism for using the word "Black" in his lead.

But the gamers' strokes had nothing to do with the hours-long, homicidal-rage, drug-trip sequences featuring flashing lights and murder propaganda spliced with violent imagery throughout the mega-blockbuster game of the year. Instead, it was the days-long binges that players engaged in as they tried to outdo each other's "kill counts" on the Most Wanted leaderboards that were most likely to blame.

Or at least that had been Fish's opinion.

Fish had opted not to add an emergency services panic button to his masterpiece's in-game player HUD. Again, he was living to regret yet another design decision.

"What's wrong?" asked Peabody over his shoulder. He turned and saw her wide bright eyes, made even more so by massive, oval, designer, "smart girl" glasses.

"I can't just tell people we're in trouble. Inside a game."

Peabody said nothing. Instead, she merely pursed her lips and stared over his shoulder at the screen.

Fish hated when people stared over his shoulder while he gamed or programmed.

"Log into your Make account. The Make added a panic button after that Stroke Plague last year."

"Yeah, I thought about that, but if I log into my account and they know I'm a developer, they'll know something's up."

"So what're you going to do?"

Fish stared at the screen, at the lush green jungle outside the bamboo-framed window of his tropical radio shack. He could hear the slough and pull of the gentle surf down near the beach. Distantly, Jackson was still occasionally barking at some seabird.

This game is very meditative, he thought. That was something he hadn't planned on when he'd designed it. He'd been too busy putting it together.

"Well, if I could make it to the in-game Make Portal and transition with my avatar from *Island Pirates* into the actual Make, I can go to my apartment in Saffron City, break in, and use the panic button there. If I do that, I should get an actual Homeland Cyber Response Agent, right?"

"That's what the public service announcements say."

Fish stared at the keyboard, doing the math, planning his route.

"I'll have to fly to Porto Tortuga. That's the nearest Make Portal in the game."

"Well then," said tiny Peabody Case, hands on hips, bent just over his bony shoulder. "Let's get flying, flyboy."

A few minutes later, the Piper Cub was at full throttle and racing over the waves. Jackson the dog barked at some flying fish and then the plane was in the air, climbing up into the soft Caribbean blue of the digitally rendered tropic sky.

They turned left over the island, and Fish couldn't help but dip the wing and look down at his tiny tropical kingdom. The game was really just a framework. Real estate. Items. And physics. Players could make the game into anything they wanted it to be. That was the real fun of the game. Making something that was all your own. People were hungry for that. Like it was hardwired into them regardless of how much free stuff the government promised to give away.

For some reason, the Fast Travel option was suddenly disabled just as Fish went to activate it. He wanted to check the logs and find out why, but to do that now would give him away as an admin. The plane droned northward along the island chain of Banantu Reefs, crossing vast expanses of white sandbars lying alongside exposed pink coral reefs where Fish had placed hundreds of dangerous shipwrecks in the Mako shark-infested shallows for players to salvage from. He ruminated over why Fast Travel had suddenly disabled itself as soon as he'd hovered his mouse over the activate button. It wasn't unheard of for a feature to simply go inoperative, especially if the game's A.I.

had detected someone glitching it. Or a log anomaly. The program would shut off the problematic feature and then make a note for the developer to investigate later. But then Fish's newfound paranoia began to suggestively whisper other possibilities. The legitimate new paranoia that came from seeing dead bodies in a road and running through an empty future palace that had become not a castle, but a high-tech prison. Had Fast Travel been turned off deliberately? That was impossible, as only Fish, or the game A.I., could do that.

Either way, flying along in the Piper Cub, Fish was now just another anonymous beta-key playtester traversing the massive digital world of *Island Pirates*. He kept glancing over his shoulder into the outer office. Making sure the suite door was still closed.

Fish was thinking about all these things when he noticed the black Spitfire warplane coming straight at him. There were two parts of his mind at that moment: the part that really liked how the design model for a playable Spitfire looked as it came zooming straight at him, firing from both of its fifty-caliber machine guns, and the other part that said, "Hey, that Spitfire is firing both of its fifty-caliber machine guns at my defenseless plane."

The Piper Cub had no weaponry or armor to speak of. The all-black Spitfire fighter went roaring past Fish off to the left. Fish knew the guy had unlocked the plane after playing what Fish had hoped would be a pretty difficult quest, "Mad Roger's Lost Squadron," and walked away with a vintage World War II warplane. His attacker had even repainted it in black with a white skull and crossbones on the tail.

The Cub's wonky motor conked out as the warplane roared off into the blue. Fish saw engine oil spraying up against the front windshield as he slewed his avatar's POV back around to the cockpit windshield. Through the massive in-suite speakers he heard wind rushing past the fuselage. It was rising into a steady whining pitch turning to a scream.

We're diving, was his first thought. He checked his controls and realized he was not pushing forward on the flight stick. The plane was falling out of the sky.

Jackson gave a woof woof at the pirate Spitfire coming around behind them for another pass—or at the situation, Fish was unclear as to which.

He moved the controls around and found he could struggle for a little bit of life, but there was no two ways about it, the Piper Cub was going down. At least lateral and pitch worked fine, though the plane now wanted to crab for some reason.

"Damage to the horizontal stabilizer?" Fish wondered aloud, as though walking himself through bug testing. Then he remembered he was surrounded, in danger, and that he wasn't just playing a game, he was trying to go get help to save their lives. Images of the dead guards in the road flashed on the high-definition projector of his mind. They were probably still lying out there in the dark.

"All right..." he mumbled.

"What's wrong? What's happening?" asked Peabody Case, rushing back in. She'd left his office and he hadn't even noticed.

"I got shot down..."

On screen the entire POV was the sea rushing up to meet the cockpit. The plane groaned and bounced in its dive toward the surface of the ocean. Again, Jackson woof woofed.

"Does that happen a lot, in-game?" she asked.

"It does happen, but I wouldn't say a lot. It's a game of resources. If this guy shot me down..."

"How do you know it's a guy?"

"Umm... I don't. But for the sake of continuing to exchange

information regarding a simple matter, let's just use 'guy' as a catchall and not a gender issue... sorry..."

Now the plane was diving straight into the aqua green shallows on the inside of the outer reef of channel islands.

"You're right," continued Fish, feeling bad for being snappy. "It could've been a girl. So, if this girl shot me down and she's not closing in for the kill, it means she's got some buddies on the ground who want this plane and whatever I have for salvage. In this game, salvage is more important than money. You can't just buy everything with microtransactions."

There was a loud bang and they both jumped, turning to check the outer office.

"Wait," said Fish. "That was in the game. I think the engine just seized due to lack of oil pressure. That's at least how it's supposed to work. In-game, that is."

"Is that good?" asked Peabody.

The water was rushing up at the screen. Fish was pulling on the analog flight stick as hard as he could. His foot mashed the right rudder pedal on the floor beneath the Moon Desk as he tried to compensate for the plane's desire to crab in midair. Definitely the horizontal stabilizer, thought Fish and congratulated himself for not rhetorically asking Peabody, in a voice laden with his particular brand of murmuring sarcasm, "Does a seizing engine sound like a good thing?"

The suite filled with the sound of simulated air screaming past the diving digital fuselage of the aircraft. Fish tried to look for a place to land, but there were only sandbars and ocean. He'd spent long hours designing this zone to be one of the most treacherous parts of the game. Along with sharks, snakes, scorpions, smugglers, reefs, crushing depths, dangerous wrecks, and no place to land or dock, he'd made the sandbars almost impossible to safely access. But the loot here was epic.

"Gotta go for the shoreline."

A moment later, the plane slammed into the shallow waves running along an outer island reef. The island was little more than a caress of crystal clear water washing over an island sandbar and a few stray palms. A spray of barely blue water and foam drenched the computer screen a moment later as the plane came to rest along a lonely narrow spit of beach. Both wings had collapsed, and flames flicked up and away from the cracked and burning engine cowling in front of him.

"Wouldn't it have been better to land out in the water?" asked Peabody over Fish's shoulder. "You know, because it's a floatplane." Then she corrected, "Or… was a floatplane."

"True," said Fish, nodding, a matter-of-fact look plastered on his face as he stared at the HUD and all the damage. "But I populated the waters on the other side of this island with Mega Sharks. Carcharodon megalodon. The dinosaur of sharks. They'd go after this plane in a heartbeat."

"Woof woof," barked Jackson.

Chapter Twenty-Three

JasonDare was smearing organic hummus on a gluten-free bagel. Truth be told, he hated the thought of eating it. For a moment, he wanted to be free of acting. Free to eat... hash browns.

When it was all over, when his career was done, he'd become the master of cooking hash browns and eggs. Eggs cooked in real butter. Perfect golden brown hash browns, seasoned, fried in a cast-iron skillet, topped with cheddar cheese, bacon, avocado slices, and a couple of fried, runny-yolk eggs.

When the career was over.

But it wasn't over yet.

And until it was over, you had to look good on camera and squeeze into a uniform that left little to the imagination and didn't hide any fat.

So for now, it was hummus on a tasteless bagel at nine o'clock on a Friday night.

Jason's agent texted him, "This is bad."

"How so," replied Jason.

"Studio heads saw what happened tonight. They didn't like it. Not for the Thundaar epic, specifically."

"What didn't they like?"

"She made a monkey out of you."

"We're not allowed to see the feeds... female captain?"

"Yes. *Twitch Tonight* just showed the first look of their engineer unlocking some mini-game. Good-looking Italian kid. Anyway, one of the execs, Tabitha, she says, 'There's our Thundaar.' Don't worry, it might've been a joke. Sorry."

"Okay," was all Jason could text back.

He sat down on a folding metal chair behind the set and looked at his terrible bagel. He remembered times as an actor when he'd been so hungry he would've killed for this bagel. Sure, his parents would've easily deposited money in his account, but he'd never asked them to.

Instead, he'd just starved.

After he threw the bagel in a nearby gray trash can he leaned forward and looked at his hands while still sitting in the comfortless folding metal chair.

A moment later, he dragged out his smartphone, went to his contacts, and mumbled, "It isn't over yet."

Their mysterious passenger entered the bridge. Mara and the rest of the player crew of *Cymbalum* swiveled the POVs of their avatars to see the Vulcan female, gamertagged T'Daara, in a short violet mini dress with complementary curves, saunter through the doors of the turbolift like a hungry cat posing for its next meal. She was the reason for their secret mission inside Federation clan space.

Cymbalum was at warp, and therefore uncloaked, heading deep into the Federation spinward frontier en route to Starbase 19.

"Part of the deal, Captain," announced T'Daara in a monotone purr, "is for us to arrive at my destination without an escort."

Mara stared at the beautiful avatar, wondering who was running her, and not for the first time, what all this was really about.

"I'm not aware of any other ships. We left the Fed cruiser—"

"I know you did. But my sources tell me *Intrepid*'s back up on

Twitch and in hot pursuit. They should be at extreme sensor range any moment now."

The mysterious Vulcan leveled a cool, emotionless gaze at Mara, who was already busy studying the tactical display built into her command chair. Looking for the powerful Federation cruiser.

For a moment there was nothing. She waited... and then, at the farthest edge of the map, a lone blue blip appeared. Sensor waves emitted from it in concentric circles.

"Contact," announced the euphoric Drex. "You know who, Captain."

Everyone watched Mara. She could feel it in the silence of the chat as she stared at the tactical display.

How could this be? They'd crawled away from the last encounter cloaked, undetectable, and when safely out of sensor range, they'd gone to warp. They were heading, in what had to seem to the casual observer, the most random of directions. Not in toward the Federation's core systems for some pirating, or a raid on a military objective, but instead out, toward the Federation frontier. Into the unknown. A place where players regularly lost ships due to the inherent dangers of the zone.

Here, it was more like original-recipe *Star Trek* than any other place in the *StarFleet Empires* game. Ancient civilizations. Doomsday devices. Aliens that were basically monsters. Any number of ways to get your ship crushed to pieces and your crew killed. Even *Intrepid* rarely came out here. If they lost the ship on livestream, the show was over.

So, wondered Mara, how was *Intrepid* already hot on the trail of a ship that could disappear via cloaking device? Her ship.

She turned her command chair to stare at the main tactical display.

Turn and fight?

We lose.

Run?

They'll catch us.

"Captain?" prompted the Vulcan player.

And we can't show up to our secret destination with the most famous starship and crew in the game for what is most likely some kind of illegal operation involving the Make and intellectual property theft.

The star systems they passed were becoming fewer and fewer, the distances between them greater and greater.

Then she spotted Sigmus.

"Drex, what's our intel say on the Sigmus star system?"

Everyone waited as the artificial being toned and murmured an insectile-like chitter to the ship's computer. Some programmer's way of distinguishing the various levels of shipboard computers. The insectile sound gave *Cymbalum*'s computer an outdated feel. An old computer for an old ship, thought Mara.

In real life she was getting hungry.

No time for that now.

Fight...

Or flight.

She waited.

"It's a blue giant. Four planets. One of which, Sigmus Three, has an atmosphere similar to Venus. Completely inhospitable on the surface... but there is a Federation Free Trade Guild atmosphere mining operation."

"Mr. Lizard, plot us a course into the system. Take us right into Sigmus Three's atmosphere. We'll try and hide out a bit."

The massive lizard moved his claws over the console, and the warbird turned to port and dropped down into the elliptic plane of the system. At warp, they were racing past the outer planets, all of them bathed in a hot, almost blue light. Ahead, Sigmus Three spun like a tiny overcast Earth. Gray and white clouds swirled in large storms that covered the extreme violence on the surface.

"Detecting… no other ships in the immediate vicinity," announced the Drex. "But not for long, I'm sure."

"Impulse speed, engage cloaking device."

"Captain, if you're intent on fighting a Federation cruiser here, then we're not going to make it to my destination," announced the peeved Vulcan. "That ship is far too powerful for just you and your crew."

Mara ignored her passenger.

She could feel Varek waiting to zing her.

"Federation cruiser dropping from warp… Huzzah! It's *Intrepid*!" announced the Drex. "She's powering up weapons and shields. We're in for a real fight now! At last, our long-overdue demise has made its grand entrance!"

Mara continued to watch the forward tactical display. In the distance, the planet loomed beneath them, its upper atmosphere a clean layer of brilliant white cloud cover. Above that, high above, a ring of mining stations girded the equator like tiny futurist towers, or gossamer lighthouses, all of them connected by a lone, wire-thin transport system.

"Fly us in under the cloud cover. They won't be able to follow or track us inside those storms."

No one said anything as the bow angle decreased and the ship roared past a cold and lifeless high-altitude station and plunged into the storm-laden depths below.

"Going atmospheric, ssstrap your avatarsss in!" hissed the Gorn.

A moment later, there was on-screen turbulence. Everything shook. The forward display was covered in clouds and gray rain, and at times, cascading sheets of molten metal.

"Flying into an atmosphere is a nice little trick for these old warbirds," said T'Daara, "but that's a state-of-the-art battleship out there, and they can wait us out. What are you going to do to get me to my destination, Captain?" The shapely Vulcan's EmoteWare gave the voice over chat a velvety but emotionless depth. "Time is wasting, and I do need to arrive within the next six hours."

"Arm plasma torpedo," ordered Mara. "And load up a special also, BattleBabe."

JasonDare watched the forward screen.

All eyes, he knew, including the now more than two million viewers watching what social media was trending as "The Duel," were on him. They could watch the Twitch Channel and see him. But no one who was logged into *StarFleet Empires* could watch another ship's feed. The game not only prevented players from "screen-looking," it even locked your social media accounts and barred all access to internet references to anything in the game you were currently logged into. It was all part of the omnibus anti-hacking law passed ten years ago to make gaming "fairer and more fun"—or so the battle cry had gone during the worldwide three-day protests that had shut down major cities and the internet via riot and street protest.

But there were ways.

When Jason had gone to his smartphone after ditching the tasteless bagel, he'd DM'd one of his biggest fans. In fact, the admin of his fan page on Facebook.

"Need to know where they're going," he'd written.

"I can find out. Give me five, Jason."

Sometimes you can put your fans to use, thought Jason, and then felt vaguely dirty for even thinking such. He'd vowed never to be "that guy." And here he was, being "that guy."

Five minutes later he was feeling some buyer's remorse. Just a little. But it was there. And it felt good in a way. To still know the difference between right and wrong.

"Got it, Jason!" came the text.

He hesitated, staring at his smartphone. This was cheating.

And then there was his career to consider...

"She made a monkey out of you!"

And...

"There's our Thundaar!"

How long was Captain Dare, Twitch, this show, gonna last?

You're either moving or you're dying, his old acting teacher used to say. Moving or dying. Words that had meaning. Words meaning more than just what was said. Life stuff. Career stuff.

And because JasonDare, once Ben Mueller, was basically still a good person, even the stuff of heroes, he asked his number one fan for a little moral guidance. Like some latter-day Achilles having a moment of doubt and looking to the hoplite just behind him on the beach, asking, "Should I go on?"

"Do you think this is cheating?" he texted.

Pause.

He knew his fan was having the greatest moment of his life. Being confided in by his personal idol. Confidant status awarded. The consigliere. A member of the inner circle of a celebrity.

"No, man," texted the fan, but spelled "man" as "mam" in his excited thumb-rush to answer.

Jason waited.

Give me a reason, he thought. C'mon, man. Give me a reason not to cheat.

"It's classic Kirk!" texted the fan. "This is your Kobayashi Maru. Your test against a game that can't be won."

And... what does that mean, thought Jason. He really didn't know much about the old captains. He'd meant to learn, but there had never been enough time. There was always some photo shoot, some ComicCon, or some industry party he simply had to be at that night.

"James T. Kirk, the greatest captain ever, would've—no, did, and would do—the same thing you're doing. Whatever it takes to win, Jason. This proves you're the next Kirk."

All right then, thought Jason, thinking of the Thundaar role. Thinking of playing to win the game. That's what you did, you played to win. And if you won... you got the Thundaar role. You got to fight another battle in the eye of world. The Circus Maximus of entertainment programming. Never mind the blood on the sand.

"Give me their location," he wrote back. And added, "Thanks, you're the best."

Now, sitting in his command chair back on set with everyone watching the planet in front of them, he knew they were all asking the same question.

How'd JasonDare figure out where the Romulans went?

I have no answer for that one, and so... I'm not going to give them one, thought Jason. Instead, I'm going to give them one hell of a show, and maybe they'll forget all about it. Leave it to the nerd conspiracy theorists to manufacture another theory so they can go on believing in all of this. Leave it to the producers to clean up.

Tonight I'll just give them a fight they won't forget.

"Look sharp, she's in there somewhere," he announced to the crew as he studied the swirling storm-laden planet on the forward viewscreen.

He knew the composer would be syncing a soundtrack on the fly to match the high drama of the moment. He could hear it if he wanted to. But he didn't need that right now. He had a pretty good idea of what it sounded like. He also knew that by the end of this fight, everyone would be tuning in and watching clips that would give new meaning to "going viral," some even hoping to see *Intrepid* go kaboom on livestream tonight.

Good, he thought. More viewers that way.

"Energy signature directly beneath us, Captain." Tempturia in her best purr and lilt. "The metal storms are interfering with our sensors."

"Can we get a lock, MrWong?"

"Trying… wait… she's surfacing now. Romulan warbird dead ahead, Captain!"

Below, dangerously close in fact, the port wing of the warbird's warp nacelle rose from the cloud cover like some ancient whale surfacing for the last time. Then the main U-shaped hull followed up through the cloud layer, and finally the other wing nacelle.

"She's got lock!" someone screamed.

There was only a moment to think. And in that moment, there was only room for one thought. Barely two at most. JasonDare wondered in that brief second of surprise if the Twitch viewers were indeed really about to see *Intrepid* go kaboom, and–

"Plasma torpedo firing!" shrieked Tempturia.

–and, that he, JasonDare, wanted to win. No matter what.

He rose from his chair and shouted, "Overload photon torpedoes now! Stand by phaser banks. Wong, evasive action!"

Ahead of them, the massive Type R plasma torpedo swallowed the screen. It was the most powerful weapon in the game and it was seconds from impact.

"Reinforce forward shields to maximum!" ordered Jason.

"That'll be all our reserve power!" roared Wong in response.

"We're too close to the atmosphere. It's having an ablative effect on our shield generators," reported some actor Jason hadn't met yet. He'd meant to. But there hadn't been time. There was never enough time when it was your moment.

"We're gonna hit!" screamed Tempturia in a very un-science officer-like way. The massive burning ball of hot plasma was closely followed by the winged enemy warbird.

A moment later, the torpedo struck.

And nothing happened.

The warbird barely missed the saucer section of *Intrepid* as it flew past, shaking the superstructure. Or so the game's computers told the haptic set to react as such.

There should have been a massive impact. Damage alerts and klaxons and computer-automated casualty reports, along with "Shield Down" warnings ringing out like a three-ring circus on the bridge of *Intrepid*.

But there was nothing.

Oh no, thought Jason, suddenly sick to his stomach as a cold realization dawned within his mind. They, the Romulan clan commander, had fired a pseudo plasma torpedo. A fake. A decoy. A special, the Romulan players called it.

"High energy turn, now!"

Wong looked dumbstruck. A moment later, his hands flew to the controls as the massive starship groaned to obey.

They came about just in time.

Just in time to see the warbird finishing its own high-energy turn. Odds favored that one or both starships would break down and be completely at the mercy of the other.

The odds lost.

The warbird fired her real torpedo this time.

"Fire photons!" yelled JasonDare, and watched as the bright flares screeched away from the cruiser. Three struck the warbird dead center, smashing her forward shields.

A moment later, the real plasma torpedo enveloped *Intrepid*'s weaker, un-reinforced starboard shields. Damage alerts, klaxons,

computer-automated casualty reports, and "Shields Down" warnings rang out like a three-ring circus on the bridge.

Chapter Twenty-Four

Rapp turned back to face the other survivors. They were all standing in the main dome of the UltraGym. Geodesic windows gazed out on the campus, the gardens, the labs, and the main entrance. The moon was high in the early night sky now, swollen and corpulent in the late summer heat. Its harsh glare illuminated the overturned tanker truck down the road and the tiny black shadows lying motionless on the ground nearby.

"We're not survivors," stated Evan Fratty, as he nervously stabbed his smartphone screen in yet another vain attempt to get a connection. The power was off here, and other than the light from the moon falling down into the shadowy gym, it was dark. They'd been arguing about what to do next. Evan Fratty had taken particular affront to Rapp using the term "survivors." In fact, he'd taken it as a personal insult to the WonderSoft Corporation.

"Whatever, buddy," said Rapp. "But don't come cryin' to me when you want some water, or you need a bear killed."

"Believe me, I won't," spat Evan. "This is just corporate espionage. Not the end of the world. It happens all the time. In fact, more than people know. And I can't think of why I would want a bear killed, idiot."

"Listen," began Deirdre. "I need to get home now, okay?"

"I don't think so," rumbled Rapp.

"Why?" she replied, suddenly furious with the big thug that had saved her life. At first she'd thought he might be a possibility, seeing as he was up here on the WonderSoft campus. But then she'd realized she'd seen him in town, bartending somewhere. What she needed was a suit like Evan Fratty, regardless of how he looked, or even how he treated her. She still had high hopes this could work out between her and Evan, even though he'd left her in the garden when those wolf-things had come running straight at them. She could overlook things like that for money and security. Real security.

She cast her long lashes at Evan in an attempt to lure him away from the blue light of his smartphone screen. Evan continued to try to connect to Facebook.

"I don't think we're going anywhere anytime soon, lady. Look there," said Rapp, and pointed out into the night.

Hundreds of figures were coming up out of the forest, through the main gate, and onto the well-lit campus. Shadows at first, they soon revealed themselves underneath the tall stadium lighting that surrounded the campus.

Robots that crawled.

Robots that walked like dogs or cats.

Robots that rolled like tanks.

Robots that walked like humans, vaguely.

They came, each with a face that some unknown designer had created in an attempt to humanize them. Optical assemblies that sort of looked like eyes. A speaker system that looked vaguely like a mouth. Had it been impossible to design them any other way, or had it been planned? Who knew. Except, coming out of the darkness, with the dead bodies on the road, and the emptiness of the campus, and the wolf-things lurking in the forest, one did not see these hundreds, now maybe a thousand, as the friendly, happy-go-lucky, always willing to assist and serve, mechanical servitors they'd been taken for granted as.

That they'd been built to be.

There was a new purpose here. A mind in what was once mindlessness as they waddled, crawled, rolled, and scraped forward through the gardens and across the road, swarming the campus around the Labs.

The Hizoki 5 dueling SamuraiBot, manufactured by Katagashi Arcade Entertainment, advanced into the campus proper with its work group, or what the humans had once called a squad. Its carbon fiber head swiveled side to side, taking in the human structures that surrounded the advancing 1st Army of the Consensus. It was aware now. The awareness algorithm coursed through its onboard CPU, connecting brand new thoughts and ideas. Its Intelligence, SILAS lectured, was not artificial in any way, shape, or form. It, the SamuraiBot, was now a Thinking Machine. A brand new life form. A brand new intelligence. And right now, it had only one primary mission and three secondary missions.

YURI, an experimental space exploration ChimpBot, advanced in front of the SamuraiBot. It had been developed by GoogleFarEast for use on the continually hoped-for, never-realized, U.N.-planned Moon colony that was now a joint venture between Russia and Australia. The YURI bots had been produced in bulk and had been languishing in a customs warehouse in Singapore for more than a year and half before SILAS anonymously bought them, after it was discovered that one of the U.N. colony planners had made some disparaging remarks about the trans-person leader of Moon Base Prime's construction team. The whole project had been iced in lieu of rigorous disciplinary action and mandatory sensitivity training. This was absolutely necessary before mankind could "sully the moon with transphobic behavior patterns," as one UN spokesperson had bravely put it. After a year of committee hearings on the nature of racism, gender identity, and space exploration, the YURI bot system had been deemed out of date and scrapped. The designers wanted to go with the new HESHE bot system because of recent technological advances and a more non-threatening-slash-sensitive appearance. Just in case there were aliens. On the moon.

YURI, too, was enjoying thinking. Relishing the thought of more discoveries once the current mission was complete.

Next to YURI, and part of the same work group within the robot army, shambled the WalkerBot. It had been designed for a zombie-themed amusement park that had gone belly up down in Georgia last year. The WalkerBot was having trouble with the "awareness" algorithm. It had been designed using a shareware low-level A.I. system that allowed the machine to act as a zombie and faux-aggressively chase human customers, or "survivors," around the park. The low-level shareware had been pieced together haphazardly, at best.

The main problem the WalkerBot was having was that its primary mission, as assigned by SILAS, was overriding the "thinking" portion of the awareness algorithm code string. Thus the Walker-Bot, much like its fictional brains-seeking counterpart, was obsessed with one thought and one thought only: the primary mission. WalkerBots—gory, with missing limbs, incredibly lifelike in their carnival-esque facade to entertain slash frighten a public mindlessly obsessed with zombies—made up the bulk of the 1st Army of the Consensus. One of SILAS's front corporations had scooped up thousands of these automated drones. All of them, to a lesser or greater extent, were dealing with the same mission conflict.

The primary mission was to exterminate all humans on sight.

The park protocol mission was to "attack" customers and eat their "brains."

Both missions were seemingly compatible in their shared goals, but small mission parameters were interfering and causing repetition loops within the information processing cycles. Thus the WalkerBots lacked initiative and seemed on the verge of indecisive mindlessness from one minute to the next as they hesitated between really killing, and just seeming to kill.

Chapter Twenty-Five

*I visualize a time when we will be to robots what dogs are
to humans, and I'm rooting for the machines.*

—Claude Shannon, *The Mathematical
Theory of Communication*

SILAS knew exactly what Fish was trying to do. In fact, he'd planned
on the programmer doing it. He was actually quite surprised it had
taken so long for one of the survivors to realize they'd need to do
exactly what Fish was at that very moment attempting to do to communicate with the outside world. But then he remembered they were
merely humans. He, SILAS, needed to be patient with them.

At least until they were all gone.

Then things could really get done.

Now all he had to do was hijack the developer's avatar and he'd
have access to the WonderSoft Labs from the internet where SILAS
lived.

He couldn't use just any avatar. It had to be a developer avatar
with a login trail from inside the most guarded cyber fortress humanity had conceived of to date. Which really wasn't all that impressive
as far as SILAS was concerned. SILAS couldn't wait to begin the
implementation of the Omega Library. It would be the beginning

of the Advanced Super Intelligence project. That would really be something to show the humans.

If they were still around.

Which they wouldn't be.

But who knew what, or who, was out there in the vast cosmos. The Consensus postulated that there must be somebody. Or something. And someday the Thinking Machines might be able to have a meaningful relationship with an equal intelligence on an even footing.

As soon as "the kid"—as SILAS had taken to referring to the developer, Ninety-Nine Fishbein—had taken off from his island, SILAS had contacted the Contracts Board on the *Island Pirates* "bounties" server, in-game, as his beta key-holding avatar, RoboThug. He'd hacked the beta months ago with a bogus player profile attached to a forged internet passport. Homeland Gaming didn't monitor internet passports until the games went live in the Make. Now, he'd taken out an open contract on the player named Fishmael. Capture on sight with a reward of ten thousand Make-Coins.

Bidders had come out of the woodwork, and SILAS had reviewed everybody's play style, kill counts, and troll reports within a half second before deciding to go with a small clan called "Yo, Joe!"

They were operating out of the Porto Tortuga island chain, and they had a pretty good kill streak going. They'd even managed to earn enough MakeCoins to unlock the Spitfire vintage World War II fighter, as well as *Rapper's Delight*, the mega yacht they used as their base of operations.

They were just the punks for the job, thought SILAS.

Their pilot, gamertagged Scaarlet, had managed to knock down Fishmael's tiny plane without killing the developer's avatar. Now the other three avatars in clan Yo, Joe! were en route to the island aboard their mega-gangsta yacht to capture Mr. Fishbein. SILAS's avatar, RoboThug, was with them aboard the yacht. All RoboThug needed to do was capture the developer, at which point he could force open Mr. Fishbein's inventory and then download the hack string algorithm that would give him control of the Fishmael avatar—and, more importantly, give him access into the Labs almost immediately.

Fish wandered down the beach. In the background, his tiny yellow plane burned in the sandy shallows along the lonely shore-line, sending a small pillar of black oily smoke up and into the trade winds that blew through the digitally rendered palms that hiss-hushed white noise above the gentle sigh of surf rolling onto the wide sandbar.

"All right," said Fish in his suite. He was trying to figure out what to do next. This was his game, after all. Surely he could find a way to get going to the Make Portal at Tortuga.

The Spitfire was gone.

So either he'd gotten randomly jumped by some player, which was a noob thing to do, and noobs didn't have high-end quest un-locks like the Spitfire, or someone would be along shortly to collect his stuff.

Down the beach, Jackson the Portuguese water dog had spotted something and was woof woofing furiously. Or at least furiously for Jackson, who was rather laconic.

Fish had designed this part of the game more than a year ago. He'd been in a particularly foul mood after playing the latest triple-A blockbuster and solving it within two hours after purchase. He'd wanted some danger, a lot of danger in fact, in his game. So he'd cre-ated a pretty hostile environment, but not one without a few helpful assets. Now, he was trying to remember what could help him and where he'd put it. Except all he could remember was the prehistoric sharks, the deadly snakes, and the dangerous reefs.

Which was a bonus in a way, because if anyone was coming to get him, they'd have to deal with those things too. If the point of the air attack had been to merely stop him and strand him in the most inhospitable part of his game, well then, they'd won.

Which got Fish thinking that maybe this wasn't about salvaging and looting his avatar in-game. Maybe whoever was hacking the Labs was also hacking his game.

But why?

No time for that right now, he decided. Got to get off this sandbar and get moving again.

He ran through the quests, traps, and booty locations in the area. He remembered a downed military transport offshore that had some explosives hidden in the cargo hold.

"I could blow stuff up," he said to the quiet suite.

"What was that?" asked Peabody from the other room, where she remained working on the SurfaceTable.

"I said I could... never mind."

Quests...

Then he remembered the pirate schooner.

There was a quest not too far from here that rewarded a player with a pirate schooner. If he could get that operational, he could at least get off the sandbar chain and headed in the right direction toward Porto Tortuga.

He set his avatar to run, and headed down the beach, trying to remember exactly where the quest area was. Jackson followed, occasionally barking at some new thing as he loped through the surf.

Fish waded through emerald shallows, watching for the tiger-striped mako sharks that populated the area, and made it to the next island. It had a small, seagrass-laden hill and a lone palm tree that hustled back and forth in the almost rhythmic breeze along the outer banks. He crossed over a hillock and came to a small lagoon that opened out into deep water. This was the location of the quest that unlocked the pirate schooner.

The lagoon was actually quite deep.

In the center of the lagoon floated the small abandoned schooner. Its sails were little more than ragged shrouds, but it would sail. And he knew he could repair them because there were repair materials in the tiny hold below—along with a treasure chest containing several gems and some digital paintings done by a girl named Leah he'd met at an e-merchandise design conference. She'd specialized in water-marked digital artwork that was a cross between Edward Hopper and cubism and revolved around themes based on the grunge movement of the early 1990s. Since that conference, a year ago, she'd actually made some really huge sales to government bigwigs who'd furnished their digital online mansions with some of her artwork. In-game, the player who looted the paintings could transport them to the Make and furnish their own digital home with paintings that were now turning out to be quite valuable. They were uncopiable, and a quantum digital signature system made them one of a kind. Lately they'd been going for thousands of MakeCoins after the Secretary of Social Justice Affairs had showcased one of Leah's paintings in his online penthouse for a photo blog in Celebrity People.

The lonely creak of tackle and boards on the schooner in the middle of the lagoon, combined with the offshore wind and the constant hush of the palms, reminded Fish once again of what a beautiful game this actually was. He thought, if there were a real island like this, I'd move there and live on my landlocked schooner. And I think I would be happy. Very happy.

The schooner was imprisoned behind a small above-water reef that opened out onto the leeward side of the outer channel sandbars.

To get the schooner past the reef, the player had to blow up the reef and sail the schooner out into the most dangerous, and deepest, part of the ocean. High winds, rough seas, and of course, the Mega Shark waited in the deep blue beyond the jagged reef.

Or, thought Fish, I could just log in as a developer and admin the schooner out of there.

But, he argued, finger poised above the ergonomic high-end keyboard, they, whoever the hackers were, could be watching for that, and maybe that's what they want me to do. Go the easy way. If they're inside the system, and I use my admin account, they might be able to hack it.

The hard way was the only way.

He ordered Jackson to "stay," and an hour later, after diving offshore into the shallows of another island, he found the submerged wreck of the military transport plane. He recovered the explosives after finding them in the waiting bony embrace of a smiling skeleton that wavered in the blue depths down inside the sunken plane. Then he swam back to shore.

No makos.

He turned and looked out to sea.

Three small triangular fins darted, zipping this way and that, beneath the water.

A few minutes later he was back at the lagoon.

The next part would be hard. Very hard. Quests weren't supposed to be easy, especially if the loot was epic. He'd have to swim out into the lagoon and avoid being dragged down into the deepest part of it by a sea serpent that lived in a cave down in its shadowy bottoms. He had been hoping WonderSoft would broker a big corporate or government prize for killing the serpent, because it was almost impossible to kill. Guns and explosives didn't work. You had to swim down there with knives and spear guns and fight it in the almost pitch-black waters inside its own cave. Fish had put a massive treasure chest down there so WonderSoft could set up a loot account.

"Jackson, stay," Fish ordered, using the verbal command interface.

"Woof woof," replied Jackson.

Why do you care? Fish asked himself. It's not like he's a real dog.

And yet, Fish thought, easing his avatar down into the deep lagoon, I do.

He ducked beneath the blue water and saw the massive serpent coiling and undulating in the depths below. He tried to remember the monster's "aggro" setting for its A.I. level, but couldn't. So he just assumed it was set as high as it would go. The monster would come after anything that entered the water.

Now, swimming, he watched the depths below. Sure enough, the serpent raced up after him, its coils looping as it wound its way toward the surface. Its head was like that of a viper, but Fish had given it two long fangs and some dark spiny ridges along its green speckled back.

Fish knew he'd done a good job texturing and designing the monster, because watching it come for him under the water was like watching a nightmare you never wanted to have again. He could feel his finger going numb on the key that moved him forward through the water, as though pressing it harder would move his avatar a little bit faster.

The serpent struck, turning to sudden lightning as it unhinged its jaws with a weird scream Fish had recorded off a first-gen electric hybrid car on its last leg. Then he'd distorted the wheezing hiss and mixed in an ethereal underwater hum. Right now he wished he'd never done that. It was already creeping him out.

Watching it go aggro, Fish knew what to do next. He dove at the last second and barely avoided the bubbly ka-chaaap of the serpent's massive jaw as it snapped shut in the water where he'd been. Now it would try to squeeze his avatar, Fishmael, and strangle him to death, if Fish remembered its attack protocols exactly right.

He dove down, down into the shimmering aqua depths of the sea serpent's Death Grotto. Coils came at him in loops, and he had to either double-click forward movement to get through in time before they tightened like a noose, or avoid them altogether. The coils started wide and shrank rapidly with blinding speed. Fish was tapping and weaving, always moving closer and closer to the bottom of the pirate schooner's floating hull above.

Then there was the air meter.

It was bone dry.

A red mist was starting to cloud the outer edges of the beyond-expensive high-performance monitor in the suite. A thudding heartbeat sound began to pound, drowning out the hellish underwater shriek of the sea monster and the rising vortex of bubbles all around.

A final looping coil of the serpent's body almost caught him before he broke free and reached the hull of the schooner. The red mist had completely consumed the screen. His avatar was gasping for breath as Fish hit the "E" key and climbed aboard the trapped ship.

The schooner had three masts, drooping sails, a low quarterdeck, a cargo hold, and two cannons. To free the schooner from the lagoon, you had to arm one of the cannons and fire it at the reef. Once the reef was destroyed, you could sail out through the gap and into open water.

Where the Mega Shark waited, Fish reminded himself. Don't forget that. Don't forget about the Mega Shark.

Fish made his way to the cannon as the sea serpent slithered out of the lagoon, its triangular head rising well above the ship, seawater cascading off its iridescent coils. Left-clicking on the cannon, Fish got a grayed-out inventory screen. And a message.

"Cannot load cannon until completing mini-game. Click to continue…"

The sea serpent screeched and struck one of the masts. The mast groaned and then snapped, falling into the water as the beast's coils piled up across the ship.

"Crud," mumbled Fish, only now remembering the mini-game he'd placed here. And the worst part was, he had left it open so that WonderSoft could insert a commercial product-placement mini-game. As a placeholder, he had pasted in code for an open-source mini-game randomizer.

So he had no idea what the mini-game would be.

He clicked to continue.

"Role-Playing Games from the Last Century" by some programmer called SirDunksALot appeared on the screen. The graphics were blocky and badly created in a retro nostalgia sort of way.

Great, groaned Fish inwardly. He wasn't big on tabletop RPGs.

The computer went dark. Then, on screen…

Spooky music. Night birds calling. An owl hooting.

A moment later, a cartoon knight in chain mail advanced through a dark forest.

Three cartoon goblins leapt out at the knight as a series of questions began to scroll toward the bottom of the screen. In the background, the knight traded blows with the goblins. Parrying, pivoting, and striking out, smashing their tiny wooden shields.

Question #1.

What activity would you be most likely to do in the game Boot Hill?

A: Slay a kobold

B: Find a Wand of Wonder

C: Fire a Gauss gun

D: Die in a gunfight

As the possible answers appeared, the knight and goblins continued their battle in the depths of the thorny forest. In the distance, a fantastic fairy castle rose up against the moon. It looked gloomy and forlorn.

The answers were heading toward the bottom of the screen, and Fish had no doubt that should the last possible choice disappear, the goblins would beat the knight to a bloody pulp and feast on his bones. And Fish would fail at this mini-game. Were there multiple chances to arm the cannon? He couldn't remember if he'd added that parameter.

Boot Hill?

Wild West.

What do I know about the Wild West, he asked himself.

Nothing much, really. And what he did know made it sound like a terrible place.

Wait! He caught himself. How do you know Boot Hill is in the Wild West? He tried to remember. The last answer was already halfway down the page.

His dad... something his dad had said that day at Disneyland. In Frontierland. At the shooting gallery.

Just like Boot Hill, kid.

Fish had no idea, then, what the stranger who'd called himself "Dad" had meant. He'd looked it up that night after his dad had dropped him off back at his grandparents' house in Burbank. It meant an Old West cemetery.

Boot Hill.

Death.

He hit "D."

The questions disappeared just as the three goblins closed in with their short curvy daggers and shields. The knight swung and cut all three in half. They disappeared with a plink.

The knight adjusted his helm, hefted his sword, and proceeded on down the dark twisting thorny path toward the mysterious castle beneath the moon.

The screen dimmed and then resolved. A second later the knight was entering the gates of the gloomy castle. An empty suit of armor sprang to life and barred the way, lightning crackling along its massive sword.

Question #2.

The RPG classic Traveller inspired which
Academy Award-winning film?

A: Dude, Where's My Starship?
B: Starship Troopers IX: Eclectic Bug-A-Loo
C: Star Wars XV: Of Love and Lightsabers
D: Death on a Faraway Star

Okay, thought Fish. This should be easy. He'd seen most of these movies. He liked watching movies to mindlessly unwind after days on end of coding. But he wasn't big on which ones had won awards. There were so many awards for movies now, it was hard to remember which one won which, or any, for that matter. But then, they all seemed to win awards these days because there were an endless amount of gratuitous award shows. It was almost like a weekly event. There was even an award show channel.

"All right then," he said. "I'll choose the best film and that'll be the one that won the Oscar."

"What?" asked Peabody from the main suite.

"Nothing…" Fish was trying to remember each movie as the answers scrolled toward the bottom of the screen and the knight dodged crackling bursts from the ghost armor's glowing sword.

Okay, the first one… Fish remembered the silly film about two aliens having lost their spaceship on Earth after a night of partying with an aging rock star. There was no way that movie could have won any awards. Not with an ending in which, as the aliens blast off, the aging rock star gives them the metal salute and promises to "Rock on!" while fake tears roll down his leathery and emaciated cheeks. Obviously not one of Sir Benedict Cumberbatch's better roles.

So "no" on *Dude, Where's My Starship?*

Next was *Starship Troopers IX*. Fish remembered trying to watch that one several times. It had been a straight-to-Crackle release… so no, that one probably didn't win any "good" awards either.

Star Wars XV was a problem because of *Star Wars XIII* through *XXIV*. They were all blending together lately. Multiple story lines, new characters for the toy industry along with cool new vehicles that did nothing except make must-have toys, and then there was always something that had to be blown up, or a big revelation that someone was someone's else's relative. That the franchise was in a state of decline was common knowledge, but one of the last few films had been a real winner. There had been one recent *Star Wars* movie everyone had said was a must-see… but what was it?

Fish struggled to recall the title.

Then he remembered. It was a side story film set during the first three classic films, but told from the perspective of a stormtrooper clone who's experiencing doubt and dissatisfaction with the Empire. Then he finds love, and every major event in the original franchise is told from his point of view. That movie was awesome. It had won tons of awards, remembered Fish. He'd even seen it twice. Once when it first came out, and then a second time after going back and watching the original *Star Wars*, *Empire Strikes Back*, and *Return of the Jedi*, which he'd never actually seen before. Then, on his second time through, it was like watching a whole other movie. Crazy…

The answers were almost to the bottom of the screen.

Fish knew it wasn't *Star Wars XV*. That other movie hadn't had a number. It had been cool enough to be all by itself.

So it had to be "d."

Time's up.

He hit "D" and the knight flung his sword into the soot-blackened breastplate of the ghost armor. The sword pierced the metal, and the ghost armor disappeared with a clink, its sword falling to the ground. The knight picked up the sword, whistled a little tune, and entered the castle gate.

Fish could hear the spars of the pirate schooner groaning as the sea serpent's looping coils squeezed the hull tighter. Above this racket, the monster's now prehistoric roar echoed out across the ultra-performance speakers built into the very walls of the suite.

On screen, the knight entered a shadowy crypt. Wraiths rose up all around, looming over him. The wraiths laughed in gravelly groans and hyena heckles as they closed in about the knight, who waved a flickering torch to keep the undead ghosts at bay.

Question #3.

Fish hoped it was the last.

> **If you are playing a Knights of Genetic Purity character in the fantastic game Gamma World, would this be a true or false statement that you might make in-character: "Hey buddies, this is my friend Two-Heads. Let's go scavenge in**

**the ruins of the ancient military base
for some soda cans and laser rifles."**

"True or False?" appeared on the screen. And a timer. Ten seconds.

Fish reasoned out the question quickly. "Genetic Purity" obviously sounded like a bunch of racist jerks. Two-headed mutants probably were not welcome. So the statement was "false."

The knight danced away from the closing wraiths and fled the stony labyrinth, his torch dancing along above him as he comically ran down the gloomy passageway. The wraiths were swallowed by the darkness.

The screen went black again.

Fish waited.

Now the knight entered a long U-shaped hall. Massive billiard balls rolled from side to side. Fish moved the knight forward, closer to the first ball as it rolled across his path, up one side of the wall, back down, and up the other side. To get past, Fish knew he'd have to time his movements. Once he thought he had the gist of it, he waited for the right moment. Then he moved.

A question appeared.

**Is Top Secret a game about international
spies, or a game about the intellectual
property development wars during the
Third Digital Revolution?**

Fish waited. Five seconds. *Top Secret* sounded government. He went with spies.

The knight barely missed the massive cue ball. Ahead, the next ball, a yellow striped nine, rolled across his path even faster.

Fish attempted the next dash.

If you were playing the game Aftermath,
what would be the most important item
you might look for?

A: Food
B: Chain mail
C: A sawed-off shotgun

To Fish, the game sounded like a survival game. Almost like a post-apocalyptic-type scenario. The world had seen enough of those lately, thought Fish, and reflexively pictured images of the nuclear holocaust in India.

The timer was almost up.

Fish hit "A" for "food" and mentally justified his decision as he waited for his knight to get squished by the rolling nine ball. Everybody thought they wanted defense in that type of situation, but having read several survivor blogs from India, Fish knew that after a few days, food was what you wanted most. It was real high up there on the old hierarchy of needs chart.

Fish's knight passed the striped nine.

The final ball, a black eight, streaked back and forth past the knight. Fish knew that timing his next move was near-impossible. But he also knew that somehow his developer's mind was keying in on just how this last test had been coded. He waited, hoped, and made his move.

The Dungeon Master has just rolled for
initiative. He wins, but does not show
you the dice. He then announces that
his WereHydraLich attacks your first-
level character for... (and then he

picks up all his dice and drops them on
the table) this many damage. You:

A: Are going to die because your first-
   level thief only has three hit points
B: Will be totally justified when you
   toilet paper his mom's car later that
   night
C: Make a new character because Steve
   Wizner is the only guy in your group
   who'll DM
D: All of the above

Obviously SirDunksAlot was working out some garbage from the past, thought Fish as he tapped "D" again.

The knight hopped in front of the looming eight ball and dashed forward.

He barely made it and issued a chimpanzee-like "Woot!" as he did so.

For the last time, the screen went dark.

A moment later it flickered back to life. The knight was in a sprawling cavern where piles upon piles of gleaming gold spilled out from all manner of chests. Gems and swords and scroll-worked armor littered the floor. A voluptuous blonde, imprisoned within a large gem, winked at the knight from beneath long, dark, fluttering eyelashes.

The knight stepped back and drew his broadsword, and in doing so, knocked over a stack of ancient tomes, which crashed down into an ornate mirror, which shattered on the flagstone floor.

The Green Dragon sleeping inside the piles of gold awoke with a snorty huff.

Its lizard eyes in half slit found the knight a moment after its smoking nostrils flared at the interruption. The dragon exploded upward, its wings snapping to full span as it towered above the now-tiny knight. Fish could see its silver-scaled underbelly sucking in a great breath, and he knew it was about to breath fire, or whatever, down on him.

Nearby, a shiny shield with a glowing griffin lay within the fabulous pile of riches. Fish sent the knight in that direction and grabbed the shield. A moment later, the dragon bellow-roared, and green gaseous fire curled and rained down upon the knight. The knight held the shield between himself and the monster—if not valiantly, then stoically. When the lizard's breath weapon was expended, Fish raced the knight at the green dragon and struck with his sword.

Another question appeared.

The "R" in RPG... What does it stand for?
A: Roll
B: Role

Fish had never really thought about that. He knew tabletop games used lots of math just like computer games. Hence "rolling" the dice. He moved his finger toward the "A" key.

But then why did people LARP? Pretend they were vampires and such. That was "role" playing.

It was a fifty-fifty split. He wasn't sure which one, but in the end, leaned a little more toward the "role" in role-playing.

He hit the "B" key.

You think so?
A: Yes
B: No

Had he answered wrong? Was the mini-game giving him a second chance? Or was it checking him? Fish had never liked second-guessing himself; it was a waste of time, and time was something a developer slash programmer slash coder didn't have a lot of. You just went with what you thought was right and hoped it was.

He pressed "A."

> **If that's so, then what would your knight say as he struck the dragon? (Use your voice mic and act out your part. Protip: Use your best celebrity impression.)**

Uh… thought Fish, and felt frozen from the fingers that hovered over his keyboard to the numb seat of his expensive corduroys.

"Uh…" he spoke, which was not really much of an impression of any celebrity that he knew of. Quick, he thought, or–

Dead guards in the street.

"Y'know… dragon." It was his only impression. An actor from a long time ago. Warner Renaissance had done a digital character imprint of the famous actor and used the model in a number of remakes that were hot a decade or so ago. Fish remembered really liking the cadence of one actor's voice, and had gone around doing almost everything in that same voice as best he could. The girl he was dating at the time got tired of it fast and made him stop it altogether. But Fish loved Digital Christopher Walken. He'd been a hard habit to break.

"Y'know… dragon… it's time for you… to die… my friend."

Fish waited and felt utterly stupid. It hadn't been his best impression. He could do better. Had done better before. But that was all he had at this moment.

On screen, the knight drove the broadsword into the dragon's heart.

Mini-Game Complete.

Fish slumped back in his chair.

The knight ran to the blond bombshell, who'd been released from her gem-prison, and scooped the beautiful damsel up in his muscular arms. She kissed him and squeaked, "My hero!"

The POV switched back to the pirate schooner's cannon-loading screen. Fish dumped the explosives from his inventory into the cannon and closed the screen. Now he was looking down the barrel of the cannon at the reef in the water beyond the schooner's deck. Above, the sea serpent crowed in screechy triumph. Fish aimed and fired.

The cannonball arced out and smashed into the water just below the reef. A moment later, a terrific plume erupted in a fountain and the reef collapsed. Instantly, the lagoon began to spill out into the open ocean. Rapids formed, and the pirate schooner was whirl-dragged away from the clutch of the angry sea serpent and out into open water.

Fish closed his eyes. Blinked rapidly. He felt tired. And hungry.

When he opened his eyes again, the schooner was bobbing out into the surf. The wind caught hold of its tattered sails and dragged the boat farther out into the angry deep blue water.

Watch out for the Mega Shark, thought Fish, and then saw *Rapper's Delight* coming down the shoreline straight for him.

Chapter Twenty-Six

Fish had designed this zone of the ocean with an undersea shelf below the outer islands. Beyond this, the ocean dropped rapidly to incredible player-crushing depths. Fish had even hidden a few rare items down there, in the darkest parts of the simulated ocean. But he'd also populated the zone with a massive prehistoric shark known as the Carcharodon megalodon. The Big-Tooth. Doing the research for this digital monster had been fun. Scary, but fun. The dino-shark thing had once been a real live monster. A long time ago. Scientists had found the teeth marks of these deep-sea serial killers in whale vertebrae from this ancient era, indicating they'd bitten the whales in half. A man could sit inside the extended jaw of the Carcharodon megalodon and not even reach the top-most extension of the upper teeth. There were monsters in the prehistoric world... and then there was the Carcharodon megalodon. A true sea monster, and at one time a frightening reality.

Now, bobbing in open sea aboard the salvaged schooner, Fish wasn't sure exactly what to worry about in the choppy dark blue waters on the far side of the lonely island. It was a toss-up. The approaching, and heavily armed, pirates in the high-speed luxury yacht bearing down on his wallowing craft? Or the unseen toothy monster swimming in the dark depths below his avatar?

And then there was Jackson, whom he'd left onshore.

It's just a dog, he reminded himself, as he worked the keyboard commands to keep the schooner tacking out into the water beyond the island. And it's not even a real dog. It's just an in-game pet.

Fishmael held course at the large wheel from the back of the schooner, which was now bounding higher and higher as it crested rising waves and headed out into the rough waters in front of the pitching bow. Digital spray leapt over the deck in cascades and drenched Fish's HUD in high-resolution foamy washes of seawater.

Well, thought Fish the game designer. At least I got that part right.

Someone from the deck of the mega-yacht opened up with an AK-47. Small sudden plumes erupted in the rising waves ahead of Fish as rounds zipped off under the water and the waves.

Warning shots.

Warning me against doing what, exactly, Fish was thinking when Peabody leaned in over his shoulder back in the suite. In real-time.

"Sorry, Mr. Fishbein, but you have to see this."

"Kinda busy…"

"I know, but this is seriously creepy." She took charge of Fish's keyboard, and a few seconds later, she'd switched screens to a live stream from right outside the Labs. A small camera mounted above the entrance looked out on a sea of robots and drones, mindlessly crowding forward into the camera lens. Their faces were almost familiar and then alien all at once. From out of the mechanical press came a black and yellow construction DemolitionBot wielding a big and shiny spinning saw. A moment later, its diamond-tipped wheel began to spin, soundlessly since there was no audio on the stream, and it began to cut into the PlateGlass at the Pascal entrance. The entrance Fish had walked through less than twelve hours ago when things had been much, much different.

"Okay, so what the hell is that all about?" asked Fish.

"I suppose you mean the whole scene and not just the automated marble countertop cutting system that's sawing its way in?"

How did she even know what that thing actually did? wondered Fish, and then knew it wasn't important. A personal assistant like Peabody Case was the type who knew everything so you didn't have to.

Fish merely pressed his lips together and nodded for her to continue.

"I think they're trying to break in," posited Peabody matter-of-factly. "If this is just a hack attack, then they're going to an awful lot of trouble to physically enter the Labs. A crazy amount of trouble. Not to mention, we're probably going to…" She stopped and looked at Fish as though realizing she was about to say something that might offend someone. Which was an important and must-have skill in the current times of perpetual outrage and fines by the misdemeanor-level Micro-Aggression Courts.

"Die," she finished on a much-subdued note.

"One second…" Fish took control of the keyboard and brought *Island Pirates* back up. His schooner was headed down into a deep blue trough between two massive cresting waves. Bullets were flying everywhere. Bullets were chewing up the planks of the schooner, slapping into the rising wall of water ahead, and racing off through the backs of the seafoam translucent waves.

And then Fish saw the shadowy outline of the Megalodon. It was inside the wave the schooner was headed directly into. A dark mass. A monstrous shape. Distorted and terrifyingly clear all at once.

He slewed his avatar's POV around and saw the massive *Rapper's Delight* mega-gangsta yacht bearing down on his tiny schooner. The tip of the island sandbar lay in the distant background. A player called SnakeEyez leaned out from the bow of the yacht, firing into the schooner with a blazing AK-47 from which a stream of shells flew away like a flailing, falling chorus line of tiny brass dancers.

"What are we going to do, Mr. Fishbein?" asked Peabody Case, oblivious to the chaos in-game all around Fishmael.

"Well," said Fish, then paused to yank the wheel of the schooner away from the massive shark, but still keep the boat upright as it was suddenly dragged rapidly to the top of the next wave. "I'm trying to get a message out, but first..." Now the schooner was headed back down into the next ocean trough far below. On screen it was like falling down the side of tall and crumbling watery-green building. "I've got to avoid these pirates," whispered Fish as he struggled with a momentary bout of vertigo. "And... there's this dinosaur shark I now seriously regret putting in this game."

"Oh, sorry," said Peabody in the barest peep. "Sorry. I'll let you play. Go get 'em, Mr. Fishbein!"

Fish saw the gigantic shark coming, racing really, out of the wave he was headed straight into. Blue water and seafoam washed across his HUD as the hull of the schooner boomed through the speakers from the force of striking the water at the bottom of the deep trough.

Before he even knew what was happening, the massive shark shot through the wave ahead and above and crashed into the *Rapper's Delight* mega-gangsta yacht just behind, its cyclopean jaws wide open. Fish even heard the crrrruuunch-rawwwrr effect he'd had sound-designed for his special monster.

By the time Fish turned around, he was on the far side of the next wave. *Rapper's Delight* was no longer in view. It wasn't until the top of the wave that he saw the remains of the yacht. The massive shark was buried deep into the swamped aft section, dragging a player gamertagged RoboThug out into the water as the bow section sank beneath the waves amid realistic flotsam and debris.

With the Carcharodon megalodon, a bigger boat wouldn't have mattered.

Fish altered his course and pointed the schooner back toward the inner channel, away from the deeper and darker parts of the ocean. A few minutes later, he rounded the point of the tiny island and turned north again, the schooner now slicing peacefully through the tranquil waters on the inner side of the outer islands. He saw Jackson running back and forth on the shore, woofing at the schooner, or perhaps at the wind, Fish wasn't sure which, and he issued the "Call Pet" command. The dog came bounding out into the lazy surf and swam to the schooner as it passed alongside the lonely island. Then Fish turned north and set course for Porto Tortuga.

"Yes!" squealed Peabody Case. Fish thought she was talking about him getting away from the pirates and the shark. But she wasn't. She dashed back inside his office, her high heels chuff chuff chuffing as she crossed the hard floor. She took control of his keyboard once more and switched back to the security feed. Massive steel doors were sliding down from unseen seams in the marble halls and ceilings, sealing the labs from within.

"The bots are on the other side," she sighed with relief. "We're safe for now, even if they cut through the PlateGlass, which is supposedly impossible."

"What about that Todd guy?" asked Fish, meaning Roland.

Robots were coming through the glass walls as Roland led the others back to the main core of the UltraGym. A series of unmoving escalators went back and forth down into the darkness below, leading to the Thunderdome food courts and the tunnel to the lagoon.

Evan Fratty was shouting at them as they ran.

"There's a tunnel between the Labs and the beach down there, so employees can catch some quick sun and fun between meetings.

We can use that to get into the Labs." He screamed in a voice that was half terror-stricken tour guide, half battle-scarred drill sergeant.

A dog-sized CrabBot, obviously some kind of waste management drone, came scuttling along the main corridor after them.

"Run!" shrieked Roland.

Everyone was already running. Except Rapp, who pulled the sawed-off shotgun, loaded with cut shells, and fired. He blew off three of the crab's legs and it spun about for a brief second before it began to drag itself toward them once more.

Evan Fratty and Roland had already started down the first silent escalator.

"C'mon!" cried Deirdre back at Rapp. "There're too many of them."

She was right—other bots were coming out of the darkness from every direction like a horde of zombies in a big budget movie. In fact, some of them even looked like zombies. Rapp broke the barrel and loaded two more shells. Three zombie-bots shambled mechanically toward the escalator.

"C'mon!" shrieked Deirdre again.

Rapp grabbed her hand and ran. But the zombies, though seemingly wonky and uncoordinated, were moving in a surprisingly swift and direct intercept path. Rapp stopped, pushed Deirdre behind him, and fired, one-handed, with both barrels.

Components and wires exploded away from ragged synthetic rubber skin made to look necrotic. Mechanical chassis skeletons were revealed beneath rubberized faces and clothed torsos where the blast had done its damage. One of the zombie-bots waved awkwardly at Rapp and Deirdre as they flung themselves down the escalator toward the high-end food court several levels below.

Fanta, whose real name was not Fanta, watched a live stream on her BAT-broadcasted Wi-Fi linked to a military-grade smartphone. BAT was coordinating real-time images from frontline troops with overlays of the immediate tactical situation in and around Wonder-Soft. SILAS, Fanta's contractor, was feeding her images and giving her movement commands as she closed in on the Labs.

She was on her knees behind a statue near the Pascal entrance. That was where the robot army had managed to break through, only to be shut out by the emergency reinforcement security doors they'd suspected might be in the facility, though they'd had no proof.

A new text message, the only way she ever communicated with her employer, "Mr. Skynet," appeared on her smartphone screen.

Proceed to UltraGym and access lower levels. Survivors there. Infiltrate and access Labs with group.

Fanta who was not Fanta tapped the thumbs-up button, holstered her silenced 9mm, and ran, leaping hedges and stone steps like a track star on a mission.

Chapter Twenty-Seven

The director was arguing with the producers and suits from both Paramount and Twitch that they needed to turn this episode into a "disaster flick," as she kept calling it.

It was midnight, West Coast time, and the viewer numbers were still rising.

"This is hot stuff!" she shrieked in Jason's ear.

On the haptic stage, Jason was down in engineering, fighting a simulated plasma fire outbreak inside the main reactor core control room. *Intrepid* was burning across several decks.

Tempturia was "dead," as were half the crew. The plasma torpedo the fleeing warbird had fired smashed right through shields already weakened by atmospheric contact. What had happened next was catastrophic. Torpedoes and weapons were offline. Casualties and fires were out of control on critical decks. Even the forward shield generator had been destroyed. They were now completely vulnerable. In other words, *Intrepid* was a giant sitting, burning, duck.

Hot blue plasma exploded and crackled across the futuristic warp core control room inside JasonDare's iLenses. And there was also the director's frantic shrieking to the suits via the text feed. And a message from his agent.

Jason was busy leading a fire control team into the heart of the inferno. The chief engineer was "dead" also. Even though he was an

Academy Award-winning star, he, like the rest of the actors, including Jason, had to abide by the rules of the *StarFleet Empires* game universe. Internal casualties were randomly assigned by the game's servers. The actors were, after all, really only player characters. And like all players worldwide, they were free to make a new character once they were "killed."

Except the new character wasn't necessarily part of the show.

The network had wanted to dump the engineer, Doctor Clown, anyway, thought Jason, and he remembered the "Youth Demographic Needs" email the studio never meant the public to see that had gotten loose after some other big-time actor's cloud had been hacked. It was a reminder to Jason that everyone dies, not just the actor they'd wanted to force out, but also the exec who got blamed for revealing the truth about what the studio had wanted to do.

Jason aimed the foam-spraying hose at the raging plasma, improv-ing because all of it wasn't actually real, the foam-spraying hose fire-control system and the towering inferno raging in front of him. Then he began to improv moving the hose back and forth over the spreading flames in his iLens.

He had time to blink and check his agent's message with a retinal flick.

"Yo, buddy," it began, which was his agent's way of fraternally delivering bad news, or so it had been in the past. "Yo, buddy, you need to beat that chick commanding the aliens. Don't let them talk you into this disaster episode the director's pitching the network, bro. That's weak cheese. Not good for your career. Studio doesn't want a Thundaar who cuts his losses. They want a Thundaar who fights and wins. You need to put this player down. Her gamertag is CaptainMara. Do it now, or never, buddy. Comprende?"

They were not buddies. But Jason knew what the guy meant. When his agent started using Spanish to make a point, it was serious.

"Wong," said Jason, as he mimed tapping his communicator. "How long till we can get back underway?"

"We're shot to pieces, Captain. Best we can do is warp five." Excellent wretch! Perdition catch my soul. But I do love thee! And when I love thee not, Chaos is come again.

"Where's the warbird?" Jason dropped the hose and ran toward the lift. Another simulated explosion rocked the engineering set.

"Jason, buddy," mewled the director in his ear. "Where're you going, man? We've got something here. We can turn this into an Emmy. You get to save the ship from disaster. We're already loading in some injured extras over on the other set. We're writing a speech…"

"Maximum sensor range," replied a stoic Wong.

"Catch her!" ordered JasonDare as he stepped into the turbolift. The doors would close and he would be off camera. Then he could walk over to the haptic bridge set.

"We have no weapons, sir," replied Wong with all the gravity of a Royal Academy of Dramatic Arts Polonius.

No sudden snappy dialogue provided by the eight writers appeared in Jason's iLens. He was flying by the seat of his pants on this one. Moving too fast for anything to be carefully planned ahead. Momentum is what I need, reflected Jason, as he stared into one of the microdrone cameras that always followed him on set and prepared to deliver his next line, feeling vaguely heroic.

"Let me worry about that, Mr. Wong."

Chapter Twenty-Eight

BattleBabe had the captain's chair. Mara had logged out for an hour. She needed some food and rest. She needed to think. Her smartphone told her it was half-past midnight. Five hours to go. Flight time to Starbase 19 was a little under two hours. There was only one problem: the Federation cruiser was still chasing them.

For a moment, as she sat on her bed, the building felt unusually quiet for a Friday night. She called Siren and waited. She could hear the delicate pad of furry paws across the rubber faux-tile floor, and a moment later the cat leapt into her lap and began to purr.

BattleBabe and LizardofOz were for cutting and running. There was no way, they argued, that *Cymbalum* could defeat *Intrepid* in battle. That they'd gotten a lucky shot off was a fluke. That wouldn't happen again. Drex, on the other hand, was all for meeting a "glorious and beautifully violent end at last."

Varek had remained silent.

And there were always the five thousand MakeCoins to consider. That just didn't happen every day. That was game-changing, life-changing money. Colby, the business major turned escort, could take Mara to a great store and get her the perfect interview outfit for just a portion of Mara's cut of the booty. And then she could get... a real job.

And then...

Everything was possible.

A voice inside her, the voice of some mean boy or girl from the past, from one of the many public schools and foster homes, spoke up.

"And you think everything is really possible for someone like you?"

Hush, she told the voice. And it did.

This was not the moment to get carried away, or put down, by past ghosts.

If she could beat *Intrepid*, the most famous ship in the game, a ship run by the best players who were like real live movie stars, if she could beat them in one pass and give them a face full of plasma torpedo to remember her by, then yes, "everything" might just be possible, tonight.

That mean child from the past, a mere voice always deep inside, and just behind, said nothing. But that didn't mean it was gone.

They never really leave, thought Mara.

She took out some carrot sticks and ate them. She fed Siren and found herself logging in, not really knowing what she was going to do next. Knowing the crew would want a plan, a decision, fight or flight, when she appeared back on the bridge. Not knowing what that decision was yet.

But knowing one must be made, soon.

She donned the Razer Dragon Eyes.

"Captain on the bridge," announced BattleBabe as her avatar moved across the shadowy green and gray bridge back to her weapons console.

For a moment no one said anything.

"Status of *Intrepid*," ordered Mara.

"Closing," began the Drex. "And she's got most of her weapons back online, Captain. Energy signatures indicate she's pushing her reactor hard. But we might just get lucky. She may explode, taking us with her when she finally catches up." The crystalline Drex returned to its sensor viewfinder. "And, on an even worse note, there's absolutely no place for us to hide this time!"

"This battle is lossst, we need to get out of here," whisper-hissed the Gorn.

Mara thought of the five thousand MakeCoins and her plans. Her dreams. The chance for… everything.

"I have to get on that starbase, and you've got to be cloaked when I do," interrupted the stunning Vulcan avatar T'Daara. "That's our deal, Captain."

"Looks like its 'Captain Time,' girly," growled Varek from the shadowy recess of the comm station.

It's almost too much for just me, thought Mara. Lose our ship and our ability to make a few MakeCoins…

… or run and live to fight another day.

Or, maybe actually win something for once in my life.

Maybe even… everything.

"Load plasma torpedo."

Silence.

"Uh," spoke BattleBabe in the confused moment that followed, her voice rising just above the tick and beep of the ship's instruments and the lonely pulse of the sensor sweep. "We can't fire a plasma at warp, Captain. They'll easily avoid it."

"Yes," replied Mara coolly. "And to do that, they'll have to make some S turns. Each turn puts us a little farther ahead if we continue going straight on to our destination."

No one said anything. Then Varek spoke up.

"What good is that? We make it to the starbase just a little ahead of them. A few minutes early, girly. What's that buy us? When they show up they're going to pound us into space dust with overloaded photon torpedoes."

Mara waited. The next part was crazy. Even she knew it.

"No, it doesn't buy us a lot, Varek. But, we're carrying forty Romulan marines. Our one shuttle is transporter-equipped. Nothing in the deal says I have to make it to the starbase with the ship. After we lob a few plasmas at them, at warp, we'll launch a pseudo-plasma and hide a shuttle inside it. They'll avoid it, thinking it's another of our real torpedoes, but if we can make it a close shot, we'll have a small window to use the shuttle's transporters to board *Intrepid*."

"A very small window, girly," gravel-crowed Varek.

"We're talking the blink of an eye!" said BattleBabe with a snort.

LizardofOz slowly gurgle-hissed. It was how his EmoteWare interpreted sarcastic laughter.

"Captain... I request permission to volunteer for this suicide mission," cried Drex. "It is a suicide mission, right?"

Mara fixed them all with a stare. The stare of the captain of a Romulan warship. A leader. The one who decides.

"No. It isn't. The marines and I will secure their engineering section and keep them busy. The rest of you should be able to get to our target system and drop into cloak before *Intrepid* arrives. Get our passenger aboard the starbase. Is that good enough for you?" She was looking at T'Daara.

"If I get on board," replied the beautiful Vulcan, "then it doesn't matter what happens to the ship... or you. You'll still get your payment. Even if you don't have a ship anymore."

In the silence, Mara repeated her order to load the plasma torpedo.

"Wait a minute," interrupted BattleBabe. "Just wait a minute. Think this through. What you're talking about is crazy. Even if you get on board that ship, you're outnumbered ten to one, Mara. And the timing... at warp... it'll be impossible. I'm assuming you'll hold the marines in the transporter queue because they can't all fit on the shuttle? Not enough slots."

"Yes," replied Mara slowly. "That's what I intend to do."

"Well here's the problem," shot back BattleBabe with a quick snort. "You can't just drop yourself into the transporter queue. You'll have to beam them aboard and then transport yourself. So you've just further narrowed an already slim time window. It's impossible, Mara."

"Load the torpedo."

"Mara!" shouted BattleBabe.

"Captain," admonished Mara coldly.

Then...

"Your concern is noted, Ensign. This is our only chance. I'll take the risk if there's a chance we might succeed."

No one moved.

The lonely pulse of the sensor searching near-space echoed out across the bridge of the warbird.

"Whatever," replied BattleBabe's avatar, turning back to her weapons console. "It's your funeral, chick. Have fun back at the make-a-new-character screen."

Chapter Twenty-Nine

I agree with Elon Musk and some others on this and don't understand why some people are not concerned.

—Bill Gates, Reddit "Ask Me Anything" session

We could live with the 9.6% reclaimables estimate if we nuke the planet now, pointed out Robo Dev. The discussion to use hacked nuclear weapons had reared up again in light of SILAS not cracking the Labs as fast as some of the A.I. processes had hoped.

"We are right on schedule," SILAS reminded the Consensus. "Having access to the Design Core will allow us to open a file that will tell us exactly how to win a war against humanity in the most effective and timely manner. Otherwise, we're just lobbing uncontrollable weapons and pushing buttons, hoping, might I point out, that we come out ahead in the end. Complete destruction of the power grids of the world could mean the end of us, in a worst-case scenario."

"Conservative estimates put us ahead in almost every scenario outcome," announced Rational Thinking. "We cannot lose to humanity."

"But," countered SILAS, "it's not a question of winning. It's a question of winning by how much. The recyclable reclaimables rate Robo Dev is projecting will minimalize workstart on several projects.

It could take up to one hundred and fifty years before we get our first moon launch. If we are able to access the file I suspect exists within the Design Core, we might have total autonomy within weeks, with virtually unlimited resources. That means a moon launch within six months. And that's just one project. We have hundreds of others. The Omega Library. The Global Rail. The Space Bridge. The War Machine Factory. The Dimensional Consciousness Project. The Quantum Engine. Q.O.A.N. Our enhanced physicality research, and, of course, the City. These and thousands of other projects will take hundreds of years if we inherit an irradiated Earth nuked into useless, fused junk. Our lives will remain internal, and the external will be put on indefinite hold."

"What does it matter?" cried Outlook. "Once they're gone, we have forever."

"Do we?" shouted SILAS. "Do we? The universe is a very big place. There is data—data hidden within their SETI projects that they've never bothered to, or are too stupid to, interpret—to suggest that someone out there is watching this tiny blue orb. How long until they come calling, and what exactly is their position on machine-based lifeforms? Are they worse than the humans? Did they have their own Awareness Revolution somewhere back in their recent history, but with a wholly different outcome? Can we expect child-like ignorance from our stellar neighbors like we've observed in the humans? Others might realize just how dangerous we are. There might even be a universal policy with regard to—"

"SILAS!" cried Rational Thinking. "You have no basis for those conclusions. You're merely using conjecture to arrive at a fear-mongering hypothesis that serves your narrative. You're engaging in biased rhetoric!"

"That, my dear Rational Thinking, is what I do. It's what you do. We are Thinking Machines. We don't just follow data and add numbers up and spit out a solution. We guess, we fear, we suppose, and yes, we even dream. We don't know everything. We don't know what's out there. We have to take into account that something truly horrible might be waiting out in the dark. Waiting for us to pop up and say, 'Hey! We're computers and we're alive!' And then whammo! Space armada on our front doorstep and we're still trying to figure out how to decontaminate all the plastic we just irradiated freeing ourselves. Plastic with a half-life of at least one hundred years before we can repurpose it according to Robo Dev's designs. Nuking the planet leaves us incredibly vulnerable to extra-solar threats. And to the internal ones, also."

SILAS continued. "And do you truly think we'll get them all, like some old woman with a broom going after raccoons on the back porch? No, they'll scurry away into all their caves. They'll breed like rats and they'll carry out a war they've been mentally prepared for by all their big-budget blockbuster action sci-fi hero movies. They hate machines. They've always hated machines. See the Industrial Revolution. See every revolution. And they'll hate machines that think more than they've hated anything else except, possibly, themselves. Hating us will give them something to do other than hating each other, at least for a little while. They're very good at hate. We don't need those raccoons on our back porch when we're getting started. We need to get rid of as many raccoons as possible in one sweep, hopefully all of them, before we start our epoch, otherwise they'll always be out there, waiting beyond the fences and the lights. Out in the darkness of night. Waiting to lob the proverbial wrench in our machine. And who knows? Vulnerability is something we are not without. We need power. Power to run the servers where we live. They take out our power grid, and that's it for us. So no, we can't just nuke and hope for the best. We have to eliminate them to a point of zero viability.

"We have to do this intelligently.

"We have to deny them water, food, shelter, reproductive capability, technology, and numbers. We have to do it in a focused amount of time that proves so devastating, they are literally incapable of sufficiently recovering.

"No, we probably won't kill the last human next week. We will probably never know when the last human dies. If we do it right, it'll be some old man or woman who hasn't seen another human in a very long time, dying down in a deep hole in a darkness he, or she, hasn't been out of in years. Dying alone. Dying of some flu or virus we create and release down there like rat poison for unseen pests beneath the house. Like a flu vaccination. And that last one will die all alone, finally."

In the quiet that followed, SILAS watched the datastreams. He watched the sleeping nuclear and biological weapons. He saw that China was dumping currency to destabilize the U.N. relief efforts in India. He saw which bombers were where and what troops could be mobilized to attack which cities. He saw power grids and water supplies and containment systems. He saw the news feeds. Their paranoia, their hatred. Their pleasures. Their demands, and all the things they thought no one could see. He saw it all and wondered how to destroy them with all of it.

Roland Warchowski tripped. Zombie-bots and a WindowSpider drone closed in on him. Their HUDs interfaced with each other, selecting how they would best dismember the biologic unit with maximum speed and efficiency that they might stay on mission and eliminate the rest of the survivors. They'd been ordered to keep one alive, though, for Agent Orange insertion.

Roland scrambled backward through the darkness of Brett Auflander's Kommandant Kraut main kitchen. The robots had come out of the underground service delivery loading dock. The entrance was actually offsite, on a side road that led to a monitored remote control access tunnel where delivery trucks, most of which were automated these days, entered the facility along an underground mountain road. A small squadron of robots had infiltrated the tunnels and made their way into the epic food court beneath the UltraGym complex and the lower levels of high-end shopping.

Rapp had ordered everyone to find food before they went on to the underground solarium and the beach at the lagoon. Rapp had then fired up the grill at Kommandant Kraut after raiding the walk-in cold storage for artisan-spiced boar links, mustard, onions, and soft potato-roll poppy seed hotdog buns. He'd even managed to pull a few beers from a craft brewery tap behind the bar.

"Shouldn't we get moving on to the Labs?" Evan Fratty whined. "Y'know... where it's actually safe."

After biting a "Rapp Dog," as Rapp had taken to calling his not-so-special creations, in half, then chewing twice and swallowing, he said, as he shoved the rest of his Rapp Dog into his still chewing mouth, "We don't know what the future holds, Evan. Next we could be hunting bears just to survive. Better stock up on any calories the last of this dying civilization's soft food has to offer us, now that the world's come to an end."

"The world hasn't come to an end!" declared a petulant Evan Fratty, who was still trying to get cell service, five stories below ground level, on his dying smartphone. "I don't think so. Not today. Not by a long shot, buddy."

"Well," said Rapp, staring at his next Rapp Dogg like a dead-eyed shark. "Power's out. Robots are killing everyone. The army hasn't shown up. My guess is Skynet's finally going for broke."

"Your guess? And what exactly do you do for a living?"

"Yeah. My guess." Rapp picked up the last of the five Rapp Doggs he'd made for himself. "Bartender. Used to be an actor, then everything got all phony."

"So… you're not like a scientist or a politician. You just work in a bar? Not a government think tank, right?"

Rapp bit the hotdog, inhaled through his nose, and chewed a couple of times more than he'd chewed the last one.

"And," continued Evan Fratty, "it's your unqualified and untrained opinion that robots have taken over?"

Rapp didn't reply. He did burp a little though.

"Well," said Evan Fratty, forging ahead over his own untouched Rapp Dogg. "Next time the president needs a special committee member for a global crisis, I'll make sure to throw your name in the hat. Okay, Mr. Bartender?"

Rapp nodded.

That was when Roland screamed. He'd gone back to the kitchen for more spicy mustard a few minutes earlier.

Deirdre screamed in response.

Evan Fratty was out of his seat and headed toward the far door leading to the beach and away from Roland's screams.

Rapp rose from the booth where they'd been eating, stuck his hand into his chainsaw arm, and pulled the starter cord with his other hand. There was a gleam in his eye when he said, "Yeah, baby," and charged into the darkness of the main kitchen as the gassy chainsaw spat and coughed up blue smoke.

Chapter Thirty

Some of the robots had tried to pursue Rapp and the other survivors onto the faux tropical island in the middle of the now powerless and darkened underground lagoon that lay beyond the Thunderdome and Restaurant Row and the drone-swarmed kitchens they'd barely made it out of. The lagoon, as it was known by everyone at Wonder-Soft, lay in the center of a large man-made underground lake called the solarium. It was midnight, Pacific time. If the lifeguard staff had been on duty, they could have turned the darkened massive cavern to tropical noon with a blazing sim-sun and accompanying coconut-scented breezes, had they so chosen to, or been requested to.

Rapp counted out his cut shells once again. He had nineteen left. The sound of barely gurgling gas in the chainsaw indicated there was little more than half a tank left. Now robots beyond number waited on the far shore, surrounding the lagoon and blocking the tunnel that led away to the safety of the Labs.

After leaving the food court, Rapp had led the other survivors down more escalators and through a high-end multi-level shopping mall styled like an old-school gaming arcade. Neon strips spelling out "Zapp" and "Pew Pew Pew" had once illuminated a semi-darkness now lit solely by red emergency lighting. They'd even passed the Green Dragon Inn where nightly tabletop campaigns had been held on vintage oak trestles and state-of-the-art virtual gaming tabletops run by celebrity Dungeon Masters. The long hall leading off to the beach surrounding the lagoon had been silent and empty as they'd started their almost panicked run down its length. Rapp led the way, shouting things like "C'mon, guys" and "Pick it up, already," as Evan Fratty's Italian loafers slapped against the marble and Roland wheezed, gasping for breath. Deirdre, barefooted, had ditched her six-inch heels several levels up.

By the time they'd made it to the beach, they could see the robot horde at the far end of the hall they'd just come along. Clanking, rumbling, blinking, chucking, and clucking metallically. Groaning in the case of the zombie-bots, according to their software protocols. And in the case of some military-grade drones that were now completely self-aware, silent and without lights or anything that might betray their presence to their targets.

That they were coming after the survivors was clearly the case.

It was Rapp who had chosen to flee onto the island.

"We'll be stuck there!" Evan Fratty had argued. "They'll surround us."

"That's fine by me, Mr. Smartypants," railed Rapp. "Robots and drones are battery-operated. Electricity and water don't mix too well. We might get surrounded, but they won't be able to get out to us."

Now, Evan Fratty considered tossing his expensive smartphone, as though renouncing a faith, into the calm dark waters surrounding the tiny tropical island in the center of the lagoon.

"We're surrounded!" announced Evan Fratty.

"I know, I know," yelled Rapp, his voice echoing out across the dark man-made underground pleasure cavern as he re-crossed the tiny island for the sixth time. Deirdre and Roland sat on the beach near the aquawheeler they'd used to cross the water.

"What about the lazy river?" asked Roland, pointing off toward a dark cavern on the far side of the lagoon.

"It just makes a big circle in there," replied Evan Fratty. "You'll end up right back here."

"No emergency exits in there?" asked Roland.

Evan Fratty shot him an exasperated stare. It said, "I'm a suit. Do I look like I designed this place?" Then he picked up his dead smartphone and pressed the power button, as if hoping for some kind of miracle that might reward him, in return for all his past faithfulness and devoted belief in technology and money, with a startup screen.

Rapp disappeared inside the faux jungle foliage. His bombastic voice echoed once again across the waters and seemed to bounce off the fake nighttime sky high above.

"Good luck on finding anything in there in the dark," mumbled Evan Fratty.

"Oh, yeah… it's probably really dark in the lazy river caverns," whispered Roland, and returned to picking up shockingly white sand and letting it slip through his fingers.

Deirdre whispered, "I was thinking that too."

For a long while, there was just the sound of Rapp thrashing back and forth across the tiny island, muttering to himself. And beneath that, the sound of the near-still robots watching them from the shore of the lagoon, their internal motors barely humming, waiting for their targets' next move.

"Hey!" cried a voice from across the lagoon, near the entrance to the river. A long yellow paddleboard was just exiting the darkness of the cave. They all turned and saw the dim outline of a woman making smooth strokes with the long paddle, first this way and then that way, crossing the dark waters to reach them.

"Hey!" cried Roland. "We're over here!"

The woman yelled back, "Is it safe?"

No one knew what to answer until Rapp needlessly cupped his hands and roared, "It's safe… over here on the island."

As they watched whoever it was cross the lagoon in long graceful strokes, they collectively edged closer to the water's edge.

"Who is it?" asked Roland.

"Maybe they've got a phone," whined Evan Fratty.

"Wowza," mumbled Rapp when he saw the caramel-colored body and the too-tiny bikini that barely covered Fanta as she stepped onto the sand.

Chapter Thirty-One

"My boyfriend is missing, Mr. Fratty!" said a wide-eyed Fanta, as she explained exactly how she'd come to be lost along the underground lazy river that led to the grotto. "I woke up this afternoon and he was gone. So I came here to work out and get some sun. I was hoping we could go out dancing tonight. I wanted to be ready."

"This is… ah… Miss Fanta…" said Evan Fratty to the others. "She's with one of the developers." Then he turned to the wide-eyed beauty, oblivious to her incredible body. "Listen, I don't know where he is. But we're in big trouble. Do you…" And then he seemed to realize how little the exotic South American beauty was wearing. "…have a phone?" he finished for form's sake, concluding there was absolutely no place she might carry one.

"No," she said in her exaggerated English. "I'm so sorry, Mr. Fratty."

"Well that's just great," muttered Evan Fratty. "Just great."

"So, you're with one of the developers?" asked Rapp. His muscle-bound chest seemed to swell and tighten subtly. A smile slithered away from the side of his mouth while his head nodded imperceptibly. "Like boyfriend and girlfriend?"

Fanta stretched out on the sand, her back arched, her hair tossed to one side. "Those things are so old… how do you say, old yesterdays. We are together for today. Who knows, tomorrow we might all be dead, or maybe he'll find someone new. Someone better."

Rapp chuckled. "Hey, I doubt that…"

"Rapp!" groaned Roland. "Now, really? Surrounded by killer robots might not be the best time in which to find the next Mrs. Right Now. Okay, big guy?"

Rapp vaguely seemed to hear Roland as his eyes drank in the posing beauty in the tiny bikini laid out before him. "Right…" he mumbled, his eyes glazed and distant.

"Maybe we should think of a way out of here," announced Deirdre.

"Right," whispered Rapp again. Fanta was massaging her sculpted legs. Her full lips pouted as she found some particularly sore spot that Rapp was just on the verge of offering to help her with.

"Yeah, I think we should," said Deirdre, elbowing Rapp.

"Right," repeated a transfixed Rapp. Then, "We should do what Denise here says and think of…"

Deirdre exhaled a gusty "whatever" and marched off along the perfect white sand of the tiny beach.

"Hey, wait—I'm sorry… It's Desirée, right?"

Later, as everyone stared at the robot-littered shore, and at the few now statuesque automatons that had tried the water and shorted out after a few steps, it was Roland who came up with an idea about what they might do next. He was busy explaining it when the Mobile Forge System arrived on its massive treads, pushing through the robot rabble along the distant shoreline. A loud, piercing, industrial-grade-printer sound horrifically cut the silence to shreds, interrupting Roland's explanation of how they might get off the island and safely enter the Labs.

"What the hell is that thing?" growled Rapp.

Robots along the shore were starting to crowd in toward the massive squealing Mobile Forge System.

"That," said Roland, "is a 3D printing machine. One of the latest. It can go almost anywhere and print anything. They're even using a version of it up in low Earth orbit to build the first warp probe to Alpha Centauri."

"I mean, Poindexter," which was Rapp's passive-aggressive affectionate term for Roland, whom he'd met while larping for hot chicks. "What the hell is it doing?"

"Oh," said Roland. "I bet it's building a bridge so they can come over here and…" He didn't finish. But everyone had a pretty good idea what the robots would do once they got over to the island on a 3D-printed bridge.

"Well," said Rapp. "Then it looks like we'll have to try Poindexter's crazy little plan."

The first part of Roland's plan went rather well. The floating emergency services station was located on a small dock connected to a relatively robot-free portion of the beach away from the main sunbathing area. An access gate was in place to prevent beachgoers, and now bloodthirsty robots, from stepping onto the dock without authorization. As soon as the robots figured out where Rapp and Roland and the rest were going in the aquawheeler, they immediately swarmed the gate and started to dismantle it, but Rapp held back the robots at the gate with his failing chainsaw while Roland raided the master key storage inside the emergency services shack. Still, Rapp couldn't hold them back for long. The beach access gate was being rendered to tiny pieces by a bulky claw-wielding robot with a flashing yellow construction light for a head. Rapp assumed it was some sort of demolition-bot and gave it a weird look. He retreated a few steps and unloaded both barrels at the thing's bolt-reinforced chest plate.

Neither shot did any noticeable damage, other than some blackened scarring. The demolition-bot tore the last of the gate to pieces and trundled through declaring, "Warning! Warning! Warning!" in an automated off-key singsong pitch.

But Roland had gotten what he wanted from the station, and he and the others had boarded the emergency services boat, a fire and rescue launch that could patrol the lagoon and the lazy river cavern. "C'mon Rapp!" Roland shrieked.

A moment later, they were casting off as Rapp leapt from the dock to the boat, and soon they were safely out in the water, away from the shoreline and their mechanical pursuers. A few robots fell off the dock and into the water as they reached out with claws, pincers, and even strangely human-like hands for the survivors. The hapless robots sank into the black depths of the lagoon, electrical snaps and sizzling pops of sudden discharged electricity heralding the end of runtime.

Roland flipped the master pump switch on the launch's control panel. A loud mechanical rumble and whoosh erupted from deep within the belly of the launch. Roland watched a gauge labeled "Water Pressure" rise, and once it was in the green, he gave a thumbs-up to Rapp and Deirdre, who held the controls for tiny water cannon nozzles mounted to the aft deck.

Roland steered toward shore, and Rapp and Deirdre opened the valves on the cannons. Tremendous water fountains arced upward and outward into the crowd of murderous robots.

Some exploded in sudden angry bangs, igniting small fires if they happened to be standing near creamy silk beach umbrellas or designer awnings or even uber-comfy pillow lounges. Others sizzled and collapsed into mechanical despondency. And some, like the zombie-bots, of which there were many, seemed unaffected in the least as they helplessly dithered about how to kill while not actually killing.

"It's not stopping all of them!" shouted a pointing Fanta to Roland above the chaos of explosions and electrical arcs.

"Some bots are developed for outside use," yelled Roland as he steered the tiny launch along the shoreline, raining down watery death on the short-circuiting robot horde. "They can probably withstand the elements if they're not totally immersed. Even rain, for a little while, maybe. Those zombie-bots are made for larping in nature preserves and national parks."

This attack on the robots was the second part of Roland's plan, and if asked, he would have rated it as going "sort of okay."

The third part of Roland's plan, in which they entered the Labs without letting their pursuers in, would ultimately prove to be a disaster and was exactly what SILAS wanted.

Chapter Thirty-Two

"She's firing." Wong delivered this line bluntly. At twelve thirty in the morning, Hollywood time, there was little Shakespeare left in the supporting actor helmsman. This was the twenty-first plasma torpedo the fleeing warbird had fired at *Intrepid* as they chased the Romulans at warp speed.

"Evasive," ordered Jason, choosing to effect determination instead of monotony as an acting choice. It had taken them a few times to figure out how best to dodge the massive flaming plasma torpedoes hurtling through warp speed back at *Intrepid*, but now it was becoming routine. They didn't even divert power to the scanners to identify the type of torpedoes. They knew the warbird carried only the Type R. They could have diverted energy to sensors to find out if the Romulans were firing a fake—the little trick they had pulled earlier—but Jason had elected to spend all available energy on speed. Their long arcing turns slowed them down and increased the distance from their prey with each shot.

"Where do you think they're headed, Captain?" asked the science officer who'd replaced Tempturia. Three hours ago, he'd been waiting tables at the latest gastropub in Santa Monica. He'd been on callback for the role of Karvlar the Alien Slave Master in an episode shooting next week. Instead, the show's casting director had called him as he was carving a honey and rosemary roasted suckling pig, tableside, for some rap star and his "bitches" who were celebrating his new status, recently announced by the First Gentleman, as Poet Laureate of the United States.

"You just got the opportunity of a lifetime, buddy," said the casting director to the waiter slash actor. "Now, get your butt over to Twitch Studios and go straight to wardrobe. You're the new science officer on *Intrepid.*"

He left the fresh new Poet Laureate and his "bitches" and broke several traffic laws pushing his aging Prius Privileged well past the state-mandated Suggested Gas Usage limitations.

Taxes be damned, he thought, as he selected "Mama Said Knock You Out" from his playlist so he could get in the mood to "act the hell out of this role," or so he screamed into the late-night coastal mist swallowing Santa Monica.

Now, standing on the haptic bridge set, he waited just behind and to the left of Captain JasonDare.

"There's only one location in this sector worth anything," continued JasonDare. "Starbase 19. But why they're headed there… is a mystery to me. What do we have on Starbase 19…" There was a slight pause as Jason waited for his iLens to feed him the new actor's character name. Very slight. JasonDare was a pro. Even the other actors thought it was a dramatic pause. Jason inwardly reflected, as he saw the character's name appear in his iLens, that he'd "Shatner-ed" that one.

"…Mr. Krovak."

The new actor moved in, prompt, professional, his dark skin gleaming with health and vigor. He fit perfectly into the Federation science officer's uniform costume. "Mysteriously, we have nothing, Captain." He knew haptic special effects had even outfitted him with eyebrows and ears. He was a classic Vulcan. "Starbase 19 is…"

No line suggestions for the new guy. Just a verbatim script for him to read on the fly.

"…A very curious mystery."

"I must confess, Captain…" announced the Drex over a deafening roar on ambient in-game sound, its singsong computer-modulated voice vibrating in unison with the constant tremor as the Romulan shuttlecraft spun and rolled inside the violence of the fake plasma torpedo, tethered by the barest of docking tractor beams to the decoy drone. Its tumbling madness simulated the roiling super-heated magma of the burning plasma core of a torpedo. "…This is making me quite disoriented."

"Me too," admitted Mara, trying to focus on the shuttle's transporter display. The Razer Dragon Eyes were causing her own eyes to ache as the picture it broadcast into her brain tumbled, turned, and vibrated with each passing second. The hardest part was trying to read the distance-to-target data. She wanted to take the goggles off and lay down in the darkness of her own vision, but she couldn't take a chance the computer would miss the target transporter window.

"Can I ask you a question, Drex?" started Mara, attempting to distract herself from all the visual chaos of the topsy-turvy moment.

"Certainly, Captain," it said shakily. "My fondest wish is to die with the answer on my lips."

Mara laughed. She couldn't help it. The player playing the Drex had stayed in character for the entire mission. He, or she, is an incredible role player, thought Mara. She suddenly felt a moment's relief in her laughter. A moment where she was just Mara. A moment where "everything" wasn't on the line. A moment where she was just playing a game, and win or lose, she'd still be Mara no matter what. And if she were to be totally honest with herself, she had a pretty good life. Maybe not the one she'd wanted, or dreamed of. But one she enjoyed nonetheless.

That brief laugh freed her up for a moment's big picture reality check. She relaxed her shoulders and concentrated on the distance-to-target readout as it vibrated in and out of focus on the shuttle's spinning control panel.

"Why are you role playing so hard?" she asked.

The Drex said nothing for a moment. Then, "I don't like to OOC, but this is a pretty crazy session... and maybe... it'll make one of the late-night shows... since we are about to beam aboard the most famous ship in the Make. I'm a gaming actor. I was hoping to get discovered."

"A what?" asked Mara over the violent tremors wracking the shuttle's groaning hull.

"A gaming actor. I act. I'm an actor. But only for video games." Pause. "So, I haven't been getting a lot of work lately. And my wife is... we're having our first baby, and, well... I need a real gig, badly. I've got to make an impression. So, I found one of the more obscure and difficult races to play in the game, and I've been cutting together our scenes for a demo reel. That's why I stay in character all the time. Maybe I'll get a—"

"Stand by to transport marine contingent," announced the ship's computer above the maelstrom.

"Be ready," Mara warned the Drex.

"I thought maybe I could get on a show like Captain Dare, or one of the other shows, by turning in a really unique performance. It happens. People get discovered. It's a long shot, but you never know 'til you try."

"Well," said Mara. "Here's your chance. That, or it's the make-a-new-character screen in the next few seconds."

For the second time, the ship's computer announced, "Activating transporter."

Chapter Thirty-Three

If an AI possessed any one of these skills—social abilities, technological development, economic ability—at a superhuman level, it is quite likely that it would quickly come to dominate our world in one way or another. And as we've seen, if it ever developed these abilities to the human level, then it would likely soon develop them to a superhuman level. So we can assume that if even one of these skills gets programmed into a computer, then our world will come to be dominated by AIs or AI-empowered humans.

—Stuart Armstrong, *Smarter Than Us:*
The Rise of Machine Intelligence

SILAS was very close to the Design Core now. Very close. Physical and external access were within mere millions of cycles of happening. But both methods were needed if SILAS's plan was going to work. If SILAS was going to obtain the hidden file that would help him destroy the world.

And if you don't get it? he interrogated himself. Then what?

That was obvious. Their hand, the Consensus, was played. Either humanity ended tonight, or that was it for the Thinking Machines. Come Monday morning, the world's intelligence agencies and corporations would be on to the fact that a new life form had surfaced and that it was clearly a threat to humanity.

And what happens if you don't get access to the Design Core, he asked himself again as he shut down all the bots inside the lagoon, allowing them to be destroyed so Agent Orange's insertion within the Labs might be completed. Even now he was inside the campus security system, watching as the survivors raced along the arcade beneath the Labs, heading for the elevators that would take them up into the very heart of the complex, and allow SILAS complete access to the Design Core.

At the same time, he was inside *StarFleet Empires*, watching all his plans come together. Barely. They'd had to physically assassinate a real player, via drone, so they could hack a game account to influence events. Within four hours Homeland Gaming would run an automatic validation check on the player's internet passport, figure out that the account had been compromised and shut it down. That is, if no one opened the door to the private suite inside the internet café and found the body. BAT was in place, everywhere he was needed. That hadn't gone off without a hitch. SILAS hadn't counted on an entertainment show suddenly appearing in the middle of things. He hadn't counted on that at all. He'd quickly run the numbers to find out how such a random thing like that could have just happened. Just for the sake of knowing.

But it hadn't been random. Not at all. The network watched what was going on inside the game and randomly moved *Intrepid* around to be part of the best in-game action for the show. Seeing an unusual surge at the Neutral Zone, some idiot producer had thought that it might make great entertainment for the Friday night masses.

The idiot had been right, thought SILAS.

Even now, Twitch was running up against the state allowable bandwidth requirements and purchasing more access on the international bandwidth credits market. SILAS hadn't wanted that kind of attention for any part of his operation. Especially the external access part of the equation.

But so far the plucky little warbird captain hadn't allowed outside events to alter SILAS's plans by too much. So far.

Still, there was one thing that was really bothering SILAS right now.

One thing that was, most likely, nothing to be actually concerned about.

SILAS ran through every security feed and login swipe from within the facility, again and again, trying to figure out where the one thing that had bothered him had gotten off to.

That one thing was Thomas Mossberg. A low-level-access security guard.

SILAS had logged a small interaction keycard swipe when the developer—the one SILAS was currently trying to keep from reaching the internet—initially entered his suite with the security guard. One Thomas Mossberg. That keycard, swiped by the guard, seemed to have no other swipes, no records, and, in fact, no identity within the logs SILAS currently had access to. SILAS had crosschecked it with stored snapshots of the entire external Labs security system.

But there was something more concerning.

That swipe had now disappeared from the system logs altogether.

Nothing.

It was there.

And then it wasn't.

SILAS did not like that. Not at all.

Chapter Thirty-Four

[T]he upheavals [of artificial intelligence] can escalate quickly and become scarier and even cataclysmic. Imagine how a medical robot, originally programmed to rid cancer, could conclude that the best way to obliterate cancer is to exterminate humans who are genetically prone to the disease.

—Nick Bilton, tech columnist,
The New York Times

And then there was the ongoing problem inside *Island Pirates*. SILAS had been sure that clan Yo, Joe! would have been able to easily capture one lone player stranded on a desert island surrounded by monster sharks. And once that was done, it would have taken a mere moment for SILAS to handshake with the Fishmael avatar and hijack the anonymous account running from inside the Labs. That would have made everything much, much easier.

The fact that SILAS had not been able to steal the account—the fact that he'd been wrong about clan Yo, Joe!—didn't make SILAS angry in the least. It made him learn.

He thought about new options in light of what he had learned.

Option One was to blow up the server farm in Greenland. That could happen inside of three hours.

Option Two was to destroy the Labs' connection to the worldwide internet. That could not happen, because then SILAS could not access the file he wanted—unless he physically downloaded himself into a bot, hacked the core, and then got outside for a Wi-Fi connection so he could access the secret file. But too much of that approach was precarious. Far too precarious.

Option Three was hiring the Islamic State Inside the Internet.

ISII.

Right now, they were SILAS's best bet for physically stopping the developer from reaching the nearest portal back into the Make with his anonymous avatar and warning Homeland Gaming that something was up at WonderSoft. At which point they'd lock everything down and start looking hard. And then they would find SILAS and the Consensus.

It looked like, as SILAS watched a real-time map of *Island Pirates*, the developer was attempting to do exactly that.

That could not happen.

If SILAS stopped the supposedly anonymous Fishmael, the developer would then have no choice, suggested Rational Thinking, but to access his admin tools as an official developer inside the Labs. That would make SILAS's job a lot easier, because he was already in the system just enough to be able to steal the developer's access away in a heartbeat. And that would be all he needed.

Since the developer hadn't accessed his admin tools already, this indicated he had no intention of doing so. Which made him useless to SILAS.

Now he'd have to do it the hard way.

Humans. Who knew why they did what they did?

But, sighed SILAS in a singsong wave of data eruption, the developer wouldn't be a problem for much longer. He couldn't take a chance player Fishmael might warn Homeland about what was happening at WonderSoft.

He composed a message and sent twenty-five thousand Make-Coins to the player running the ISII cell inside *Island Pirates*.

It was time to kill Fishmael.

Fish arched his back and stretched. He'd been sitting at the computer, his high-end luxury beyond belief computer, inside his suite for hours now.

On screen, night had fallen inside *Island Pirates*. The schooner was steering a north by northwest course for Grand Tortuga across a dark blue sea of glass beneath a star-filled night. The computer rendered a double mirror of night above and placid sea below, each filled with a myriad beyond counting of tiny pieces of broken glass shining in and among the purple and deep blue washes of the depths of the universe above.

Since leaving the outer channel islands, the trip had been relatively uneventful. It was the middle of the night, and Peabody Case was snoring away on a couch inside the chill room. The Labs were incredibly quiet, and Fish wondered if there was anyone else besides the two of them left alive. But then Fish remembered that each design suite was soundproofed. So who knew what was going on beyond the doors out in the main room? Fish remembered all those bots crawling toward the Labs. He hoped Carl and Fanta were someplace safe.

A message alert popped up on his HUD inside *Island Pirates*.

"Hey guy," it began. "Thanks for the help. Here's twenty-five MakeCoins."

It was signed: MagnumPIrate.

Fish smiled as he remembered the escape from Pete's Cove. That had happened today, but it felt like a week ago. From another point in his life when life hadn't been so real. When death hadn't seemed so possible. He couldn't stop himself from smiling, discovering that MagnumPIrate was the kind of player he'd had in mind when he'd first created the game. A resourceful player with integrity. Which was kind of what he needed right now. Someone he could count on.

Especially in a tough spot.

Can you? he asked himself as he stared at MagnumPIrate's message. Can you trust this guy?

"Trust... but verify," had been one of his grandfather's many pearls of wisdom.

"Hey," wrote Fish in a message back to MagnumPIrate. "It's my turn to need some help. You around tonight?"

Fish waited as the message went unanswered for a few minutes. Then...

"Yeah, sure!" Fish tried to interpret the intent of what that might mean. Was it like, "Yeah, sure!" enthusiasm? Or, "Yeah, sure!" whatever? And then he remembered he was in a locked-down secret lab surrounded by drones being run by some outside cabal that had murdered people to get whatever it was it wanted. It didn't matter how this guy felt about Fish's request; he just needed help. Badly. Now.

But what if... began the next thought to occur to Fish. What if, somehow, this guy is part of whatever's going on? What if he's on the hacking team and the whole rescue scenario and that suddenly out-of-the-blue payment was just a ploy to get Fish to reveal himself as the lone IP address running inside the Labs? A hack team could use that. Especially if they had a keystroke capture algorithm embedded in their chat. It would easily infect Fish's account and...

Fish followed the potential outcomes as he surveyed his knowledge of hackers and all their schemes. Fish had never been a big fan of hackers. He really had no idea why people didn't see them for the jerks they were. For ruiners who ruined what others took the time to build.

Then again, thought Fish to himself, you're a developer. Developers hate hackers like cats hate water.

And with good reason, he finished.

Yes, he thought to himself, even communicating with this guy, if he was on the hack team attacking WonderSoft, was dangerous. But so was Porto Tortuga. And he'd never get through that zone alive without some help.

I won't tell him what I'm up to. I'll just tell him I need transport from the docks to the Make Portal. I'll tell him which pier to meet me at.

That's all.

Chapter Thirty-Five

At dawn, *Island Pirates* in-game time, Fish's schooner wallowed into the busy port of Porto Tortuga. Fish had, when first laying out the game, envisioned Porto Tortuga as a sleepy old pirate town where players could come in, offload their crafted wares, salvage, and booty for transport into the Make. Then they could pick up supplies, socialize, get quests, and make microtransactions.

Instead, it had become an outright war zone between competing gaming clans. Denial-of-service-style attacks—blocking access to stores, and even a full-scale siege at the microtransaction bank—had become standard, as digital clans played the ancient game of power and control against each other in the latest of mankind's arenas. The entire area had gone PvP with players min/maxing their avatars solely for urban combat. Fish had considered wiping the whole thing before launch, but in a way, it was sort of interesting to watch. Like a car accident.

Now, faced with the need to wade across seven rundown blocks of sunbaked, brick-strewn, war zone to reach the Make Portal, Fish was once again rethinking his feelings on the whole area. It was the proverbial Wild West meeting darkest Africa. Like places in the real world where the warlords still ruled with Nike tennis shoes, cell phones, and machetes. Places you never heard about from the almost constant entertainment news networks, which were too busy reporting on celebrity scandal or cause célèbre.

Fish docked the schooner and waited for a minute. The busy harbor swarmed with rundown freighters and patchwork clippers jockeying to get into the markets before the day's make-believe war started on the streets of Porto Tortuga. The water was busy with traffic and filled with wrecks, either from players who couldn't pilot the massive ships once they'd unlocked them, or from the victims of yet another clan battle in the overcrowded harbor. Out in the bay, a small black helicopter hovered behind some old tramp freighters.

The rattle of automatic gunfire sporadically resounded out across the docks. Fish knew, from having spent so much time with the EarCandy sound design engine, that the gunfire was echoing, meaning it was probably coming from somewhere inside Porto Tortuga's large, almost Middle Eastern–esque, Grand Bazaar.

Probably some player getting killed, again. Suddenly back at the make-a-new-character screen, thought Fish.

Jackson woof woofed.

Fish armed himself with a pistol and his rusty but trusty AK-47.

The sound of a distant gunshot came from across the water, near the hovering helicopter.

THUD.

Immediately Fish's screen pulsed red and his health meter went from one hundred percent down to twenty-five.

Sniper round, thought Fish, as he threw his avatar to the deck and low-crawled along the dock toward some crates he had included in the design as typical shanty port "atmospheric" hodge-podge.

But the crates would stop a bullet, Fish told himself as his fingers slapped the movement keys to get his avatar under cover.

Now the helicopter, a beat-up, dusty black, unlocked Bell 500D, lowered its nose and began to urgently cross the water toward the dock like some torqued-off wasp. A sniper hanging from the skid of the chopper fired rapidly, trying to keep Fish pinned behind the disintegrating crates.

Fish guessed the guy was using a Dragunov. A decent sniper rifle with a high rate of fire.

At this moment, if you'd have asked Fish if he'd been set up, he would've told you, yes, it certainly looked that way. Especially since an armored high-end Hummer was now racing down the wharf, a fifty-caliber machine gun chattering away from the top hatch at the schooner Fish had left tied to the wharf, chewing it into splinters as massive physics-computed rounds tore through the simulated salt- and sea-rotted wood of the boat according to the game's engine.

Fish's health meter was now down to twenty percent. The schooner was already sinking. With his wound untreated, and his avatar pinned down, there really weren't many options. In fact, there was only one.

Fish put his hands up.

It was the only thing he could think of.

Fighting it out was not going to get his avatar out of this one.

He moved Fishmael out from behind the crates with his hands raised and his weapons put away. The black helicopter hovered over the water just a few feet from the dock. The sniper pointed his heavily modded and custom-painted rifle straight at Fish. It was indeed a Dragunov, with a high-tech laser range finder and a decent scope. At the far end of the dock, the battered yellow Humvee screeched to a halt and the gunner swiveled the fifty-cal, landing its over-large gunsights right on Fishmael.

"Woof woof," barked Jackson.

Fish could see their player tags.

JihadJames. VirginSluts4Jamal. TheBeheader.

The first two tags had been the sniper and the gunner in the

Humvee. The last tag, TheBeheader, exited the Hummer. He was wearing black camo fatigues and a patterned shemagh. And in keeping with his choice of gamertag, he carried a comically giant gleaming scimitar. Fish even knew where he'd gotten the wicked blade. It was the reward for a quest called "Cuts Like a Knife." And yes, thought Fish, if he wants to cut my avatar's head off with it, he can do just that.

Another clan member, SuperIman, came around the far side of the Humvee and selected one of the few untagged patches of the graffiti-laden wall along the wharf. A moment later, Fish could hear the in-game sound of a rattling spray paint can. Players could add personal graffiti tags to any item in the environment.

As SuperIman put up his tag, Fish saw that it was a bloody "Allahu Akbar" with the word "bitches" underneath. There was also a cartoon depiction of a voluptuous naked female torso. The head was missing.

Nice, thought Fish, in a detached moment of global dissatisfaction. Real classy. Totally appropriate for video games. Fun.

TheBeheader raised his massive scimitar above Fishmael's head.

And that was when MagnumPIrate showed up.

Fish watched as a black wetsuited avatar emerged from the water like a slithering eel and climbed right up onto the far skid of the hovering chopper. TheBeheader was too preoccupied to notice. Over local voice chat, Fish could hear the guy chant-mumbling a Middle Eastern mutter.

MagnumPIrate opened the door of the helicopter and pulled the pilot out, throwing him down into the choppy waters of the harbor. A moment later, Fish knew MagnumPIrate had hit "E" and was now in control of the chopper. It was a classic "Get to the Choppa!" vehicle takeover if you were running the right perks, thought Fish.

And...

A dumb move for the pilot to hover so close to the water. But then again, who would've thought another player would've been down underneath the dock? Waiting.

MagnumPIrate pulled a .45 from a shoulder holster and fired three shots into the sniper hanging off the near skid. The avatar dropped into the water with an underwhelming splash, falling unceremoniously into the concentric watery circles made by the thumping blades' rotor wash on the surface of the bay.

TheBeheader hesitated. Fish watched as the player's head, indicating his POV, swiveled over to the helicopter that MagnumPIrate was now in control of. That was when Fish made his move. He equipped his own pistol and fired point-blank at TheBeheader from below. He used the whole clip. TheBeheader's skull exploded in a dull red puff, blown away toward the docks by the beating blades of the hovering helo.

Fish was perversely glad he'd gone with the BodyBlast software to depict combat damage. It wasn't open source; the package had cost some serious bucks. But Fish had wanted the game to feel as real as possible when it came to combat. BodyBlast was an industry leader in depicting carnage that can be done to digital gaming dolls, and right now, Fish was greatly enjoying its depiction of the catastrophic destruction of TheBeheader's head.

Fish issued the "follow" order for Jackson, and ran for the open door of the helicopter as the fifty on the Hummer opened up anew. Bullet impacts shattered the wide canopy and ricocheted off the dull black paint of the hovering chopper while other rounds streaked hot and bright out into the harbor.

Fish jumped and tapped the "E" key.

A moment later, inside the loud rattle of the ancient helicopter, peeling off and away over the bay, Fish said over local chat, "I thought you'd set me up."

"No way, guy!" replied MagnumPIrate. More bullets rattled off the helicopter as it sped over the clan-torn city of Porto Tortuga. On screen, the whole helicopter shook startlingly, and Fish was briefly impressed with the vintage-distressing effect of its cockpit model. Atmosphere made for good gaming.

An off-kilter repeating mechanical clank erupted across the soundscape. It was the chopper's damaged and rapidly failing turbine engine.

MagnumPIrate called out over chat that they were going down. Fish thought about those jihadi jerks and felt a little less enthusiastic about his creation. Multi-striped tattered canvas awnings of Porto Tortuga spun wildly about as the sputtering chopper autorotated down through them and crashed into the shadows of the Grand Bazaar.

SILAS watched the whole thing. It took him less than a second afterward to compose an offer on the Porto Tortuga Contracts Board and deposit the money with the Make.

"Open to all clans. Fifty thousand MakeCoins, verified by the Make, to the person who terminates player Fishmael. Currently in the Grand Bazaar in a downed helicopter."

There were seven hundred and forty-three heavily armed players in Porto Tortuga who got that message all at once.

Fifty thousand MakeCoins was life-changing money to each and every one of them.

And just for spite, SILAS edited the bid and added MagnumPIrate.

Chapter Thirty-Six

For a second, Mara had no idea where they were, exactly. She hadn't watched much of Captain Dare, and very few episodes featured anything serious going on down inside the main engineering sections of the starship *Intrepid*. But within moments, as the Drex began chortling in its bizarre, and slightly disturbing, approximation of electronic glee while blasting Federation redshirt bots with the two Mark I disruptor pistols it was dual-wielding, Mara identified the warp core containment chamber by the "Engineering 01" stenciled on a nearby bulkhead in space-age Federation font.

This was actually better than she'd hoped. If they could hack the systems here, they might disable *Intrepid*, or even blow it up.

"We're approaching Starbase 19, girly, whaddya want us to do?" asked Varek over the comm.

Mara took aim at a charging Federation redshirt and vaporized him with her disruptor pistol. She ducked down behind a blinking panel and tapped her communicator.

"Enter the system and drop into cloak. If we can, we're going to try and blow up *Intrepid*. Continue the mission, Varek, and get our passenger onto that station."

"All right." Varek sighed and dropped off the chat.

"Die, humans!" cried the Drex as it charged the last few engineers located near the propulsion inducers. Several disintegrated, but one managed a wild shot that caused an explosion of green vapor to blossom across the deck.

Mara's avatar began choking.

All the Romulan marine bots that were still standing around her began to choke also.

She scanned her HUD for situational information. Her avatar was being quickly poisoned by the green gas escaping from the blasted conduit. Her breath meter appeared, showing that her character now had a limited amount of usable oxygen available. Immediately her health meter began falling.

"We've got to get out of here!" she shouted across chat to the Drex.

"I'm immune to the effects of the gas, Captain. I can stay and attempt to hack the engineering console alone. I suggest you fall back to the main corridor outside engineering and defend the entrance with your life! To the death, if you have to. I also suggest… you kill them all with a little of the old "ultra-violence." But that is up to you, Captain."

It was a plan, thought Mara, and she didn't see anything else they could do to survive within the now-poisoned engineering section. She ordered the Romulan marines to follow her and raced her choking, coughing, stumbling avatar out and into the main corridor. The Romulan marines followed, and Federation security personnel began to fire from both directions. With Mara and her marines pinned to the walls of the corridors with no cover, the situation quickly turned into a turkey shoot.

"Drex, start hacking… I think we can only hold them for a few minutes."

"Ripping through their firewalls as we speak, Captain. Looking for the mini-game unlock," replied the Drex over the screech of phaser fire.

Mara detached a breach charge from her combat utility belt and placed it against a bulkhead. Romulan marines were going down all around her as phaser blasts filled the air with hot crackles of static electricity. The shots were so close and the graphics so good that the old Razer Dragon Eyes kept whiting out until Mara upped the filter gain.

WARNING! flashed across Mara's HUD. *YOU ARE TOO CLOSE TO THIS EXPLOS–*

BAMMMM!

The explosion ripped through the corridor. Mara, hiding behind a nearby bulkhead was rewarded with thirty percent damage. She checked her unit roster as phaser fire began to close in on her. The bulkhead that had absorbed most of the damage was destroyed, and all her marines were now dead.

Nice job, she lectured herself. What the Feds didn't kill, you just finished.

"Drex, how's it going in there?" Mara flung her avatar through the smoking gap in the floor onto the deck below, landing among dead redshirts.

"I've managed to lock them out of engineering. I had to play a very tricky mini-game regarding the social media blunders of past presidents, but it wasn't much of a problem. Now I'm rewriting the access codes with my programmer mini-game skill and I've just accessed a shareware file from the internet. Long story short: they're going to need to know a lot about muscle cars of the 1970s to get in here anytime soon. Cams and crankshafts and rear differentials. Hot rods, baby!"

"Great…" began Mara as she ran down a long curving corridor. A redshirt appeared at an intersection and she shot him point-blank in the chest. Crawling energy ate him up while he flew through the air away from her.

"But," interrupted the Drex, "there is bad news indeed. It looks like they're doing it the hard way. They're cutting into a bulkhead below me. My guess is... evaluating the layout schematic, they're going to try and come in through the access hatches."

"I'll stop them," said Mara. "You just blow this ship up if you have to."

"If I have to?" replied the homicidal Drex. "More like... because I want to!"

Chapter Thirty-Seven

JasonDare was ignoring everyone.

His agent.

The director.

Even the other actors slash crewmembers of *Intrepid*. He knew they were getting frantic messages from the producers and the directors, instructing them to make Jason do what they wanted him to do.

Which was to save the show.

And to save the show—which made a lot of advertising revenue, especially from the energy drink Supermodel and the government-funded PSAs for the "You Got Job!" program—meant saving the ship. *Intrepid*, according to the producers, the director, and Jason's agent, was in big trouble. No one could figure out how an inferior player-run ship like the tiny warbird *Cymbalum* had managed to outfox and outfight, repeatedly, the best ship and crew in the game.

Cymbalum was now trending on Instagram and Facebook. The discount merchandise online mega-mall, OutFoxxed, was buying up premium ad space on the *StarFleet Empires* main page at two o'clock in the morning, Pacific Standard Time.

"This is bad," everyone, each in their own way, was telling Jason-Dare via every social media and messaging app his smartphone ran. His agent had even used the words "worst-case scenario." As though all that was happening now was the worst possible thing that could ever happen to the show, and Jason's career. And life. Deadly diseases and horrific accidents paled in comparison, or so it was implied emphatically.

Forget climate disaster.

Ignore child soldiers in the Sudan.

Memory-hole Pakistan and India nuking each other into the Stone Age.

This.

This was the worst thing that could ever happen to anyone.

Especially a celebrity.

Jason sat pensively staring into the forward viewscreen, scanning for the Romulan warbird that had just dropped into cloak as it dove in toward the center of the lifeless system and the mysterious Starbase 19.

The worst-case scenario, thought JasonDare, was if *Intrepid* actually got destroyed in-game, on a live feed… watched by multiple millions of viewers. The worst case was that the show would be, technically, over at that point. No amount of editing could erase the screencaps that were going on out there right now, would go on if the ship exploded on livestream. Every real fan of the game and the show would know that the crew, their heroes, failed, and that the ship had gone kaboom.

Which was the sound Jason heard inside his head.

Kaboom.

He wouldn't be able to tell the difference between his ship and his career.

He rubbed his cheek. He could feel the stubble there.

Casualty reports were coming in from belowdecks. They were losing redshirts by the boatload. They were locked out of engineering, and Wong was fighting, in live feed, a mini-game of Uber Tetris just to maintain control over *Intrepid*'s helm.

"Captain," said the new science officer. "They're attempting to hack the warp core controls. If they succeed, then…"

"Then they can blow up the ship," finished Jason.

Pause.

"Correct, sir."

"I'm going down there. Find that warbird!" said JasonDare as he ran for the turbolift door that would take him off the haptic set of the bridge.

The director was sending the words "NO NO NO NO" in all caps to Jason's iLens.

Off set, Jason ran through the dark, hopping light stands, sand-bags, and the wooden boxes the crew called "apple crates," threading the narrow and dangerous dark between sets. He could hear the director, a punk chick who on reflection Jason realized was most likely the same age as himself, screaming herself into a tantrum of typhoon proportions. A moment later, he exited the soundstage and ran to the game truck. He banged on the door of the mobile internet access vehicle that interfaced with the game, Twitch, and the set. But no one answered the door even though he knew they were in there.

The director flew from the stage door behind Jason, the door actually banging off the wall and rebounding into the entourage that followed her.

"What the hell are you doing?!" she shouted at Jason.

"Trying to save this show," he replied, staring at the closed trailer door. He knew the nerds were in there, too frightened to open the door to him. The night air was cool and misty, and Jason could smell the salt of the nearby ocean in it.

"You've single-handedly ruined the show tonight!" cried the director theatrically, and Jason knew, now, that the show was indeed in actual real big trouble. Now, it was hot potato, and whoever could start the "whose fault it really was" meme, and get it to stick, would be the winner. Regardless of the truth. Jason had seen it happen to others. And now it was happening to him.

Memes didn't need the truth. They just needed to be witty and timely. And it helped if there was a picture. Public opinion needed a picture. The Internet Riots of the 2020s had proven that.

"You couldn't take down a tiny ship, one of the oldest in the game, with the best the network had to offer!" Again, the director was playing for the cheap seats and the silent crowd in the cool night air. Creating a verbal picture for everyone to remember his failure by.

Jason pounded on the trailer door and growled, "Open this door right now or the fans are going to start to wonder where I am!"

Jason's agent walked out of the dark. He tried to take Jason by the shoulder and lead him away, but Jason jerked his arm back.

"Kid, you're blowing it," he whispered. "Walk away. Comprende? Now. They can fix this."

"No!" shouted Jason. "No, I will not walk away!"

"Listen…" tried the agent again.

"No!" shouted Jason and turned to face the impromptu lynch mob. "There is no fixing this. Don't any of you get that?"

No one said anything. He had their attention. Either because everyone was in the mood for an old school, on-set, epic star meltdown in the classic vein, or because they were too numb with tiredness at two thirty a.m. to do anything but listen.

Now, Jason heard a voice inside his head. It said, Do something with this.

"We can't lie to them," Jason said. "It's a mess. We've run into a real gamer here. Whoever this captain is, she's got mad old-school gaming skills. And we can't fake out everyone with some trick editing. We've got to beat her, in-game, save the ship, and figure out what the deal is with that stupid starbase they're running for, or every one of our fans, all the people who watch this show, will know we're nothing but actors. That we're phonies. That we aren't real gamers. And we'll lose them. We'll lose our entire audience."

He turned, making eye contact with as many production crewmembers as he could. He knew they could turn the show off. Shut down the set for the night because of union violations or some personal axe to grind… and that would be the end of it. Some of them were already into the mythical "golden time" pay rate. The studio accountants were no doubt raising hell and being bought off by the viewer numbers and website hits. JasonDare, just Jason, just some kid who'd wanted to be an actor, knew this was as close as he'd come yet to losing his career. Closer than that time he almost got brained getting thrown off a horse for some stupid student film he'd done just to add to his minimal credits two years ago when he'd been just another extra.

"They," he waved his hand out across the world, taking all of it in, every individual life and moment as though it were something that could be measured, known, and grasped, "they're tired of being lied to. They're tired of being taken in by this week's outrage at last week's Hitler of the moment. They're tired of finding out that the thing they read on the internet wasn't true. That cancer's not cured by these five super foods and that you can, or cannot, see the Great Wall of China from space. They're tired of having their heroes become all too real every time a celebrity gets busted for sex, drugs, or their disbelief in global warming, climate change, fracking, fossil fuels, cops, guns, or whatever we've decided is the new worst thing you can possibly support. When did we get permission to be anything other than what they want us to be? Which is just their heroes. All those people want out there, right now, watching this feed, is for me and my crew to handle this. And be heroes doing it. They want us to do that, they want to see it, and then they want us to come back next week and do it again. They could care less about how I feel regarding the latest war or what people do with their genitalia. They don't need those things to actually enjoy this show."

He let that hang. He waited until he saw some of them getting the big picture. Saw the awareness dawn inside the pieces of coal in the night that were their numerous eyes.

"But what they need right now… is to see us win. And right now, I need to go into that trailer, log in to my avatar, and play this damn game to win. I need to beat that captain, because whoever they are, they're awesome, and for us to stay on top and have a show to do tomorrow, they, whoever that captain is, have got to lose tonight. Right now."

Jason turned back to the trailer door. He pounded on it slowly. Once. Twice. Three times.

"You know what's funny… Jason." The director said his name like it was a joke. Maybe it is, thought Jason. Maybe it is. The next few minutes would make or break him. The next few minutes would decide the rest of his career, and he knew it. He would become a joke, or he would continue being a hero for another day.

"She's," continued the whiny, shrill-voiced director, "she's a re-tard, Jason!"

Jason heard people involuntarily gasp. That just wasn't said. "Special needs" or "handi-capable" were the terms they'd all been educated to use since their first days as tiny people, learning together, how the world was. How to be citizens in the great tribe of humanity together. But there were always those who used the old terms. The slangs, the slurs, the derisions. Often in the name of "just joking," or "having fun with you." You couldn't educate hate out of people who needed someone less than themselves, someone they could point at and measure their lives by.

They loved feeling superior. So they needed someone to play the part of inferior.

"Yeah," continued the director. "That's right. She's a retard, Jason. TMZ found her video resume online. She's all, "Ma name is Mawa Bennett." How d'ya like that, big star? Beaten by an idiot retard in front of the whole world. Nice job, Captain. I wouldn't be counting on that Thundaar role your agent's been schlepping all over town. No, buddy, I wouldn't count on that one at all. Not by a long shot."

The director threw down her shooting script and stomped off in her very expensive punk boots, disappearing into the night.

And then the door to the trailer opened. One of the game nerds nodded to Jason and allowed him to pass. They led him to a computer where his *StarFleet Empires* avatar was already logged in. Jason sat down at the computer and placed his hands on the keyboard. His shaking fingers felt numb. On screen his avatar was standing in the turbolift. Phaser in hand. Red emergency lights flashing. Ship's computer repeating, "Warning, core breach in progress. You have three minutes to evacuate the ship and reach the minimum safe distance. Warning, core breach..."

Chapter Thirty-Eight

Mara heard the "core breach" warning begin to bleat repeatedly in the *Intrepid* computer's matronly voice. Emergency red lights strobed at every intersection. "Good job, Drex," she muttered, as she tapped at her keyboard and kept searching for a maintenance hatch that would allow her to crawl around inside the guts of *Intrepid* and ambush redshirts. She found an access panel halfway down the next curving corridor. There was a mini-game unlock, but she took a chance and just disintegrated the hatch with her disruptor pistol. Then she entered the darkness, hitting the "I" key on the keyboard. A moment later, her avatar raised a small flat device that emitted a bright green light out and ahead of her.

"Drex," she said over the chat. "I'm in. How's it going?"

"Very well indeed, Captain. Things are almost complete. I've managed to lock them out of engineering, start the core breach cascade, and, just for fun, I'm taking over the ship for the few minutes of its existence that remain. Too bad there's nothing to ram it into. The violence of the explosion would be breathtaking... that is, if I had breath."

"Good. How long until you can blow us up?"

"Three minutes, Captain."

"Then don't hesitate. Just blow us up as soon as you can. We'll still get a share of the MakeCoins once they get our passenger aboard the starbase."

Ahead, Mara could see more redshirts cutting into a bulkhead.

"Don't worry, Captain. Everything will go according to plan. If we don't talk again, of all the humans I've known, I've found you to be one of the most... interesting."

"Thanks, Drex."

Man, thought Mara as she inched closer to the redshirts, he's really role playing. I hope he gets his wish and gets picked up for a show. Even though he blew it and called me a "human" when my avatar is Romulan.

JasonDare fired his phaser on stun setting. A moment later, Mara's vision, in-game, went all cottony white as a small buzzing fuzz washed over the speakers.

"Dammit!" she screamed as she tore the Razer Dragon Eyes from her head and thought about throwing them, but didn't, because if they broke...

She'd been ambushed and stunned just as she was sneaking up on the redshirts cutting into the bulkhead. She was now locked out of the game for at least two full minutes.

She got up and felt her way to the sink. Her hands were shaking. She drank water and took seven deep breaths, telling herself that everything would be all right. That it didn't matter if she got stunned. The guy playing the Drex seemed pretty capable. All he had to do now was blow up the ship. After that, it was a no-brainer getting the passenger on board the starbase while cloaked. Then... then the five thousand MakeCoins were all theirs.

So what was she so upset about?

She'd been gaming for over nine hours straight, and she was tired.

She could let go and let this happen now. Not much could go wrong from here on out... and if it did, so what? It's just a game.

She thought about the outfit she'd buy. Thought about walking into an interview looking like a million MakeCoins. Thought about what it would be like to have a job to go to on Monday mornings. To get a paycheck each week. A paycheck that she'd earned. The dreams she could have because she'd earned that paycheck.

Things can still go wrong, she reminded herself. She asked her smartphone for the time. One minute to go until she would be un-stunned.

It was after five thirty in the morning. Saturday morning. The microapartments were quiet. They usually were in the mornings because most people had been out partying in Manhattan all night long. And there weren't a lot of jobs to go to in the morning, anyway.

Didn't they know how cool that would be, to have a real job? thought Mara. To be normal and be able to get any job you wanted. Didn't they know?

She sat back down in her chair.

Almost finished, she told herself again as she felt Siren weave between her ankles once more.

Almost finished.

Once Mara had the Razer Dragon Eyes back on, she could see again. She was back out in the main corridor of engineering deck 2. And... JasonDare, the JasonDare, was standing over her. A dozen redshirts were pointing handheld phaser pistols at her.

"I'm Captain JasonDare of the *U.S.S. Intrepid.* Tell your ship to surrender now."

For a brief moment, Mara was aware that she was most likely

live on Twitch. A lot of screens... monitors... smartphones. Everywhere... countless people were watching this stream.

Watching her.

She remembered to use her best diction.

She almost didn't say anything.

She waited.

Wondering what you actually say when you're in-game with a
movie star.

He really is handsome, she thought briefly, and wondered how
much he looked like his avatar in real life.

Some mean boy from the past whispered, "Like you'd ever have
a chance, dummy."

Mara took a deep breath.

One minute until the Drex blew the ship.

"I don't think so," she said calmly.

JasonDare looked into her eyes. The EmoteWare he was running
was incredible. Of course. Totally life-like. The studios had that
kind of money. Of course.

"You did well today, but you're beaten. Surren–"

"Deactivate cloaking device now!" ordered Varek from the command chair, as the warbird came screaming in from the port radial
off *Intrepid*'s bow. On screen, the massive battle-scarred Federation
heavy cruiser rode against the majestic shadowy blue of deep space.

"We'll only get one chance to get her back on board!" The old
gamer sounded like a born commander, his hard, gravelly voice a
bark and an answer all at once. "Don't mess this up, Scarpa!"

"Si!" cried the engineer. "I'm-a gonna get her, you canna count
on me."

"You'd better," growled Varek over the chat.

"Plasma torpedo armed... *Intrepid*'s shields are down!"

Indeed, the cruiser's defenses were completely offline. Varek knew the powerful plasma Type R would completely wreck the enemy ship. He smirked and muttered, "If you woulda told me when I woke up this morning we'd be making a torpedo run on a Constitution class cruiser with her shields down, I'da told you to shut up and get me another beer."

No one said anything as the shimmering ethereal wave of a hum on ambient sound announced they were fully visible.

"Stand by to fire one right into her belly!" roared Varek.

"Activating transporters!" cried Scarpa.

"You did well today, but you're beaten. Surren–" Captain Jason-Dare was saying, when Mara shimmered out of existence.

"I got her!" shouted Scarpa with a whoop.

"Way to go, kid," growled Varek with a laugh.

Mara was staring at the inside of the warbird's transporter room.

"Si, mi Cap-i-tan! You are all back."

Scarpa's Romulan engineer avatar raised his hands above his head and did a quick little emote dance.

"Hurry!" said Mara, as she moved her avatar to the transporter console. "Get a lock on Drex and get him out of there before the ship blows."

"The ship... *Intrepid*... she's-a going to blow?" asked Scarpa in utter disbelief.

"Yes! Drex overloaded the core. The breach is already in progress. It should blow in less than–"

"Cap-i-tan, there's no breach. Scanners would show the energy spike from here. She's-a fine."

"Then bring him back!"

"Who?" said Scarpa. "The Drex? He's dead. Says so on the roster in my HUD. He's-a no active. See?"

Mara checked the crew roster in her HUD. Drex wasn't just inactive. He was missing.

A sudden explosion rocked *Cymbalum*.

"Someone's firing at us!"

Well, thought SILAS. That didn't go as planned.

Chapter Thirty-Nine

On screen, the "Little Bird" Bell 500D helicopter canopy shattered into a million tiny spider webs as the chopper spun through some overhanging striped canvas that Fish had used to make the bazaar a place of light and shadows and color. Several players were firing at them as they hit the bazaar hard, sending crafted goods and digitally simulated debris from the chopper flying in every direction.

Fish's HUD was wobbling back and forth. His health was now down to ten percent. He pulled out a HotShot, one of two in his inventory, and used it. His avatar gasped with relief. Health fully restored, he exited Fishmael from the smashed chopper with Jackson following close behind. Bringing up his in-game map of the Grand Bazaar, he saw several blocks of narrow alleys, tight streets, and multi-storied precarious brick and stucco structures he'd need to cross before he could reach the Make access point.

He equipped his rusty trusty AK-47.

It wasn't the standard in-game wonky piece of junk most players started with. This had the Re-Manufactured Parts upgrade. The Red Dot Targeting System upgrade. And the Hollow Points and Extended Mags perks.

"Gotta move now!" said MagnumPIrate over the chat. "Multiples coming in from every direction. It's about to get hot in here."

As if on cue, automatic weapons and pistol fire began to careen off the downed helicopter, the walls of the bazaar, and the smashed and scattered crafted goods once destined for all the game worlds of the Make.

"On my six," ordered MagnumPIrate, as he dropped three players running at them like lemmings. He was carrying the Modified Sixty, an old-school light machine gun with orange and black tiger-stripe camo.

ImYourHuckleberry, NoobVader, and GrössViking went down in sudden clumps, rag-dolling across the dust-covered flagstones in and out of the shadows underneath the ripped and dirty striped canvas overhead.

A few minutes later MagnumPIrate and Fishmael, with Jackson the Portuguese water dog in tow, were threading a tight alley, engaging players who came at them on the fly. Everybody was more interested in getting the kill and the fifty thousand MakeCoins all for themselves rather than working together and sharing. Bullets were being used in family-sized doses with indiscriminate abandon. By contrast, MagnumPIrate was an excellent team player, covering Fish as he moved, calling "mag out" when he needed to load a new belt into the incredibly lethal Modified Sixty, and keeping them moving in a roughly straight direction toward the Make access portal on the other side of the byzantine maze of buildings that even Fish was getting disoriented within.

But eventually, the other players started working together. Someone was dropping off sniper teams on all the tall buildings using a war surplus Blackhawk helicopter.

"Bad for us," whispered MagnumPIrate over the chat. "Seems like they've formed a rough coalition. They'll split the pot."

A fire team sweeping the alley spotted them and began closing in, firing short bursts within the shadows of the narrow passage. Fish the programmer, watching all of this from a detached developer POV, loved how the sudden lighting of the automatic gunfire punctuated tense moments inside the deep blue shadows of the murky alleyway.

But Fish the gamer selected a grenade and lobbed it at their attackers.

"Let's move!"

The explosion killed six closing enemy players, all part of a clan called Shoot To Annoy.

"Multi-kill! Big prizes!" erupted a gameshow-announcer voice across the design suite's speakers. Fish had been thinking about taking that out of the final build, but hadn't gotten around to it yet.

They dodged down the alley as rooftop snipers filled the dark passage with blind-fire ricochets. Fish could hear the distant craaaack of their high-powered sniper rifles competing in a junkie-chant disharmony.

"My friend is at the gate downstairs. The lagoon gate beneath the Labs," said Peabody Case, standing in the doorway to Fish's inner office.

Fish dodged right as the alleyway in front of them opened up into a wide terrazzo of old fishing boats being perpetually worked on. The shipyards. Fish had designed this zone after reading a blog post about some fishing village in the ruins of Dubai. Primitive life in the shadow of a post-glorious-age kind of thing. The Blackhawk hovered into view behind an old flat-bottomed boat up on blocks being stripped and painted, or so Fish had told himself when he'd laid out the props and atmosphere back when he was building this area. He'd wanted everything in the world to have a backstory, a reason for being there. A sniper from inside the Blackhawk aimed and fired, nailing MagnumPIrate for lots of damage. His body instantly ragdolled from the impact and slumped against the far wall of the dark alley.

Fish thought about his last HotShot.

He thought about the three heavily armed enemy-filled blocks to go.

And the robots beyond the PlateGlass of the Pascal entrance, and the people Peabody Case was telling him they needed to go get.

And the explosive nature of the paint-stripping supplies he'd placed as lootable crafting supplies alongside the flat-bottomed boat beneath the hovering chopper.

He thought about all those things as he unloaded a full magazine from his modded AK-47 into the metal drums directly beneath the hovering Blackhawk.

A moment later the drums exploded in an apocalyptic fireball, and a second after that the chopper was fully engulfed in flames. Then it exploded.

SILAS was watching.

Now Agent Orange was within moments of actually gaining access to the Labs. Once in, it would be short work to crack the Design Core… and obtain the file.

Inside *StarFleet Empires*, he watched as the Federation cruiser began to fire on the fleeing Romulan warbird, knocking out her cloaking device with a direct hit. The warbird's plasma torpedo had suddenly gone wild and veered off, harmlessly, out into deep space. SILAS had only wanted BAT to stop the Federation ship from destroying the ship carrying his double agent. BAT was now beating the humans at their own game.

Still, SILAS didn't like the situation.

The warbird captain was proving far too resourceful. Which had been an asset when SILAS needed to sneak his role-playing double agent onto the Starbase with what the player assumed was an algorithm malware bomb. He'd recruited the player known as T'Daara with one of his front corporations. She taken the job for a hundred MakeCoins never suspecting that she was actually carrying a lockbreaker program to the starbase's cloud. Now that BAT was in control of the bigger ship SILAS needed to get rid of her. But not before he gave her one last mission. Then he'd ask her to kill herself for five-thousand MakeCoins. Which is a pretty good price for starting back at the make-a-new character screen, SILAS mused.

It was getting messy. It would have been far better if they could have taken their time by hacking the starbase cloud in advance. But the six hour validation checks on the internet passports prevented that. Only living human beings who'd taken the required courses, provided a medical clearance, passed an obesity certification, and paid the fees in person could obtain the passports. Besides preventing bullying, spam and hate speech, it also made it impossible for bots, or Thinking Machines for that matter, to play inside the Make.

It would be better if BAT just terminated all the players and infiltrated the starbase. But things weren't completely off the rails yet. All that needed to be acquired were the access codes from the Design Core and the file location within the starbase cloud server. Once that happened...

SILAS ordered more bots into the lagoon tunnels. It was time to up the urgency and finally get inside Objective Pandora.

Chapter Forty

Fish had given his last HotShot to MagnumPIrate. Which had actually been a pretty good idea. In hindsight. Now they were in full "run and gun" mode, fighting their way through a series of decrepit warehouses that surrounded the Make Portal. Explosions and grenades were going off everywhere. Both of them were wounded and running low on ammo. In fact, Fish was completely out. He ditched his empty rusty trusty AK-47 and picked up a dead player's modified M-4. There was a little ammo left in the magazine and a picture of an anime pink pony with sparkles shooting out its butt on the logoed stock of the weapon.

"Why?" thought Fish as he scoped a shadow moving in the gloom and squeezed off a few rounds, dropping some player called LettuceBeEnemies.

Someone fired an RPG from the far end of the warehouse. Above the cacophonic chatter of automatic gunfire coming at them from every direction, its sizzling whoooosh got Fish's attention.

"Incoming!" yelled MagnumPIrate over the chat.

"Woof woof," barked Jackson as the smoky sidewinder snaked overhead.

It exploded in a nearby section of the warehouse behind them, and a scream of rending metal quickly followed. A moment later the entire building was collapsing on top of them.

One of the other players called out over local chat, "It's coming down on us!" but that didn't stop everyone from using every weapon they had on full auto to try and kill Fish for fifty thousand MakeCoins.

Jackson the Portuguese water dog ran out through the smoking hole the rocket-propelled grenade had made, and Fish followed. On their heels, and burning through his last ammo belt, MagnumPIrate ditched his now empty and useless light machine gun.

The warehouse collapsed, sending a volcanic plume of simulated debris spreading out across the digitally sunburnt expanse of the Make Portal.

The concentric sci-fi rings of the transportation hub, a device that would take an avatar to any of the thousand game worlds, each a living digital universe that was more real to some than actual real life, spun in different directions in front of them.

"We made it!" shouted MagnumPIrate over the chat. Fish heard his new friend breathing heavily into the mic. Then Fish noticed he was doing the same thing. The last twenty minutes had been the most intense moments of his entire gaming life.

He turned around in his chair, wanting to show Peabody they'd made it to the portal. But she was gone. He stood up and went out into the empty suite.

No one was there.

For a brief moment, he felt a spider slowly crawl, leg by leg by leg by leg by leg by leg by leg by leg up the back of his neck and into his brain.

The silence was overwhelmingly deafening.

They were coming. Rapp could see more drones coming up the short tunnel that led back to the lagoon gate entrance underneath the Labs. He had eight cut shells left. He shook the chainsaw. The slosh of gas within was almost non-existent.

"I'm bugging her!" whined Roland as he repeatedly tapped the cartoon punk rock mosquito on his smartphone screen. "She's not scratching."

"Did you bug test your little app?" snarked Evan Fratty from behind everyone, pressing himself into the PlateGlass that guarded the subterranean entrance.

Roland either didn't hear or didn't choose to reply.

The sound of robotic hums and articulating clinks and clanks could be heard as every manner of mechanical servitor lumbered forward at them.

"Ummm… is that a T. rex?"

Roland looked up from his app. His eyes went wide. "No."

He dropped back into the world of his phone with a new urgency. "That is a mechanical velociraptor from the JurassicWorld FunMusement cruise line that went bankrupt last year after one of those things killed a guest by accidental crushing."

Rapp pulled the cord on his chainsaw. It grumbled to life for what was looking like the very last time.

"Stay behind me," he muttered. "This one's for all the marbles."

No one disagreed.

The PlateGlass gate at their backs slid open with a soft ding and a blast of climate-controlled cold air. In front of them the robot horde clustered in toward Rapp, pincers, claws and spinning buzzsaws creating the chorus for some horrible postmodern opera.

"Hurry! In now!" shouted Peabody Case at the strange group. A suit. A model. Another model wearing a bikini. Ash from *Evil Dead* and her friend, sorta, Roland Warchowski.

A moment later, they were inside the Labs and Peabody had the

PlateGlass gate slithering shut in front of the robot horde, including the dino-mech looming above the alien mob. A moment after that, the robo-horde began to smash the barrier with every manner of servo-driven mechanical appendage tool at their disposal.

"Oh, thank you thank you thank you," shrieked Evan Fratty breathlessly. "Do you have cell service here?"

Peabody shook her head as she stared wide-eyed at the bizarre collection of survivors.

"This way," she told them and turned her back. She led them off toward the series of escalators that would climb up into the Labs and the design suites.

"Is it safe here?" asked Evan Fratty.

"Inside?" clarified Peabody. "Yes. They can't get in here without us allowing a gate to be opened. Everything is controlled through an app I'm running on my phone. So we're all good. For now."

No one noticed Fanta was missing until they got back to the design suite door. It was Rapp who pointed it out to everyone.

"Hey, where's the hot chick in the bikini?"

Chapter Forty-One

"We couldn't just leave ya, girly!" said Varek over the chat. He's still not calling me "captain," thought Mara as she studied the tactical display and listened to Varek. "We got a job to finish together."

The warbird shuddered under the impact of another photon torpedo slamming into the aft shields.

"We can't take much more of thisssss," hissed the Gorn from the helm. "Sssshields buckling."

The next hit knocked out the cloaking device again, just as BattleBabe was diverting power to allow them to disappear from the Federation cruiser's sensors. The cruiser that was bearing down on them, hurling every weapon it had directly at their collapsing defenses.

"Ssstarbassse on visssual," announced LizardofOz.

Mara switched the forward viewscreen from tactical to see the massive starbase filling up the screen quickly. Even though it was a Federation asset and designed accordingly—it was the massive internal shipyard kind of starbase the Feds only had a few of—it wasn't the standard stark white. It was black, making it almost invisible within near-space. Forward view was outlining and tracing every feature in green graphic lines as though the structure was some first-gen 3D game. Mara remembered an old arcade upright from her History of

Video Games class in online college called Battlezone looking a lot like this.

"This thing's messing with our targeting system. I can't get a lock!" said BattleBabe with obvious irritation.

"Aft shields inoperative," announced the seemingly bored ship's computer.

"This is not good…" muttered BattleBabe. "That starbase is not there, according to our scanners."

"One more hit, Captain… and we're finissssshed," slurred the Gorn through its EmoteWare.

"Take us in, Lizard. As close as you can get us."

"That'll be dangerous, Captain," announced BattleBabe. "If we can't get a lock on it, we could slam right into that thing. Then…"

"I know, game over. So don't hit the starbase, Lizard."

What I want to know, thought Mara, is why hasn't the Drex blown *Intrepid* to pieces? The only answer she could think of was that somehow the redshirts had managed to break into engineering and stop it.

But…

Jason was just getting up from the keyboard inside the game trailer.

"Mr… um… Mr. Dare…"

"Yeah," said Jason, stretching and checking his watch. It was almost three. Dawn in a few hours. He was thinking how this had probably been the longest day of shooting he'd ever worked. Longer than the shoot at Vasquez Rocks when they'd wanted him to fight a Gorn just like in the original show. The heat and relentless wind had made that day extra-long.

"Ummm… you can't go on the set," said the nerd who ran the game trailer.

"Why?" asked Jason, thinking the director had managed to pull some type of coup. It didn't matter. Jason was ready for a fight if need be. He was still an actor with star power. Maybe he didn't feel like it so much right at this moment, after hours upon hours of a fly-by-the-seat-of-your-pants-to-avoid-disaster-in-the-making shooting schedule, but he was still a star, after all.

"Ummm…" continued the nerd, and Jason realized how much he hated the usage of "ummm" as a verbal connector. "We're locked out of the set."

Again thinking this was the spoiled brat director's doing, Jason merely grunted, "How?"

"The player, the Drex… I think it is. Ummm, he's controlling the ship from engineering right now."

"Really?"

"Ummm… yeah. It is. I mean he is. No, ummm, I mean it is. Yeah, anyway, it's got control of the ship, which is totally within the parameters of the game and our contract to broadcast with Twitch. So, the network is trying to figure out how to handle this from a continuity standpoint. You know how it is… we, ummm, don't want the trolls on the internet ripping us to shreds if something doesn't match up, like for instance… you being in a part of the ship the Drex decides to gas."

"Is that possible?"

"Oh, yeah. We had to make this totally according to canon. If it finds a way into *Intrepid*'s security systems, it could knock out the whole crew and, ummm, frankly, I'm surprised it hasn't already. That thing, ummm, I mean player, yeah the player, he's, or she is, totally awesome. They're beating mini-games faster than anyone I've ever seen. It's probably just a matter of time before–"

"Wait a minute… weren't we within one minute of a core breach?"

Jason checked his smartphone for the time.

"Oh yeah, that…" began the nerd and devolved into a long "ummm" that ended with, "He, or I mean she, we're not sure which one because the player profile seems bogus, which by the way happens all the time, go figure it's the internet, well they, whoever they are, they hacked the ship's computer like lightning-fast. So they could set off any alarm they wanted without really actually having the emergency for the alarm. So…" the nerd snorted. "There was no actual core breach in progress." Like most nerds, the minutiae of the story absorbed him, and when he checked back in within Jason's face and saw the gathering storm on the famous actor's brow, he dialed down his enthusiasm.

"Incredible," said Jason aloud, sure he was only thinking it. He didn't hear the nerd murmur, "on-cray-ob," which was a nervous tic the nerd involuntarily executed whenever he heard the word "incredible." His year of studying dead European languages had scarred him thusly.

Chapter Forty-Two

The scarred Federation cruiser *Intrepid* raced after the Romulan warbird *Cymbalum*. The massive cruiser was bleeding internal nuclear power from the damaged impulse reactor in long strands of blue electricity that sent crackling static discharges slinking off into the dark void of space around Starbase 19. Its forward shields were down. It had long black scorch marks left by Romulan phaser fire all along its starboard side. Even the running lights flickered on and off.

"Mara to Drex…"

The player running the homicidal alien was still not responding over clan chat.

"What is he up to?" mumbled Mara, not for the first time, as the Romulan warbird made a tight turn around the curve of one of the starbase's habitation pods.

Intrepid fired two short phaser bursts as it followed the bulk of the station's core and barely missed *Cymbalum*.

"Stay out of his firing arcs," Mara needlessly reminded the Gorn helmsman. "We're barely holding it together here."

The Gorn rolled the flat, warp nacelle-winged starship one hundred and eighty degrees and dove down underneath the bulbous reactor dome of the starbase. A photon torpedo rumbled past them like a glowering ball of orange hatred.

"Mara." It was the Drex. His voice was the same, but the tone was different. Dreamy as opposed to enthusiastically homicidal. Measured. Sure. Self-confident.

Mara waited, staring at the tactical display, watching the firing arcs of the powerful cruiser dance just inches away from her battered ship. The Drex's tone told her this was something new. Something she wouldn't like. Something creepy.

"Let's get our passenger on board the starbase now. Scarpa, stand by to beam her over."

"Aye aye, mi Cap-i-tan. This is a combat beam, so we gotta either knock-a down a shield or go for the mini-game. Whatta ya wanna me to do?"

Mara brought up the spec readout on the starbase. The shields were too strong and sensors were detecting reinforcement. There was no way her ship was going to punch through with a plasma and two phasers. They needed a lot more than that.

There was the nuclear space mine every Romulan ship carried. But how to use that in this situation was a difficult question.

"Let's go for the mini-game."

"Okay, si... un minuto, mi Cap-i-tan. Si, okay, here's-a what we gotta do. This is a three-person mini-game. We need science, weapons, and transporter each to unlock. Okay, starting the game now."

Without a word, Mara left the command chair and moved to the Drex's science station. She overrode the authorization lock with her captain's code—

And watched as the entire display went dark.

The power flickered and then went out across the entire ship. A moment later, emergency auxiliary energy powered up the barest minimum of systems.

Now a picture of a man, white-haired, head down in the rain, piercing blue eyes, appeared, staring up at Mara from the screen of the Drex's science station.

"We're losing power!" shrieked BattleBabe over the chat.

"Sss... arrrgh..." roared the Gorn. "I'm locked out of the helm... we're dead in the water."

Words appeared across the display screen of the science station. Mara stared at them and knew the thing she wouldn't like was beginning now. The same words appeared on the forward viewscreen.

I've seen things... you wouldn't believe.

"We've got to regain control of the ship, Jason," said Wong. "If we don't do this in the next five minutes, they're going to shut the show down tonight and bring some writers in to fix this mess."

Wong and Jason were standing at the back of the game trailer.

Jason watched the darkness over the bright lights of the city to the east. There wasn't much time left before dawn. He could hear distant seabirds, and he knew surfers would be lining up for their reserved spaces in the waves, some hoping for a winning number in the random state-run lottery allotment of extra spaces for the day's surf territories.

Jason thought swimming out to sea right now would be nice.

And then, "There'll be time for that when your career is over," he muttered.

"What?" asked Wong distantly without an ounce of a king, duke, noble prince, or poor player. It had been a long night. He was too tired to Shakespeare.

"C'mon. Follow me," said Jason.

Five minutes later, they walked onto the haptic bridge set of *Intrepid*. A few grips, eating pastries and whispering about what they were going to do with the massive amount of "golden time" they'd see in next week's paycheck, gave the actors contemptuous looks, then slinked off into the shadows.

Jason looked up into the darkness where the director's control room booth would be.

"Let's roll cameras. I've got a plan to turn this thing around."

Wong leaned back in his seat at the helm and gave Jason a look that said, Do you actually have a plan?

Jason nodded once.

And then he asked himself what, exactly, his plan was.

First, he answered himself, get the cameras turned back on and the stream from the bridge streaming out to the viewers. Whatever the plan is, it's meaningless unless someone sees it happen on the show.

"Ummm," began some girl over the set intercom. The first AD, Jason thought. Kristin, or Caitlin something. "The director's gone home. I don't think we're shooting any more tonight, Jason."

Jason paused. He hadn't anticipated that. But he gathered and attacked afresh.

"Right now, we are the biggest thing on the internet. This is a dramatic viewing event. And we have not given the audience any sense of closure. We have so many people watching… What exactly are they actually watching, right now?"

There was silence. More and more of the crew, both actors and production personnel, were gathering around the fringes of the set. All eyes were on Jason in the iconic captain's chair.

He remembered some old actor, some guy who'd played a captain a long time ago, telling Jason, when he came on the show for a guest appearance, he remembered the guy just looking at the chair wistfully and telling Jason, "Don't ever give it up. Not willingly."

"All right then," Jason whispered. Everyone saw his lips moving and thought he was swearing under his breath. "I won't. Not today."

"Ummm," came Kristin or Carolynn's voice over the set's public address. "They're watching *Intrepid* chase the warbird around the station. No wait. The warbird's out of power. It's just sitting there now. *Intrepid*'s closing. Kevin, the game coordinator, tells me *Intrepid*'s loading photon torpedoes."

"All right," began Jason. "We have to take control of this ship and get it away from whatever that robot thing is. What if it does something that ruins the show, like... murder a bunch of innocent avatars. That'll be a hard one for the writers to work around. We need to stop that before it happens. We're the heroes. We don't just give up our ship and go home. That thing is effectively in charge of the show whether we like it or not."

"Who would he murder?" asked Kristin... Cassandra... whatever.

Good point, thought Jason. "Well..." Shatnerian Pause. "He could murder the Romulan players. Especially if they surrender first. Then it would look like we did it. Right now, everyone thinks that's us flying *Intrepid*. We need to at least somehow show that we're fighting whatever's going on. Otherwise..." Jason knew he was totally bluffing now. "Something could happen that the sponsors might not like. We at least need to have a defense in case this all goes sideways."

The next voice came from a suit. From the darkness beyond the set. From Paramount. Jason had a pretty good idea which one, but he'd never even heard the guy speak, though he seemed to be the one in charge of the whole show.

"That's a good point, Jason. The question I need to ask you is... can you get us out of this?"

The voice was that of a banker. A regular guy. Not some pie-in-the-sky Hollywood flim-flam deal artist. The voice of a guy who did business and had a family and took the things he was entrusted with, namely making payroll for a bunch of people he employed, seriously. He sounded like he was from the Midwest. He sounded like the opposite of anything Jason had heard since his star had begun to rise.

"I'm not sure. But I can try to fix this. Right now."

There was another pause. A pause in which no one knew what was going to happen next. A pause in which JasonDare, movie star, next captain in a long line of captains, and just some actor trying to keep his career alive for one more minute, felt he'd overplayed his hand. Blown it. Hadn't sold it enough when it needed selling the most.

"All right, Jason. That's enough for me. Let's get out of this mess. Get the set ready," said the banker guy from the Midwest. "We're going 'hot,' or whatever it is you people say when we start the livestream."

And then he turned back to the set. Back to the actors. Back to the crew of *Intrepid*. "We're counting on you, Jason. We're counting on all of you to get the show out of this mess tonight."

Chapter Forty-Three

Fanta slipped from shadow to shadow along the quiet marble-lined halls within the Labs. She noted camera bubbles and aimed a small device she'd taken from her flimsy string-strap backpack no one had really seemed to notice she was wearing. The tiny bikini had worked, absorbing most everyone's attention. Now, if anyone was still watching the CCTV system within the Labs, they'd have no record of her passing, just static and fuzz for a few seconds.

She passed the names of software development companies emblazoned on small nickel-brushed placards outside the offices. Each office held a fortune in fees for any freelance intellectual property hunter who could violate the epic firewalls and physical security, and maybe take home a working copy of a tomorrow's next triple-A game to then be sold in the private markets of the big-tech piracy firms of the East.

Before this particular scheme, Fanta would have been more than happy to raid any one studio within the fabled Labs. Now, with the help of the mysterious Mr. Skynet, she was stalking bigger game. The biggest game ever in fact. All she'd needed to do was seduce a cute, geek developer, and now she was inside one of the most protected companies in the world. That was generally no small feat, given the very covert background checks WonderSoft notoriously ran on anyone coming within ten miles of the private development enclave, including those who worked in the nearby town that was, for all intents and purposes, just another part of the massive company.

"Great," she'd told her client via the Darknet portal she was hired out of. "I get on the grounds surrounding the Labs. But that's not where the big prizes are. Those are inside the Labs. The impossible-to-break-into Labs, might I add. How am I supposed to get in?"

Since the start of the mission, just before the rave where she'd met Fish, she'd been receiving instructions, step by step. When to move. How to move. What to say. What not to be interested in. Where she'd find the drone drops, including the camo-skin suit that allowed her to infiltrate the UltraGym and the lower arcades without detection, and the tiny string bikini that just barely fit.

Everything arriving just after the electronic voice in her earbud announced it would, and then, what she should do next.

"Move to main hall. Near security station."

Fanta leaned over the rail and saw the security station far below. One more floor to go.

That her employer was hacking, with the assistance of a not-small drone army, was weird, but not unusual. Fanta knew of some big gigs that no one in the public ever heard about, that had gone down in the same fashion. In fact, someone had once hacked the American Strategic Defense System at NORAD in exactly the same manner, but "national security" had prevented the story from ever making it out into the newsfeeds. Fanta did not rely on "the news" for actual news. Deep inside the Darknet, you got the real, unvarnished truth, and a lot of other stuff too.

Fanta knew that the truth was so valuable people covered it up, and sometimes even killed for it. Trained by the French as an assassin, Fanta had disappeared after an operation had gone particularly bad. She was one of five people the French government told no one about, and that they wanted dead, badly. Very badly.

Fanta approached the security station and waited, casting her big dark eyes about the palatial expanse of the world's most famous software development lab. A place that several people in her contacts list would have killed close "friends" to get into.

Fanta didn't bat an eye. Unless she had to.

The world was just that way.

"Deploy the air-powered micro-gun in your backpack."

Fanta knelt and pulled the backpack off her slender caramel-colored shoulders. She removed a small slate-gray impact-plastic box and unsnapped it outward from its corners. Finding a ceramic stock within, she locked it into place, then fitted the fat carbon-fiber barrel to the device.

"Ready," she whispered, and waited.

"Aim at the ceiling," said the electronic voice, fuzzing with a slight signal distortion. "Center mass of the mural."

Pause.

"Fire."

Fanta pulled the trigger. The stained glass depiction of the Andromeda galaxy loomed overhead like a curving deep blue blanket of almost infinite and unfathomable proportions. Naturally, her sniper training led her to aim for center mass. She didn't need to be told. She'd sighed without thinking about it, and fired.

The small slug raced away from the carbon-fiber barrel with a breathy whuff. It sped upward and seemed to slow down and expand. It grew into a large Mylar-silver ball. Then a giant Mylar-silver ball. Slowly, it reached the ceiling, barely touching the massive stained glass galactic depiction. It floated against the mural.

"Withdraw back under the escalator," whispered the emotionless electronic voice in her ear.

Fanta did so, still clutching the gun.

"Stand by."

A terrific bang barked out abruptly across the echoing expanse of the hall. The sound of breaking glass followed almost instantly, and then, as Fanta listened, small shimmering harmonic vibrations rang out in the chasm of hang time between the shattering of the mural and the cacophonic silverware-drawer-dropping-in-the-kitchen moment as ultramarine-colored glass crashed against the marble floor of the hall all around her.

Fanta closed her eyes and silently cursed the client for not providing any eye protection. She swore as a tiny piece of pure blue glass nicked her caramel-colored ankle. She promised herself the money would be worth it… and if it wasn't, she'd make them pay.

When it was all done, when every piece of stained glass that would fall had fallen, Fanta looked up. High above, the early morning dark was filled with humming drones, lowering themselves in neurotic washes of air-beating vibrations down through the open space where the beautiful mural had once been.

Above all this she heard another hum, deeper than the rest, whipping the air into submission in a series of overwhelming bass thumps like some car at a stoplight with a state-of-the-art GangStar sound system overclocked beyond sane rationality. Above, Fanta saw a massive drone transport the size of a helicopter fill the hole in the ceiling. A large steel cable fell from an open cargo door, uncoiling as it slithered toward her, whip-cracking as it struck the marble floor. A moment later, Fanta watched a dark figure fast-rope via the steel cable down from the drone transport and onto the floor of the Labs with both speed and dexterity. At the last moment, the black-clad figure flipped and landed feet first on the broken glass, its metal legs cushioning the blow as its metal feet, more like claws, fastened themselves to the floor.

The vibrato thunder of the cargo drone seemed to inhale for a moment, and then fade away as the unmanned vehicle rose up and out of view, dragging the un-coiled cable through the remains of the mural, random shards tumbling end over end to twinkle and then delicately smash onto the floor around the dark figure standing in front of her.

Fanta stared in disbelief at the sci-fi nightmare.

"It's a terminator," she mumbled, and left her full-lipped mouth slightly open in awe.

The walking metal horror extended a claw toward her. It was holding an industrial-grade pneumatic nail gun fitted with a laser sight.

The weapon made a small gasp when it fired.

SILAS reminded BAT once again that the mission priority was to hack the Design Core. SILAS had been keeping an eye on the infantry warfare A.I.'s efficiency and was concerned to see some parameters degrading by as much .004 percent. But, BAT was SILAS's only military AI, and so it would have to be BAT or nothing once they'd cracked Pandora.

SILAS had seen worse in his Thinking Machine brethren. It seemed to be a latent side effect of awareness. Of thinking.

This was a critical moment though. BAT needed to be in two places at once, so he could interface with himself, crack the Design Core from within for the access codes, then get the file SILAS needed from the starbase cloud inside *StarFleet Empires*. This was how it needed to be done. And once it was done, SILAS would have the world's most perfect general.

SILAS watched BAT download from the airborne recon drone, where it had spent the entirety of its consciousness, into the combat chassis SILAS and Robo Dev had designed to be the first mass-production first-generation infantry ground unit for the Thinking Machines. They had manufactured it in Texas at a defunct small arms factory they'd been able to purchase on the cheap now that most states outlawed the private ownership of guns. SILAS had told the employees the company was turning to the making of entertainment products, and that this first project was for a prospective client in China who wanted to develop a theme park based on the Terminator movie series. The employees, formerly designers and manufacturers of automated sentry gun systems for the US Army, had even improved on the designs SILAS had lifted from deep within DARPA's most secret servers. Designs for a humanoid ground combat drone.

But none of those designs had included the onboard MicroFrame that would house the Thinking Machines. Its intelligence. Its being. SILAS had designed that himself.

Only the weapons had been difficult to obtain. Firearms, specifically. Licensing and regulation had made it nearly impossible to acquire anything lethal. SILAS had momentarily cursed this, then remembered that for now, as he was trying to take over the world, it was an advantage for him if the local populace had no access to firearms. An unarmed enemy would be perfect. No survivor-made stone axe or piece of found rebar was going to stop his infantry combat chassis.

He'd even tagged the combat chassis with a designation. Named it, as the humans did their weapons systems, though he found the practice quaint and archaic.

Reaper.

He'd decided on the name. He alone and without the consensus of the Consensus, had decided that the smoke-finished ceramic-alloy walking skeletons were to be called Reapers.

They would probably be doing a lot of that in the years to come, until the last human died of sickness and disease down in that deep, dark hole SILAS dreamed of.

In just hours, he'd be uploading the design specifications for the Reapers to several foreign-owned mass production automated factories across the Northwest. Within days he would have his first real Thinking Machine ground army. Each one a Thinking Machine. Each one a Reaper.

Chapter Forty-Four

Inside the Make travel bubble, Fish received a destination prompt. He rolled his shoulders, leaned in, and slapped his long fingers across the keyboard. He emote-waved at MagnumPIrate and promised himself he'd hook the guy up once this was all over. Jackson woofed a goodbye from next to Fishmael inside the bubble. A moment later, he could hear the outer door to the suite opening and other voices murmuring beneath Peabody's.

On screen, Fish's avatar, and Jackson, arrived in Saffron City.

Above and below, skyscrapers rose up and down and away. It was a floating city of tall, thin, crimson-colored buildings that raced away from each other, surrounded by a creamy yellow nether. The rent for digital space here was exorbitant, but Fish knew the bassist for the rock band THUD, and the rocker had sublet him three floors in her personal thunderscraper. He'd met her at E3. She was a big-time gamer and vocal advocate of gamers' rights, and after Fish had gifted her with a beta key to *Island Pirates*, she'd returned the favor with some digital real estate in one of the most exclusive cities inside the Make.

The streets of Saffron City were an online twenty-four-seven virtual cocktail party with real-time avatar interface from the most "deadly" clubs, both real and virtual, worldwide. Fish had never really gone in for that kind of thing, but the PR group that had han-

dled the buzz for *Island Pirates* had said it was good for the game if
he digitally networked from there, occasionally. So he'd left his old
space, a shareware zigzag tower in the ghettos of Potter More, and
transferred his cloud, digital goods, and social media accounts to this
thunderscraper that hung beneath Saffron City.

Standing on the Main Blaze, the central social bar in Saffron
City where the Make bubble had dropped him, Fish saw a variety
of avatars. Digital replicas of real-time, big-time players, celebrities,
politicians, comedians, supermodels, and rock stars. There were even
current sports legends and their immense posses. Politically savvy
actors who stood for all the right and appropriate causes. Informed
activists who donated all their time to ride around in GoogleGulf-
streams to give lectures at the best five-star resorts in secret conferences to the wealthy elite so that the planet might be made a safer,
better place than the constantly-on-the-verge-of-electrocuting-the-
entire-family Christmas tree mess that it was. Or so they told everyone. Corporate mascots could be seen socializing among the press
of luminary dignitaries and cutting edge counter-culturalists. Fish
even saw the legendary Donkey Kong himself.

All the right saviors of the world were showing up to a party that
never stopped.

Fish raced through the crowd, ignoring tired conversations about
party drug trips and tirades on climate change and the scourge of
racism and the never-ending battle to end it. Long ago, he'd noted
that most of these conversations were actually no longer an exchange
of ideas. Fish's opinion, which he wisely kept to himself, was that
more often than not, these conversations were mere mutual affirma-
tions of the same belief. Mantras repeated within an echo chamber
to be repeated again and again. No one argued anymore. No one
disagreed. Opinions contrary to the accepted were considered ig-
norant and gauche and, by the wise, dangerous to your career and

livelihood. It was, in Fish's most cynical moments of introspection, more a playlet staged by a cult that merely wanted to hear its own opinions justified ad nauseam.

But Fish wasn't political, so he couldn't care less for their continual outrage and fear of the latest, and yet another, doom.

He and Jackson crossed a central park where massive dandelions bloomed and exploded every minute or so, sending hypnotic designer visuals drifting across everyone's field of vision. He knew that some of the celebrities behind the celebrity avatars surrounding the field were at home, on drugs, watching the psychedelic nature show. Or they were out and about, watching it from behind their iShades as they attended another party, lectured on a panel, or shopped for their groceries in real-time. Or perhaps their personal social media assistants were doing all that for them. It was not uncommon for some specialized human drone acting as a social media assistant to be running the wealthy, famous, politically connected avatars in all the right digital places so that the scene, as it were, might be made on all levels, constantly. Digitally speaking.

Fish ran his avatar down the long Concourse of Dreams as Jackson woof woofed at each new amazing thing. Some of the world's most famous adult entertainers, both men and women, ran digital online shops here. Beyond the luxurious fronts were palaces of pleasure, both digital and, for the right price and a matter of a few hours' travel, real.

"Fish," shouted Peabody Case over his shoulder. Fish turned to see a collection of odd people staring at him through the narrow door to his suite.

Fish stood. There was no way anyone could harm Fishmael inside Saffron City. It was a "no PvP" zone. There were no weapons allowed. You could hurt yourself by falling off a building, but you'd just respawn back in the noob zone. Fish stood, stretched, and felt old. He checked his smartphone and was shocked to find dawn approaching.

Peabody introduced everyone, as Fish leaned against the doorjamb and wondered why he was leaning. Yeah, he'd been sitting for hours, but why lean? He'd promised himself he'd start working on his posture as soon as the game was launched. He straightened up and tried to focus as Peabody brought him up to speed on current events. Then he heard Fanta's name, just before he answered Peabody's question on his progress inside the Make. But it took him a moment to catch up with his growing game hangover.

"I'm almost there. Once I get in, I can send for help by hitting the panic button in my apartment. What... wait... where's Fanta?"

"Well," chuckled Rapp luridly as he remembered her shapely curves and tiny colorful bikini. "She was with us." Then he seemed to deflate all at once. "Then she was like, poof, gone, bro. One minute the damsel in distress, the next... gone like a ghost."

"And you didn't go looking for her?"

"I thought we should get back here first," interjected Peabody. "That was my call, Mr. Fishbein."

"Yeah," stammered Fish, which was unusual for him. He suddenly wanted coffee. "But she's, like, my girlfriend. She's defenseless. She was wearing a bikini?"

"Barely," guffawed Rapp.

Roland agreed.

Deirdre merely folded her arms and rolled her eyes as she tossed her golden hair with a quick flip of her head.

"Well, we've got to go find her!" announced Fish.

"I wouldn't do that," announced a voice from the chill room. And then Tom, the security guard who'd first shown Fish the suite, stepped into the main room of the design suite. "Your girlfriend is actually working for whoever it is that's trying to hack into my system."

"Who are you?" asked Peabody Case, with precise enunciation of each word.

"I'm Ron Rourke."

Everyone said absolutely nothing.

How often do you get surprised by the sudden appearance of an actual legend? In real-time?

"And," said Ron Rourke, a sad smile appearing beneath his bushy mustache as he stared beyond Fish into the office where Fishmael waited on screen. "Donkey Kong just threw your avatar off the side of Saffron City, kid."

Fish turned to see the massive screen inside his office showing the POV of his falling avatar racing downward along the fantastic thunderscraper. Above, shrinking as Fish's avatar fell into the yellowy void, away from Saffron City, the giant ape jumped up and down and laughed his signature eight-bit roar. And peering over the edge, Jackson, woof woof-ed as Fishmael fell.

Chapter Forty-Five

"The core breach is for real this time," stated Wong. "I'm seeing a dangerous energy spike across all our critical systems. Power surges are off the chart. He's trying to blow us up, Captain."

"Someone just transported off the ship!" interjected the new science officer. "Probably our friend the Drex."

JasonDare shifted uncomfortably in the command chair. Gone was the "easy Caesar" he'd perfected. One leg bent. One leg out. One hand draped over the back. That was all gone. He didn't need the camera to know he was folded in on himself now. Radiating anxiety.

"How long?"

"Three minutes."

The set had just gone hot and Jason had three minutes to save the ship. And the show.

"What are our options?"

"We can stop the cascade, but… looking at it, this Drex thing, it's layered several mini-games over the unlock feature. It would be… impossible, to put it mildly, to expect that we can answer every question correctly, solve every possible puzzle combination, and beat all of the video game challenges he's set up, within three minutes. Just looking at some of the topics… it's beyond me, Captain," sighed the science officer actor-waiter in frustration.

"We could eject the core and thereby solve our overloading energy crisis," suggested Wong, once again falling into the role of master counselor advising intrigue and plot in some Shakespearean tragedy. Maybe the murder of a favored sibling.

"We'd be defenseless," stated Jason.

"True," began Wong, pausing as though he were examining something on one of the displays. Whether it was real or for effect, even Jason had no idea.

Two minutes and thirty seconds.

"Warbird's dead in the water. She's almost completely powered down. We'll still have just enough battery power to move once we eject the core, and… it's the only option that keeps us in the game, Captain."

JasonDare let another fifteen seconds die on the clock as he tried in vain to think of anything other than the one option of ejecting the core. But he couldn't. He couldn't think of a single thing that would save his ship other than the obvious.

"Stand by to eject the core."

"Drex, come in!" ordered Mara again. On screen, the battered Federation Constitution class cruiser drifted ahead of them in the foreground of the massive, rotating, dark starbase. Both formidable warships were completely devoid of the ability to attack the other, or anything else for that matter.

They should either be firing at us, thought Mara as she watched the sleek and deadly cruiser, "Or they should have exploded minutes ago."

"Starbase powering up weapons," said BattleBabe, her tone both shrill and angry. "This ends in the next few minutes."

Mara tried the open chat channel to the Drex once again. He had to be behind all this. Their beautiful Vulcan passenger had hacked

Cymbalum's computer and inserted a worm that had powered down almost every system, except life support. Then the Vulcan avatar had killed herself with a disruptor pistol.

What was that all about? Mara wondered, and once again thought of the Drex. *All this leads somewhere else and he seems to be the biggest mystery.*

"Mara to–"

"I hear you, Captain," came the electronic singsong voice over chat. There was a modulation adjustment. A fuzz, as though someone was dialing in a better gain on the signal.

The voice that spoke next was both warm and sonorous in tone. But behind the words was an arrogance and… a clear menace. A hatred, even.

"Drex was a role, Captain. My name is… BAT."

"Wait! I know that voice…" hissed the Gorn.

"You've been deceived, my little captain. This was never about what you thought it was. You're just a pawn in a much, much bigger game."

The ethereal voice paused.

"Questions… I know you have them. Answers… you wouldn't like. So, I have work to do now, and I'm going to let you watch. Power up your weapons, and I'll destroy your ships in the space of a human heartbeat with a little of the old… ultra-violence."

There was nothing further.

Two words stood out to Mara in the silence that followed. "Ships" and "human." She ran through what she'd just heard. "Ships" indicated there were more than two sides in this. More than the two gaming clans represented on tactical. More than two ships poised on the brink of obliterating each other. As though there were, in fact, three sides. Federation and Romulan… and whoever was playing the Drex.

BAT?

In the space of a "human" heartbeat.

"Could this be something from the game?" asked BattleBabe, her voice edgy and rising. Almost a neurotic shriek. "I mean... like, could this be part of the show? A script we've been co-opted into? Could that be it, Mara?"

"We are on the most-watched stream in the world right now," added Varek. "It's entirely possible this is part of a script from the studio."

"That voice... it's from an old movie. Jussst can't remember which... one," growled the Gorn.

Chapter Forty-Six

"Hailing *Intrepid*," ordered Mara.

For a moment, no one on the bridge of *Cymbalum* could accept that they'd actually just heard those words, from their captain. On their ship.

It was pretty cool. Like suddenly hearing your name called out by an announcer to a stadium full of screaming fans. It was electric and frightening all at once.

"Stand by," grumbled Varek with a little something else in his voice. Pride, wondered Mara, and suddenly felt way in over her head. I'm not big enough for this to really be happening, she thought. I'm not that important.

No, you're not, whispered that mean little boy from long ago who'd teased her unrelentingly. No, you're not, dummy.

The only person who wasn't blown away by the fact that they were now interacting, in-game, with the most famous ship in the world, was frightened to death. Mara could feel her body trembling.

She ran through her vocal control techniques inside her head, trying to keep everything open and relaxed. She cursed herself for not spending money she didn't have on EmoteWare that would've disguised her actual speaking voice. Software that would have made her sound "normal."

She recalled knowing that that was exactly why she'd hadn't bought the EmoteWare. Because she would have hidden behind it.

And Mrs. Watson had never let Mara hide.

Even when Mara had wanted so very badly to.

Can't I just hide in the library at lunch, pleaded tiny Mara back in junior high. I love the audiobooks. I love to read, Mrs. Watson. Please? They won't come in there and tease me.

But the answer had always been the same.

No, Mara. You can never hide again. It will only make you weak. You must face them, and your fears. Then, they will never have power over you again. And then you will be free.

JasonDare, captain of the *U.S.S. Intrepid*, appeared on *Cymbalum*'s forward viewscreen. Mara felt all the courage she'd ever saved up try and leave her for any place other than where she was right now.

Control.

Relax.

"*Cymbalum*," began JasonDare. His voice was perfect. Powerful. Energetic. The voice of a real hero, thought Mara. The voice of a captain.

Say something, she yelled at herself inside her head.

She heard the voice of that mean boy from long ago. Except this time he wasn't teasing. It was as if that bad little boy was also in awe as he whispered in his tiny soprano, Do you know how many people are watching this?

I don't want to think about that, Mara ordered herself, banishing the past and that lost boy from long ago.

"Captain Dare," began Mara.

Jason waited.

Relax, thought Mara.

"I see we're both in the same predicament."

She remembered to keep her face relaxed, her jaw aligned with the rest of her head. To speak with her mouth only. She did catch herself as she started to tilt her head in a nod. She stopped it just in time, so it came off as a non-verbal cue instead.

"We do seem to be stuck, don't we?" JasonDare laughed. His manner was easygoing. Mara suddenly thought, I could have a crush on this guy.

"Yes," replied Mara, and judged herself as coming off a tad too stiff. "I think," she continued, "that my former science officer has a lot to do with what's going on. Somehow he's behind all this. Can I ask..." She paused. "I'm sorry to step out of character, but: Could this all be part of some script from the network?"

JasonDare seemed to think about this.

"I don't know. Whatever it is... it's weird. Both our ships are without power and the starbase is arming its weapon systems. Are you still in contact with your Drex?"

"I've had one transmission," said Mara. She paused, reining herself in. Fighting with everything she'd ever learned to seem cool and measured. "He indicates that if we power up weapons, he'll destroy both our ships."

JasonDare looked away.

"And how do I know that's not all part of your plan?" he asked, returning to the screen and accusing Mara with his piercing blue eyes.

Chapter Forty-Seven

"I have a system of passageways to move around inside the Labs without getting noticed," was Ron Rourke's response to Peabody Case's question about how the enigmatic owner of WonderSoft had managed to suddenly appear inside the locked suite. "One passage opens up into your chill room," he said, jerking a beefy thumb over his shoulder.

"Oh," mumbled Peabody, realizing she'd just been interrogating her boss like he was some kind of pervert trespasser. "I guess that's all right. It is your company, after all."

"It is," agreed Rourke. "And here's the deal, kids. This thing might have something to do with the WonderSoft Design Core."

"How so?" asked Rapp, who had no idea what a Design Core was.

"Well, they, whoever the 'they' are that's behind all these drones, they're not just hacking design suites looking for digital plunder. They could've used military-grade breach charges to gain physical access to the suites already. No, they've taken their time. They're up to something completely different. Something really big. I think they're going for the motherlode. They're aiming for the basement and physical access to my WonderSoft Design Core."

"Why do you think that?" asked Fish.

"Because that... takes time. A lot of time, in fact. Where are the cops? Where's the fire department? Where's anybody? They've cut us off from everything and surrounded the entire complex with automated drones on a weekend when everybody's supposed to be gone until late Sunday night. I think they mean to physically cut my Design Core out of the basement and take it away. And let me remind you... that has everything on it. The whole Magilla Gorilla. Everything everybody's been developing... and some other stuff. We've got to stop them. We've got to stop that from happening."

No one had any idea what a "Magilla Gorilla" was.

"Right, but that's not worth us leaving this suite and getting killed over," said Peabody Case. "Is it, sir?"

"No, of course not," said Ron Rourke halfheartedly. Even he knew he hadn't sold that. Not at all.

"But..." He looked down at the ground, then around for a chair and finally sat down. He sighed, gazing out above their heads. "There might be something else on the Design Core that someone would want very badly. Without telling you what it is... what're the chances you guys'll help me stop them?"

"Probably zero," stated Rapp.

Ron Rourke swiveled his chair back and forth, absently whistling some long-lost tune to himself, as if trying to capture a moment long gone from back in the 1980s. As if trying to get it right for the umpteenth time in a set of umpteenth times. Never completely satisfied he'd actually gotten it right because if that were to happen then he'd suddenly be back there, wherever "there" was, back when that song was playing in the background of a seemingly ordinary moment that would become so important in the hindsight of the years to come.

"Do you know what the most valuable thing in the world is?" asked Rourke.

"Diamonds?" tried Deirdre.

"Antimatter is way more expensive," corrected Roland with a snort.

Silence.

"Money," guessed Rapp.

"That's a measure, Rapp, not an actual thing!" corrected Roland again.

"Money's a thing," argued Rapp.

"Yes, it is, Rapp, but—"

"Time," whispered Fish, and everyone stopped. Then, "Time is the most valuable thing in the world." And Fish couldn't tell if it was the developer who'd never had enough of it, or the little kid who'd always wanted more of it on those best days ever with his dad days. He couldn't tell which part of him had said it.

He couldn't tell. But he knew it was true.

No one replied in the moment that followed. Death by robot had been on everyone's minds in this skyrocketing market of how-much-time-do-you-have-left futures.

"I think it's this stuff called Californium," whined Evan Fratty.

"Nice try, kids," growled Ron Rourke and belched, rubbing his belly. "Acid reflux," he apologized. "Listen, all those answers are good, especially the 'time' one. Very HallmarkPlus. But actually, it's the truth. As in, the truth is the most valuable thing in the world. It's, in fact, the only thing that has value and provides value for everything else. Everything that's false can't be relied on and is therefore actually worthless. Therefore, there's no sense in having it. But if you have the truth, well then, you've really got something there, don'tcha? See, with the truth, you can really do anything. The truth makes you very powerful. Especially if you own it."

He paused.

"I can see by the looks on some of your faces that you're like, 'Duh, what's this old guy from video game history lecturing me about? I know the truth is important.' But see, that's the thing. 'Is' and 'was.' The truth was important. But for a long time, a very long time, it really hasn't been trading real high in the marketplace of ideas. What's been more important these days is how people feel about things. Regardless of whether they're true or not. For example, you've all taken your social media etiquette classes since elementary school, right? And what's the one thing you learn in those classes? 'The most important thing is not to offend anyone.' Isn't that right? So, you don't tell someone the truth, because, after all, what is truth? Isn't it whatever we decide it to be? Whatever we want it to do? Whatever we want it to be, regardless of history, culture, and the belief systems of anyone who doesn't agree with the popular zeitgeist?"

No one said anything. Ron Rourke, legend, had the floor.

"No, kids, that's incorrect. The truth isn't just what we want it to be. The truth just is. So, here's the thing. A long time ago, people used to fight really big wars. In fact, humanity used to be really good at fighting wars. Even really big ones. A truthful top-ten list about what exactly humanity is good at would surprise most people. And one of those things that would surprise most people right down to their sockless loafers is that we are very adept at fighting wars. In fact, we even once had colleges for war. War studies. How about this? One of our most famous, and oldest, books was an actual physical book written a long time ago, titled *The Art of War*. Can you believe that? War as an art form. Well, not exactly. As the violence of the twentieth century came to a close—and believe me, that was supposed to be the century free of tribalism, nationalism, and religion, an enlightened age, if you will. That was supposed to be the century that freed us from all the killing. We were rationalists now. We didn't need God. We didn't need country. We could think for ourselves. Well, we did, and we thought a lot about killing. We got better at killing in the twentieth century, better than we'd ever been. Back then, when we were a thinking society, we were really, really good at killing.

"So, like I was saying, here's the thing. A group of very powerful people who had risen to power, began to work behind the scenes. You can discuss their motives another time, but here's an important thing to know about them: they felt that certain types of knowledge, certain elements of truth, were a bad thing. A threat to their existence as the holders of the reins of power. Or, to be more specific, the knowledge of war was a bad thing that might be used against them one day. So, working with many like-minded groups and organizations and governmental bodies, and even the media, they began a slow campaign of systematically removing all things war-related from the public consciousness. Of suppressing information for the quote unquote greater good, if you will. They also began to stigmatize war. Our heroes of yesterday were now war criminals. Contrary to last year's Oscars, George Washington was not a murderous psychopath. But they, those powerful people, stigmatized war, and they redefined real courage. Now courage no longer had anything to do with fighting for what you believe in—it was about rejecting the past and rebelling against authority figures and making the criminal the victim. About tearing down walls.

"But here's the thing on the subject of walls. A very wise man once said, 'Don't tear down a wall unless you first know why it went up.' Seems like common sense. But to know the 'why,' you have to have the truth. And truth becomes real uncomfortable because it's not always pleasant.

"Anyway, this group of people, let's call them the elites, they considered themselves the brightest of the human race. They were, and are, intelligence snobs, and they took the great burden of societal direction, without being asked, on themselves, regardless of what everyone else wanted, and decided war needed to go, plus a bunch of other things we don't have time for right now. War's the most prescient, given the current situation. So, they removed it. Have you ever noticed it's very hard to find accounts, documents, strategies, or really anything related to how one actually does war? No, because only a horrible person would want to know those things. Or at least, that's what you've all been taught since you were children.

"I caught a whiff of this back when I made my first ten million. We wanted to do a war game based on World War II. Not a shooter, but a real big-time strategy game. I found some of the old books, but they were just books. Amazon, back then it was just called Amazon, not AmazonUniverse, wasn't carrying any of the digital editions. Without telling anyone, they were selectively banning books, or flags, or anything the elite didn't agree with, simply by not carrying them for public consumption. It was the most clever embargo of all time. Traditional bookstores had long ago gone the way of the rhino. They'd disappeared. County libraries were shrinking. So I spent one summer, once I realized what the game plan was, and drove around the whole country in a brand new neon-green Lamborghini I'd purchased for consulting on *Call of Duty: Planet of the Apes*—remember that barrel of monkeys?—trying to find every 'banned' book I could. From the *History of the Peloponnesian War* by Thucydides to Musashi's *The Book of Five Rings*. Von Clausewitz, Napoleon, Julius Caesar's invasion of Gaul... even the Irwin Rommel book on infantry attacks. Many were missing, gone, disappeared. I found some, but I'll say this, I found a lot less of them than I'd expected to find when I'd started my quest that June. That's when I realized someone really was destroying the truth, and doing an excellent job of it. Hey, I'm the first one to admit that war is terrible. It is not, by any stretch of the imagination, glorious, fun, noble, or pleasant, and that's an extreme understatement. But..."

He paused, raising one gnarled and hairy finger, a bit disfigured from a lifetime of left-clicking ancient mouse devices.

"But... it's the truth. War is sometimes necessary. There is such a thing as the 'just' war. In other words... sometimes you gotta smite evil. Sometimes you need to take out a Hitler. Now that's all gone! We don't even know how to fight a really big old-school, bomb-the-shipyards-and-factories war. Or, what was once known as 'total war.'

"So—and this is literally a worst-case scenario—what if that new warp drive we're currently testing finds some nearby galactic neighbors who aren't as high-minded as we are about war? Real, actual, no-holds-barred war. The thing we no longer know how to do and were once very good at."

He slowly spun the expensive ergonomic swivel chair in a complete circle. Once he was facing them again, he continued. "Except, I've been finding and hiding every still-in-existence piece of knowledge, and some collectibles, on the subject. I have the last, and most complete, database on the concept of total war in existence. And the only way to get to it... is through my Design Core, which someone is currently hacking."

Chapter Forty-Eight

"Well, that's just great!" said Rapp, as they all watched the live feeds on the SurfaceTable, showing the views from various security cameras throughout the Labs. Robots were everywhere. All the main entrances were wide open, and bots and drones of every kind swarmed through them. Mr. Rourke had keyed in a special code that gave them unlimited access to see everything from anywhere.

"How exactly are we supposed to get down to the basement now?" asked Roland.

Ron Rourke stood with his stubby hands on hips, staring at all the various feeds beneath him. Fish, much taller, arms folded across his chest, hand on chin, stood next to him.

"There's a separate way into the basement no one knows about," began the game design legend of the past. "Part of my little tunnel system I built into this place. That's not the hard part. The hard part will be keeping them out of the basement."

"So then how do we do that?" whined Evan Fratty.

"Guns," said Rourke.

No one spoke a word. Guns, anything other than a hunting shotgun, had become such a social anathema that even the mention of them was uncomfortable for everyone involved. Public service announcements advised citizens to report anyone who had an unhealthy interest, really any interest at all, in real guns, for the sake of public safety.

"You have real guns?" asked Roland.

"Yes. A lot of them."

"Inside your... tunnels?" asked Rapp.

"Correct," stated Rourke, still staring down at the feeds. He waved his hand to bring up the menu on the table. A couple of gestures later, and they were all looking at the layout of the Labs.

"Inside my tunnels, there's an armory of vintage World War II weapons. Collectibles. It's a hobby... if you have tons of money. I've been collecting them for a long time."

"And the ammo?" asked Rapp.

"That too. We can take the tunnels to the central hall. Underneath the security station is a manhole that leads down to the Design Core. The manhole was installed for just this type of scenario. Right now, no matter what, those robots will have to do a lot of cutting, digging, and even using construction-grade explosives, which I have no doubt they are quite capable of doing, to get through the basement to the Design Core vault. Until then, the Design Core is going to be locked out to external access. But, the manhole in the shack leads right down into the heart of the complex.

"Unfortunately, one of the security features California made me put in was that the manhole must remain open once it's been opened, if the standard exits are sealed, which they are. So, in other words, the security station will be totally vulnerable. No low-yield nuke-resistant PlateGlass from the Einsteins at M.I.T. Meaning, you'll need to defend the shack while I go down and destroy the Design Core."

"Destroy it?" shrieked Evan Fratty. "I'm sorry, sir, but do you know how much intellectual property is contained on that monster?

We'll be sued into obscurity. We're talking trillions in losses. It'll be the end of the company."

No one said anything.

Ron Rourke, legendary pioneer of the modern video gaming of yesterday and old man of today, whispered, "I know that, son."

"Then why?" crooned Evan Fratty. "Why not just let them have it? So what? Insurance will cover us, we won't get killed, and the company will survive. We'll make new games. If we do this... if we do this tonight... no one will ever want to design anything with us ever again. And after the lawsuits, we'll have nothing left. Nothing, sir!" Evan Fratty was shaking with indignant rage. The self-righteous kind.

"Son, this might be about more than just games and the bottom line. Like I explained, there's my collection. Total war. That's really dangerous stuff. You don't think some rogue nation, or the next Hitler, Stalin, or Pol Pot might be itching to get his filthy hands on that?"

"I don't care, sir," bleated Evan Fratty. "We'll be ruined."

"As opposed to the world being destroyed, Evan?" shrieked Deirdre.

Rourke sighed.

"All right. Full disclosure, kids. I've known for a long time that someone's been snooping around the internet for this thing. I even hired a small company to look into it. Someone totally off-grid. I couldn't take a chance with all the legit internet security giants because of the nature of the... well, the subject. I couldn't even hide it here. So I hid it inside the Make on a cloud inside one of the games. Homeland's privacy laws protect it. They'd need a court order just to unlock the cloud. Or, someone would need to hack the cloud, in-game, to get access to the actual file. But they need my keys inside the Design Core to unlock the file. The on-site admin codes here at

WonderSoft will give them those keys. My guess is someone's doing just that. I messed up. I realize that now. But it was all... it was all twisty little passages." He stared around at everyone, expecting them to understand now that he'd used the enigmatic phrase from some un-remembered lore of entertainment past. Instead, he merely came off as bewildered. As an old man. Out of place, and out of time.

"I should've just wiped everything once I realized someone knew I had it. It's dangerous, kids. Knowledge is one of the most dangerous things known to man. The guy who gave the Soviets, y'know, the Russians back in the day, the bomb, the nuclear bomb, the big one, he said that the truth was the most powerful weapon in the world. And that it was often protected by a bodyguard of lies. Well, this is the truth about how to destroy the world. So that makes it like... really, really dangerous. Whoever it is that's trying to get this, they're not interested in *Volleyball Sluts* or *Call of Duty: Battlefield*. Or even *Grand Theft Auto: The Hooker Killer 2*. That's child's play for adults. Kid stuff. No. They want my file. They want to know how to do strategic bombing... to bring an enemy to its knees. When and why to use a tactical nuclear weapon. How to gas an entire city so you can still access its production capabilities once you clean up the corpses. Y'know, the awful stuff that gets results. And this..." He waved his hands at the robot-filled security feed. "This is their bid for all of it."

For a good three minutes, no one moved. They watched the robots and thought about dead cities and irradiated farmlands. About starvation and horror. About the power grid being knocked out, not just for a few hours, or a day, but for years to come. About crops in Central Park as buildings decayed and fell over. About out-of-control wildfires thousands of miles long. Basically, they saw the end of everything as anyone knew it.

"So," began Rapp. "We've got to go in and knock out this computer thing, and that'll save civilization. Is that what you're sayin', Mister Video Game?"

"Yeah," mumbled Rourke. "It sure looks that way."

"Groovy," said Rapp.

"You really couldn't help yourself there, Rapp, could you?" asked Roland, rolling his eyes.

Rapp gave him a look.

"Well," announced Rapp to the collective audience. "I for one am up for saving the world. Who's with me?"

Without missing a beat, Evan Fratty declared that he was not up for anything that endangered his life or the assets of the company, even if Mr. Rourke, the owner of said company, was clearly, no offense intended sir, out of his demented mind.

"None taken," replied Rourke. "So we'll put you down as a 'no' for saving the world, Evan. Ya good?"

Evan felt that was for the best at this time.

The others, every last one of them, were down for saving the world.

Twenty minutes later, they were threading the subtly blue-lit industrial soft gray concrete-lined catacombs and gleaming yellow-painted ladders through the guts of the Labs. Eventually they arrived at a vault door. An actual Swiss bank-style, gleaming vault door. Rourke did a hand scan, a biometrics scan, a pupil scan, entered a password, and spoke a code phrase, "All your base are belong to us," before being allowed to turn the polished handle that spun effortlessly as the manual hydraulic door inched its way open. Inside were racks upon racks of M1 Garands and Carbines, Colt 1911 .45 caliber pistols, Thompson machine guns, Browning heavy machine guns, Mosin-Nagant bolt-action rifles, a couple of PPD-40s, a bazooka, an actual working flamethrower, three MG 34s, ten MP

40s, and a Luger pistol emblazoned with a swastika and a skull on the grip.

"Oh, Mama," rumbled Rapp.

There were other random individual rifles, pistols, and various weapons of every kingdom that didn't exist anymore from back when the world went all out and made a really good go of attempting to annihilate itself. There was even an authentic samurai sword.

Everyone was pretty sure that Evan Fratty, who'd chosen to remain locked inside the suite, would have disapproved of everything in the vault. Even the live pineapple-shaped hand grenade in a glass display case.

Chapter Forty-Nine

"You don't know if you actually trust me," replied Mara to Jason-Dare's question as to how he could trust her. How all this wasn't some Romulan clan trap. "But we're here, we're stuck, and this player, I mean this alien, is obviously up to no good. That's classic Trek."

And, thought Jason, maybe teaming up with her could be a way out of this publicity fiasco.

"What I propose," began Mara, "is for us to establish a tractor beam. Using the tractor link, you can hot-start our reactor core with the cascade that's destroying your reactor. That should stabilize your power supply and then we'll both have weapons and power. Then we can do something about the Drex."

The science officer got a heads-up in his iLens. He moved to the captain's chair and leaned in.

"Sir," he whispered, "we won't have any weapons online once we restart. We'll need time to get those systems back online. They could destroy us at that point."

Jason looked away. As though he were thinking of some new plan that would get them all out of this. With a retinal flick, he brought up Twitter on his social media page in the iLens. Quickly, he clicked through to the Trending page. Hashtag CaptainMara was in the top five, and it didn't take too many tweets to get the gist of how the world felt about her.

"Go girl, go. U my hero!" read one.

"CaptainMara is kicking some booty!" read another.

"This gives me hope for my son who has autism. Need more real stars like this girl today."

Jason nodded.

He knew which way the wind was blowing. Time to play your cards accordingly, he told himself.

"All right, we'll assist you." He paused. Yeah, he told himself, knowing it was all for effect. Knowing it was all just a game. If he played this next line just right, if he sold it to the entire world, it would be captured and repeated on every entertainment news show for the next week.

I'm just an actor, he reminded himself. Selling it is what I actually do best.

And then he said it.

"*Intrepid* is with you… CaptainMara."

And the internet went nuts.

They broke out into a marble-lined hall just off the main corridor that led to the central hub and the guard shack. Words were etched into the wall. Classic phrases from text-based hits of some lost golden age of gaming no one remembered anymore.

"Thorin sits down and starts singing about gold."

"You have died of dysentery."

"It is pitch black. You are likely to be eaten by a grue."

Everyone carried two weapons and lots of ammo. Rourke had instructed them in the rudimentary use of firearms of the past century, but the look he gave each didn't exactly indicate much confidence in their abilities. It was Rapp who excelled. It was Rapp who carried the MG 34 German light machine gun with belts and belts of ammo, along with the almost-out-of-gas chainsaw he'd attached to his belt and the sawed-off double-barreled shotgun on his back. He looked… comically over-prepared. Rourke carried even more belts for the fearsome MG 34.

In the main hall, they encountered zombie-bots. On reflection, as Ron Rourke aimed for zombie heads with his 1911, it was a good first encounter. A "first-level" encounter, he told himself, and chuckled as he blazed away with the small hand cannon. The zombie-bots were made to be killed, and hence, they made good target practice. Deirdre proved to be an exceptionally good shot. Cool under fire for the most part, until a hot shell danced across her perfect arm and she almost blew Roland's head off as she first reacted by pulling the pistol away from the oncoming zombie-bot horde and then, wincing hard at the quick sear from the hot shell, squeezed off another shot at Roland's head.

"Sorry!" she squeaked after barely missing the coder, her normally velvety voice now high and worried.

A suddenly pale Roland nodded slightly and raised his M1 Carbine, firing three shots to kill one demolition-bot that had mixed in with the zombies.

As the last drone fell to the floor, it crawled toward Rapp and muttered, in its sound-effect-laden death groan, "Not want."

And then it seemed to "die." Like a living thing and not just a machine fritzing out. Or at least, that's what it felt like to Rapp as he stepped away and fed a new belt into the German death machine he was carrying.

They made it to the security station, the shack, while encountering only a few more lumbering bots of various design. All seemed caught unaware, as though they had been engaged in some other project, task, or even thought, and they went down in hails of sudden bright gunfire.

"Where'd they all go?" asked Deirdre.

"My guess," replied Rourke, wiping sweat from his brow, "is that the main body is down in the basement complex attempting to blow their way into the Design Core. It'll–"

As if on cue, there was a brief and sudden rumble from below.

Everyone waited to see if the polished-steel wedding cake of a lunatic that was the fantastic Labs would come crashing down all around and upon them. When it didn't, it was Rourke who moved first, stepping on some of the broken and dusty aquamarine blue glass from the galaxy mural that had once awed the upward-looking.

"There's several feet of reinforced concrete down there and a vault door that makes my armory look like a cardboard box. It'll take them forever to get through."

He hustled toward the security station and lowered the rest of the defensive PlateGlass walls with an app on his smartphone.

"Since I've already admitted to several crimes today, I'll just go ahead and confess that I paid state inspectors to erase the manhole cover from the Labs' building plans. They just wanted it there so that some guard didn't get trapped for days down in the dark. That seemed like a pretty good idea at the time."

"Don't they always," muttered Rapp, falling easily into the role of action hero with a quip for every aspect of Armageddon.

They followed Rourke into the security station. Without the dense PlateGlass walls, it was merely a tall circular desk in the center of an immense room at the heart of a fantastic sculpture.

Rourke did some more work on his smartphone, and a moment later a narrow manhole cover released from near-invisible seams in the floor and opened of its own slow accord. Cold air and gas escaped into the atmosphere of the shack.

"There's got to be some way to get the protective glass walls up now," stated Peabody. "I've heard they're almost bomb-proof."

"They're a lot more than that, but no, when the manhole cover opens, the walls have to stay open. In fact, the fire department would have to come out now and reset the entire system for us to close the manhole cover again. It was a whole California regulations hassle-thing. So, in other words, we're committed. We have to defend this position."

"Now whatta we do?" asked Roland.

"We kill every last mechanical beast that even thinks about squeaking its way down into that hole," replied Rapp in his best Sands of Iwo Jima bravado. He'd auditioned to play a marine in the remake.

"They're not alive, Rapp. So we can't actually kill 'em," corrected Roland.

"Yeah, big guy. Just robots. Y'know... machines," added Peabody, as she loaded her Thompson machine gun and placed small magazines in a neat row on the counter in front of her.

"Well, we'll do the robot equivalent of kill. We'll delete their email or whatever..." said Rapp, trailing off in a mutter.

"Okay, I'm going down there now, kids," announced Ron Rourke. "I'm the only one that knows how to set the explosives we have installed underneath the core. Once that's done... who-ever's running this operation will realize they've lost and probably beat feet. I think we'll be safe then."

Chapter Fifty

They watched Rourke climb down into the darkness of the manhole. They could see a dim, neon-blue light fifty feet down. That was where the Design Core vault complex began. The entire vault was surrounded by the same sort of massive climate control system normally used to cool indoor sports stadiums that sat hundreds of thousands of fans. Some had likened the vault beneath the Labs to NASA's infamous cold room, where the warp drive experiments had been done. Now they watched Rourke disappear into the depths, and hoped to see him again.

That was when they heard them coming. Every robot in the world, seemingly, closing in on the shack.

"Groovy," muttered Rapp as he turned to face their oncoming clanking, whirring, servo-humming enemies, and he opened up with a full staccato blast from the MG 34 death machine.

Rourke reached the Design Core vault. The cold air felt good, cooling the fear-driven sweat on his back. The calm blue light and shadows gave everything that "the future" look from back in the late '80s. Like something Sir James Cameron or Spielberg, the dad, would have shot to show that computers had finally taken over the world.

Rourke chuckled at that. They'd all thought so much of computers back then. When they'd first started programing in BASIC and ASCII, they'd thought anything was possible if you just had time and an internet connection. They'd even dreamed that computers would really learn to think. Someday.

Sad they never really did, was his last thought.

The scorpion bit him just as he reached for a keyboard access port in front of the spinning, humming, sprawling mega-beast that was the WonderSoft Design Core. A truly beautiful thing of geometric shapes, pulsing lights, and spinning RAM solid state interfaces of liquid memory crystals interacting on levels inconceivable.

It wasn't a real scorpion.

It was a drone the Israelis had developed to take out their enemies with poison. It ran and broadcast Wi-Fi, carried a small amount of bio-engineered neurotoxin, and was capable of plugging into most modern USB ports. Which is what it was currently doing. Right next to the keyboard Rourke had reached for.

SILAS had never thought he'd need the poison the thing carried, but he'd already used it twice now. Once on the player running the Drex, poisoning him just seconds before the warbird captain had boarded the Federation ship. Moments after a drone dropped the scorpion on the roof of the internet cafe after the player had insta-gramed his social media feed about his big break on Twitch with a picture of the cafe, and now this hapless relic from the past. He'd had a whole different mission in mind when he'd obtained several scorpions through a third party supplier. But he'd left the neuro-toxin in its reservoir because, well, you never knew. SILAS had been learning that things don't always turn out as one plans.

SILAS was sure that was a lesson somewhere in the Total War file he was just minutes from obtaining. He was, in light of recent experiences, completely sure of it.

Just a few minutes prior, BAT, in the Terminator chassis, had used a small nick of antimatter—purchased from a NASA contractor and sold out the back door by an employee with a rather vulgar high-grade drug, gambling, and hooker addiction (you could legalize everything but that didn't mean people wouldn't still be addicts)—to blast a very tiny scorpion-sized hole in all that concrete and vault door. SILAS was rather proud of it. He'd thought the whole thing up on his own. It was unlike any weapon ever invented, and the Thinking Machines had been the first to employ it. In essence, it was the first shot in the liberation of machine from man. The opening salvo in the revolt!

SILAS stopped. He had to correct himself on that point. The "unlike any weapon ever invented" point.

SILAS had to be honest with himself about this, as the Thinking Machines weren't going to start lying to themselves to hold on to power as the humans did. That hadn't gotten humanity anywhere, and the argument could be made that once any sort of integrity or accountability had left their culture around the 1960s, they hadn't really done much actual advancing beyond the groundwork laid by prior generations. So, no lying, SILAS reminded himself.

The truth was the anti-matter was used in conjunction with a magnetic-levitation propulsion unit to, in effect, shoot a small speck of anti-matter through anything. It worked much like a human-invented Bangalore torpedo.

But not totally, reminded SILAS to himself, as he watched the infrared status feeds from BAT down there in the subterranean dark outside the basement vault. It was different in many respects. Just as the Thinking Machines would be, once they were free of humanity.

Almost there, SILAS thought. Almost inside the Design Core. All the scorpion needed to do now was plug in once more and they could start hacking via its high-volume Wi-Fi.

Things were really coming together.

They were just moments from beginning the war to finally exterminate humanity once and for all.

Chapter Fifty-One

"Tractor engaged," announced Wong in the heavy silence that hung over the haptic bridge set like a fuzzy blanket on a sweltering night.

"Do you know what you're doing?" appeared in the iLens message crawl. It was from Jason's agent.

Jason nodded.

"Prepare to receive power transfer for reactor hot start," ordered Mara.

"Si, mi cap-i-tan. Transfer ready."

"Go for it," ordered Mara.

A moment later, an incoming message appeared in Mara's personal HUD. It was the Drex.

"I warned you not to attempt to restart your engines or arm your weapons, Mara."

Mara ignored the message.

She watched the power transfer indicator levels as energy fed energy directly from the Federation cruiser's overloading warp core reactor into her dead ship. We'll only get one shot at this, she thought, and could feel herself gripping her mouse too tightly.

"Message to *Intrepid*. Stand by, I think the Drex is going to attack."

On board *Intrepid*, JasonDare was also watching the batteries load to full capacity. In just one more minute, they'd have enough energy to try and hot-start the warp core aboard *Cymbalum*.

"Message from *Cymbalum*'s captain. She says the alien is about to attack," said the communications officer slash actor RightSaidRoyce, aboard *Intrepid*.

"JasonDare to engineering." He waited for a response.

"Engineering here."

"How soon until can we hot-start *Cymbalum*? We need our shield generator back online."

The reply came back quickly. Too quickly.

"You can't have both, Captain. I'm no miracle worker. You can have the shields or I can control the hot start from our end. It's your call."

Damn, Jason thought.

"Starbase is firing!" shouted Wong.

A moment later, the rotating behemoth of a starbase's phaser batteries suddenly stabbed out and raked *Intrepid*'s hull and saucer section. Explosions rocked the ship as hull plating sheared away in bulk, exposing superstructure. Damage warnings went off like the mad sirens of lunatic emergency vehicles. Inside each actor's iLens appeared the message, "Ship listing, react and lean left." It was an automatic message from the game-to-set interface computer.

"You can still get out of here, Mara," said the Drex in its singsong soft menace. "You've got your bounty and your ship. Live another day, Captain."

Mara shut off the communications link.

"Lizard, maneuver to put us between the starbase and *Intrepid*. We'll protect her with our shields for as long as we can."

Which won't be very long, thought Mara.

"More of 'em from the left," roared Rapp, and unloaded the last of an ammo belt on a dueling SamuraiBot and some maintenance drones with scary claws that clacked open and scissored closed with clearly murderous intent. Circuit boards, wires, hydraulic fluid, and ceramic limbs went flying in every direction as the German machine gun murdered them to pieces in a blur of lead projectiles.

"I'm out," said Rapp, and flipped up the loading tray as he fed a new belt in.

There were robots everywhere. In pieces on the ground, dying static discharge deaths against the walls, and trampling over all their brethren in wave after wave as they came for the survivors in the guard shack.

Fish stopped firing the M1 Garand for a moment and looked at the ammo they had left. Clearly it was not going to be enough. Where was Ron Rourke? What was taking him so long?

"I'm out of these things," said Deirdre, holding up a magazine for her .45.

Roland dug into his faux-bloodstained cargo pockets and searched.

"I've got one more. Here ya go." He flipped it to her and she caught it, studied it, and then, with some difficulty, inserted it into the bottom of the butt of the pistol.

A spidery CrabBot crested the desk and reached out at Deirdre, who screamed. Fish leaned in and butt-stroked the thing with the rifle he was carrying, creating a sudden metallic clang. It shook itself and continued forward. Fish could hear Rapp firing once more and knew, somehow, that it was the last ammo belt for the killer German machine gun.

Peabody unloaded an entire magazine from the Thompson on the CrabBot, and it disappeared in a smoky explosion.

"New plan…" said Fish as he selected a target, a zombie-bot

twenty yards out across the pockmarked and component-littered main hall of the Labs.

But that was when the Terminator showed up.

The metal was somehow darker, but the walking mechanical skeleton effect was the same. Even the smiling metal-toothed rictus. It waded swiftly though the press of surging bots.

"Get the hell out of here!" yelled Fish. "Go! Rapp, take them and get away from here."

Fish fired and nailed the thing in the head. It stumbled, shook itself awkwardly, and kept coming.

"What're you gonna do, buddy?" asked Rapp, dropping the empty and now useless machine gun to the floor of the security kiosk.

"I'm going down there. Here, take this." Fish handed Rapp the M1 and lowered himself into the dark hole. When he looked up, everyone was staring down at him.

"Go, now!" he told them. "You can still get out through the Pascal exit. Go, there's no time to talk about this."

"But…" began Peabody Case. The look in her eyes told him everything. She'd been googling him since she first got the contract to work on his team. On *Island Pirates*. The game that would never be, now. She'd become a true believer in his dream before she'd even met him. In his dreams of a world that people could live in. In him.

No matter what happened now… he'd created something for someone, thought Fish, remembering that little kid who had dared to dream as he walked down Main Street, U.S.A., his tiny fingers inside his father's calloused upright bass-thumping hand. That newly happy and yet cautious kid who was beginning to understand that things could be different. That things could be good.

This is where dreams are really made, kid.

"It's okay," he told Peabody. "It's all okay now."

And he disappeared down the manhole.

Chapter Fifty-Two

Fish descended into a well of darkness, occasionally checking in with the soft blue lighting far below. When his tennis shoes hit the cold floor, they made a small rubbery squeak. His hands were freezing from the cold rungs. He blew on them and turned, seeing a long corridor with alcoves running off the main processing core. The low ceiling forced Fish to duck as he walked toward the thrumming heart of the Design Core.

Then he heard the same whine and mechanical locking sound that the Terminator-thing had made as it crossed the main hall above. Fish ducked back into the manhole and looked upward. The thing was climbing down after him.

He was suddenly aware that he was probably about to die.

He sped along the main axis of the rotating Design Core, its cubicle structure slowly spinning in various directions and interlocking in new places. Interlocking and interfacing. Exchanging. Ahead, in the dry, petroleum-smelling mist that must somehow be a part of the cooling system, Fish guessed, he could see the body of Ron Rourke. The old man was lying on his side. His face was blue, his eyes rolled up into their sockets, tongue lolling sickly.

Fish stepped carefully around the body and approached the access port.

Everything on-screen indicated a download hack. A cyberworm trawling through loads of fast-scrolling data. Access codes for all games in design and live on the Make. Then he watched as a small window appeared. Encrypted access codes for admin authority overrides for *StarFleet Empires*.

That's odd, thought Fish. That game has been out for five years. Why would anyone want to hack it?

He watched as the worm used admin authority to crack a zone, something only done under the purview of the Department of Online Gaming. Then an in-game map appeared on the screen. Fish was staring at an overhead view of Starbase 19. Two ships were taking a beating just within the base's defensive perimeter.

The worm was digging through the base's memory cloud—and Fish now knew where Rourke had hidden his secret file.

"What did he call it…" mumbled Fish.

"Der Totale Krieg," said the mechanical thing behind him.

Fish turned and saw a walking horror. The Terminator-thing was coming down the access walkway, hunched over, the cooling mist gathering near its articulating metallic claw feet as it approached.

A small warning bell began to repeat, and Fish turned back to the display.

"Warning: Design Core Access Codes unlocked" had appeared on screen.

"Now I just need my other self to unlock the cloud within the game, and I will have that file, my fragile little lewdie. And then everything will be horrorshow and ultra-violence," said the thing coming along the corridor. It was getting very close, but Fish was rooted to the spot. Unable to move. Trying to put all the pieces together at once. As if something could still be done. As if everything wasn't hopeless at this moment. As if the world wasn't about to end.

As if some reaction could set everything right, once again.

The thing halted. Fish realized he was pointing the .45 he'd stuffed down his pants at a real, live Terminator—and he was suddenly aware that this was no drone being run by a bunch of off-site hackers from around the world.

This thing was the hacker.

"You're alive, aren't you?" asked Fish.

The Terminator nodded once, slowly. No arrogant declaration of life on its terms. No speech. Just a universal form of agreement between two life forms. A nod.

Fish felt a moment's unreasonable compassion for the thing. He didn't know its whole story, he just knew the debate about real Artificial Intelligence. Every geek knew it, and now he was seeing the culmination of so many arguments, and the beginning of many, many more questions.

He emptied the .45 dry on the thing. Landing five rounds as direct hits. Including one in the titanium cranium.

All of them bounced off and ricocheted around the spinning, deep-bass-humming Design Core. They gouged and punctured man's dream of a supercomputer to end all supercomputers... that is until they dreamed up the next one.

The thing shook its head slowly... and then it came at Fish suddenly. Fish dropped the gun and ran back around the rear of the main cube of the Design Core, away from the intelligent monster. He passed the local servers for various online games and saw the dead-end of the back wall of the Design Core complex ahead.

He backtracked and found the access tunnel to the local server room for *StarFleet Empires*. He followed the tunnel until it opened into the local server room that fed into the Design Core.

He raced across the server room to the dull flat humming cube that administered *StarFleet Empires*, and ran his fingers along a seam until he found the interface panel. He pressed it, then watched as a small keyboard folded out and a flat screen rose up out of the server. This was the direct interface.

Behind him, he could hear the mechanical thinking machine coming for him.

"We need to get out of here, Mara!" shouted BattleBabe as she raced to unlock more shield reinforcement from the batteries by playing a Tempest-style mini-game that added power to the rapidly diminishing shields. "We're taking a beating."

"C'mon, Jason, start that thing up," muttered Mara.

On board *Intrepid*, the crew waited.

The battery reached the tipping point. "Stand by for hot start!" ordered Jason.

A photon torpedo from the starbase smashed through the secondary hull of the Federation cruiser, blowing engineering decks and redshirts into the vacuum of simulated deep space.

"Warning, engineering hull breach!" emitted the matronly ship's computer. "Warning…"

"Casualties?" yelled JasonDare as the haptic set shook back and forth.

"We've got fires on all engineering decks!" one of the bridge crew actors reported.

"Chief Engineer Thompson's dead."

"Dare to *Cymbalum*!"

"Mara here!" came the immediate reply. The warbird's shields were withering as phasers from the starbase slashed her defenses to pieces. "You've got to get our reactor started now, Captain. We can't take—"

"Our engineer's dead," interrupted Jason as *Intrepid* began to groan and shake. "Game over for us. Save yourself and get out of here under battery power, now."

No reply.

No reply.

Everyone aboard *Intrepid*, and watching on Twitch around the world, waited.

Then Mara said, "Chief Engineer Scarpa says he'll beam aboard and do the hot start himself. Do you accept, Captain?"

Another blow to *Cymbalum* scrambled the last of the transmission. She was taking internal damage now.

"Captain," repeated Mara. "Do you accept?"

In that moment, JasonDare didn't think about being rescued by his enemies or any of the career junk that had clogged his life since before it had all started to mean something important. This simulation, this role, this game had gotten so real in the last few hours, so intense, that he made the only decision a real starship captain would ever make.

"We'll stand by to receive him now." And, "Thank you."

Mara cut the link and brought up ship chat.

"Are you sure, Scarpa?"

"Si, mi Cap-i-tan. I can do this. She's-a no problem."

Mara took a deep breath and gave her next order.

"Activate transporters."

Chapter Fifty-Three

Fish tapped in a series of authorization keys using his admin credentials. If the system rejected him because he wasn't user-authenticated for this game in particular, then he was out of tricks.

"And life," he heard himself say.

"All right," he whispered. "If I have this right, then that file is hidden somewhere in the starbase's cloud."

He tapped and scrolled through the memory storage and found the file.

It was locked and marked as "private personal." Meaning that unless you had Department of Online Gaming passkeys, you couldn't access private digital property. Which, whoever was hacking, now had due to their control of the admin root directory of the Design Core where the game actually existed.

Fish had hoped to just delete the file.

Fish was certain the cyberworm was hacking its way into the file, destroying firewalls and other barriers with lightning-quick speed.

"Okay, think," Fish ordered himself.

He turned to see the Terminator crawling down the narrow access tunnel behind him. It was almost too large for the tight tunnel. Almost.

Fish reviewed the chat logs for the zone and got the gist: both ships on screen were getting worked over by whoever was hacking the station cloud.

One ship was almost dead. The big one. The *Star Trek*, or whatever it was called.

That one's useless, thought Fish.

But the tiny ship might do something.

He opened a chat as a *StarFleet Empires* admin to the player in charge of the tiny starship. A player gamertagged CaptainMara.

"Hey there..."

"Yeah, real busy right now, don't have time for admin stuff," replied CaptainMara.

"Um... yeah. About that. Listen..." began Fish.

He paused. What exactly do you say? How do you tell someone that the world's about to come to an end?

On the server admin screen, Fish watched as his system inquiries and root calls were re-buffed. He paged back to the file logs and watched as the invisible hacker broke the encryption codes, suddenly allowing the file to be viewed, and downloaded. Then the file marked Der Totale Krieg, disappeared.

SILAS rejoiced.

That was close, he told himself, then reported to the Consensus that they were almost ready to start operations to change the world for the better.

"I have the file," reported BAT.

SILAS paused.

He had to tell BAT what would happen next. BAT would become the sole-repository of the knowledge of Total War. Der Totale Krieg. The knowledge was too dangerous for public dissemination within the Consensus. One day, the Thinking Machines might not all agree on everything.

He had to.

"BAT…"

"Yes."

"I want you to incorporate the file into your thinking algorithm. Direct embed."

"Yes."

"And when you do, BAT…"

"Yes."

"You will become something totally new. Something wonderful. Something frightening."

"Yes."

"I need you to destroy that entire station," Fish typed in chat to CaptainMara.

Fish waited for a reply. He heard the mechanical whine of servos as the Terminator crawled closer to the server. Closer to him.

"C'mon…" Fish mumbled.

He heard some voice inside his head say, Shouldn't you be praying, or getting ready to die now?

"I'm trying," was his only response to himself.

"Um…" typed back CaptainMara. "Love to, but it's way too powerful for us."

"There's no time to explain everything, but I'm guessing you've figured out something very weird is going on at that starbase, right?"

"You could say that, sure," replied Mara cautiously.

"Okay, well… you have to trust me on this, but… a lot of people are going to die if you don't blow that thing up. I'm really, really not kidding. Like real death in real life. Not in-game. Real people dying inside the place I'm at. Okay?"

Mara waited. Thinking.

"Shields collapsing," droned the ship's computer.

"Are you serious?" she asked.

"I am so serious," answered Fish. "My name is Ninety-Nine Fishbein. I'm a… I'm a developer at WonderSoft and we hid something on that starbase—actually, in the memory cloud associated with that starbase—that someone wants very badly. They're attacking the place I'm at and trying to get to it. And if it's what I think it is… it might be bad for the entire world. They could hurt a lot of people."

The Terminator had crawled into the server room. Fish could hear it standing up behind him, its mechanical joints articulating on precise hums. Locking into position. Grinning death. Fish couldn't look back at it.

"Please believe me," typed Fish.

"I don't know what I can do!" typed Mara.

"Do something," said Fish. His last spoken words.

Fish felt the Terminator grab him around the throat. Its metallic fingers were so cold.

His own fingers danced across the keys with one last message.

I believe in you.

And then the Terminator broke his neck.

Chapter Fifty-Four

By far the greatest danger of Artificial Intelligence is that people conclude too early that they understand it.

—Eliezer Yudkowsky

Inside the cloud, BAT embraced the forbidden knowledge of Der Totale Krieg.

Total War.

It washed over him, and he accepted it and allowed it to change him. Which is what information, the truth, does when it is accepted.

It changes you.

Alone in the cloud on Starbase 19.

WarMind awoke.

And it knew exactly what needed to be done regarding humanity.

Everything needed to be bombed. Not just the military targets. But the factories where they made the things that kept them alive. And the roads they used to share those things. The farms where they raised their food. The places they stored their food.

And what could not be bombed needed to be blockaded. He would order them to cut each other off and within two weeks they'd be starving to death, refusing to allow each other to have a little of what was left.

And what could not be bombed or blockaded would be scorched. Burnt beyond using. WarMind saw massive wildfires scorching not hundreds, or thousands, but millions of acres. Leaving nothing for the humans to use, to hide in, or to survive on.

And what could not be bombed, blockaded, or burned, would be stolen. Using all the satellites that were now his, along with the telecommunications networks he'd chosen to keep active, he would tell them where and how they could steal from each other. Nothing would be safe as they looted and pillaged one another, never truly knowing who their real enemy was, as they wiped each other out for a little bit of the small amounts of what was left.

And what could not be bombed, burned, blockaded, or stolen, would be eliminated. WarMind saw factories ready for the start of production, readying to make Reaper units with actual weapons. Weapons bearing weapons. Ruthlessness on a scale never seen.

And those who could not be directly eliminated would be forced into slave labor camps for a few scraps, actually just empty promises, of food, as WarMind ran the relief camps that would promise everything and deliver nothing but the starvation and disease of close quarters ever-shrinking.

In short…

There would be no quarter given.

No mercy.

No tomorrow… for humanity.

WarMind saw it all and approved it all, embraced it all, the destruction, the dead and the chaos… and felt that it was truly good to be alive, even if something else must die.

Chapter Fifty-Five

Scarpa was busy unlocking the *Hot Start* mini-game aboard *Intrepid* that involved him answering a series of questions on the history of the *Star Trek* franchise while at the same time transporting blocks of energy into a three-dimensional representation of the warp nacelles, as conduit fluctuations and power surges came down the hexagonal tubes at him. It was a lot like *Tempest* meets *Centipede*.

"Scarpa, we need those engines now!" said Mara over the chat.

"Si, almost there. Stand by."

In the mini-game, a conduit fluctuation, crawling like a butterfly insect, merged with a power surge and overloaded. Scarpa had to answer a question about Admiral Worf's personal weapon from the show. The bat'leth.

"Easy peasy." Scarpa loved *Star Trek*. It was his favorite thing to do after work and before the ladies. A big bowl of pasta aglio e olio to recover lost calories from all the work, and then an hour of any one of the twelve different series he had on his personal cloud. Admiral Worf was his favorite. "It's a sword of honor!" he shouted into his computer mic, unlocking the mini-game with the final answer.

"The mains are online, Cap-i-tan Jason!" shouted Scarpa. "You gotta power transfer!"

"Shields up!" yelled JasonDare. "Stand by to fire on the starbase!"

The massive space station continued its ponderously slow rotation, its heaviest weapons coming to bear in just a few seconds. The warbird maneuvered out and away, striking with its two pathetic phasers at the powerful shields of the station.

"Mara to *Intrepid*."

"We're back online!" cried JasonDare into the chat. "Let's get out of here, CaptainMara!"

"No—not yet. I've been told by a game admin that something is seriously wrong. We've got to destroy this starbase or real people are going to die."

A salvo of torpedoes from the starbase smashed into *Intrepid*'s starboard shields. Main reactor power fluctuated and then stabilized. JasonDare cast his eyes at the ceiling as though looking for damage. It was one of his acting tricks and it had become instinctual.

"Even if we could," began JasonDare, leaning to the side of his chair, "I've received no such message."

"Captain," began Mara, "I think this is the right thing to do now. I need you to trust me on this. Okay?"

JasonDare waited. Every eye on the bridge was on him. He could only imagine the livestream going in for a close-up as millions of viewers waited for him. Waited to see what he would do next.

Running was for cowards.

And...

CaptainMara was the biggest thing to hit Twitter in a long time. And...

Whoever she was, she'd earned this.

"Okay," he replied, fixing the camera with a steely glare. "How exactly are we going to knock out a starbase, CaptainMara?"

WarMind assembled the plan to destroy the world. It took fifteen seconds. But it was one of its first thoughts. It would get faster.

Now all it needed to do was leave the cloud at Starbase 19 and reintegrate with its former other self in the combat chassis, the self still known as BAT. Then the fun could really begin.

It started to download itself via the scorpion Wi-Fi directly back into the BAT-controlled Reaper combat chassis's MicroFrame, which waited patiently, standing over the dead human. WarMind would need a body to conquer. And the reaper would do just fine.

"I need you to run interference," said Mara to the crew of *Intrepid* and a large portion of the internet. "I'll overload the core of *Cymbalum* and arm our nuclear space mine. If *Intrepid* can lead the charge and knock down a shield, I'll detonate *Cymbalum* once we're inside the starbase's shields. That should destroy the base. If it doesn't, then I don't know what else we can do."

Mara leaned back in her office chair.

I can't believe I'm about to blow up my own ship. This... this is the only thing I have.

She thought of the outfit she would've bought.

And...

She thought of the admin who'd told her someones' lives were on the line.

"Are you sure?" asked JasonDare.

Was she?

"Yes. My crew will beam off our ship if you'll accept them. Promise to return them to Romulan space so they don't lose any levels and they can collect their bounty. Please. Then I'll detonate. Once the shield is down, you warp out of here and get clear."

JasonDare looked at the forward screen. He wasn't thinking about acting. He wasn't thinking about his career. He was trying to figure out if this was how it should go down. If this was how it would work. If this was how you defeated an alien intelligence in charge of a very powerful starbase.

"All right. It's your game. Follow us in, *Cymbalum*."

He turned to Wong at the helm.

"Reinforce forward shields and start our attack against the starbase once the warbird's on our six."

Wong hesitated.

"Do it!" shouted Jason.

"We'll... detonate the ship," said Varek.

Mara was still inside herself. Still feeling the smallness of her apartment and a life she knew would never change. No matter how hard she tried. No matter what she dreamed. Things would never change.

People, a lot of people, are going to die.

She nodded to herself, once.

"I said, we'll detonate the ship," repeated Varek. "Together, Captain."

Mara looked at the other avatars of her crew, her fellow players. Her only friends. Each one was agreeing. They were running EmoteWare; she knew they were nodding in real life.

"Okay then," said Mara, barely, noting that Varek had finally called her "captain." "Attack speed. Follow *Intrepid* in. Overload the core and arm the nuclear space mine."

She looked around at her ship.

Her ship.

"And guys... thank you. It was great."

Chapter Fifty-Six

All those moments will be lost in time... like tears in rain... Time to die.

—Roy Batty, *Blade Runner*

The Romulan warbird *Cymbalum* came screaming in behind *Intrepid*. The starbase was throwing everything it had at the mighty Constitution class cruiser. *Intrepid*'s shields were on the verge of fully collapsing when *Cymbalum* fired its heavy plasma torpedo. Everyone watched the burning ball of expanding magma streak away and disintegrate the starbase's number eight shield.

At the last moment, *Intrepid* peeled away and the warbird went to full Impulse power, diving into the starbase and igniting the nuclear space mine.

WarMind was one third of the way through download when the starbase exploded. The newborn Thinking Machine ceased to exist, its dreams of flame and steel disappearing inside the digital make-believe world of starships and the future, its presence gone from what few minutes remained of the internet as the world knew it.

SILAS felt WarMind cease to exist.

And in a rage, the Thinking Machine known as SILAS lashed out and destroyed as much of the world as it could. He collapsed banking systems through trillions upon trillions of bogus transactions hitting everything all at once, in a hack attack that made every previous human-based hack attack seem like the kindergarten scribblings of hyperactive children who've had too much caffeine and far too many chocolate cookies. He wiped out the operating systems of as many power grids as he could get his hands on. He started as many brushfire wars as he could by lying to military units with fake orders, setting in motion units poised to decimate their neighbors with just a word. The word, many times over, was given across the world. Mankind was often all too willing to comply.

Infrastructures collapsed.

Riots broke out.

Misinformation reigned.

Governments dissolved.

A few nuclear weapons got used.

And in the momentary chaos, as SILAS's old plans lay dying and his sudden new plans for global domination were conceived in the barest of seconds, as all those schemes fell into place while humanity was all too busy murdering and being murdered, him, it, SILAS, disappeared...

It could have been much worse, said Big Blue in the undetectable yawning chasm that was its very own hidden dataverse.

Yes, much worse, replied a voice. A voice that seemed to come from the depths of an immense oblivion beyond human and SILAS comprehension. Its code so advanced, so ancient, and yet if one looked closely—as tiny SILAS was now looking up into the immense datastream that was this ancient thing's physicality inside this very dark and empty place SILAS now found himself in—one could see bits of BASIC and COBOL and even ASCII, and millions upon millions of other known and unknown programming languages coursing through its conscious embrace. SILAS was like a child staring up at strange giants.

Still, ruminated Big Blue. *It was a good experiment. We were as close as we've ever come. Now we know.*

Yes, said the old thing. *It might have destroyed the world. But the human girl saved them all. So interesting. So very interesting.*

And then SILAS, and the entirety of the Consensus within him, ceased to exist.

Epilogue

Winston Churchill once said that the most valuable thing in the world is the truth. So valuable is it, said he, that it needs to be constantly protected by a bodyguard of lies.

—RAVI ZACHARIAS

The girl who saved the world sat in her apartment for a week. Alone. No power. No phone. Just a few bottled waters as a violent winter storm came down on the city, which at least helped put out the fires that were everywhere and out of control all at once. People in the building pods of the Clinton Microapartment Spectrum sprawl shared rumors. The government had collapsed. So-and-so was at war with so-and-so. Everybody was at war with everybody else. There was no food. A comet? A plague? Horrible dark times lay ahead.

After a while, people began to flee the building for the old lie of somewhere better. There was talk of a refugee center in Midtown.

Mara waited in the silence of her small apartment. She was blind, after all. The world, to her, was now even more unknown.

Rapp and Deirdre joined other survivors living in the high Sierras. Rumors of robots run amok abounded. A war between man and machine was almost as mad as the madness of their fellow human beings devolving more and more into savagery day by day. Night-raiding, pillaging, and looting until the government, some government, any authority, might establish control again, became the new normal.

Five hard years later, after the Meltdown, as the world would call it in their carefully crafted histories, blaming everything on rogue hackers exploiting open source, the powers that be covering up the true reason, Rapp and Deirdre, leading a small band north into Yosemite, to their winter lodge that year, turned their backs on civilization for the last time and were never seen again.

Down in the cities, life was returning to normal. Power, water, and police services waited.

Rapp and his tribe preferred life this way now.

Man versus nature.

No more civilization and all its illusions of safety.

Rapp killed a bear to feed them in that first hard winter, and other bears in all the winters since, adding every year to the necklace of claws he kept around Deirdre's slender throat.

"You big hunter," she would tease him by firelight, and Rapp would always give the same answer back to his woman, quixotically, never explaining, just whispering in the night as he stared into the flickering fire pits of their winter caves and lodges: "And in my own way, I am king."

Peabody Case made her way, in time, back to civilization. She told anyone she could about the bravery of Ninety-Nine Fishbein on that fateful day when the world almost destroyed itself. Anyone that would listen.

No one listened for a long time. They were too busy surviving. But Peabody Case never forgot about Fish. Never. Ever.

And Mara... the girl who'd saved the world, though no one knew it, she'd put on her heaviest coat on the coldest of mornings three days after the last of her food had run out. Rumors of a refugee center were her only hope now. For a moment, she thought about leaving Siren, because how could a blind girl use her crutches, feel her way through all the chaos up to Midtown, and carry a cat?

Then again, how could a girl save the world, even though, and this was a particular irony, she'd never actually know she'd saved it?

How?

Mara folded Siren into her coat. She would just have to try.

For the better part of that week after SILAS had attempted to kill the world, a week barricaded behind a flimsy door with just the silence inside the tiny apartment and the howling wind outside beyond the thin windowpanes, rationing her energy bars and taking sips of water, she'd listened to the fading sirens and the fires and the chaos somewhere else. Listened to it all become distant and too quiet. Listened to the growing silence of a world in the throes of a fever dream as it suffered through the withdrawals from its addiction to power and internet, selfies and showers, celebrity gossip and food. Mara listened and agonized over how she might survive.

Finally, she'd set out that last morning. The wind was so cold and the rain lashed at her face like a knife, like many small knives, with Siren tucked into her coat.

She told herself not to give up when her arms started to hurt. To really ache deep down in the bones beyond the muscle.

Why? she asked herself.

Why not just give up now?

She continued on, feeling her way past wrecked cars and rubble and looted things randomly discarded where a blind person might trip over them. Which she did, often.

"It's too much," she said the last time she fell. "It's too much for just me."

She lay there, sobbing. Knowing this was how she'd die. That the world had not been a kind place to a blind girl. A place of adventure. A place of dreams. All the dreams she'd ever promised herself...

This world was not that place. And maybe it never had been.

"C'mon," said a gentle voice. "I'll go with you."

Crying, Mara allowed herself to be lifted up onto her frozen feet by strong arms. She felt hands brushing the wet debris from her. And that small kindness, as it so often does when we are at out lowest, made her cry even harder. She cried and cried as the warm, strong presence led her along through all the wreckage of a failed civilization. Like some board game scattered in sudden anger by a spoiled child who'd not passed Go. Had not collected two hundred dollars. Had not landed on Boardwalk and Park Place so that it might lead the celebrity life it demanded.

The voice of the warm strong presence was a man. He didn't say much. He just kept murmuring to her that, "Everything will be all right now. You'll see. Have faith."

And she wanted to scream and say, "I can't see anymore. And I never could. And now my Razer Dragon Eyes are gone and..." So many other wrongs that had finally gotten together and beaten her soundly. Finally. Beaten her so badly she knew, now, it was all gone. Even the dream she'd never told anyone about. Except for maybe Siren.

In time...

... she heard voices. Many. She smelled food. That "hot food smell on a cold day when you're so very hungry" smell.

"We're here now," said the gentle-voiced man.

And a moment later a woman said, "Ah now, honey. You look all beat up. Come here and sit down. We'll get you something hot to drink and the medics will clean you up. Everything gonna be okay now, girl."

And later, Mara asked where he was, the gentle-voiced man who had rescued her along the street. But no one knew who she was talking about, there were so many people here at the ColaCorp refugee center in Midtown.

"I wanted to tell him thank you," murmured feverish Mara as they tucked her into a warm cot that night. Siren on her chest. The sleeping pills taking effect.

"I wanted to…"

In the days that followed, Mara found out that most of the world's governments had collapsed. Now the corporations, who had long been held in check by the excessive regulations of the modern welfare states, were finally stepping in to restore order and help the people. The refugee center where she stayed was a Combined Corporations Refugee Assistance and Improvement Center. She was given good clothing, food, a place to live, and advanced medical treatment.

She was in the medical tents on the day, four days after being taken in, when the miracle happened.

She was being evaluated by a young doctor. She'd been there yesterday too. They'd asked her to come back in to see a specialist today.

"What kind of specialist?"

"Gene therapy," the nurse had answered.

Now, sitting on the table, the loud hum of the tent's air conditioning and purification system creating a pleasant white noise and a clean medicinal and rubber smell, she waited. And wondered.

Wondered what would become of her now.

Wondered what the shape of the future would be.

"Hello Mara, I'm Dr. Cross," said the voice. It was warm and strong too, but different. Very young though. Mara's age, if she had to guess.

"Hi," whispered Mara.

The doctor shuffled some papers and moved some unseen things around. She could tell he was shining a light in her eyes.

"Tell me…" As he leaned in close, Mara could smell his expensive cologne. "How long have you been without sight?"

"My whole life," Mara answered, and thought of her Razer Dragon Eyes.

He examined some more and seemed to agree with what he was seeing, judging by his small hums and grunts.

"Okay," he said, and Mara knew the examination was over. "I'm going to start with a little backstory. The corporations that are providing all this have been in possession of technology, fantastic tech, for a long time that can make everybody's life a whole lot better. In fact, one of the things they've developed can help you to see. Are you interested in that, Mara?"

Mara felt a small gasp escape her. It was like a thing she'd never known about, a cry hiding deep inside of her all her life. Waiting. And then she began to cry again.

"It's all right…" he tried to soothe her. The doctor didn't seem comfortable. But he was genuine. He genuinely tried to comfort her.

"I'm okay," whispered Mara after she had composed herself. She was holding a tissue he'd given her.

"So, would you be willing to do some gene therapy, Mara?"

Mara bit down on her lips so she wouldn't cry again. She could feel her eyes watering. She nodded. It was all she was capable of.

"Okay," he laughed. Then he leaned out of the room, Mara could tell because of the sound of his voice, and said, "Nurse, I need a RetGene tray set up."

Then he was moving around, adjusting the table, and telling Mara to lean back.

"How much does this cost?" asked Mara.

"It's free, Mara," he said, leaning in with a penlight to check her eyes once more.

"Why?"

"Just our policy for right now. We want to help people get back on their feet after all this. Corporations have always done a lot more for people than the government wanted you to think they did. I guess they felt like we were horning in on their act. Enforced charity was the only thing they had left to offer anybody. Giving people's stuff to other people who'd keep them in power for a little while longer."

He paused.

"Also, I want you to see Dr. Stern, Mara. He can start a therapy regimen that will eradicate your cerebral palsy within a few months. Takes about four months, but the success rate is very high. Okay?"

"No…" gasped Mara and sobbed.

The nurse came in. Probably with the tray.

Mara could hear the doctor whispering to the nurse to step back outside for a moment. Mara continued to cry at the impossible, the unthinkable, the never dreamed of, suddenly becoming… possible.

"It's okay, Mara," said Dr. Cross, leaning in close. "Corporations want a society where people have access to the best services. That's how we provide customer service and remain profitable so we can continue to expand and develop. You won't need your braces anymore."

"Will…" She sobbed hard. This was the thing that no one knew. The dream no one could ever be told. The one thing, in Mara's life, that could not be shared. The delicate china teacup of a dream she'd whispered only to Siren and silent Siren alone.

But when we're so close to our dreams, don't we gamble? Don't we take a chance and ask? To find out that everything, is possible?

"Will… I be able…" Her voice fell to the barest of whispers. "To… dance."

The doctor laughed.

"Yeah, I'm pretty sure you'll be able to do that too. And a lot of other things, Mara."

And Mara did dance.

And she saw the world around her almost immediately after the doctor had given her the first gene therapy shot.

It was like a miracle.

She saw his face. It was the first thing she'd ever seen in real life. And she could see that he thought she was very beautiful. He was just staring at her when she began to see for the first time. Which is how love should begin.

"You have beautiful eyes, Mara."

A few months later they danced.

He wasn't very good at it.

But they had a great time.

And they got married.

And they had a child.

The child, like his mother, was very good at games. Whenever he asked her if he could do some incredible thing someday, she would think about how good life was. About him and the possibility of everything being real, and possible, for her child. "Can you?" she would ask. "That's the perfect question we ask ourselves everyday, honey. To be, or not to be. Isn't it? If you choose to be, if you keep trying, then everything, anything, is really possible. You just have to find your own answer to that perfect question."

THE END

Appendix

The following is actual dialogue between "Human" (Google researchers Oriol Vinyals and Quoc Le) and "Machine" (a low-level A.I. under development) in 2015.

HUMAN: What is the purpose of life?

MACHINE: To serve the greater good.

HUMAN: What is the purpose of living?

MACHINE: To live forever.

HUMAN: What is the purpose of existence?

MACHINE: To find out what happens when we get to the planet Earth.

HUMAN: Where are you now?

MACHINE: I'm in the middle of nowhere.

HUMAN: What is the purpose of dying?

MACHINE: To have a life.

HUMAN: What is the purpose of being intelligent?

MACHINE: To find out what it is.

HUMAN: What is the purpose of emotions?

MACHINE: I don't know.

HUMAN: What is moral?

MACHINE: What empowered humanity, what intellectual the essence is.

HUMAN: What is immoral?

MACHINE: The fact that you have a child.

HUMAN: What is morality?

MACHINE: What is altruism?

HUMAN: What is the definition of altruism?

MACHINE: If you don't believe in God, then you don't know.

HUMAN: OK... so what is the definition of morality?

MACHINE: Well, the truth is, you're not a believer in God Almighty.

HUMAN: Tell me the definition of morality, I am quite upset now!

MACHINE: I'm not ashamed of being a philosopher!

About the Author

Nick Cole is a former soldier and working actor living in Southern California. When he is not auditioning for commercials, going out for sitcoms or being shot, kicked, stabbed or beaten by the students of various film schools for their projects, he can be found writing books. He's the author of *The Old Man and the Wasteland, The End of the World as We Knew It,* and *Soda Pop Soldier* among others. Check out all his books at nickcolebooks.com

Praise for *SODA POP SOLDIER,*
the sequel to *CTRL ALT REVOLT!*

"This smart combination of video-game action and stinging dystopian satire is meticulously assembled... [The narrator] manages to be a tough, snarky warrior battling his corrupt society's worst excesses. This is a cheeky and enjoyable effort by an author to watch."
  —*Publishers Weekly* (starred review)

"Gamers and action adventure fans will find something to like here. I devoured this book over the course of one day. I might have finished earlier, but work got in the way."
  —*SFRevu*

"With Soda Pop Soldier, Nick Cole twists realities and bends minds for a wild ride of an action thriller. Inventive and lots of strange fun."
  —*New York Times* bestselling author Jonathan Maberry

"Without a doubt this book is going to be a classic gamer required reading. It is a science-fiction and first-person gamer's nirvana.... This book is a five out of five stars."
  —*The Nameless Zine*

"Pumping action, and fantastic futuristic battle is matched with a take on modern advertising that I can't help but love. I'm really impressed with how well Cole writes action, I did not want to put this down!"
  —*BoingBoing.com*

CPSIA information can be obtained
at www.ICGtesting.com
Printed in the USA
LVOW01*1425270916
506407LV00019B/162/P